Sigrid Undset

The Son Avenger

Sigrid Undset was born to Norwegian parents in Denmark in 1882. Between 1920 and 1922, she published her magnificent and widely acclaimed trilogy of fourteenth-century Norway, *Kristin Lavransdatter* (composed of *The Bridal Wreath*, *The Mistress of Husaby*, and *The Cross*). And between 1925 and 1927, she published the four volumes of *The Master of Hestviken* (composed of *The Axe*, *The Snake Pit*, *In the Wilderness*, and *The Son Avenger*). Ms. Undset, the author of numerous other novels, essays, short stories, and tales for young readers, was awarded the Nobel Prize for Literature in 1928. During the Second World War, she worked with the Norwegian underground before having to flee to Sweden and then to the United States. After the war, she returned to Norway, where she died in 1949.

ALSO BY Sigrid Undset

KRISTIN LAVRANSDATTER

The Bridal Wreath (VOLUME I)

The Mistress of Husaby (VOLUME II)

The Cross (VOLUME III)

THE MASTER OF HESTVIKEN

The Axe (VOLUME I)

The Snake Pit (VOLUME II)

In the Wilderness (VOLUME III)

The Son Avenger (VOLUME IV)

THE SON
AVENGER

THE SON AVENGER

THE MASTER OF HESTVIKEN, VOLUME IV

SIGRID UNDSET

VINTAGE BOOKS

A DIVISION OF RANDOM HOUSE, INC.

NEW YORK

All rights reserved under International and Pan-American Copyright
Conventions. Published in the United States by Vintage Books, a division of
Random House, Inc., New York, and simultaneously in Canada by Random House
of Canada Limited, Toronto. Originally published in hardcover in Norwegian in
two volumes as *Olav Audunsson I Hestviken* and *Olav Audunsson og Hans Born* by
H. Ascheboug & Company, Oslo. Copyright © 1925, 1927
by H. Ascheboug & Company, Oslo. This translation was published in
hardcover as part of *The Master of Hestviken* by
Alfred A. Knopf, Inc., New York, in 1930.

Translated from the Norwegian by Arthur G. Chater.

Library of Congress Cataloging-in-Publication Data
Undset, Sigrid, 1882–1949.
[Olav Audunssøn og hans born. II. English]
The son avenger / Sigrid Undset.
p. cm — (Master of Hestviken ; v. 4)
Originally published in Norwegian as pt. 2 of Olav Audunssøn og hans
born (2 v.).
ISBN 978-0-679-75552-4
1. Middle Ages—History—Fiction. 2. Norway—History—1030–1397—Fiction.
I. Title. II. Series: Undset, Sigrid, 1882–1949.
Master of Hestviken ; v. 4.
PT8950.U506313 1995
839.8'2372—dc20
94-42542
CIP

THE SON
AVENGER

PART ONE

Winter

ᴏɴᴇ evening in late autumn Olav Audunsson went down to his sheds at the waterside to see that all was made fast and well closed. It had been blowing hard during the day and the tide was high, and now on the approach of night the wind was rising. Going out on the pier, he saw that a little sailboat had put in under its lee. There was only one man in the boat, and so Olav went up to see if the stranger might need a hand.

"Now luck is with me," said the new-comer, shaking the water from his clothes, while Olav took charge of his arms and wiped the worst of the wet from them. "My wish was to speak with you alone, Olav, as soon as might be; and here you come yourself to meet me."

He talked as if they had known each other of old, and Olav thought he had seen this young lad before, but could not put a name to him—his face was fair and bold-featured, with a delicate, thin-lipped mouth; a little spoiled by the bulging, pale-blue eyes, but in spite of that he was good-looking. The hair clung to his forehead under the waxed linen hat from which the water poured, but it could be seen that it had a reddish tinge. The stranger was tall and well grown.

Olav took the man into one of the sheds and bade him declare his errand.

"Ay, 'tis best I say how it is, master; I have had the mischance to slay a man, and no atonement has yet been made—the case may drag on. And so I could think of no better way than to put myself in your hands: I know you for a man who will not refuse to hide me while my kinsmen make terms on my behalf."

Olav was silent. It had become a far more risky matter to harbour outlaws of late years since the country had grown quieter and King Haakon enforced the laws more strictly. But on the other hand he could not send the young man away—the fiord was white with foam, and night was already falling.

"Where did this thing happen?" he asked. "And what manner of man was it you slew?"

" 'Twas at home, and the man was Hallvard Bratte, the Warden's nephew."

"At home—where may that be?" asked Olav rather impatiently.

"I see—you do not know me," said the young man, seeming hurt. "Although I was with you as your trusty comrade both in the fight by Skeidis church and at Frysja bridge—"

"Ah, yes—now I mind me where I have seen you before—Aslak Gunnarsson from Yttre Dal. But you have grown much since that time, Aslak, 'tis nigh four years ago."

Aslak went on with his tale. The way of it was that Aslak's father had given summer pasturage to some cows for the lady Signe, Hallvard Bratte's sister, and two of these had been struck down by the bear. When the dalesmen came back to Hamar with the lady's cattle, she had been very unreasonable, and so one word had led to another. At last Hallvard, the lady's brother, who was standing by, had uttered words of Gunnar of Yttre Dal to which Aslak could not listen with patience. He had got away after the slaying, had ridden south, and first sought refuge with the White Friars at Tunsberg. But on coming to the convent he learned that his kinsman Prior Sigurd was lately dead, and he quickly guessed that the monks were loath to give him shelter: they had been compelled to abandon their claim that the right of asylum enjoyed by the convent of Mariskog also applied to the house of their order in Tunsberg. The Abbot said he might indeed repair to Mariskog, but it was becoming somewhat too common for King Haakon's enemies to take sanctuary there, and Aslak had remarked that the monks were a little uneasy, since the King no longer looked with favour on this monastery which possessed the right of asylum. That being so, Aslak had no great mind to betake himself thither: "and then I bethought me of you, Olav. A man without fear I know you to be, and one that is wont to do as he thinks fit. You yourself have roamed as an outlaw in your youth—so I thought you would not refuse me help."

Olav was not more favourably disposed to hide the manslayer by what he had just heard—that the lad was from the Upplands and seemed to know more about Olav's youth in that part of the country than Olav cared to be reminded of; *how* much it was not easy to guess. Until now he had believed that folk in the north had long ago forgotten him and his affairs, it was so many years now since he had shown himself in those regions. Eirik had been there awhile two years ago and had visited Steinfinn Haaksonsson at Berg; Olav had not been pleased when he heard of it, nor did he grieve overmuch when it came to his ears that the cousins had fallen out a few months later, so that Eirik had not stayed long in the Upplands. But as for refusing to receive Aslak Gunnarsson, there could be no question of that.

So he said they had better go up to the houses; Aslak must need some warm food and dry clothes.

At any rate, thought Olav as he helped to carry the other's gear, it was a lucky thing that nobody at home would try to ferret out who their guest was. Since Lady Mærta's death in the spring, Bothild Asgersdatter and Cecilia managed his house, and the two young maids were so well brought up that they never troubled their father with unnecessary questions.

Aslak Gunnarsson settled down at Hestviken. It had not been Olav's intention that he should remain there, but he could not bring himself to say anything about the matter, and when spring came Aslak was still there, bearing himself in every way as if he belonged to the household. They called him Jon Toresson—it was Olav who hit upon this name, from which no one could guess who he was.

Otherwise Olav was quite willing to admit that Aslak, or Jon, was a most agreeable house-mate, and he had a way of making himself useful. He was strong and industrious, incredibly handy besides—an excellent worker in both wood and iron, and he always found something to occupy him. Olav himself had never been more than a moderately skilful craftsman; he could accomplish all that was needed about the farm, but not such things as required special cunning or deftness of hand and a delicate eye. And since he had lost Bodvar, the house-carl who fell at Frysja bridge, he had not had a man who was practised in such crafts. And then Aslak was always cheerful and of good humour; he had a fine voice for singing, but above all he could whistle so sweetly and truly that it was a pleasure to hear him—he almost always whistled at his work. He could read a little too, so Olav got him to look at some of the writings he had concerning his estates and privileges—there were one or two matters about which he could not trust his memory.

Withal Aslak was quiet in his ways, so that he did not too roughly disturb the muffled tone that prevailed at Hestviken.

Life at the manor was calm and still. Little was said among the household, and all spoke low: the master's silence lay like a damper on all these people who had lived with him so long—they were for the most part the same. Nevertheless the life of Hestviken seemed to have taken on a brighter hue since Mærta Birgersdatter's sharp voice was hushed and her keen eyes closed. The two young foster-sisters, who now shared the duties of housewife between them, were the most demure and courteous maids a man could see; yet there was a youthful joy and brightness about them, they were so fair and so well beloved of all.

Bothild Asgersdatter was now in her eighteenth year, quick and capable beyond her age, and not strong in health, blithe and gentle at home, but very shy among strangers.

As to Cecilia Olavsdatter, no one ever thought of putting it down to bashfulness or timidity that she was so retiring in folks' company: she looked everyone straight in the face with her clear, cool, pale-grey eyes. Olav's young daughter was as taciturn as her father, and just as fair-skinned as he had been in his youth. The shining, flaxen hair lay in soft curls about the girl's head when she wore it loose on holy-days; her complexion was white as the kernel of a nut, and her skin seemed so firm and close that sun and wind made little impression on it, and the full young lips were pink as the pale brier-rose. She was short for her fifteen years, and rather broadly built, but round and shapely, with small hands and feet, but strong of hand and sure of foot. It was rarely that Cecilia Olavsdatter smiled, and her laugh was rarer yet; but she had never been heard to weep. In her actions she was kind with her own people and charitable to the poor and sick, but rather sullen and short-spoken in her manner.

The foster-sisters were always good friends and of one mind; they seemed to be bound together in intimate affection.

The Hestvik maids were never abroad, except to the annual feastings within Olav's own circle of friends; otherwise they were not to be seen at such meetings as were frequented by young people. But they went to mass every Sunday and holy-day unless the weather was very bad. And then they were so handsomely dressed and adorned that no other woman had better clothes or heavier silver belts and buckles than Olav's maids—both were called so among the folk—and they rode, one on each side of their father, on good, well-groomed horses with newly clipped hog-manes.

Olav's heart was filled with deep and silent joy as he walked up the church with his daughters. Their coloured mantles of foreign cloth trailed after them; through the thin church veils shimmered the maidens' unbound hair, Bothild's smooth and copper-brown, Cecilia's silky mane bright as silver. He stood during the mass and never once looked over to the women's side; nevertheless it was as though all his thoughts were centred on their presence in that place.

He no longer thought of himself and his own affairs; he was now an old man, it seemed to him, had made his choice of what was to become of him. But, for that very reason, all that he might yet achieve ere evening fell upon him had but one object: to brighten the lives of these two children. How their future would shape itself—of this he scarcely thought; it would surely fall out for the best. In course of time he would marry them off, and it would be a strange man indeed who would not bear such treasures safely through the world when once he had had the good fortune to win them. But still he had time enough to look about him—they were yet so very young, both of them.

There was Eirik. But it was as though the figure of Eirik had faded into unreality in Olav's mind; he seldom gave him a thought. He had not seen him since that day at Oslo. Olav had been away from home the only time Eirik had visited Hestviken since—it would be four years ago this summer, and then his father had gone with Ivar Jonsson on the campaign in Sweden, where that brave young leader fell. And it had grown almost to a certainty in Olav's mind that Eirik would never possess Hestviken after him—*that* sin God had taken from him; the false heir was not to take over the old manor. God Himself would defend Cecilia's rights.

Then there came a morning in early summer. Olav and one of his men were down on the beach by the pier, busy hanging up some nets. The weather was as fine as could be. The sunlight lay in great white flakes on the sea; around the bay, fields and meadows shone with a wealth of green, and the leaves of the alders were dark already with their summer hue, while the firs had long, fresh shoots.

Cecilia knelt on the sun-baked rock by the pier with a heap of bright, floundering fish beside her. In the morning sun the girl's old rusty-brown everyday frock was quite resplendent; her thick, fair plaits hung over her shoulders—they were not very long, and her hair was so curly that the plaits escaped from the red ribbons that bound them. Her knife flashed as she raised it and tried the edge against her finger.

It gave a sound of summer and mild weather in the morning stillness as Aslak loaded his boat. The water splashed and gurgled as he moved about and arranged the goods he was to take with him—Olav had sent him on an errand south to Saltviken.

"Jon!" called Cecilia softly. The man looked up—Olav saw his healthy young face light up in a quiet smile. As the girl beckoned to him with her knife, he drew the boat up to her along the edge of the pier; she was now standing on the rock.

She wanted him to sharpen the knife for her. She sat down as he did so, looking out across the water, with her hands resting in her lap. They were not talking together, that Olav could see—but when he had finished and took his place in the boat again, the same quiet, warm smile played across Aslak's face. And as Cecilia went back to her work, a reflection as it were of the same smile lay upon her fair features.

She began to clean the fish. As Aslak rowed past the rock, he dropped the oars for a stroke and waved his hand to the maid. And Cecilia raised a hand slightly in reply. Then she bent over her work again with a furtive little smile.

Olav stared—it had given him a shock: something was passing before his eyes of which he had had no suspicion.

Cecilia threw the cleaned fish into the bucket and straightened herself a moment. She turned her lovely white face up toward the sun and sat with closed eyes. And the smile that spread over the child's stubborn little face was like nothing her father had ever seen before; it beamed with a sweet and secret joy—no fairer sight had Olav seen in his life.

Afterwards he tried to shake it off. Go and take a fancy to a man who lived here at Hestviken as a servant; nay, his daughter could never do that. She could not even have known who this Jon Toresson was.

Nevertheless Olav determined to be rid of Aslak as soon as might be. The lad was now free to remain in the country; during the past winter he had received news through the monks of Tunsberg that the ban of outlawry had been removed. So now there was no reason for Olav's keeping him longer than he had use for his services.

But a week went by ere Olav found occasion to broach the matter to Aslak. Covertly he kept an eye on the two young people; but he could see no sign that they were closer friends with each other than with the rest of the household. He comforted himself with the thought that he had been mistaken that morning by the pier.

—Until the Saturday evening, when Olav and the men were to go to the bath-house, but the women would wash themselves in the cook-house; they had been preparing juniper water. Olav and the men were crossing the yard when Cecilia called to Aslak from the cook-house door.

It struck her father that she knew their guest's real name.

Aslak went over to the maid, took from her two pails, and dashed past Olav. In the golden afternoon sunshine he ran light-footed down the meadow to the spring. He was a big man, slight and loose of limb, handsome and cheerful; his curly, reddish hair shone gaily in the evening sun.

Olav stood still. Now Cecilia appeared again at the cook-house door. She had put off her kirtle and stood in her blue undergarment, which fell about her in rich folds down to her little bare feet as she stood warming one with the other, for the stone was cold in the shadow. While waiting for the water she let down her plaits, shook out her hair, and combed it, so that it waved about her face and arms.

Aslak came up with the pails of water. The two young people exchanged a few words, which Olav could not hear, but again Cecilia's face beamed with that new and lovely light. And Aslak was smiling as he left her.

On Monday evening Olav went out to the smithy and spoke to Aslak:

9

"Your mind will be set toward home, Aslak, now that your
atonement is made. And I think perchance you would do well to
profit by the fine weather while it lasts—you reckon it a four days'
journey, do you not?"

Aslak laid down what he had in his hands and looked at the
older man. "I have thought the same myself, Olav, that I would
go home ere long. If I shall not be leaving you in the lurch—will
you then let me go before the haymaking?"

"You may be sure I will. 'Tis not my wish that you stay here
as my serving-man, now that you no longer need my harbouring."

"No, no," said Aslak; "I am not that sort of man either. You
know well that I will stay as long as you have use for me."

Olav shook his head. Aslak removed some scythe-blades he had
been sharpening; he seemed somewhat agitated. Then he turned
and faced Olav. He had a serious look: the fellow *was* handsome,
his bold-featured, ruddy face was frank and honest; it was re-
markable how little it was spoiled by the prominent eyes.

"If I were to come back, Olav, so soon as my father or my
eldest brother can make ready to accompany me south—you can
guess what it is I would have my kinsmen ask of you?"

Olav made no reply.

Aslak went on: "You can guess what our business would be
with you? How would you receive us, and what answer might
my father expect of you?"

"If your meaning is what I believe it to be," said Olav very low
and indistinctly, "then I will tell you that you shall not trouble
your kinsmen to make the long journey for naught."

Aslak gave a little start.

"Can you say that so surely, Olav—before you have heard what
conditions we could offer you? 'Tis true, you might find a richer
son-in-law, but you might also find a poorer. And the richest men
are seldom those of best birth or repute—as times are now—unless
you should look for them among those knights and nobles with
whom you yourself have not cared to associate in all the time you
have dwelt here at Hestviken. I come of such good kin, so old in
all its branches, that I may claim on that score to be a match for
your daughter, and there are not many men in Heidmark who
enjoy such honour as my father."

Olav shrugged his shoulders slightly. He could not find an answer to this, offhand; it was not quite clear to his mind *why* he

would not at any price marry Cecilia to a man from the Upplands.

"There is this too," said Aslak again; "it may be a good enough
thing to marry one's child to wealth, but this avails little if the
son-in-law be such a one as knows not how to husband his estate
and improve his position. I think I may promise you this: in my
hands it shall not decrease, if God do grant me health and save us
from great misfortunes. Ay, now I have been with you more than
half a year, and you know me."

"I say naught else but that I like you, Aslak—but that is not
reason enough for giving away one's only daughter to the first
man who asks for her. I know little more of you than that you
have many brothers and sisters, and you yourself have said that
Gunnar's lot is not an easy one—though indeed I have never heard
aught but good of your house, the little I have heard of it. But 'tis
another matter that, young as you are, you have already been the
death of a man—and it was as an outlaw you came hither to me"—
Olav felt a strange relief in every reason he found for refusing the
lad. "Moreover it seems to me you are far too young to think of
marriage without having asked the advice of your kinsfolk."

"I have repented and atoned for my sin," said Aslak; "and as to
my having slain a man so early in life—that surely is the more
reason for thinking I have learned to command myself better, so
that I shall not fall into the like another time, unless I be strongly
provoked. But you should be the last man to blame me for that,
Olav Audunsson; nor can *you* rightly deem me too young to seek
a bride. For I am full nineteen winters old—you were fifteen or
sixteen, I have heard, when you took a wife by force and cut
down her cousin who sought to deny her to you."

"The one case is not like the other, Aslak." Olav succeeded in
speaking quite coolly. "The maid whom I took to myself was
affianced to me and I to her; there was a legally binding act between her father and my father while we were yet of tender age,
and afterwards her kinsmen tried to set at naught the rights of us
two fatherless children. *You* will lose neither honour nor rights
if you fail to win the first young maid you have cast your eyes
upon, without your kinsmen so much as knowing what you have
in mind.

"No, no," said Olav hotly; "your father shall never have leave
to say of me that I received you when you came hither, a friend-

less outlaw, and then treated with you, a young lad under age, for the hand of my daughter, without even knowing whether your kinsfolk were minded to ally themselves with my house."

"You know yourself," replied Aslak coolly, " 'tis not likely my father woud be loath to see me wed the daughter of Olav Audunsson of Hestviken. I know not what you mean! Is it on account of those rumours that were abroad concerning you at the time when your marriage with Ingunn Steinfinnsdatter was at issue? So much water has flowed into the fiord since then that no man cares any more what you did or left undone in your young days—for since that time you have lived peaceably for more than twenty years and have won renown for honourable conduct in both peace and war."

Olav felt his heart beating with terrible force. But he broke off, cold as ice: "That is well and good, Aslak—but 'tis vain for you to say more on this subject. For Cecilia I have other designs."

"Of that she knows nothing!" exclaimed Aslak hotly.

"Is it so"—Olav felt relieved at being given just cause for breaking out in anger—"that you have made bold to woo my daughter behind my back?"

"You surely do not believe that of me. Not one word have I spoken to Cecilia with which you could have found fault. But that I like her she has seen; and I have seen that she likes me—neither of us can help that, such things cannot be hid. If you would listen to us, Olav, Cecilia would give her consent without sorrow—so much I have guessed."

Olav said: "Nor will it bring so much sorrow upon either of you if I refuse to listen to your suit. The maid is but a child—and you are not so old either."

"Say you so! You yourself and her mother held fast to each other for ten years or more and would not suffer her kinsmen to part the love that was between you—I have heard you spoken of it at home, Olav, as patterns of loyalty in love!"

Olav was silent a moment. The boy's words went strangely to his heart—while at the same time he was yet more unshakably determined that he would never have Cecilia married to a man from that part of the country. Then he replied in a low and faltering voice:

"That was different, Aslak—I had a *right* to her. And we had grown up together like two berries on a twig—loved each other as brother and sister from early childhood. You two, Cecilia and you, have known each other for one winter, and there is no compact between you. So it cannot be so great a grief to either of you if you now must part."

Aslak flushed deeply. He stood for a moment with bowed head, his hand on his breast, his fingers plucking at his brooch.

"For your daughter *I* cannot answer," he then said shortly. "I—" He shrugged his shoulders, then turned on his heel and went out.

Next day he was already prepared for the road. He took it with a good grace, thanked Olav in well-chosen words for the help and friendship he had shown, and bade him farewell. He went round and took leave of all his fellows. Privily Olav kept an anxious watch on the two young people when they said farewell to each other. But they took it well: they did not look at each other, and their hands dropped with a strange slackness after they had joined them; otherwise there was no sign, for one who did not know.

Then Aslak rode away from Hestviken.

Olav continually watched his daughter in secret. But Cecilia was like her usual self, and her father tried to make himself believe that she did not regret Aslak—not much, anyway. And she was only fifteen.—Fifteen had been Ingunn's age. But that was different altogether.

He had nothing to regret. The youngest son from Yttre Dal—Cecilia Olavsdatter of Hestviken might well look for a better match than that. It was natural that she should like Aslak; she had seen so few young men, and the boy had winning ways; but she would forget him sure enough when she met others.

It had made a stir in Olav's mind, an insufferable welter of conflicting emotions, to find that there were still folk in the north who remembered his and Ingunn's love and talked about it. As a pattern.— And rumours—he knew not what sort of rumours they might be. He had believed them both forgotten in those parts, both himself and her. Here none remembered Ingunn save himself alone, and he no longer remembered her so well that he thought of her often; it was only that he knew of all that had been, that he was aware of the origin of all that had befallen him.

Sin and sorrow and shame, and, beneath it all, the memories of a sweetness which might well up as water wells up over the ice and flood his whole soul whenever a break was made in the crust of his peace of mind.—And there in the north all this lived among folk as a legend, true or false. Not for anything in the world would he resume fellowship with men who perhaps talked behind his back of his youth's adventures.

And this merely for a young maid's fancy, which she would surely have forgotten ere a year was out, if only none reminded her of it. Was he to return alive to such a purgatory for the sake of two children's childishness? Never would he consent.

2

A month later Eirik Olavsson came home to Hestviken. He had sent word in advance that he was bringing with him a friend, Jörund Kolbeinsson from Gunnarsby, and he begged his father to receive the guest kindly.

The sun-warmed air of the valley was charged with the scent of hay and of lime blossoms as Eirik rode down by the side of the Hestvik stream. At Rundmyr the hay was still lying in swaths, dark and already somewhat spoiled, in the little meadows; around the poor homestead stood the forest, deep and still, drinking in the sunlight. Anki came out when he heard the horseman, shading his eyes with his hand, and then he broke into a run, with his thin neck stretched out, his back bent, swinging his overlong arms. After him came the whole flock of half-naked, barelegged children, and last of all waddled Liv herself, carrying her last baby in her arms and with the next one already under her shift; she was so marked with age that with her chinless face she looked like a plucked hen.

Eirik stayed in the saddle, so that they might have a good sight of him. But when the first greetings were over, he had to dismount, and Anki looked his horse over and felt him, while Liv sang the praises of Eirik and his companion. He had to go back to the hut with them.

The very smell within, sour and putrid as it was, seemed grateful and familiar. The round mud hut, with no walls and a pointed roof like a tent, was divided into two raised floors with a passage between, and this passage was wet like a ditch of stinking mud:

one had to sit with legs drawn up. The dark hole was full of a litter of rubbish. Eirik's memories were of all that was strange and lawless: here he had lain listening, all ears, to vagabonds' tales of a life that lurked, darkly and secretly, like the slime of Liv's floor, beyond the pale of law-abiding, workaday men, in bothies and caves in summertime, on the fringe of the great farms—the life of husbandmen, townsmen, priests, as seen from the beggar's pallet. He heard of smuggling in wares banned by the King, of robbery and of secret arts, of illicit intercourse between men and women who kept company for a while and then parted, of St. Olav's feast and the consecration of churches, and of sheer heathendom, sacred stones and trees. Here he had won in gaming a silver-mounted knife, which he gave away, for he dared not keep it. And over there in the corner they had once found a dead child—the mother had overlain it in the night, and then she had simply gone her way. Liv had got rid of the corpse. Eirik had been sick with suspense—what if his father came to hear that such a thing had happened in a croft that belonged to Hestviken! It was a dire thought, but at the same time there was solace in it! It would be a sort of redress for his miserable, everlasting rebuffs—his father ought just to know what things he dared to see and hear and do at Rundmyr. As yet his father knew nothing of his defying him in this way. Even when he first misconducted himself with a woman it was more to avenge himself on his father than for anything else. Afterwards he had been sick with shame and fright when he had to creep home in the dark and steal from the storehouse the piece of meat he had promised her; and he knew not which was the stronger, his remorse or a kind of joy that he had ventured to do a thing at which his father would be beside himself with wrath—if he knew of it.

Eirik picked the flies out of the old wooden bowl and drank. The milk was villainously sour and acrid, but it had the familiar taste that was proper to Liv's cabin. After that he sat with his knees drawn up and his hands clasped about them, listening to the talk of Anki and Liv: ay, they were well off, now that Cecilia and Bothild ruled the house; nay, Olav himself never had a hand in it, either when Mærta refused them or when his daughter gave. In-terwoven with their talk came news of deaths and births and feast-ings throughout the countryside, of Hestviken and the ravages of the Swedes, so far as these things had affected their life.

Eirik listened to them with half an ear. Rather sleepily he allowed his memories to drift through his mind, wondering with a faint smile what was to come now. He had buffeted about the world so long that he felt old and invulnerable. Outside the door the sun shone upon rock and mossy meadow; lower down the bog-holes glistened among the osier thickets, and behind him rose the dark wall of the spruce forest. It was *his* land and *his* forest, the cabin here was his, and these people were his: his heart warmed toward them in all their wretchedness of body and soul. He would be good to them, for they had been true to him when he was a child.

Jörund Rypa called to him from outside—he lay taking his ease in the grass, had refused to enter the foul hut. Anki and Liv and their whole flock of children followed at Eirik's heels as he came out.

The millstream trickled, narrow and shrunken, among the rocks. Eirik recognized pool after pool where he used to take trout. The sheeny green flies that darted hither and thither under the overhanging foliage might have been the same as of old, and the same tufts of setwall and clusters of bluebells were to be found as he remembered them. He rode past one meadow after another; in some places the haycocks were still out. The scent was overpowering; screes and bluffs were covered with lime trees that clung fast to the cliff with their honey-coloured bunches of blossom showing beneath the dark overlapping leaves. Where a tongue of the forest intruded on the bridle-path, the shingles-grass [1] carpeted the whole ground with little pale-pink bells.

There was the little overhanging rock under which he had found thunderbolts lying in the sand—Lapps' arrows his father had called them. He forded the stream near its mouth and rode out of the thicket, and there lay the old creek before him, glittering in the sun. On the north the Bull rose with the reflection of the water like a luminous net on its rusty, smooth-worn cliff; on the south side the land sloped upward, meadows already cut and bright, waving cornfields under the steep black wall of the Horse, and against the blue summer sky the roofs of the manor showed up on the knee of the hill, below the crag. Smoke whirled above the roofs up there; outside there was a glimpse of the fiord, dark

[1] *Linnæa borealis*—reputed to be a cure for shingles.

blue in the fair-weather breeze. Every stone of the path and every straw in the fields was his and he loved it.

There stood the bath-house, a little apart, and the great barn above it. He rode up the steep little bend that was so hard to get round with a loaded sledge when there was no snow on the ground. And now the horses' hoofs were striking against the bare rock of the courtyard.

From the door of the living-room came his father, followed by his sister. His father was in holiday dress, a green kirtle reaching to the feet with a silver belt about his waist; he went to meet his son, erect and dignified. He was freshly shaved and combed, and about his square-cut, stone-grey face with its bloodshot, pale-blue eyes, a wealth of hair lay curled. It was now quite grey, with pale-yellow strands floating here and there in the softly waving locks. Eirik had always pictured to himself God the Father Almighty in his father's likeness.

He was the handsomest and manliest man in the world. He was that still, though his head had grown grey and the right side of his face seemed driven in and the cheek was wrinkled and furrowed all over by the great scar. The two young men sprang from their horses; Eirik took his father's outstretched hand and kissed it.

Then Olav greeted Jörund and bade him welcome.

Cecilia came forward. She bore the old drinking-horn in both hands, and she too was in festival attire with her flowing hair bright about her grave little face. She stood there in doubt, looking from one young man to the other, when her father gave a nod: she must offer it first to the son of the house.

A wave as of the final, perfect joy came over Eirik—this was his sister! Young and erect, fair and fresh and pure as the noble damsels he had never been able to approach—here was one, the fairest, the brightest of all high-born maids, meeting him at the door of his home; and she was his own sister.

"Our guest first, sister mine," said Eirik joyfully, and Cecilia greeted Jörund and drank to him.

Indoors a fire had been lighted on the hearth; the flame played palely in the sunshine that made its way through the smoke-vent and turned the smoke blue under the rafters. The floor was thickly strewn with leaves and flowers; on the northern bed, which had been Eirik's when he was a boy, a new red and yellow coverlet had been spread over the skins. The table was laid as for a banquet, and on each side of Olav's high seat were set the two silver-mounted griffin's claws from which he and Jörund were to drink; never before had Eirik been allowed to drink from these horns.

After sunset they sat on the lookout rock, the three young people. Eirik lay in the heather, in a little dry hollow among the rocks; his sister sat higher up, straight in the back, with her little, short hands folded in her lap. With quiet delight Eirik listened to her talk—she was sparing of words and judicious beyond her years.

It was dead calm; the ripples gently licked the base of the cliff. The sky was perfectly clear but for some strips of red-tinged cloud down in the south-west. A flood of light from the fiord and the pale vault of heaven shone upon his sister's white face, as she turned it upward to see if any stars were visible tonight.

Jörund sat a little apart. He too was unusually silent this evening; he listened to the others' talk and looked at Cecilia.

Nay, said Cecilia, it was on Bothild that most of the household duties fell, Bothild was a far better housewife. And she had left everything in such good order that it was easy for Cecilia to work single-handed for a time. 'Twas always so that Signe Arnesdatter took one of them with her when she went to visit her married children, and this time it was Bothild who was to go—nay, she would not be home for a good while yet; Helga did not expect to be brought to bed before St. Margaret's Mass [2] or thereabouts, and Signe always made a long stay with that daughter.

Nay, Bothild was not yet betrothed, but no doubt their father would soon look about for a husband for her. And Bothild might well look to make a good match; she had inherited not a few chattels from her aunt, and Olav would add to her dowry, and with her gifts and her goodness, and her beauty—ah, beauty! There were not many maidens hereabout who were so fair as Bothild Asgersdatter, so said all the countryside. Her hair was fine as silk, and so long and thick "she can scarce comb it herself; I do that for her; we are wont to plait each other's hair."

Eirik lay smiling to himself from pure joy. He rejoiced too that Jörund could see what his ancestral home was like: a great manor and a house of gentlefolk, maintained in lordly fashion—but after the old usage; the houses were small and old, here were no new-

[2] July 20.

fangled courtiers' ways, but it was the more dignified on that account. Such things might be suitable for the new families who had risen from a poor estate, but there was no need of them here at Hestviken; Olav Audunsson and his children had no need of ostentation.

Eirik saw his father come out of the stable in the yard below. Olav stopped, looked up at the rock where the young people were sitting, but went indoors without calling to them or saying anything.

Cecilia, however, rose at once. "I am sure Father thinks 'tis time we go in and go to bed. And you may well be tired too, brother."

Eirik awoke next morning to the sound of bells and lowing—leaped up, into his clothes, and out.

The sun had just risen above the ridge in the north-east; it shone in splendour upon the green that clung fast to the clefts of the rock. Outside, the sea lay bright and smooth as a mirror; over the meadows at the entrance to the valley lay long shadows of trees and bushes in the morning sunlight.

The feeble warmth of the beams was grateful in the early coolness. Eirik came out in time to see the last of the cattle disappear into the woods. Cecilia stood by the gate, fastening the hasp of withy and calling to the herdsmen. Now she came back, walking along the high balk of the cornfield, for she was barefooted and the path was muddy. She was dressed like a workingwoman, in an old blue smock she had kilted up to her knees, and her feet were red with cold in the dewy grass.

"Are *you* up already?" she greeted her brother. Ay, she was always early up: "the first morning hours are the busiest." There was a smell of the byre about her, and her white arms were soiled from milking; the wrists were as round as if they had been turned in a lathe. The two stiff plaits that hung over her bosom were short and thick, and ruffled in the knots, so curly was her hair.

Cecilia had to go off to the bleaching-ground; Eirik sat on the step of the barn and watched her laying out her linen. She went into the dairy and spoke to Ragna, and he stood at the door meanwhile—she was so brisk and prompt in all that she did.

Her brother followed at her heels, sitting on the threshold of the women's house while she washed herself in the water-butt outside and rinsed her feet. She stepped past him over the threshold and called from within: would he come in and see the room?

The women's bower was the largest room in the manor; with its walls of fresh yellow logs it was much finer than the dark hall, and its furniture was richly carved; the beam from which the pot hung over the hearth ended in a wild, gaping horse's head. Along the wall stood weaving-frames, reels of yarn, and chests; over the crossbeams hung folded blankets and cushions for the benches. Cecilia, who had now put on shoes and stockings, took down the best of them to show him.

From a carved box his sister fetched a stone jar and a little silver goblet, filled it, and drank to her brother.

"Father gave us this last year—we were to have it, he said, in case one day we might have to receive a guest. And now you are the first."

"Thanks! It was good wine too."

"But strong? We were all drunken on it one evening last autumn, Bothild and I and the maids." She looked up at her brother with a bashful little laugh, as though unused to tell strangers of her own affairs. "There was one whose name was Yngvild, she is not here any more; 'twas she who thought of it—we danced in here. There were to be games on the green by the shore to the northward, and they would have had us with them when they came down to take boat, Gaute Sigurdsson and Jon Tasall and a few more; but Father said no, though there were two from Rynjul among them—'twas of no use. Yngvild was angry; she said Father kept us stricter than Lady Groa keeps the children who are sent to her convent to be taught. So she persuaded us to lay aside our sewing, and we danced in here, and then we drank of the wine that was meant for our guests."

"What said Father to that?" Eirik smiled. He felt nothing beyond his bright new-born love for this sweet young sister. Every word she spoke and every gesture she made filled his soul with joy.

"Father? He said nothing, as you may well guess. But two days after, he came and ordered us to move into the hall and sleep in the upper chamber there; 'twas too unsafe for young maids to sleep alone in a bower that lay so near the shore. Until then we had lived here night and day. And next time Yngvild offered to oppose him, he answered that 'twas best she went home to her own father, for belike she would obey him."

"Is he so strict with you, Father?"

Cecilia had put on her kirtle; it was red, handsomely embroidered. She fastened her belt about her and hung on its scissors and knife, purse and bunch of keys. The little barefooted dairymaid was now a fine young franklin's daughter.

"Strict he is, in that he holds so firmly to customs and manners as they were observed in old time—we may not open our mouths or move our eyes when strangers are present. But he bears us goodwill withal." She took out of her chest and spread on the bed a sleeveless, low-necked kirtle of brown velvet, embroidered with rings and crosses of yellow silk. The long-sleeved shift that belonged to it was of red silk and had gilt hooks to fasten it over the bosom. "Such dresses he gave both to Bothild and me—'twas after he had refused us leave to go into Oslo to see the damsels' wedding with the Swedish dukes. Meseems 'tis high time we came to town one day—to the fair or to Halvard's Vigil. But father will not have it."

"Have you never been up to Oslo?"

Cecilia shook her head and wrapped her finery in its covering of homespun cloth. "God knows when we shall have a chance to wear these trappings."

"That will come when we are to drink your betrothal ale."

Cecilia's face changed in an instant; she turned to her chest and put away her finery. "I know naught of that."

The beauty and charm of his sister went to Eirik's head like a slight intoxication. He did not know how it was he had never thought of *her* in all these years; had he done so, he would surely have kept himself from one thing and another, from drinking and gaming, brawling, wenching, and debauchery. He regretted now that he had had so little thought of curbing himself—he had never thought of it—had yielded to every temptation and obeyed the fancy of the moment. Thus he had been carried away by what soon became habit, and he got the reputation of being a man of immoral ways, one who haunted taverns and worse places. Nor was this reputation undeserved. But the result was that he enjoyed no more respect than other hired servants, a man-at-arms in his lord's retinue.

Now that it was too late, he saw that he ought to have followed his father's advice; then he could have asserted himself so that none would ever forget he was the son of Olav of Hestviken. If he had kept himself more from dice and ale-houses, bought himself clothes and arms instead, kept his own horse—and then he should have stayed indoors, in the company of older men of good report, sat still and modestly listened to their talk. Then he might also have been received in the ladies' hall, where high-born damsels sat; he might have borne them company to the dance and to mass.

He had kept himself a stranger to all such women, dreaming of them, in pale, harmless dreams. But he was too shy in their presence, and far too lazy and irresolute to compel himself to break with his evil habits.

Yet in a way he did not *believe* they were so pure and grand as he liked to *think* they were. Jörund told a different tale, and he was just as welcome in their bower as in other places. And Jörund used to say that he dallied with them freely and boldly. There was only one thing they were afraid of, he sneered—short of that they liked a man to handle them somewhat rudely.

This was one of the things Eirik disliked in his friend—that he could speak thus of the damsels of his own estate. It took away Eirik's desire to try his fortune there—he did not realize that he was unwilling to hazard his own good opinion of good women. There were plenty of the other sort for other uses.

But the truth was that every maid would gladly have married Jörund—he never let people forget who he was: one of the sons of Gunnarsby, and that he had only taken service in a lord's retinue in order to see something of the world before settling down at home on his own estate. His morals were no better than Eirik Olavsson's, he was no more squeamish in the choice of those he drank with, and at the sight of dice and gaming-tables he went clean mad—but luck was with him more often than not. Nevertheless no one ever forgot that Jörund was no less a man than any of the King's body-guard, for all that he had chosen to serve a lord whose followers enjoyed a freer life.—But then it was true that Jörund had not left home at enmity with his kinsfolk.

At the bottom of Eirik's mind lay the thought that one day he would break with this retainer's life. One day he would return to his ancestral home, be reconciled to his father, recover his position as the heir of Hestviken. And then no doubt it would be time to marry—it would be for his father to find a suitable bride for him.

· · ·

Winter

Eirik had been on a ride round the parish, had visited his kins-woman Una Arnesdatter and met others of his acquaintance. In the evening Eirik mentioned at home that on the next day there would be dancing on the green by the shore to the northward, where young people from north and south were sometimes wont to assemble.

"Cecilia may go with us to the games, may she not?"

Olav answered: "They are unused to taking part in such gather-ings, the children here. Nor can we stay up so late at home on a Saturday evening—we have a long way to church."

Eirik protested: there were many other houses that lay just as far from the church, and they could rest when they came home from mass. Olav muttered something—a refusal—and made as though he did not notice that Cecilia was looking at him.

Jörund guessed it was of no use to pursue this subject with the master of the house and took up another. But a little later Eirik asked suddenly:

"What was that, Father, that I heard from Una? She said you had that Aslak Gunnarsson from Yttre Dal here last winter—he called himself by another name, and you kept him hid, so that the Sheriff never knew you were harbouring an outlaw."

"Did he not?" said Olav with a faint smile.

"One cannot say your father hid him so well as that," said old Tore laughing. "Reidulf is not fond of trouble. And since the winter of the Swedish broil I trow he is more afraid of Olav dis-turbing him than minded to disturb Olav."

"Nevertheless it was unmanly to fling himself upon strangers in such a case," said Eirik. "But those red-polls of Yttre Dal are like that—proud in spite of their poverty, but ready to accept help where they can find it, when they are hard pressed. I met his brother, that time I was in the Upplands, a haughty and ungra-cious fellow he was—"

"Then Aslak is not like him," said one of the house-carls warmly; "we were all fond of him." At this Olav interrupted the man, sent him out for something, and began to talk to Tore about a horse that had some boils under its mane.

Olav had gone down to the waterside before going to rest. As he came back he saw Cecilia standing on the lookout rock. Her father went up to her.

23

"You must come in now, Cecilia—'tis late."

The girl turned round to him. In the pale gleam of the summer night her father saw that her face was discomposed—the stubborn features were slackened in irresolution. But she said nothing and followed him obediently down to the houses.

Next morning, when Cecilia brought in the food, Olav said to his daughter: "You know, if you have a mind to go with them for once and listen to the dancing, I will not deny you—now that you can have your brother's company."

Cecilia looked at him rather doubtfully.

"But perhaps you have no mind to go—?"

"Oh, yes. Gladly would I be there for once," said Cecilia.

The thin new moon floated in summer whiteness in the rosy grey of the sky above Hudrheimsland as Olav rowed round the foot of the Bull. A reflection of daylight still rested on the rocky wall of the promontory. Olav rowed with cautious strokes in the evening stillness. He put in at a little cove where there was a strip of sand, drew up the boat, and made his way up through the wooded cleft in the rock.

He had bow and arrows with him, and he stole along quietly. On reaching the height, where the trees thinned out and the moss-grown rocks sloped down to the Otter Stone, he paused for a moment, but then resumed his way northward into the forest. After a while the sound of singing came up to him and the smell of smoke.

As he came out on a little knoll, he saw the fire blazing far below; beneath him he had the bay with the clear curve of its sandy beach, and higher up between the flat rocks lay the dancing-green, burned yellow by the summer sun. Around the great bonfire the chain moved in a ring, black against the flames; the dancers' feet drummed on the dry ground, and their song rang sweetly in the still evening air. Olav could not catch the words, for he did not know this ballad by heart, but he recognized the tune and knew that it was the lay of Charlemagne and Roland. The one who sang for them had a deep, warm voice; Olav wondered if it might be Eirik—he had always been singing when he was a boy. They were too far off for Olav to recognize any of the dancers in the twilight. Some were sitting down to rest outside the circle.

Olav stretched himself on the crisp bog-moss, which still felt warm from the heat of the sun. The ballads were wafted up to him, and the sound of the tramping in time to the song:

> It was dum-dum dumdelideia
> dum-dum dumdelidei—

Now and again he heard the crackling sound of the fire, and, far below, the fiord murmured and lapped against the rocks. The moon had gone down long ago; above him the summer night grew dark. Nor were there many stars out tonight—it was already a little past midsummer.

At last the man rose, picked up his bow and arrows, and walked quietly back, down through the forest.

He lay in his bed within the dark closet, dozing and losing himself in a web of vague dreams, but every time he was on the point of falling asleep, he woke up with a start. Each time it was nothing, only a feeling that he had been waked by something from without. But there was no one in the hearth-room, and it was growing lighter and lighter—they had forgotten to close the smoke-vent.

At last he heard them in the yard—they were taking leave of the other young people who were going farther inland. Then his own folk came in. From the closet Olav could hear them talking and yawning as the men took off their footgear. Cecilia had not gone up; once or twice she gave a little laugh.

" 'Tis morning already," her father heard her say. "In three hours we must ride away to church. 'Tis not worth while to go up to the loft—I think I will lie down in here."

There was a slight creaking in the south bed as she got up into it, then came the louder sound of the men getting into the other. A few words passed between them. Cecilia's voice grew faint with sleepiness, then she left off answering, and soon after, one of the men began to snore.

Olav got up after a while; he would go into the hearth-room and close the vent. In the north bed he saw the heads of the young men; they had rolled the coverlet about them.

Cecilia was asleep in the other bed; she lay right on her back, her delicate, flower-like face showed white among the masses of loosened hair. Olav was reminded of her mother, who had lain thus, in the same bed, year after year, flung down like a corpse, paralysed to the waist, slowly withering to death.

But the sleeping child was radiant with health. She was white in the face, but it was fresh and round as pearls; a little stubborn and self-willed she looked, even when asleep, and the long, pale lashes cast a shadow on the rounded cheeks. The short, straight nose and the broad curve of the chin betokened obstinacy or steadfastness—one could not say which it was at her age.

One of the hands hung down over the side of the bed—it looked uncomfortable. Olav cautiously raised it and laid it on her bosom. Her breasts were rounded firmly and delicately under the red woollen gown, making a wide gape at the opening and showing an embroidered kerchief under the silver lacing. She had outgrown this gown in the sleeves too—they did not reach nearly to her wrists.

Olav stood looking at his daughter till he felt himself shivering in the chilly morning air with only a cloak about him. He bent down and made the sign of the cross over her. Then he picked up the little red shoes; they were dark with wet from the water in the bottom of the boat—her father set them on the edge of the cold hearth.

3

Eirik and Jörund went much abroad to feastings and merry-makings and often Cecilia was with them; Olav had nothing to say to it.

The two friends were handsome men; at any rate they made a handsome pair when they went about together; they brought life and gaiety with them, and they were well liked. When folk met Olav they said he might feel honoured in his son.

Now that he had stopped growing, Eirik was very tall, long and big of limb, but shapely, narrow in the hips and thin about the waist, though the upper part of his body seemed somewhat too broad and heavy—he had grown so broad-shouldered that he stooped a little, so that folk said in jest that he was rather top-heavy—but his head was small in comparison.

He had grown very dark of hair and complexion, and he had

a long, narrow face; his features were not so handsome: the nose hooked, or rather indented, first between the eyes, and then another dent over the bridge; the mouth was so big and the upper jaw so sharply curved that his great white teeth made one think of a horse's mouth; the long, flat chin lacked roundness. But he had such matchless eyes, said folk—Eirik's eyes were large and light brown and seemed full of an inner light. And then he had youth, so that he passed for a handsome young man, even if his features might have been better.

Jörund Rypa was such as most call handsome, tall and well grown, with smooth flaxen hair, blue eyes, a ruddy face, and a large, rather pointed nose, a fresh, rather thick-lipped mouth. He was quiet and retiring enough among the neighbours here—Eirik was far more winning in his ways. So the one was thought handsome because he was lively, and the other's good looks were held to excuse his being somewhat indolent or haughty.

It was this subdued manner of Jörund's that made Olav like him, so long as he was in the room with him. But if he chanced to think of Jörund Rypa when he no longer had him before his eyes, Olav felt a profound, obscure ill will toward his son's friend.

With unreasonable clarity he recalled an ugly little act he had seen this man do when he was a boy—one day when he and some other lads were snowballing here in the yard; Jörund had then behaved disloyally to Eirik. It was a small thing to lay so much stress on, a child's trick during a children's game; but at the time it had revolted Olav like the blackest treason, and the impression had remained with him, so that he could not think of Jörund without antipathy.

But when he was in Jörund's company this feeling vanished almost entirely—he could see the injustice of laying a long-past boyish trick to the charge of this grown man. Jörund conducted himself becomingly, was quiet in his manner, looked folk frankly in the face, and never spoke without need. Olav saw therefore that he was unjust in thinking of the young man as though there were something underhand about him, for there *was* nothing underhand about Jörund Rypa, either in his speech or in his face or in his eyes.

One day Olav chanced to hear a scrap of talk between brother and sister. He was busy in the smithy when Eirik came to the door with Cecilia. They stopped outside.

"—every maid would be glad to be married to Jörund Kolbeinsson," said Eirik.

"Then 'twill not be hard for him to find a match."

"But how comes it, sister, that *you* like not Jörund?"

"I never said that I like him not," replied Cecilia.

"You said so but now, when I asked you."

" 'Tis not to say I like him *not*"—there was a laugh in Cecilia's voice—"if I answer no when you ask me do I *like* your friend!"

"But is it not one and the same thing? If you do not like him, then surely you like him *not*?"

"No, 'tis *not* the same!" The girl was laughing now; Olav heard her run on down the field. Eirik opened the door and came in, smiling at his sister's words.

This new, exhilarating fondness for his sister filled Eirik's heart entirely. It was as though all his childhood's unrequited affection for his father, his anxious and burning passion for Hestviken, had dissolved in the sunny warmth and peaceful well-being of these summer days; the evil in it ran away, and the good was left behind, remoulded as a warm and golden joy in this little sister's winning brightness and pert girlish charm. He followed her about at home, he had to have her with him whenever he went abroad, he lavished gifts on her—the best jewels and clothes he possessed, which he had never thought to part with.

He rejoiced in everything wherever he went over his father's land—his love for this land, which was to be always his, was increased by a vague memory of his strange thought, as a child, that he might lose it in the end. It was the same as with Hestviken itself when the sun returned after a long spell of bad weather: never did the fields and the manor gleam with so bright a glance as then.

It was almost the same with his love for his father. It had been the groundwork of Eirik's whole life that no man in the world was like his father; the only change was that he no longer *thought* about it. He no longer took it to heart that his father was taciturn and could by no means be called a man of good cheer—they were now friends in spite of that. Eirik did not see that it harmed anyone if his father was gloomy and cross; he himself had now grown out of the shadow that Olav cast around him.

He took his ease and disported himself in the glory of his own youth. His sister had grown into a winsome maid; he could share his joy in life with her. He had his best friend with him, and the three together enjoyed the happiness that each day brought.

Thus it was that he had already half formed the thought that Jörund spoke one evening when the two were out fishing in the fiord.

"I have been thinking, Eirik—what if we two bound our friendship in a closer tie? Think you Olav would receive it well if I let my kinsfolk ask for the hand of your sister?"

"You know right well," replied Eirik gladly, "Father could but esteem so good an offer—and I know none to whom I would so gladly see her given, dear as I hold her; never would I advise her betrothal to a lesser man than you. And Father sets great store by my advice—" No sooner had he said it than Eirik believed his own words.

From that time it was a settled matter in Eirik's mind that Jörund and he were to be brothers-in-law. And unconsciously he began from that moment to regard his friend in a slightly different light.

It escaped him altogether that, though he had loved Jörund Rypa ever since he first knew him as a child, it was nevertheless true that he had never entirely liked him, nor had he ever trusted Jörund so well as not to have a care—how far he might venture with him. Unsure as Eirik himself had been in everything, he was drawn to the other boy, who was so unshakably sure. But all the time he had known that what made Jörund so secure was that he was firmly resolved to keep himself safe, at whatever cost to others. Jörund Rypa would neither blink nor waver if it came to leaving a friend in the lurch. Jörund's was not a timid nature, nor was he afraid of how folk might judge him.

But this power of Jörund's of being sufficient to himself had clean bewitched Eirik when they were boys. And when Jörund Rypa turned up in Ragnvald Torvaldsson's following, Eirik had pressed himself upon him, claiming the right to call himself Jörund's best friend from childhood. There was no one in the company with whom he was better friends than another in spite of all his efforts to please his comrades; they liked him well enough—he was ready to do them a turn, brave, a daredevil in many ways, though in other things he would show himself strangely and unexpectedly petty-minded. But they laughed a little at him too—he was altogether too credulous for them, and he made too great demands on plain folk's credulity when he told a story.

Jörund accepted the position of Eirik's best friend, and Eirik did not haggle about the price; in the course of time he had had more than once to serve as a cat's-paw to Jörund. But Jörund affected complete ignorance when Eirik took the blame for the other's wrongdoing, and at the sight of his friend's innocent, blue-eyed look Eirik himself believed in Jörund's good faith—it would be unworthy to think otherwise. He was so good-natured in his ways, was Jörund, with his genial voice and his prompt smile, when Eirik talked nonsense to him. Careless he was in many ways, to the downright alarm of Eirik—for Eirik himself was scrupulous in the performance of his duty, though he was too short of memory to do it well always, and he was hurt at any disparaging word of his conduct. Jörund knew how to take care of himself better than Eirik liked or would have admitted to be the case; Jörund spoke of women in coarser terms than Eirik could have brought himself to use even of the loose wenches who were all he yet knew. But in spite of all this, Eirik loved Jörund.

In this way they had now kept fellowship for several years. Now and again they had been parted, for Eirik from time to time would take himself off and seek service with another lord; but it always ended in his coming back to Sir Ragnvald, with whom Jörund stayed.

There was but one thing about his friend which Eirik could never put up with, and that was Jörund's singing. Jörund comported himself well in a dance, and he had a powerful voice, so that he often led the dance; that was his pride. But he did not sing true. Eirik himself had a fine ear for music, and his singing voice was not so full as his friend's, but warm and soft—and when Jörund broke into a ballad, Eirik felt quite sick with shame on his friend's behalf.

The very next day Eirik told Olav that Jörund seemed to have thoughts of Cecilia. The two men were walking together across the ridge to Saltviken.

Olav listened to his son in silence and walked on without answering.

"You may be sure," Eirik went on, "that Jörund is a man who is attended by good fortune. And you must have heard a good report of the house of Gunnarsby—"

"I know they are called rich." Olav walked a few paces in silence. "Have you been there—at Gunnarsby?"

At once it struck Eirik that this was a thing Jörund might well have done—asked him to bear him company some time or other when he went home to see his kinsfolk. It gave him a little pang: "It never happened that I was able, when Jörund wished to have me home with him."

"What do *you* think of the man *himself?*" asked Olav. "Is he such a one that you would deem Cecilia and her welfare safe in his hands?"

Involuntarily the old disquietude returned, vague and distant. But he had thought all this over, Jörund's faults were such as a man may lay aside when he sets up house; and if they were to be brothers-in-law they must be loyal to each other. So Eirik answered yes, and began to sing Jörund's praises loudly—cool-headed he was, good-natured, cheerful, mettlesome—his father had seen that for himself.

"Ay, I have seen naught but good in him." Olav heaved a sigh. They walked on in silence. Then the father said:

"I shall speak with Baard—ask what he knows. Baard must be able to find out about these folks; he has kinsmen of his own in that part. Till then I look to hear no more said of the matter. Jörund is our guest and he must know enough of good manners not to bring forward his suit again before his brothers can take it up."

"You may be sure of that." Eirik was at once mortally afraid lest Jörund should upset the whole plan, if he gave any hint of it in speaking to his father, who insisted so strictly that all should proceed in seemly fashion. Or that he might scare away Cecilia if he approached her with the rather rough and aggressive good humour with which Eirik had seen him win the favour of other maids. But Cecilia would not like such ways, he saw that at once; she had been brought up by this father and she had far too much of both pride and modesty. He would have to speak of this to Jörund.

· · ·

The day before Laurence-mass,[3] Eirik had been on an errand up the fiord. It was a dead calm as he rowed homeward—in the north and east heat clouds with gleaming edges surged up over the hills; their reflection darkened the pale blue of the fiord and gave the water a leaden hue, while the patches of sunlight beyond were bright as silver. Eirik rowed fast—he had his best coat on and was trying to be home before the storm burst. It was warm; the sun scorched him, and the reflection on the water dazzled his eyes.

He looked over his shoulder—down in the south the sky was clear and blue, and the sea was all aglitter. Hestviken lay in sunshine—the fields of ripe corn and those which had been already cut, where the corn stood in shooks among the stubble, showed white amidst all the green. Eirik thought he would have to see to getting in all that was nearly dry, in any case—his father and Tore were not at home. He remembered storms that had threshed out the sheaves over the ground.

The sky was blue-black over toward Oslo, and the thunder rolled far away—it looked as if perhaps the storm would pass farther north. From the quay Eirik took the path by the side of the "good acre"; he leaped the fence, felt the sheaves and tore off a handful of the white barley, rubbed it between his hands and stuffed the sweet grains into his mouth. Then he heard someone singing above, on the lookout rock—a soft, veiled female voice. It could not be Cecilia, she had no voice for singing.

Eirik went up to see. On the rock lay a strange young woman; she lay with her back to him, and her face turned toward the sea. Her heavy tresses, dark with wet, were spread over the rock to dry. As she lay resting at full length on her side, with one hip raised, there was something about her that stirred Eirik's senses, so that he came to a standstill, as though he had taken the wrong track.

In indolent repose the woman lay humming to herself as she gazed into the sunlight over the fiord. Then it struck Eirik who she must be. He came toward her.

On hearing footsteps on the rock she turned and rose on her knees. Eirik saw that her figure was full in all its outlines, but without firmness, as though overripe for a young maid, and when she rose to her feet, her movements were heavy and lacked elasticity. She flushed deeply as she looked up at him with a hesitating,

[3] August 10.

evasive look of her great dark eyes, while her hands struggled to throw her heavy, dark hair back over her shoulders.

Eirik went up to her and gave her his hand.

"Have you come home now, Bothild? Welcome!"

She did not return the pressure of his hand, but withdrew hers quickly and shyly; she stood with bent head, looking down, and her voice was toneless and veiled.

Eirik himself felt confused and heavy at heart because he had been so suddenly disquieted at the sight of this girl—her doubtful attitude, her drooping head, and her hushed voice were enough to warn him that the days of their innocent and carefree life together were gone. Bothild's startled air as she stood with her shoulders rounded, full-bosomed and broad of hip, the strong scent of her hair, wet with sea-water—it seemed as though both his conscience and hers were already darkened.

They said a few words about her journey and then spoke of the weather, which looked so threatening. Eirik told her he meant to get in what he could of the corn before the storm burst. Bothild whispered yes—if it did not come before, they would have it at night. Now and then there was a faint blink of lightning far to the north, followed by a distant rumble.

Eirik stole glances at her as they walked side by side toward the manor. She was tall, but did not hold herself erect; her hair was very thick and long, but seemed stiff now from the sea-water. But her face was fair, round, and white, with red roses in her cheeks; she had a broad forehead, smooth and white; black, curved eyebrows; and her dark-blue eyes looked up with a covert, side-long glance under thick white lashes; her mouth was big, her chin small and round as an apple. Once she smiled at something he said, and then he saw that she had small short teeth with gaps between them, like a child's milk teeth, and she showed her gums as she smiled—he felt he would like to take and kiss her, but roughly, without kindness.

He got in all the corn off the "good acre" that afternoon; the storm passed round to the north over the fiord, but did not reach Hestviken. It was already dark outside and distant lightnings flashed in the evening sky; between the claps of thunder the stillness of the fiord seemed uncannily hushed beneath the cliffs in the close evening air of late summer. The men went indoors. Bothild brought in supper, hanging her head, as in all she did. But it was easy to see that Cecilia was delighted to have her foster-sister back again. This added to the touch of hostility that was part of Eirik's uneasy feeling toward Bothild; she was not a seemly play-mate for his sister, he thought—a woman who excited his desire in this way.

In the course of the night he was awakened by the crash of thunder; now the rain was pouring down: it drummed dully on the turf of the roof, ran off and splashed on the rocky floor of the yard, streamed over the foliage of the trees. From one corner of the smoke-vent it ran down into the room. The vivid flashes lighted up chinks in the wall at the end of the house; the logs were no longer weather-tight after the long drought. And clap after clap of thunder crashed and rattled right above the houses.

Eirik remembered Bothild the moment he woke—now she would be lying in the loft above the closet. Jörund slept like a stone on the inside of the bed, against the wall; Eirik lay outside. He was tempted to get up and go to the ladder—call up to hear if the girls were also awake; perhaps they would be frightened by the storm. But he lay where he was.

He tried to think of other things—of the fields farther up the valley, and the corn that stood there ready for the sickle; how would it fare in this weather? He could not remember that he had noticed Bothild Asgersdatter when he was last at home, the year of the Swedish troubles—it must be three years ago now. Cecilia was only a child at that time, his father was with Ivar Jonsson in Sweden, Bothild was helping her aunt in the housework; both the girls did so. He had not seen much of them, nor had he heeded them greatly.

He could not tell what had put it into his head that Bothild was not a pure maiden like Cecilia.

4

For Eirik there was an end of the peaceful home life and the pure, innocent summer days. They were now a company of four young people—for it never occurred to Cecilia to go anywhere without her sister. But to Eirik's fevered senses it seemed that Bothild clung to the younger girl. She was always a little in the rear, dropping behind with her indolent tongue and voluptuous gestures and her everlasting shy and stolen sidelong glances—it was at himself they were aimed, and he felt them as if she had touched him with her hand; but as soon as he looked at her, her eyes were turned away. It roused a kind of fury in the man—that she would never leave him in peace. He was ashamed of his own thoughts—here he was at home, with his father and his sister, but through Bothild's fault he was harried and beset with desire.

He felt inclined to deal harshly and cruelly with her when he got her in his power—to send her away from him in tears and overcome. It was a senseless whim, this spiteful prompting which sprang from an unknown depth in his soul—the blind and witless caprice of a master who is angry with a slave because he is irritated by the slave's frightened looks and humble efforts to conceal his sorrow.

For it was of a thrall she reminded him, a woman captive. Even the two thick plaits she wore hanging over her full, rather flaccid bosom made him think of chains; they reached nearly to her knees, and their weight seemed to force her head forward and give her a stoop in walking. And Bothild's hair was not black and stiff as he had thought at first, when he saw it wet; it had a soft brown hue, with a tinge of red, and went well with her red and white complexion and her dark-blue eyes. But not even her fairness sufficed to soften Eirik's mind toward her.

He scarcely spoke to her—it was only in his thoughts, all this of Bothild. To do anything to a woman who lived in his father's house was not to be thought of. Besides, he was afraid of his father; now that the peace and purity within him had been bemired, his childhood's dread of his father was also reawakened in full force.

Either Olav and Cecilia were ignorant that anything was passing in secret between Eirik and Bothild Asgersdatter, or they misinterpreted what they saw—thought that the two disliked each other, or were shy of each other. In any case neither the father nor the sister showed any sign that they thought about the matter.

Jörund had quickly guessed what was wrong with Eirik, but he contented himself with hinting at it once or twice in jest.

"I cannot make out," he said one day, with the sneering smile that Eirik disliked, "why you have such a mighty fancy to her. She sweats so."

Another time he said—it was one evening after they were in bed: "'Tis a great pity you cannot have her for a leman, since Olav is her guardian—and she cannot be rich enough for you to think of marrying her!"

Eirik was silent, overwhelmed with agitation. Marry *her*—she was the last woman in the world he would take to wife! 'Twas not *thus* he had thought of Bothild.

Jörund made ready for his departure—he was to be home for the Nativity of Mary.[4] Baard of Skikkjustad had made inquiries about Jörund. He must be reckoned a good match, said Baard. There was wealth at Gunnarsby, and Gunhild Rypa's sons might look to inherit more; Kolbein had been like a chief in those parts and a man held in honour. The sons who were now in possession of the manor were not so well liked, but what folk had to say of them was for the most part such envious talk as is always heard when rich men stand on their rights. The two elder brothers were married to daughters of high-born men of good repute—"so I will not seek to dissuade you from listening to them, if in other ways you hold Jörund to be worthy your alliance," said Baard to Olav.

Olav then let fall a few words to Eirik: if Jörund was so minded, and his kinsmen would consider the matter, there would be no harm in discussing it.

When it came to the point, Eirik was a little dispirited. He did not know why, but now he thought all at once that there was no such hurry in getting Cecilia married. She was not much more than a child, his good little sister.

One morning Cecilia said to her father that now she and Bothild must move out and sleep in the women's house awhile—they had to repair the winter clothing for the folk of the manor and they would be working till late at night.

Before Eirik went to bed that evening, he took out the clothes he was to wear next morning on the fiord—Olav and the house-carls were going out after mackerel at dawn. Then he saw that the woollen shirt he meant to put on was ragged at the elbows. Eirik took the shirt and went out to ask his sister to mend it—the

[4] September 8.

36

maids were still up, he had heard, as he went by their door just now.

It was pitch-dark in the anteroom. On the other side of the thin boarding he heard his sister clattering with chests and boxes; she called to Bothild to open, as Eirik knocked at the door of the room.

Then the door was opened, and the room was light behind her. The dark female figure in the doorway seemed to collapse with fright when she saw who stood outside. In her toneless whisper she said that Cecilia was busy turning out the clothes: "I will sew this for you." She put out her hand for the shirt.

"Come hither," Eirik bade her in a low voice, and seized her by the wrist. With a little gasp as of fear the girl obeyed: she bent her head under the lintel and let him draw her out into the anteroom. Instantly he took her in his arms and thrust her against the wall, pressed her close and searched with his lips for her face in the dark, came upon her plaits and found the soft, ice-cold rounding of her cheek. With his kisses he nailed her head, which struggled to be free, against the wall.

"Come with me," he whispered; "come out with me—"

She gulped with terror, he heard her teeth chattering and her soft, cold hands struggled in vain; she tried to defend herself, but had no strength. Eirik took both her hands in one of his and pressed them, as though he would squeeze the blood out under the roots of her nails. So terrified was she that Eirik scarcely knew whether she understood a word of his wild and shameless whispering—

Then Olav called through the outer door. They had not heard him coming. He called for Cecilia. Eirik let go of Bothild—he himself was trembling—as Cecilia came to the inner door.

"Are you two *here*?" she asked in surprise, and then spoke past them: "What is it, Father?"

Olav asked for the little bucket he had brought up the week before to be cleaned.

"Inga has surely forgotten it—I will find another for you, Father."

She went back for a lantern and came out again. "Have you been quarrelling?" she asked, half smiling, as the light fell on the faces of the two in the anteroom. Then she ran off.

Eirik heard the sound of his father's iron-shod heels die away on the rocks of the yard. He had caught a glimpse of Bothild's face, deadly pale, as she slunk through the door of the room. Now he went and looked in.

She was crouching on her knees over a chest of clothes, her head sunk in her clasped hands. It made him furious to see her kneeling thus—as though in prayer.

"Stand up," he said, and his voice was rude and harsh, "before Cecilia comes. Do you wish *her* to find out about this?" Then he went out.

As he went down to the waterside at dawn next morning, he saw her in front of him, carrying a great box. When he reached the boat, she had taken it on board and was just returning over the gangplank. Eirik put out a hand to help her. As he touched her for a moment, her body shrank up and he saw she was dead-white in the face, but under her eyes there were deep black rings. But she often had those, it struck him—no doubt that was why her eyes looked so big.

But scarcely had Eirik stepped aboard when Olav came and told him he had better stay ashore. It might be they would stay out two days, and he half expected Reidulf, the Sheriff, to come on the morrow about a case. Olav gave Eirik orders as to what he should say and do if the Sheriff came.

Eirik stood watching the boat till it was lost in the morning mist. He could just see across the creek—the leaves of the little trees in the crevices of the rock were yellow already—he had scarcely noticed it, but here was autumn well on the way. He listened for the sound of oars in the mist; the little craft could still be seen, like a shadow. Eirik shivered a little—it was chilly—he turned to go up to the houses.

As he passed the shed he heard someone within. Instantly he halted and listened, stiff and tense—could it be she?

He stole up to the door and peeped in. Bothild stood with her back to him, taking dried fish out of a bundle. In two bounds he was upon her, throwing his arms about her from behind. He felt her body give way, as though every bone in it were dissolved; she hung powerless over his arms, which were crossed below her bosom. Then he flung her from him, so that she fell on the floor. Eirik ran to the door and barred it.

As he turned, she stood up and faced him, erect, with face

aflame. "What are you doing!" Her eyes were big and black as coal. "You act like a—you are not acting like a *man*—oh!" Bothild gave one scream, loud and shrill, and then her tears gushed out.

A chill gust passed over Eirik—the sight of the girl's anger sobered him at once. But her tears plunged him headlong into a fresh tumult—he was bewildered by a sense of shame and misfortune, and her weeping frightened him.

"Do not weep so—" he muttered in his agitation.

But Bothild continued to sob, so that the tears poured down her distorted features. Once she threw her hands before her face, but the next moment she let them drop heavily again.

"What have I *done* to you?" she cried; "what sort of man are you become?"

"Bothild!" Eirik begged, miserably. "You surely cannot think I meant it in earnest—'twas only jesting."

"Jesting!" Flashing with anger, she looked him full in the eyes. "Is that what *you* call jesting?" Then her tears got the better of her again. She wept so that she had to sit down—sank down on a chest and turned her face from him. With her forehead leaned against the wall, she now wept more quietly, in bitter lamentation.

Eirik stood still. He could not find a word to say.

At long last Bothild half turned round to him again; she heaved a long, quaking sigh. "Ah me! It was not this I had looked for, when you came home to us again."

"When I came home?" asked Eirik weakly.

"We thought you would surely come home again one day," she said almost scornfully. "We often spoke of it, Cecilia and I—" Now she was weeping again.

"Do not weep so," Eirik begged at last.

Bothild got up, passed her hands over her tear-stained face.

"Open the door for me," she bade him curtly.

Eirik did so, but did not move from the doorway.

"Stand aside," she said as before. "Let me out now!"

Eirik stepped aside. Bothild went out past him. Eirik did not move—his surprise felt like a gleam of light within him, faint at first, then growing stronger and stronger. Now he was utterly unable to understand how he could have treated her as he had done.

A little way up the hill he overtook Bothild. She stood holding

dewy leaves to her tear-stained cheeks and red eyes. As he stopped
before her, she charged him, with looking round: "Go—" He hesitated. Bothild said impatiently: "Go now—I cannot show myself
like this, all tears—you must see that!"

Eirik made no reply, walked on.

He could not understand what had gone wrong with him. The
moment the defenceless maid had turned to resist, it was as though
a devil had gone from him. He was bewildered and ashamed, but
not deeply, for already his own evil thoughts appeared to him un-
real—nothing but an ugly dream.

The sun shone brilliantly in the course of the day and it was
warm as summer. Eirik and the house-carl who was left at home
were busy on the newly broken ground under the woods. Eirik
worked hard—he always did so when once he had taken anything
in hand. But at the same time he was deep in thought—Bothild was
in his mind the whole time. He could not forget her quivering
rage and her bitter tears. And now for the first time he realized
what she had said: she and Cecilia had often spoken of his coming
home.

A lingering, painful shame pierced him at the thought. Had
these two poor little maids waited here all this time for their
brother? Bothild must have expected that he would look on her
as another sister.

The rude and turbulent thoughts he had conceived of her lay
dead at the bottom of his soul like the dried mud left by a flooded
stream. And as new and tender green struggles up through the
hardened grey slime, so did new thoughts of Bothild shoot up in
him unceasingly.

That day he did not see her again till he came in to supper. She
busied herself gently, holding her fair head bent as usual under
the weight of her plaits, but the cowed and secret air that had
been upon her and had provoked him to evil and sensual thoughts
was now gone. She was merely a gentle young housewife going
calmly about her duties.

Even her beauty now stirred him in another way: now he saw
nothing but sweetness and gentleness in her rounded, red and
white face, dignity in her languid movements and in the fullness
of her form.

.   .   .

40

The Sheriff did not come next day, and by noon on the following day he was not yet there. An hour or two later Eirik went down to get a bite of food. As he came out with a piece of bread in his hand he heard Inga calling to Bothild, who was sitting outside by the north wall of the house, toward the sea. He went thither—she sat in the sunshine, sewing the shirt he had given her that evening.

She looked up for a moment as he came, but there was none of the anxious, clinging look in her glance now. Bothild bent over her sewing again; she looked melancholy, but calm and sweet.

Eirik stood there, leaning against the corner of the house. When he had eaten his bread and she had neither spoken nor looked up again, he had to break the silence himself.

"Are you still angry with me, Bothild?"

"Angry—" she repeated in a low voice, and went on sewing in silence for a while. "I hardly know myself *what* I am, Eirik—for I cannot understand it. Nay, I cannot understand why you should treat me thus!"

Eirik was at a loss. For as he was about to reply that he had believed she was trying to allure him, he saw that he must not say such a thing—it would make the matter far worse.

"I can promise you now," he said softly, with a little sigh, "I shall not hurt you again."

Bothild let her sewing drop into her lap and slowly turned up her face toward him. And now Eirik was moved by it in quite a new way: the round, white face with the two bright roses in the cheeks, the dark, thoughtful eyes, the fine mouth, which seemed small when she was distressed. Now his only desire was to pat her cheek, to pass his hand tenderly and kindly over the long, white curve of her throat—he felt he wished her well with so warm a heart.

"Is it for my aunt's sake," she asked him earnestly, "that you were so—spiteful toward me?"

Eirik seized upon this eagerly. "Yes—but now I cannot understand how I could think you were like Mærta—"

"Even so, my aunt never desired aught else than Olav's welfare," said Bothild meekly. "She would ever bid me be mindful of how great were the thanks we owed your father—God must reward him, we cannot. And I too wish him naught but well—I am not greedy of authority, Eirik, but consult Cecilia in all I do."

Eirik felt a thrill of intense joy and relief. God be thanked for her innocence—she believed no more than that he was bad to her because he was jealous on his sister's account, or would avenge himself on her for the old ogress, her aunt—beyond that she had no thought. She firmly believed he had only meant to humiliate her.

He had heard sounds of horsemen coming down from Kverndal, and now he thought he must go and see who was coming. So there was no help for it, he had to tear himself away.

The horsemen were already in the court. They were Ragnvald Jonsson, the Sheriff's young brother from Galaby, and Gaute Sigurdsson, whom folk called Virvir; Eirik had often met them in the two months he had spent at home. He called to Bothild, and she appeared at the corner of the house.

"Heh!" said Ragnvald with a laugh. "So you were not alone! Then our coming is untimely, I fear."

"Are you sewing that shirt for Eirik, Bothild?" Gaute Virvir rallied her.

And now she hung her head again, and her eyes hovered this way and that. She hurried away, as though she would avoid them.

Ragnvald and the other had come by land, for they had had business up in the church town, and they were not altogether unrefreshed, so Eirik guessed it would be well to settle the matter in hand ere they went to table. The sisters had spread the cloth and laid the table when they returned from the upper chamber, and by that time the guests were hungry and not a little thirsty. While the men ate and drank, the two young maids sat in another part of the room. Ragnvald tried conclusions with Cecilia the whole time, and Cecilia gave him sharp and snappish answers; but Eirik could see that this word-play amused her—he had remarked the same thing before, his sister was ready enough for a wrangle. But Bothild had relapsed into her diffidence and shyness and seemed utterly miserable when Gaute teased her about a certain Einar from Tegneby whom she was supposed to have met in the summer, while staying with Signe Arnesdatter at her daughter's house. Eirik did not like to hear her teased about another man, and he did not like her looking as though she had a bad conscience.

Ragnvald and Gaute delayed their leave-taking for some while after sundown. Then they would have Eirik and the maids to bear them company a part of the way.

"Nay, I dare not go with you, Ragnvald," said Cecilia Olavs-datter; "I might meet with the same misfortune as befell Tora Paalsdatter—you jested with her so long that she put out her jaw with yawning. It may be Father and the men will soon come in, I cannot leave the houses. But you, Bothild, might go up to Liv, since Eirik can bring you back."

So the four set off. Ragnvald and Gaute let their horses walk in front, the three young men chatted together, and Bothild followed a little way behind with her box and her bundle. Dusk was already falling; a thin white mist lay over the pale autumnal fields, and the orange glow in the sky faded and turned to rust-red. A bitter, withered scent hung about the alder thicket along the river, and the path was wet with the dew from falling leaves.

At Rundmyr Bothild left the path; before the men were aware of it the dark, bent figure was already darting across the fields. Eirik would have gone on with the others, but they begged him with a laugh not to give himself the trouble. Then they mounted their horses.

"Bitter cold to sport in the grove with one's lady fair," said Ragnvald laughing. "But I dare say you cannot choose your own time, you two—with the old man always about you down yonder."

"Good night," they both cried. "Beware, Eirik, lest the trolls snatch away your ladylove tonight!"

Eirik stood listening to the beat of their horses' hoofs as the two rode away into the dusk. Then he turned and went up to the cabin.

There was a good fire burning on the hearth by the door, and a candle stood in an iron clip by Liv's couch on one of the raised floors. Bothild sat at the mother's feet swathing the child. On the other side sat Anki and the six older children, eating the food Cecilia had sent; the savoury smell of a boiling pot of meat almost overcame the wonted evil odour of the hut. Comfort and uncon-cern in the midst of poverty met Eirik as he entered, ducking his head, from the raw autumn evening outside.

He sat for a while talking to Anki, while Bothild tended the child—she dawdled over it till Eirik grew impatient: now she must come, 'twas already black night outside.

They went, he in front and she behind, across the Rundmyr fields, which showed faintly grey in the darkness, and down to the bridle path through the woods. They walked by the side of the river, which rippled and gurgled very softly among the bushes; there was hardly any water in it that autumn.

Now and again Eirik heard that she was hanging behind; then he stopped and waited till she came up. And every time he had to halt and wait like this in the dark under the trees, his evil will seemed to grow more irresistible.

At last, when he had halted thus, she did not come. Eirik held his breath as he went back, treading as noiselessly as he could. He ran against her in the dark; as he took hold of her shoulder he felt she was trembling like one sick of a fever.

"What is it?" His pulses were throbbing so that he could hardly command his voice.

"I can go no farther," she whispered miserably.

"Then we must rest awhile." He took her in his arms and drew her to the edge of the road, where there was a little clearing among the trees. " 'Tis your own wish!" he muttered threateningly.

Instantly Bothild tore herself away from him. It was a moment before Eirik recovered himself—he heard her flying footfalls on the path ahead, ran after her; then came a dull thud—Eirik nearly stumbled over the prostrate body. He knelt beside her—she had fallen face forward. Eirik took hold of her, put his hand over her mouth, and felt it wet with a scalding stream that came bubbling out. At first he did not know what it was; disgust and rage boiled up in him—was the bitch lying there vomiting! Then with a shock of horror he knew that it was blood.

He turned her on her back, knelt in the mire of the path, and supported her against his chest. It was so dark that he could only just make out the pale round of her face and the dark flood that poured in pulse-beats from her mouth.

"Bothild—what is it—have you hurt yourself so badly?"

He could get no answer, but beneath his hand he felt the girl's heart throbbing as fast as his own. In vain he begged, time after time: "Can you not answer, Bothild—Bothild, have you hurt yourself?"

At last he had to lay her down. He tore his way through the bushes; stones scattered and gravel crunched under his feet as he floundered in the darkness, searching for a pool in the river-bed where he could fill his hat. The water oozed through the felt crown; he had but a few drops when he found her again, and dashed them over her. And now he could smell the blood; his own clothes were drenched with blood, and he felt sick with horror and disgust. And Bothild lay silent as though she were dead already.

Then he saw there was nothing else to be done—he lifted her up in his arms. He was forced to get her home; but heavy she was, as she hung lifeless in his embrace. That little distance, over stocks and stones in pitch-darkness, was as long as eternity. And he himself was worn out inwardly—with the wild desire that was shattered on this terrible mystery.

After an age, it seemed to him, he reached the manor with his burden. He managed to open the door of the women's house, found his way to the bed and laid her on it. Then he went out in search of help—Cecilia, where was she?

In the living-room—as he came in he saw his father and the three boatmen were sitting at the table over their porridge. His sister and the serving-maid were hanging up clothes by the hearth.

"Bothild is sick, I think—"

Cecilia turned sharply—saw her brother standing there, just in the firelight, with blood on his face, and hands as though they had been plunged in blood. With a loud groan she dropped the garment she was hanging on the bar, darted past him and out of the door.

But Olav too had leaped up. He sprang over the table and out after his daughter.

And the men had risen and came out into the room.

"Jesus, Mary!" old Tore wailed, "Jesus, Mary—has it come upon her again?"

Inga, the serving-maid, sighed as one who knew: "What else could we look for?—'tis ever thus with the wasting sickness, it will not give up its hold, when it has fastened on a young body. I have thought this the whole time—for Bothild, poor thing, there is no hope of cure."

"Cecilia will take this sorely to heart," said one of the men. "Olav too—they love her as their own flesh and blood."

"Far too red and white," said Tore; "I was sure of it—no long life was in store for her. Like a stranger she was here—little use was it that Olav had masses sung for her and was a father to her."

45

Eirik had sunk on the beggar's bench by the door. Without knowing it he had hidden his face in his arms. It was as though veil after veil was being drawn from before his eyes. The wasting sickness, they said, she had had these blood vomits before—she had been sick the whole time, and no one had said a word to him of it. The whole time, while he had had such thoughts of her, had played his cruel game with her, she had been a sick child.

Such were his thoughts when someone took him by the shoulder.

"How did it come about—that she was stricken so sorely?" Olav had spoken in a low voice. Eirik looked up. His father seemed already to have forgotten his question. He gazed vacantly before him, in bitter grief. Eirik could not bear to look at him more than an instant.

Now Cecilia came in. The house-folk swarmed about her with their questions. The maid merely shook her head—her face seemed compressed; she would not weep. In haste she took out of her chest a little box and was going out again.

"I will watch with you tonight," said Olav in a low voice.

His daughter paused and nodded. Olav took her in his arms and held her face against his breast a moment. Then he went out with her.

Eirik was outside the door of the women's house but dared not go in. He thought of that other evening, when he stood with her between the doors—he had not guessed it was a sick woman.

Inga came out after something. It was ill with Bothild, she replied to Eirik's question. The smell of blood from his own clothes wellnigh choked him.

He went in and to bed. He had not guessed that she was sick—and now he began to understand what had lain behind her strange manner—till he was afraid and resisted and would not be forced to see it all. Beware lest the troll snatch away your ladylove, they had said—Ragnvald, or was it Gaute?

He had fancied she was not as she should be, pure and undefiled. But he had never dreamed that he who had defiled her was Death.

Cecilia came into the room with red eyes next morning. Nay, Bothild had slept but little, she answered—nay, she had not spoken either, seemed to have no strength for that—she must have lost more blood this time than ever before.

Cecilia took the clothes that her brother had worn the evening before. "I will take charge of these and have them washed clean."

" 'Twill be best for me to take myself away now," said Eirik doubtfully —"back to Sir Ragnvald—since you have sickness in the house—"

"Is there any need for that?" asked Cecilia in surprise.

Eirik said the same to his father when he met him later in the day. Olav gave a start—looked at Eirik so strangely that the young man felt all his old fear of his father awakening. What if *he* had guessed—or Bothild had said something to him. Eirik turned red, and was furious with his father for causing him to blush. Olav answered not a word, but went out.

Two days later Eirik was ready for the road.

He wished to set out early in the day; so he had to go and visit Bothild—he must bid her farewell before he left the manor.

She lay with red roses in her cheeks, but when he came near the bed, he saw that her face had sunk in, especially under the eyes. She had been holding a rosary in her hands; now she hid it hastily under the coverlet. Eirik felt a choking pang of grief as he saw it.

The sharp and acrid odour of sweat that had inflamed him so— oh, now he knew what it meant; in the wasting sickness they sweat so profusely, for it devours them with the heat within. And that little cough of hers which had vexed him so—

He stood still, resting both hands on the hilt of his sword. He found it impossible to say anything—if he were to ask her forgiveness, there would be no end to it. Rather would he have thrown himself on his knees, laid his head on her sick bosom.

"You must not believe worse things of me than— My intent was not so evil as it must have seemed. With all my faults I am not such as you believe me now."

The sick girl lay looking at him with great dark eyes.

"You must tell me, Bothild—can you forgive me?"

"Yes," was all she answered. Eirik waited yet a little while.

Then he went right up to the bed, took her hand—it was cold and clammy.

"Fare you well, then." He ventured so far as to stroke her cheek

—but her face was hot as fire. "God give you health again—that you may be well when we next meet."

"Farewell, Eirik. God be with you."

His father and sister went with him no farther than to the barn. Alone he had to ride from home. And he could not shake off his heaviness—he felt like one who rode away an outlaw and accursed.

5

BOTHILD lay abed through the autumn. It was up and down with her.

Olav watched his young daughter moving about, silent and serious, divided between her sick sister and all the household work of the great manor. She was brave and loyal, Cecilia. Her father saw that her heart was oppressed with sorrow and anxiety; she was often not far from tears, but she would not give up—capable and diligent, she performed the work they had shared between them.

Then Olav said that Cecilia must sleep at night. He himself would watch by the sick girl.

The cough and the fever left Bothild little sleep—on her worst nights Olav sat by her bedside. For the first time in his life Olav found himself regretting that he had no practice in such things as pass the time—he knew no games, he could not sing, nor tell tales. And to speak to his foster-daughter of death and of heaven was not in his power.

He had not felt the silence as a burden when he watched over his wife. Between him and Ingunn there had been a life—of childish games and youthful joys and sorrow and shame, and love stronger than death; the silence between them had been a living one, with a murmur like that of the sea. But this child was both known and unknown to her foster-father; all he had seen of her was that she had grown up in his house, grown fair and winsome so that it was a delight to look upon her; he had taken such care of her as he could—and now she was dying as a young tree withers and dies.

She had let him feel, more plainly than the other children, that she needed his protection; that made it all the more bitter for him now to *know* that she must die. Though he knew it would have been even worse, had it been his own daughter that lay here.

So he sat in the log chair between the hearth and the bed, nodding and dozing, got up and supported the sick girl when the fits of coughing came, drew the bedspread up to her chin lest she should take cold, bathed in perspiration as she was, held the dipper to her lips as she drank, and then went back to his seat.

He was tired, and he was heavy at heart—and yet he felt that this sorrow dwelt in his soul as a stranger in an empty house—only an echo and a shadow of the sorrow he had borne for his mate. That had been so much worse, and yet it had been a thousand times better when she was parted from him, like the tearing asunder of living bonds of flesh and blood—than now, when he sat waiting for the frail and slender bond between him and this stranger's child to be dissolved.

She had spat blood more than once—not so much as that evening when she fell sick on the way home from Rundmyr. But it was easy to see that she was going downhill, and rapidly.

One morning at the beginning of Advent she had another severe fit of coughing and brought up blood. As the day went on, Olav saw that she was now very weak. She fell asleep at evening; her father stayed up. And when Bothild woke again about midnight, and he had settled her so that she lay comfortably, he said what he thought he *must* say:

"When daylight comes, my Bothild, 'twill be best I fetch a priest to you."

"Oh, no, oh, no—" she clutched the man's arm with both hands in an agony of supplication; "oh, no, say not so! Foster-father, do you think I am going to die?"

No other thought had ever crossed Olav's mind but that the child herself must have known this long ago.

"Child, child," he said, hushing her, "why should you not die? You are young and good—why need you fear death? God's holy angels will meet you and lead you before God's high seat, to join the blessed virgins to whom it is given to follow the Lamb of God eternally—"

But the tears welled forth under Bothild's sunken eyelids. "I am not ready to die, foster-father—all I long for is to live on here in this world. I am *afraid* to die!"

"Afraid you must not be. 'Tis better to dwell in heaven and follow Mary as the least of her handmaids than if you possessed the whole round ball of earth and had command of all that is in it."

"You say that because you are a righteous man and a good Christian," said Bothild, weeping.

"So folk believe me to be," replied Olav, greatly agitated. "Daughter, my dear one, I am not so; God knows what I am. And yet, Bothild—I could tell you such things of God's mercy, of His patience with our sins and of the love that our Lord shows us in His five holy wounds, in His bloody stripes and blows— Years have now gone by since I myself turned aside from that path, and my own path is overgrown with weeds and wild bushes— Could I but tell you what I myself once saw and learned—it is the worse for me that I dared not live in the way I know to be right—foster-daughter, I know that you ought to be glad to die now, ere you have acquired a greater share of guilt in our Lord's death and wounds—"

Bothild looked at her foster-father in terrified wonder. But then she began to weep again. "Sins I may have to answer for, though I be young—"

"You will tell them tomorrow to Sira Eyvind and then you may rest with an easy mind—"

Olav seated himself on the side of the bed, holding Bothild's hand in his; she was weeping quietly and miserably.

"The Christmas feast is better kept in heaven," he said softly.

"You may fetch him, then," she whispered at last, utterly broken, and then she wept again.

Next day Olav fetched the priest. Bothild was shriven, and when it was done she sent for her foster-father and sister and the whole household, begged their forgiveness if she had offended them, wittingly or unwittingly. Then Sira Eyvind gave her extreme unction and the bread of parting.

After the priest had ridden away, Olav went in and sat by the dying girl.

"Now, my Bothild, you will soon be gathered to your father. And then you must beg my friend Asger to forgive me for not keeping my word to him so well as I ought—the word I gave him on the day when I received you at his hands and promised to be to you as a father. Do you remember that day?—you sat outside the door of the room where your father lay, it was raining and snowing; you were blue with cold. A good, obedient child you have always been, foster-daughter—God grant you may not have cause to complain too bitterly of me when you come before the judgment-seat."

"Toward me you were ever the most loving father." She paused awhile, then whispered as though she feared to broach this other subject: "Would you were never harder toward any other—"

"What mean you?" asked her father rather coldly.

"Eirik," said Bothild very softly. "Toward him meseems you were often hard."

"I trow not," replied Olav, dismissing the matter. "I know not that I have been stricter with Eirik than there was need."

Bothild was silent for some moments. Then she summoned up courage:

"There is Cecilia too, Father. I would wish that you do not give her to Jörund Kolbeinsson, if this be too grievously against her will."

"Is it so?" Olav asked reluctantly after a moment.

"She liked Aslak better," whispered her sister.

To that Olav made no answer.

"I had not thought to force Cecilia," he said at last. "I will not marry her to a man she is loath to take. But I cannot promise therefore to give her to any man on whom her fancy may light, if I have reason to count him no good match for her."

Olav's tone was such that the sick girl dared say no more of the subject.

It vexed Olav that his foster-daughter had spoken of these things. Eirik's departure from Hestviken had been too like a flight for Olav not to wonder at it. And there was one thing and another that he had seen—his suspicions were dawning. Only Olav would not admit them. No, such a thing one ought not to believe of any man, nor of Eirik either: that he could engage in clandestine commerce with a young maid who was under his own father's protection, his foster-sister. It was true that foster-brothers and sisters —but that of himself and Ingunn was another matter; they had been called an affianced pair from childhood; that it grew to love between them, that they even forgot themselves in each other's

arms—that was bound to come when there was none to take care
of them and lead them aright, as inevitably as that two young sap-
lings growing side by side should blend their twigs and leaves into
one crown of foliage. Neither Eirik nor Bothild had ever been
told of such plans in their case. It was true that he had *thought* of
it at times: if it turned out that Eirik came home, and that Cecilia
would not inherit Hestviken after him—then he might marry her,
who was scarcely less dear to him than his own daughter, to
Eirik. It might be a sort of consolation that the new race would be
her children. But these had been but the vaguest thoughts, he had
spoken of them to none; so far as he recalled he had only given
Bothild's youth and poverty as his reasons when he let Ragnvald
of Galaby know that he not be at the trouble of sending his suitors
for her.

Then there was that about Cecilia. No word had come from
Jörund's kinsmen, and in his heart Olav was bitterly offended;
'twas not good manners that Jörund should first feel his way in a
matter of this kind, and when he was told he might try his luck,
should do no more. In secret Olav was angry both with Jörund
and with Eirik, who was to blame in this.

That affair of Aslak was not worth further thought. He could
see no sign that Cecilia thought any more of their guest.

But nevertheless Olav was disturbed in mind. He was by no
means so sure that there had not been something between Eirik
and Bothild of which he knew nothing—he could not tell *what* it
had been. A feeling of uncertainty stole in upon him during the
long nights of watching.

Cecilia— Folk said it was always thus: if a woman has bastards,
the same fate will befall her daughters as far as the third generation. Ingebjörg Jonsdatter, Ingunn— 'Twas monstrous to think of
such a thing with Cecilia, cool and chaste as the day at dawn: un-
thinkable that any man could decoy that steadfast child from
the right way. There was nothing about her to remind him
of her grandmother's ardent waywardness or her mother's defenceless weakness. But God, my God! can one human ever
answer for another in such things? He had only to think of himself—

In any case he would be glad when the day came that he had
Cecilia married and safely disposed of—he knew that now.

• • •

In the evening, as he sat with the sick girl, Bothild asked a question about her father—a little thing she thought perhaps Olav would know.

It had never occurred to Olav to speak of his friend to that friend's daughter. He was now surprised to find that Bothild had faithfully remembered her father all these years. Olav was glad that at last he had found a subject on which he could talk to the sick girl. Now one youthful memory after another came up—as far back as the time he was in Denmark with his uncle. Indeed, there was a great deal he could tell Bothild about Asger Magnusson and the kinsfolk they had in common.

"How near akin are we then, Eirik and I—and Cecilia?" asked Bothild after a while.

Olav unravelled the relationship. It was very distant. But to Eirik, of course, Bothild was not related at all, he thought to himself.

Surely she could never have asked that in order to find out whether there were kinship within the prohibited degrees?—for she must now have reconciled herself to the thought of death.

Never again did he bring himself to speak as he had spoken that night when for the first time he had seen that the poor child was unwilling to die—of the kingdom of God and Christ's love and of the paths he had once followed but had allowed to become grass-grown.

Then, ten nights before Yule, Bothild Agersdatter died in the arms of her foster-sister.

Sir Ragnvald Torvaldsson spent that winter at his manor near Konungahella. He was a little surprised when Eirik Olavsson returned, since, for all he knew, the lad this time had meant to leave his service for good. But he received the young man well—he was used by now to Eirik's fitfulness and love of change; but the man was brave, loyal and active when on duty, and Sir Ragnvald liked his ways.

So Eirik was given his old place in Sir Ragnvald's hall; and then he went about among his old comrades like a man who has been bewitched. There was neither song nor sport in Eirik that winter.

The more he struggled to tear himself out of his own thoughts, the worse it was—he was like a fish in the net: the more he tossed and floundered to be free, the faster he was caught.

If he tried to think of the first happy, innocent days at home with Jörund and Cecilia, their gaiety and summer work at the beloved manor, it only aggravated his pain: he himself had destroyed all this for ever. The sorrowing figure of Bothild came before him—the frightened child whom he had betrayed and profaned and hunted like a wolf, though he loved her—she was the first and only one he had loved.

He did not understand how he could have acted thus to her. It was not like him— But he had an obscure feeling that some ancient evil met him wherever he went at Hestviken last summer, welling up from the ground and the water and the old houses and from Liv's cabin—as the black water oozes up in a man's footsteps as he passes over marshy ground. And like the fumes of stagnant, putrid bog-water it had made him feverish and light-headed.

But now there was an end of *that*—to Hestviken he could never return. Now he was an outlaw, exiled from his home. For now his father must have heard all. And the thought of meeting his father after this, of being called to account by him—that terrified Eirik much more than the thought of doomsday.

In vain, in vain that Bothild held him dear. He knew now that she did so, and she had been waiting for him all these years while he was abroad in the world. It was her timid, faithful, waiting love that he had seen in those humble glances, in her helpless submission, when they were together. And now he had wasted it all.

At times he tried to take heart of grace. In the first place it was not *true* that he had profaned and betrayed his beloved. For he had never *done* her any ill—and surely thought is free in this world. He had behaved rudely and discourteously more than once—'twas bad enough, but no worse than that.

It availed nothing that he said such things to himself. That evening in the doorway of the women's house, the horror of that night in the wood—these were not to be surmounted. He could not shake off the feeling that much more had happened than he knew to be the actual fact. And it was like sinking into an abyss of horror.

And then came the temptation to make an end of it. To set his sword-hilt against a stone and aim the point at his heart; then the cold steel might quench the burning anguish in his breast. It was toward Yule that this thought haunted him; he had no peace, day or night—it must be such a relief to take one's life.

But one morning in the new year he awoke in a mood so changed that it seemed a mist had been blown away. It had suddenly become incomprehensible to himself that he could have had such thoughts.

Bothild, his poor sweet wife—was she to wait in vain! Of course she was waiting now for him to come back to her. He had been cruel and bad toward her—but he had not outraged her, God be praised! And when they parted—they had parted as friends; he had promised to come back to her.

His father—he could not understand how he had been so mortally afraid of him. Was he not a grown man? If his father wished to fly into a rage, then let him! Besides, why should Bothild have said anything to his father? Nothing had taken place between him and her that would give her ground for complaining to her foster-father. What if he had taken her in his arms rather roughly once or twice, given her a kiss—no maid need be distressed at that!

Cecilia had said that their father would seek out a good marriage for Bothild—he loved Bothild as though she were his own child. And even if he should deem her not rich enough to be his daughter-in-law—Eirik would make his father change his mind!

It was glorious winter weather, the snow gleamed in the sunshine, and the sky was as blue as if spring were on the way. As he went about, Eirik hummed or sang aloud. And in the evening, when he accompanied his lord to his bedchamber, he asked to be relieved of his service. To Sir Ragnvald's question what it was *this* time, Eirik replied that he had received word that he was to come home and be married.

Sir Ragnvald had drunk freely and was in good humour; he rallied the young man and drew him out, and Eirik told him a tale:

It was his foster-sister—daughter of that Asger Magnusson who had gotten Eirikstad by his marriage with Knuthild Holgeirsdatter —Sir Ragnvald knew this story and how he had slain Paal Galt and been made an outlaw. Well, Olav of Hestviken had taken to himself both the old she-bear and the little maid—Olav and Asger had been brothers-in-arms. Now she was grown up, fair and bonny, a mirror for all women, but possessed of neither land nor rich kinsfolk; so Olav would not hear of the marriage. 'Twas for that Eirik had returned to Sir Ragnvald in the autumn—he would give his father time to change his mind, for he had declared they should not see him at Hestviken again until his father was willing to give him Bothild. And Olav knew from of old that Eirik was not one to give in.—And now his father was well on in years; he found it hard to cope single-handed with the whole charge of the manor; he needed his son at home. So he had sent a message: Eirik must come home; he should have Bothild to wife, and now his father wished it to take place as soon as might be—no doubt the betrothal would be held at once and the wedding as soon as the fast was at an end. Ay, truly, said Eirik, he had received the message yesterday at church; a man from Maastrand who had been with the Minorites, and he had spoken to him after mass. Some of the folk from his home parish were always engaged in the herring fishery at Maastrand. Therefore he would fain go at once; he could then accompany this man as far as Maastrand and get a passage home in one of the fishing-boats.

Sir Ragnvald wished him joy and gave him as a parting gift the horse Eirik was wont to ride, with saddle and harness, and a red cloak with a hooded cape of black silk.

No later than the next day but one Eirik rode northward; he was bound for Maastrand. It did not trouble him that the story he had told Sir Ragnvald was untrue; but it was a fact that fisherfolk from near his home were often to be found there in winter, so he was sure to meet with some who could take him up to Folden.[5]

The fishing was in full swing, and besides, Eirik wished to take his horse on board with him, for now he had the idea of giving it to Bothild as a bridal gift. So more than a week went by before he could get a passage—with some men from Drafn who had been at Maastrand selling salt.

They had rough weather on the voyage along the coast, and when they came to Stavern the traders had to put in to shore and lie there. Folden was full of drift-ice to the northward, and long stretches were frozen over; there was no crossing the fiord either by boat or on horseback.

[5] The Oslo Fiord.

Eirik's impatience had increased hourly during the whole voyage. Bothild, Bothild, ran constantly in his mind; he imagined her waiting for him at home in Hestviken. There was none to whom he could pour out his cares.—Or else they were sitting in the women's house, she and Cecilia, spinning and sewing, and talking of him. He could see her face and her eyes as she stepped into the room—when it had been cried over the whole manor that Eirik had come home. And when he thought how he would hold her in his arms, the first moment they were alone together, every drop of blood in him thrilled and laughed in joyful longing; his evil mood was only recalled as a spell from which he had been set free. Now she too had been set free from sorrow and sickness, and they would live together in joy and amity all the days of their life. He doubted not that his father would yield, when first he had had time to growl and show his black looks. But when he saw that his son would *not* give in—!

So Eirik Olavsson saddled his horse and took the road northward along the western shore of Folden. At Tunsberg folk said the same: 'twas useless to attempt to cross the fiord to Hestviken. So he rode on. Right up into the hundred of Skogheim he had to go; the head of the Oslo Fiord was firmly frozen over. Eirik had no time to go round by the town; he turned his horse southward.

It was afternoon as he rode through the church town at home. There he met Ragnvald Jonsson with a loaded sledge; they stopped and greeted each other. Eirik asked whether Ragnvald had been out at Hestviken lately.

"Not since the funeral ale," said Ragnvald.

As Eirik made no reply, Ragnvald thought he must break the silence:

"I have not spoken with your father or Cecilia since—I have not seen them elsewhere than at church. 'Twas a heavy sorrow for them—though not unlooked for; but she was young and good, God rest her soul! He could not have made a fairer funeral ale if it had been for his own child—and he spoke handsomely over the bier, did Olav, as she was borne out of the house."

"I knew not that my sister was dead—"

Eirik was motionless, gazing before him. Ragnvald felt ill at ease, for he guessed that this was a great blow. Then he gathered up the reins and urged on his horse.

"Nay, if I am to reach home ere dark— Farewell, Eirik, we shall meet again if you mean to stay at home awhile."

Eirik came to where he could see the little houses of Rundmyr snowed under beyond the white expanse. A shudder of disgust and sickly fear assailed his stricken soul.

The endless grey frost-fog from the fiord grew denser over the smoke-coloured clouds in the west, behind which the sun had gone down. There was so little depth of snow that stones and roots showed bare in the track under the alders; dark bristles left from the summer's meadowsweet and yellow, withered grass bordered the path beside the frozen stream.

Light, bare, and open the woods were now. But somewhere upon this very path it had happened—and Eirik vividly recalled the rank and clammy darkness of the autumn night as a night of wickedness in which they two had been imprisoned.

It was growing dark as he rode into the yard at home. Olav himself was out of doors. He went to meet the stranger; on recognizing his son he gave him a surprised but friendly greeting: "Is it you—?"

His father's close-knit figure, not very tall, looked broad and bulky in his sheepskin coat; he was bareheaded. In the dusk Eirik could just make out his hair and face, grey all over, the clear-cut features gashed and drawn in on one side. Eirik did not know whether his despair grew worse or better at the sight of the other. A kind of hope sprang up in him that he might find help in his father, but he checked it as one checks a hound on the leash: so many a time he had hoped in vain of Olav.

Then came old Tore, greeted him and took his horse. Olav bade his son go in.

6

Olav and Eirik lived but moderately well together for the rest of the winter.

Eirik knew no peace. He could not bear Hestviken; he had forgotten what his father was like in daily life—silent, with a far-off look in his eyes; if one spoke to him it was often like calling over hill and dale. And then it might happen that Eirik felt his father staring at him, and Eirik could never be sure whether his father was looking at him or whether he glared like this without knowing it. Eirik could not stand him. And his sister was always so quiet and distant.

So Eirik went about among their neighbours, and when he came home he had usually been drinking. Olav knew that the men whose company the lad sought were fit for nothing but drinking and gaming; immoral in other ways they were too. Most of them were younger sons on the great manors, such as stayed at home and refused to do what might be held the work of a servant. But Olav said nothing to Eirik about the company he kept—he ignored him.

It was Ragnvald Jonsson, the Sheriff's brother, who had now become Eirik's best friend. At first Eirik had associated with Ragnvald because in a vague way he hoped or expected that the other would tell him more, since it was from his lips that he had first heard of Bothild's death. Even if Ragnvald had not known his sisters very well, he had nevertheless seen more of them than most other young men thereabout.

Later, as the torment gnawed and gnawed at Eirik's soul, there arose within him a morbid desire to question his friend: had rumours ever been abroad concerning Bothild? By degrees he had been ground down to such a depth of misery that he believed it would be easier to live if he could hear that she had had a name for being light or wanton. For it was more than he could bear, if he had shed innocent blood.

But no one ever spoke of Bothild Asgersdatter. And at last he swallowed his shame, one night when he slept at Galaby and shared a bed with Ragnvald.

Eirik then asked his friend: "What meant you by what you said, that day you were out at Hestviken last autumn? Of Bothild?"

"I cannot recall that I said anything—"

"Oh, yes. You spoke of her, so lightly—"

"Are you out of your wits—I spoke lightly of your sister?"

"She was only my foster-sister. Your words made me think that maybe Bothild was no more steadfast than that folk deemed she might let herself be tempted by a man—"

"He would have to turn himself into a bird, like the knight in the ballad, the man who would tempt one of Olav's daughters, so well are they herded! I think you are out of your wits, Eirik!

Maybe I said a word or two in jest—now you speak of it, I believe I remember. To tell the truth, I myself liked Bothild so well that I got Reidulf to make inquiry of Ólav one time. But the answer he was given was such that we could only suppose Olav had chosen her to be your bride" Ragnvald gave a little laugh—"unless he meant to take her himself, old as he is."

Some days later, when Olav and Eirik were alone in the great room, Eirik asked suddenly: "Father—is it true what folk say in the parish—that you were to marry Bothild?"

Olav looked up sharply from the thongs he was plaiting into a rope. He *looked* at his son for a moment, then went on with his work, said nothing.

Eirik insisted, almost pleading: "I have been told it for sure—"

"I wonder," said Olav quietly, "*what* thing you could be told that was too foolish for you to believe it!"

Eirik whispered: "You—or I. They say that, from the way you spoke of her, they could only deem you to have chosen her to be mistress here at Hestviken one day."

Again Olav looked up. Still he made no answer, but Eirik saw the changing expression in the elder man's ravaged face—surprise, or pain, or both.

"Father—is it true—was it your purpose that Bothild and I should possess this house in common?"

"It may be," Olav said in a low voice, "I had purposed something of the sort. That it would be for the good of the manor—after my time—that you took a wife whom I knew to be well fitted and not idle, when the time came for you to be master—"

"Had we but known that!" Eirik smote his hands together, clasped them. "Had we but known that! But we both thought you would never hear of such a thing—since she was a poor orphan, without kinsfolk, without a foot of land—'twas vain to think of it—"

Olav leaned forward, resting his elbows on his knees and letting his hands hang down.

"Then you spoke of this?" he asked at last, quietly, without looking up.

"We spoke of it that last evening, on the way home from Rundmyr."

"Ah, well," sighed Olav after a long pause. "But she had been sick ere that. So God alone knows how it would have turned out."

They sat in silence for a while.

" 'Tis not easy either, for a woman," said Olav in a low and earnest voice, "if she be weak in health—to have the charge of a great house like this, to take part in her husband's cares and counsels, to bear maybe one child after another, though she be weary and sick. I saw that with your mother, Eirik—her lot was a hard one here—"

Eirik rose and stood before his father. "That may be, Father. But now I have lost all desire to deal with the things of this world. So now I mean to betake myself to a convent."

Olav raised his head—stared at the young man in astonishment.

Eirik said: "I feel, Father, this is a heavy blow to you. You have but one son to be your heir, and he is to be a monk. But you must not oppose me in this!"

"Oppose you— But it comes unlooked for."

At that moment Eirik was aware that it had come unlooked for upon himself. He had not thought of it until the instant he uttered the words. But then God Himself must have put them in his mouth.

"After the holy days I had purposed to go in to Oslo, to speak with the guardian."

"Is it to *them* you will go—to the begging friars?"

Eirik nodded.

"Do others know of this—do they await you at the convent?"

Eirik shook his head.

"Then you must give me time—to think the matter over," said Olav.

Eirik nodded. They said no more to each other, and soon after Cecilia came in with the maids.

No sooner had Olav gone into the closet than Eirik threw himself down before the crucifix. His state of mind was that of a man who has lost his way in bogs and wastes and suddenly comes upon a firm path—and he prayed as a man astray hurries toward the haunts of men. It seemed to him almost a miracle—never before in all his days had he thought for a single instant of entering a convent—and the longer he prayed, the more clearly he seemed to see the path before him and the lighter it grew about him.

He did not think even now of what the words meant, any more

than he did when he repeated them morning and evening and every time he entered a church. But they bore his soul up like a stream, and he floated upon it on and on toward new scenes.

Little had he learned of the Christian religion, and of that little he no longer remembered much. But as he now tried to call forth what he had once known—of our Lord's life and death, the story of Mary, the words of the Prophets and the songs of David, the prayers of the mass—he felt as though he had come into a noble gallery where massive, fairly carven chests and coffers stood in every corner. He himself was now the young heir, who had entered for the first time with the keys in his hand. Full of impatient zeal, he was scarce able to await the hour when he might unlock and possess and handle all the hidden treasures of the faith.

Perhaps it would be his lot to be made a priest—he was no slower at learning than other men, so he must be able to achieve this. Eirik had a vision of a man standing before an altar; garbed in fine linen and gold embroidery he lifted up his hands to receive heaven's deepest mystery, incomprehensibly united with Christ Himself in the miracle of the mass. It was as though the angel of the Lord had seized him by the hair, raised him out of his wonted world, placed him there—as he remembered to have heard of one of the wise men of the Jews: he went out into the fields with his porridge-bowl to bring food to his mowers, when the angel of the Lord came, seized him by the hair, and carried him away to Babylon.

They would be astonished, the brethren of Konungahella, when they heard that Eirik Olavsson had entered their order—little had either they or he dreamed that one day he would be a barefoot friar! Now he recalled that this had also come to him as an inspiration, without his having to think or choose—to the Minorites of Oslo he was to go. And in this too he was satisfied with God's choice. He had always made his confession to the Minorites, both in Oslo and in Konungahella—folk said they prayed far more for their penitents than did the secular priests. Though he had seldom made up his mind to be shriven more than once a year, before Easter—he had dealt unwarily with his soul, he saw that now. But he had always liked these brethren, and looked forward to seeing their joy when he came and asked to be admitted to their company.

Olav lay awake. And as he strove to see clearly in the welter of thoughts to which his son's words had given rise, he heard the hurried whispering stream of words—Pater, Ave, Credo, Laudate Dominum. The young voice rose and fell, the words ran faster or slower, as the stream ebbed and flowed in Eirik's mind.

The lad had lighted a candle when he went to his prayers. It was so placed that Olav could not see it from where he lay, but beyond the open door the room swam in a soft golden light.

Olav's heart was oppressed. Yet he said to himself that it was a great godsend if Eirik so utterly unexpectedly and of his own accord had now found a call for the monastic life. A godsend for the lad himself, a godsend for Cecilia. And he would be freed from the rankling thought of the bastard heir whom he had falsely brought into his kindred.

Great as was the injustice he had committed in giving out another man's child for his own, had he *not* done so, but let the boy stay where his mother had hidden him away in the wilds—then indeed Eirik's lot would never have been other than that of a poor man's child. That too would have been an injustice—on *her* part. Now he would be a servant of God—and he might bring the convent a rich dower; if he wished to bestow on it the whole of his mother's inheritance, Olav would not oppose it. Then *that* sin would be undone. And this child of her misfortune would be made a life dedicated to the glory of God and many men's profit; for in times such as these, when so many seemed indifferent, uncharitable, and froward in their attitude to God, it was good and salutary to see a young man of Eirik's condition give up all for the sake of the kingdom of heaven. And now he might be an aid to his mother, maybe. Perhaps to him too—

Nevertheless his father's heart was heavy.

He could not rid himself of the thought of what Eirik had said of a marriage with Bothild. An unwise match it would have been —Olav was not sure whether he would have consented to it. But he could not help thinking of the grief of the two young people —of all the nights he had watched beside his foster-daughter. Had the child had this sorrow upon her as she lay there? It almost made him wish they had spoken to him. And yet the sickness must have had a good hold on her—'twould only have been the misery of Ingunn over again. And Eirik had been vouchsafed a better lot. It was better as it was.

But, but, but— Often as he had thought it would be better if Eirik never returned to Hestviken—intensely as the lad's ways had often irritated him, rousing him a thousand times to wrath, contempt, perplexity in his dealings with this strange bird he had taken into his nest—there had been so much else blended with these feelings while he had under his protection the offspring of that disaster which had wrecked his own and Ingunn's lives. He had taken charge of Eirik since the lad was a child, had cared for him as he grew up into a man. And now that he was to relinquish his charge, it was as though the young man had been his own son.

The voice within was hushed, but the candle was still burning—and now and again he heard a sound of snoring. Olav got up and looked into the room. Eirik was still on his knees, sunk forward on a chest with his head buried in his arms. The lighted candle stood just by his elbow. It might easily have been overturned into the straw.

His father took hold of Eirik and aroused him as gently as he could. Barely half-awake, his dreamy eyes heavy with sleep, Eirik undressed without a sound, lay down on his bed, and fell asleep at once. Like a child he had been, as in a deep torpor he obediently did as his father told him.

Olav blew out the light, pinched the wick between wet fingers, and stole quietly back to the closet. Lying awake in the dark, he resumed the contest with his unreasoning heart.

7

ONE evening in the following week, as Eirik was at his prayers—and now it seemed to him an immemorial custom that when the rest of the household had gone to rest he abandoned himself every night to hours of praying—he was aroused by a sharp whisper:

"Eirik—?"

He turned. Halfway down the ladder that led to the room above the closet and anteroom the white form of his sister appeared.

Eirik broke off abruptly with "*In nomine—*" and crossed himself, as though throwing a cloak about him. Then he sprang up and went to her.

"Do I keep you awake, Cecilia?"

"Yes—I am afraid you will fall asleep and forget the candle. You have done so many times—and yesternight I had to come down and put it out, for Father was asleep too."

The girl was shivering with cold in her thin nightdress. Eirik stood before her, looking up at her bright form: he thought she was like an angel, and he bowed his head forward, breathing affectionately on the bare toes, red with cold, that protruded below the long ample garment, clinging to the step of the ladder.

"Go up now, Cecilia, and lie down," he said gaily. And there came upon him a desire to speak with his sister of all the new thoughts that filled him. "Then I will come up to you anon."

He slipped in under her coverlet, crooked an arm around the head of the bed, and began, in an eager voice:

"Now you shall hear news that will surprise you, Cecilia—I am to go into a monastery."

"Ay, that I have heard."

Eirik checked himself, taken aback.

"You have heard it! Has father told you?"

"No, Ragna told me."

Ragna, the dairy-woman. Ah yes, he had chanced to mention it to her too. It dawned on Eirik that he had already mentioned it to not a few. But Ragna had always shown him kindness, and so he had said to her that when he was a monk he would pray specially for her eldest child, the sick girl. Ragna's three children had all been such good friends with Eirik last summer.

"Ah—" said Eirik. "Have you never thought the like, Cecilia— have you never been minded to become a nun and serve Mary maid?"

"No," said Cecilia. It sounded like a lock shutting with a snap, and Eirik was silenced.

"Nay, nay," he said meekly after a moment, "nor did this thought come to me of myself—'twas sent me by God's mercy."

"This came upon you rather suddenly?" asked Cecilia with hesitation.

"Yes," replied Eirik gleefully. "Like a knock at the door by night and a voice calling on me to rise and go out. Like you, I had never thought upon such things before. And so it may be with you too, sister."

"I know not," said Cecilia quietly. "I cannot think it. But 'twill be stilled here now," she whispered, and all at once her voice sounded pitifully small and weak. "First I lost Bothild—and now you are going from us—"

Eirik lay still, struck by his sister's words. He had almost forgotten their summer in all that had followed after; he seemed to have travelled a long way from the memory of Bothild in these last days. But now he called to mind how she had been wont to sleep by Cecilia's side, where he was now lying. All his memories, suddenly released, filled him with melancholy beyond bounds. He could not utter a word.

"Are you weeping?" he asked at last, as Cecilia did not break the silence either.

"No," replied his sister as curtly as before.

Ay, now Bothild slept under the sod, and his feet were set upon a path that led far away from all this. But Cecilia, she would be left here, lonely as a bird when all its fellows have flown, alone with her sad and silent father.

"Have you heard no more of Jörund this winter?" it occurred to him to ask.

"We have not." He could hear by her voice that she was in a ferment.

"That is strange. He let me suppose he would be here some time this winter."

Cecilia gave a start; she turned abruptly to the wall. Eirik noticed that the girl was trembling. He raised himself on his elbow, leaning over his sister.

"What ails you?" he asked anxiously.

"Nothing ails me," she whispered, half choking. "I do not ask how it is with Jörund Kolbeinsson. *I* have not set my mind on him."

Eirik said doubtfully: "I cannot make this out. You speak as if you were angry with him."

"Angry?" She flung herself round again, facing her brother. "Maybe I am. For I am not wont to hear such speech from a man as Jörund used to me. And I gave him such answer that he—that he— I am unused to put up with a slight."

"Now you must tell me how this is," Eirik begged her quietly.

"Nay, I know not—maybe it counts for little among folk now-adays, and 'tis only I, a home-bred maid, who deem that the word of a noble damsel is worth so high a price. But he came to me in the women's house, the evening before he was to ride away. And then he said—ay, he let me know that he would come back together with his kinsmen and sue for me. Then he asked if this was against my will. To that I said no. He also asked leave to kiss me," she whispered almost inaudibly. "Again I did not refuse him. God knows I would rather have been left unkissed. God knows I had not set my mind on him. But his speech was such that I could but think it was Father's wish—and yours. And so I would not set myself against it. At that time I thought so well of Jörund that I believed he might be better than most others. Since I can clearly see that Father is little minded to let me have a say in my own marriage. But Jörund, I ween, counts a word and a kiss for little worth."

With a sudden impulse Eirik bent over his sister and kissed her on her lips. Then he lay down quietly again.

"Maybe Jörund could not decide for himself," he said, finding an excuse on the spur of the moment. "Maybe his kinsmen had already treated of another marriage for him, without his knowing it."

"Then he should not have spoken," replied Cecilia angrily—"if he knew not whether he were bought or sold."

"That may be so. But—ay, he spoke to me of this matter as though it lay very near his heart—that he got you to wife, I mean. But you know, he had to go home and consult his brothers—"

"Then do they think we are not good enough for Jörund?"

Eirik did not know what to say. His sister had reason to be angry. And now he seemed to remember speaking of this to Jörund, and Jörund had promised him not to say anything of the matter to Cecilia before he came as a suitor. But he could guess that Jörund might easily forget that promise, Cecilia being so fair and sweet. So he took her hand, laid it on his breast, and stroked it, while he fell back upon the first excuse he had tried to offer for his friend:

"They must have designed another marriage for him, without his knowing it."

Cecilia did not answer. Eirik lay patting her hand—but now he found he was getting very sleepy. She must be already asleep.

Once more Eirik bent over her, cautiously kissed his young sister, then stole out of the bed and down. He was already on the ladder when the chilly little voice asked in the darkness above:

"You will say no more prayers tonight, will you?"

"No," replied Eirik feelingly; "now I will go to rest."

"Then you will put out the light?"

Eirik did so. He lay in bed feeling angry with Jörund for having shown his sister and all of them so little respect. But at the same time he had in some sort conceived an aversion for the thought of giving Cecilia to Jörund. This one week of his conversion had altered his view of many things. He now thought of his whole life since he had run away from home with repugnance, nay, with sorrow. He repented his sins, that was well enough—but beyond that he wished, now that his life was to be consecrated to God, that it had been less defiled.

But Jörund, to whom no such call had come—of him no man could require that he should be better than other men. And Jörund was no *worse*. But Cecilia—she was so *good*.

Olav had not meant very much by it when he hinted that he had no very great esteem for the order of the Minorites. He had grown somewhat tired of them, like many other folk in the neighbourhood, in Sira Hallbjörn's time—because the priest constantly had them at his house. The Grey Friars had long been at strife with the cathedral chapter and the priests of Oslo, but it was not certain that the brethren had been chiefly to blame for the quarrel. And there had been some ugly talk of one of the Minorites and Eldrid Bersesdatter of the Ness—but there had always been ugly talk about Eldrid, ever since her father gave the reluctant maid to old Harald Jonsson, though no one could give clear proof of it; she was barren as the sole of an old shoe. She was moreover the daughter of a nephew of old Sira Benedikt and a second cousin of the daughters of Arne, but her kinsfolk never spoke of her; she had quite dropped out of good company. The young friar, Brother Gunnar, who had been too often with her at the Ness, had been sent out of the country, to a school of learning, it was said.

The only men of the order whom Olav knew something of were the Richardsons' brother, Edvin the painter, and Brother Stevne, who used to come out to Hestviken once a year, in Lent—he had done so ever since he attended Ingunn in her hour of death.

Olav did not like Brother Stevne's appearance: he was a little crook-backed man with a face like a bad fairy; one intuitively expected him to wag his long, flexible nose. But Olav had never heard or seen anything but good of the man.

And as Eirik seemed so fixed in his desire to enter this order, his father was quite willing to give him to the Minorites with a fitting endowment.

Olav gave much thought to the question of Eirik's birth. But he had never heard of dispensation for bastard birth being denied to any man who was otherwise well suited to be a monk or priest. And he had already burdened his conscience with so much that he might well add this to the load—hold his peace about his secret. This burden had grown into his flesh and into his soul—he felt it was beyond his power to rid himself of it.

Eirik felt his father's changed attitude toward him as part of his new happiness. Although Olav had not much more to say to his son than usual, Eirik was aware of the new warmth with which he was met whenever he was in the elder man's company. Most of the sayings and preaching of pious men that Eirik had heard of late years had gone in at one ear and out at the other, but now one thing and another recurred to his memory. "Seek ye first the kingdom of God and His righteousness, then shall all other good things be added unto you"—something like this Christ had once said to His disciples, he had heard. Eirik remembered it now. All his life he thought there was one thing he had desired more than all else in the world: to force his father to acknowledge him with loving pride. Now, when he was about to renounce all the good things of this world in order to win heaven, he received as a parting gift that for which he had begged from his childhood's days.

So it was only the thought of his sister that caused Eirik uneasiness. He said to himself that after all none but his father and sister could have thought of taking this matter of Jörund's suit so seriously, calling it an affront and a broken promise. For nowadays folk were not so scrupulous about every word spoken at random—he himself had never been so. But now it seemed to him that his father was right—life would be much better if folk were more prone to keep their word.

. . .

One day when Olav and Eirik were down on the beach engaged in tarring a boat, and Cecilia had brought them their afternoon meal, her brother said, after she had gone:

" 'Twill be lonely for her when I have left."

"Maybe." Olav followed the girl with a thoughtful look as she went up the hill.

Eirik said: "That is the only care on my mind, that I must go away before her future is assured."

"I think you may leave me to deal with that." Olav's lips twitched with the little crooked smile that had been so habitual to him of old when answering his son. "For many years we have seen no sign that you troubled yourself about your sister's welfare."

"Nay, nay. But I had to see the world first, like other men. And I knew she was safe in your care."

"Think you that is no longer good enough?"

Eirik paused, pressing the scraping-iron against the boat's side and looking down.

"You know, Father, you begin to grow old, so—" Eirik stole an embarrassed glance at his father. Olav's mien was now cold and unfriendly. Nevertheless he went on: "My sister is not so cheerful and easy in her mind as she should be—at her age."

Olav could not forbear, though he was loath to put the question. "Has she complained—to you?" he asked suspiciously.

It was Aslak he had in his mind. But Eirik answered: "I think she marvels that she has heard no more of Jörund."

Olav went savagely at the work he was doing, but said nothing.

"Have you had no message from them?" asked Eirik at last.

"Does she *know* that Jörund—? If I remember aright, I bade you tell your friend that I enjoined him not to give the child any hint of the matter till it had advanced much farther. I call it unmanly and little consonant with honour if he has spoken to so young a maid ere his kinsmen and I have come to an agreement."

Olav's tone was so disdainful that something of Eirik's old feeling of comradeship with Jörund was awakened.

"*Spoken* he has not, for sure. But when two young people have a kindness for one another, 'tis not easily hidden, so that the one knows not the other's mind—"

Olav worked on in silence.

Jörund!" he exclaimed all at once, so gruffly and scornfully that Eirik dared not ask another question when his father relapsed into silence.

It was not one year since Aslak had used the same words—such things could not be hidden. Then he had kept an eye on his daughter, fearing she might regret Aslak too deeply. But he might safely have spared himself that. It was well she had not taken it so sadly but that she could now think of Jörund—so she would surely get over this fresh sorrow. And indeed she was little more than a child. —But, for all that, Olav felt it as a disappointment that his daughter could be so quick to forget.

Eirik wished to sail up to the convent before Easter—he could find no peace in his soul till he was admitted to the monastic life.

It had been Olav's intention to accompany his son. But he fell sick. He had got an inward hurt in the fight at Frysja bridge; he had taken little heed of it at the time, but ever and anon it showed itself in a bloody flux and vomiting. This time he had to take to his bed. But Eirik could not wait. So he promised to send his father word in good time, when the day was appointed for him to take the habit.

On the morning of his departure he went into the closet to take leave of his father. He knelt beside the bed and asked his father's blessing.

Olav said: "One thing I will ask of you, Eirik—that you learn the office for the dead and say it each week for your mother's soul and for your father."

"That I promise. To the best of my power I shall pray for my mother and for you."

In a low voice Olav answered: "For your father you must pray. But you are not to utter my name."

Deeply moved by his father's humility, Eirik kissed his hand.

Eirik Olavsson was received most affectionately by the Minorites. And so eager was he that he could not wait till after the holy-days; he began at once to seek instruction of the brethren regarding his new life, accompanied them to the choir, and took part in the singing as far as he could.

But in the week after Easter he went to the guardian and said he had a friend of whom he would take leave before he renounced the world. And he wished to ride thither at once; then perhaps there might still be time for him to take the habit on St. Eirik's Day,[6] as had been proposed.

Eirik had become convinced that his sister's agitation, on the night when he had talked to her, must be due to a feeling of love for Jörund. And now at any rate he would see whether he could render his beloved sister a service before he took his vows—in any case he would try to find out how the land lay.

At Gunnarsby he was well received, but Jörund was somewhat reserved. But when Eirik told him that he was to enter a convent and had come hither to bid his friend good-bye, both Jörund and his brothers seemed mightily surprised.

Two nights before Eirik was to leave, he and Jörund went out together to find a haunt of wood grouse. As they walked through the wood Jörund Rypa said to his friend:

"Howbeit, Eirik, it seems to me you should wait awhile and prove yourself ere you give up Hestviken and all the good things of this world."

He could hear by Eirik's voice that he was smiling in the darkness. "Why so? What should it avail, think you, that I proved myself, when I know this has not come from myself? You would not have me let Him wait who has called me?"

"This too you must lay aside," said Jörund as if in jest, nudging the bow that Eirik carried. "You were always a keen hunter, Eirik."

"I change it for a bow that shoots higher."

"Ay, so it is, no doubt. But will you not wait till we have time to speak with your father of that matter you know of—put in a word for me with Olav and Cecilia?"

Eirik could scarcely conceal his joy. And now Jörund said he had been uneasy the whole winter with longing for Cecilia. But he had waited because there had been a talk that Steinar and Brynhild should move to Norderheim, and he would rather the young Cecilia were spared having to dwell under the same roof with Brynhild, who was a shrew. But now that matter was in order.

Eirik nevertheless held to his purpose and left at the time he had appointed with the guardian. He gave Jörund a brooch to take to Cecilia as a token.

[6] May 18.

8

OLAV AUDUNSSON had barely risen from his bed after his sickness when the brothers from Gunnarsby came riding to visit him.

Olav received them well. He did not think his guests would notice that he was still unwell and could take little food—and his spirit was also weary within him: he found it hard to come to a decision as to what answer he should make, when the strangers set forth their errand.

In his anger with this Jörund Rypa, who had first lured him into giving a half-promise and then allowed three quarters of a year to go by without making a sign, Olav had thought: nay, he did not like the fellow, he did not trust him farther than he could see him; Cecilia might find ten husbands that were better than Jörund. But now these Rypungs had come, and he could not deny that they were courtly and well-born men. Aake, the eldest, was married to Lucia Toresdatter from Leikvin, and Steinar to Brynhild Bergsdatter from Hof in Lautin—so it was difficult for him to find any pretext, if he was to reject Jörund's suit. He had no other reason than his unwillingness to say yes.

So he sent a message privily to Baard of Skikkjustad and made a tryst with him at a place within his forest, not far from the manor.

Baard came and repeated all that he knew of the Gunnarsby folk.

The old oaks showed their tiny new leaves, reddish brown against the mild blue sky, and the grass sprouted up through the pale crust of withered leaves wherever the sun could reach it. Around the great embedded rocks that gathered its rays bloomed greater clusters of violets. Olav had stretched himself on the ground, and Baard, who sat watching his friend, thought he looked as if he might well be fey. He was grey and sunken in the face, his eyes as pale as milk and water, and yellow in the whites, the fine silvery sheen of his hair and stubbly beard was as it were tarnished. Then said Baard:

"You know, kinsman, Torgrim and I will protect Cecilia and her estate as well as we are able, if it should happen that she were left alone. But now all you possess will be hers, since Eirik is to enter a convent. And, after all, a husband takes better care of an estate than any other—"

Olav nodded.

He knew it. However good may be the intentions of a child's guardians, an estate fares best in the hands of an owner. If Jörund got Cecilia to wife, they would move out to Hestviken as soon as he died or grew too old to have sole charge; already there dwelt two married sons at Gunnarsby. Without a doubt it was the rumour that the son and heir was to become a monk that had induced the brothers to bring forward their suit at this time. But since the two young people had conceived a love for each other so long ago as last summer, as Eirik said, then Jörund would scarcely love her less now, when he was to get the manor with her. And all the Rypungs had the name of being active and prudent husbandmen, said Baard.

Olav himself had thought the child might be left alone before they were aware of it; he had been very low this spring. True, Cecilia would be in good hands with Baard and Signe, and, young as she was, she had good sense enough. But nevertheless her father was ridden by a kind of anxiety—what was it she might take after —her mother, and himself, God mend him—

"Then you advise me to it, I perceive," said Olav in a low voice.

"Mm—not that either," replied Baard. "But as matters stand now, with Eirik away, I will not *dissuade* you from it either, Olav!"

So when Aake Kolbeinsson brought forward the brothers' errand, Olav listened to him graciously and showed himself well disposed. The final agreement was that the betrothal feast should be held at Hestviken on the eve of St. Columba, and the bride should be brought to Gunnarsby four days before St. Laurence.[7]

Olav Audunsson had not been inside the church of the Minorite convent since the building was finished.

It was a bright and fresh May morning, and spring had come early this year, so that the wild cherry stood in full bloom by the roadside as Olav went up the hill from the wharf to the convent. He was early abroad—the bells were only beginning to ring in the steeple as he stepped upon the green before the church. Their

[7] St. Columba's Day is June 9; St. Laurence's August 10.

sonorous pealing right above his head sent a cold thrill down his back.

Within the church the sunlight entered the windows aslant like broad beams, in which the dust-motes danced. Olav threw a rapid glance around him, but it was not at all as he remembered the Franciscans' church—from that evening—dark and cold and desolate, still in disorder from the building, with the gaping chancel arch and black night beyond. Now the choir was flooded with light of many colours; the windows were already filled with stained glass; images were painted on the whitewash of the walls, and the high altar was very richly and handsomely adorned. Behind it, farther up the choir, he had a glimpse of the brown-frocked brethren standing in their stalls, they were already at their prayers.

By the wall to the left of the arch, where he remembered the strangely living crucifix had been placed, were now two small side altars with tapestries on the wall behind them. It was no doubt the same crucifix that now stood on the rood-beam, but it had a different look by daylight.

The church was still almost empty, so Olav seated himself on the bench near the door to wait for the time of mass. Idly he looked about him—'twas true, as folk said, the barefoot friars' church was now a fair one. Above him the bells were calling, and the guests flowed in, more and more of them. His own party came, Baard in his bravest array, Anki and Tore in the new clothes he had given them for the journey to town. They knelt awhile; when they rose Olav went forward with them toward the choir arch. Signe and Una were already kneeling at the head of the women's side, with Cecilia between them. The young girl was closely veiled. The church began to fill—it always drew many folk when a novice was to take the habit.

A monk came in with the long candlestick and lighted the tapers on the altar, and most of those who stood at the upper end of the nave knelt down. Olav felt ill at ease standing up, the mark of all eyes, so he too knelt and covered his face with a corner of his cloak. The soft coolness of the silk felt unfamiliar, for of late years he had not often worn his festival attire.

From habit he began to mumble the prayers, because he found himself on his knees—he always did so when custom and good manners demanded that he should seem to be praying. At the same time there was a sort of purpose in it: he passed for a pious Christian, and he *wished* to pass for one. He would keep his apostasy hidden as a secret of his heart; openly he would not be numbered with those who scorned or defied God. It was not their victory or success he desired; even as he was, he knew that he desired Christ's victory and honour—as a leader, outlawed in a foreign land, may secretly rejoice over the victories of his countrymen, secretly hope for the success of the banner under which he himself may never fight again.

But he knew too that these words which flowed from his lips were like seed-corn in which the germinating power had been killed, and he scattered them abroad nevertheless, because he did not wish his neighbours to know of his poverty.

But now, when he called to mind that next winter he would be alone at Hestviken, he could no longer steel himself against the soundlessness and emptiness within by the thought that he was working for others, all those whose welfare depended on his effort. It would be a gain to Cecilia, Olav saw that well enough, if her husband could take over without delay all that she was to bring him. And Eirik was gone, and Bothild was gone—

Then he would be left alone with his own soul, as a captive in the deepest dungeon is left alone with the corpse of his fellow prisoner.

Olav felt that these thoughts had brought him into a whirlpool; with desperate rapidity he was being sucked under. A sort of dizziness at the vision of the loneliness that would now prevail at Hestviken; then a stillness, as though he had sunk to the bottom of a sea, a clear and motionless abyss of darkness, and then the certainty that even in this abyss he was not alone. When everything on which he had been able to fix his thoughts was plucked out of his reach, he would again be alone with the Living One Himself, from whom he had sought to fly away and hide.

God, my God, hast Thou pursued me up into the sky and down into the depths of the sea? Once he had found himself face to face with God under the vault of pale-blue winter night—when he lost the other half of his life. Now, when he was losing all that he had tried to put in her place, he was forced to feel that God's eyes were looking upon him as though out of a forest of weed in the dark depths of the sea.

What if the seed-corn he had thought dead were not dead after all, what if the murdered child stirred on its bed of withered leaves and awakened?

Olav knew not whether there were more of terror or of hope in it; but in the vision that again overwhelmed him he saw that he had never been afraid to bear terror and pains when he believed he could save a life from being wasted or ruined. The only thing he had always been afraid of was to see a life brought to destruction, rot away. And with marvellous clearness he saw on a sudden that the same instinct that had forced him to take care of all who came in his way would now force him to be mindful of his own soul. That a man should love his even Christian as himself he had always heard and seen to be right, and the more one could follow that precept, the better. But as when a painted window is lighted up by the sun, so that one can distinguish the images in it, so did he perceive in a flash the meaning of God's command, clear and straightforward, that a man must also love himself.

He was aroused by a hand on his shoulder. One of the monks signed to him to move forward—Olav had not noticed how far the mass had progressed, but the priest was already at *Orate, fratres*—and now he saw Eirik; he had not remarked his son's coming.

But there under the choir arch lay Eirik, with his hands extended on either side, his forehead touching the pavement. His dark-red velvet cloak covered the kneeling figure, spreading out over the grey stones of the floor, and below it could be seen the outline of his sword; for today, when he was to offer himself and all that he owned to God, Eirik alone of all men was permitted to bear arms in God's house.

Olav stood up and advanced the few steps, then knelt in his place at the young man's left side. And at the last his affection for this son burst all bonds. It was his own son he was giving away today.—Olav hid his face again in the folds of his cloak.

His daughter he had promised—her he was to give away to a man whom he trusted no more than halfway, to all that was uncertain and transitory in this world; but for that reason it seemed to him that he was not taking his hand entirely from Cecilia; he might yet be compelled to intervene in her destiny. But Eirik was to be given to God, to what is firmer than all rocks, more certain than death and judgment—this was complete severance, for all time, for eternity, it might be.

"My son, my son, who is to make amends for my failure—"

Olav was too absorbed to follow the mass—he was aware of nothing around him until he heard the voice just above his head. The guardian stood in the centre under the arch; before him Eirik now knelt upright and erect, his young face turned upward, his cloak thrown back, so that the brooches and the bridegroom's chain flashed on his silken jerkin. Eirik was clad entirely in red, for his garments were to be offered to the altar, and they had most need of a new set of red vestments.

Olav heard Eirik say the responses—loudly and clearly so that he was heard over the whole church. Some women at the back wept aloud—but there are always some women who do that, Olav tried to persuade himself, so as not to be unmanned.—Eirik was of full age, so Olav was not called upon to answer.

He saw Eirik raised to his feet by the hand of the guardian. His spurs jingled faintly as the young man followed the monk up to the high altar. Olav saw the bundle of coarse, ashy-grey homespun that lay on the altar—the novice's habit was being blessed. Now it was given to Eirik, who took it and clasped it to his breast.

The contracting pain in his throat became unbearable—and Olav felt his burning eyes dimmed with tears. He drew his cloak before his face again. When he looked up once more, Eirik was gone.

Olav rose and went back to his place by Baard's side. He took in nothing of the prayers and lessons that followed. They had sung the *Veni Creator* to the end without his hearing it.

And at last they came back. Olav thought he did not know this young monk. The fine, narrow skull shone smooth and newly shaven above the black fringe of close-cropped hair, and was it Eirik's dark and mobile face that was now so changed, pale as bast beneath the brown complexion? His great yellow eyes blazed like stars. He looked even taller and broader in the shoulders in the grey frock with the knotted rope around his slender waist. Below the edge of the frock Olav saw his son's feet naked in the sandals.

For a moment Eirik stood still, beaming. Then he turned, passed round the choir, was greeted by his new brethren with the kiss of peace. When his father looked up again, the last of the monks were disappearing through the door leading to the convent.

Outside the church Olav met with his company. One after another they took him by the hand, wishing him joy of his son. Several of the townsmen who knew Olav Audunsson came up and greeted him.

The daughters of Arne were wiping their tear-stained faces with the flaps of their coifs. Cecilia wore her veil down—she had certainly never raised it once while in church.

"What think you of this, my daughter?" Olav asked her as they went round to the guest-house; they had all been bidden to break their fast there.

" 'Tis well," the maid said simply.

Oh, nay, but then 'twas true she had seen so little of her brother for many years, thought Olav.

9

OLAV had spared nothing in making his daughter's betrothal feast, and folk who had been present spoke well of it afterwards. Laughter and merriment were always somewhat rare at Olav Audunsson's banquets, but all was done in a handsome and worthy manner.

Signe and Una stayed on with two of their daughters and some serving-maids, and now there was a busy time at Hestviken. Cecilia's rich dowry was to be inspected and to receive its last touches, and festival garments were to be prepared for those of his household whom Olav was to take with him on the bridal journey.

One morning Signe came and said to Olav that now they must look through those things which the child was to inherit from her mother.

Ingunn Steinfinnsdatter's bridal chest had stood during all these years in the closet where Olav slept; he had never answered when anyone had suggested removing it to the storehouse. So when he and old Tore carried it into the light, the women were afraid that the stuffs might have suffered damage. Olav had indeed kept it resting on the ends of two beams, but the air of the closet was always so raw.

Olav saw that Cecilia was filled with expectation, though she appeared as calm as usual. His daughter had never set eyes on the goods she was to inherit from her mother; the chest had not been opened since the days Olav took his wife's grave-clothes out of it.

Olav gave the key to Signe. But the women could not cope with the lock—he had to do it himself. Then he stood by and looked at what they took out of the chest.

The first thing that met his eyes was a folded cloth of reddish-brown wool. A glimpse of the wrong side was enough: they had used it in his childhood at Frettastein, when they hung the walls of the hall. It was embroidered with the New Jerusalem and saints adoring the Lamb, according to the vision of Saint John. Above and below the images there were borders of vines, with beasts and hunters between.

The women shook it out, and there fell from it a shower of dried flowers that had been put in to guard against moth. It had taken no hurt.

"But beautiful you cannot call it," said Una; "it must be old as the hills." The saints were stumpy and broad and all the men had beards. "This cannot be anything for Cecilia to take to Gunnarsby?"

" 'Tis only laid over for a covering." Olav took the tapestry, rolled it up, and laid it on the bench behind him.

Piece by piece the things were lifted into the daylight and shaken out, making the bystanders sneeze with the herbs and spices that filled the air. Cushions and tapestries, kirtles and mantles, chaperons of velvet and Flemish cloth, shifts with embroidered fronts of silk and linen, and many vests to which the skirts had not been attached.

"Deft with her hands was Ingunn," said Una, handing one of these vests to Cecilia. "Have you ever seen such fine sewing?"

Cecilia fingered the costly piece: it was of white silk, embroidered in black and gold thread at the wrists and neck. "Nay, I have never seen the like. Mother had great skill!"

Her father nodded—he had no wish to enter the conversation. But in fact it was not Ingunn who had sewed this shirt body; he had bought it when he was in Stockholm with the Earl, of a man who said it came from Micklegarth.[8] Ingunn had never finished it for wear.

The women took out the carved coffer and spread the jewels over the table—finger-rings fastened together with a ribbon,

[8] Constantinople.

80

brooches white and gilt, but blackened and tarnished for want of use, a decayed leather belt studded with plates of chased metal. A ring-brooch of pure gold, which he himself had given her; he had inherited it of his father. Around the ring was inscribed the Angel's Greeting and "*Amor vincit omnia.*" Then Signe handed Olav a faded band of green velvet, thickly set with gilt roses—Ingunn's bridal garland, the symbol of inviolate maidenhood and gentle birth.

"I wonder that you did not give this to Cecilia for her betrothal," said Signe.

"The other garland that I gave her is better," replied Olav, turning the matter aside. "This one weighs scarce the half of it."

The women brought forward into the light a kirtle of green silk, woven with golden flowers and birds. Down to the waist it was fairly close-fitting, but wide below and exceedingly long. All the women broke into exclamations of delight at the beautiful stuff —'twas great pity that they must cut it shorter, if Cecilia was to wear it at her bridal.

Olav remembered that Ingunn had had to lift it as she went round the table pouring wine—she had caught her foot in it as they ran hand in hand across the wet courtyard that summer night—and in the dark bower he had felt the soft silk about her slender body as a part of the lawless sweetness of the adventure. His heart grew hot within him at the thought that that man should embrace his daughter in this very garb.

" 'Twould be a shame to cut up and spoil such costly silk," he said. "Cecilia is not so old but that she may grow taller yet—her mother was a tall woman. Better to let this gown lie by a few years longer."

Olav had arranged with Aake Kolbeinsson that he was to visit Gunnarsby before the haymaking, in order to become acquainted with the home of the Rypungs before he brought his daughter thither. He went by way of Oslo, taking a number of jewels and vessels to the goldsmith—Cecilia would have to bring a share of such into the estate, but there was such good store at Hestviken that he needed only to have some of the old vessels remade. His daughter's marriage entailed expense enough without his having to buy new silver for her dowry.

The last day he was in the town he went out into the fields and

heard vespers in the Minorites' church. After the service he went
to the gate and asked leave to speak with his son.

Brother Eirik came down to the gate—again Olav gave a start
on seeing the young monk, he was so unlike his old self. He had
already acquired the monastic air, but in such a way that it suited
him. At home Eirik had never seemed to know how to bear himself—now he was too noisy and now too abrupt, now too courteous and now too rude; but however he might be, there was too
much effort in all he did. Now he seemed to have learned to com-
port himself calmly, and he talked as though he had thought of
what he was to say.

He had little time, he said—'twas this sickness that was rife, they
had it here too. Father Einar said it came from the water; it turned
rotten in the heat. So now he and Brother Arne were busy in the
garden. But he would ask leave to bring his father thither, so that
they might talk as he worked.

It was cool in the shade of the great birches, and the grass grew
high and rank under the drip from the hollowed logs that carried
a stream from Eikaberg down to the convent garden. Olav sat
taking his ease as he watched the two young friars in grey frocks
watering rows of beans and beds of celery. In the flower-beds
beyond, a rose bloomed already here and there, and round about
them yellow lilies swayed, and some blue flowers the name of
which Olav did not know.

Now and then as Eirik went to the water-butt he said a few
words to his father. Father Einar, the master of the novices, had
already begun teaching him to read in a book and to write; it
came easy to him.

In one thing and another Olav recognized his son as of old—he
had always had such a strong belief in himself when he was to do
anything, before he had really set about it. But Eirik had not been
here more than six weeks, and already Olav could see a great
change in him. He sat there letting his affection for Eirik thaw and
warm his heart: after all, he had always been fond of this child
in a way, and it was good to feel that this battered and crippled
affection might now be suffered to grow healthy and strong.

At Gunnarsby Olav was received with such marks of friendship and honour by the Kolbeinssons that he could not help liking
the place.

The manor was a fair one and a great, and lying as it did on the sunny slope above a little lake, with broad acres and meadows about it and many new and well-built houses, it might well support three brothers in lordly fashion. Here the household was ordered more after the custom of the new nobles—as was to be expected with young masters and a greater range of husbandry. Between the masters themselves and the labourers in farmyard and workyard a crowd of serving-men and maids passed to and fro—some of these were poor kinsfolk of the Rypungs.

Olav had seen none of the women of Gunnarsby before now. Gunhild Rypa, the mother of the Kolbeinssons, was infirm and in her dotage. So Cecilia would have no mother-in-law above her. Aake's and Steinar's wives had just been brought to bed, both of them, when the betrothal feast was held at Hestviken. Olav liked them least of all the folk of Gunnarsby. Brynhild had a hard look, but Lucia was far too mild—she promised Olav that Cecilia should have milk to wash in and wine to drink, as the saying goes. Olav smiled to himself—Cecilia would be able to hold her own with them well enough; his child lacked neither wit nor will, and she bore herself in just as courtly a fashion as these two knights' daughters. Moreover, it was only natural that these brothers' wives should be glad to see the youngest of the family marry a franklin's daughter; then he could leave Gunnarsby with wife and children, when the time came.

So Olav was not ill pleased with what he had seen, when he rode from Gunnarsby.

The summer heat held on day after day. Toward nones the sky was often overcast—a dark-blue wall, flecked with flame-coloured clouds, rose above the wooded ridges; within the blue darkness gleamed distant lightnings, as when a candle is moved within a tent, and the thunder rolled faintly far up the country. Sometimes a shred of cloud brought a scud of rain over the dried-up fields, but the storm that was to clear the air was long in coming. And every evening it cleared up, and every morning dawned with a hazy blue sky that heralded a hot day.

And broiling hot it was even in the middle of the morning, the day Olav and Tore rode home through the woods that divide the districts of Eyjavatn and Folden. And toward nones, as they were riding high up on a hillside, the thunder-clouds again rolled up in the north and east, casting shadows over the sun-drenched woods, and darkening the tarns scattered over the pale bogs that stretched everywhere on the lower land.

The path led across some mountain pastures at the top of the ridge, and here they would unsaddle their horses and rest a few hours. Outside one of the sæters they found a young woman sitting and spinning, while she kept an eye on a caldron that hung over a fire close by. When she saw that the new-comers were peaceful wayfarers, she was overjoyed at having guests; she pressed upon them both fresh milk and curds to take on their journey. After they had talked awhile it came out that old Tore had known some kinsfolk of her master. So they two sat and talked, while Olav went down toward the brook they heard murmuring in the wood near by—he would look for a cool place where he could lie down and sleep.

He had to go some way down; up near the sæters the banks were trodden into mire round the watering-places, and the ants swarmed on the moss where he had first flung himself down under the firs. But then he came to a little patch of dry, close-cropped grass, thyme, and ground ivy, and there he stretched himself at the edge of the wood.

He was not so sleepy—lay looking up at the great dark, silver-bordered clouds that drifted over the tree-tops, causing a succession of shadows and sharp yellow sunlight. The thunder muttered far away, and at the bottom of the slope the brook swirled and gurgled among great stones.

On the other side of the stream the wood rose steeply to the rounded summit, but right opposite to him was a scree, where masses of red-flowered willow-herb grew among the stones. And all at once it flashed on Olav that he had been here once before—he recognized the scree and the cascade of flowers and these black clouds silently rising, and the murmur of the brook and the distant thunder—all had been present before.

Then the mirage vanished as suddenly as it had come. The place looked like any other watercourse in a wood. Olav lay down again, dozed with eyes half-open to the sunshine, and breathed in the scent of herbs that floated about him and made him sleepy.

Then all at once he was roused, broad awake, by a little whirring sound—before he had time to grasp what it was, a shadow flitted past him as swiftly as the shadow of a bird in flight. He opened his eyes, looked about him, and was aware of Ingunn standing in the scree on the other side of the brook among the red flowers.

Olav felt no surprise—as he rose on his knees he saw in a flash every detail he afterwards called to mind. A gust of warm wind passed through the wood at that moment, and the tall red tufts of flowers waved, the trees leaned over with a yielding droop of their tops and a soughing in their branches, but her mantle of flowing light-brown hair never stirred. She stood motionless, with her long, pale hands crossed on her bosom. Her white face was also perfectly motionless; she gazed at him with a strange, beseeching look in her great, wide eyes. Although he was so far away, he could see that her skin was pale and as it were bedewed —as it always was when she felt the heat.

It did not occur to him to marvel that he saw her as she had been at the time when they were newly grown up. It did not occur to him that he was of any age either, as he rose and ran toward the vision. Time seemed to be no more.

As he crossed the brook she stretched out her hands toward him —he could not tell whether it was to receive him or forbid him to come nearer. But now he could read a great dread in her snow-white face.

Then a stone slipped under his foot. Olav fell on his knee, and behind him there was a splash in the water. When he raised his head again, the vision was gone, but the tall swaying willow-herbs scattered over the scree stirred as though someone had fled that way.

For a moment he remained as he had fallen, on one knee, trying to collect himself. Then it came upon him, a wave of blood that seemed ready to burst his heart and his brain—and the scree was whirling upward, while dark patches fell one by one before his eyes, and he sank forward in a swoon.

He was roused by spots of rain—the first he saw was that the stones were thickly splashed, but not all wet; he saw there was blood on the stones where he had lain, and he felt his face stiffened and wet with blood. He saw the grey trail of the shower as it swept up the course of the stream, while the wood was whitened by a gust that reversed the leaves.

Olav stood up, feeling as if all the marrow had been taken from his bones. He had a terrible pain in the head—not from the fall, but from within—and in the heart, as he realized that she had been here and was gone, and that the vision had been a revelation of other times than these, times that he believed to have gone by more than a generation ago. Body and soul were rent with a pain unlike any other he had known, and he thought: "This is Death."

Then the fit of pain passed over; he got back his breath and shook himself under the pouring rain. As he leaped back across the brook, he found he was trembling and weak all over.

The rain streamed down as Olav a moment later hurried across the pasture. Tore and the woman were peeping out through the door of the shed. "What have you *done* to yourself, Olav?" asked the house-carl in surprise.

Olav had forgotten the blood on his face. He answered that he had run his forehead against the trunk of a fir. He flung himself down on the couch at the far end of the sæter hut and lay prone with his hands before his face, trying to get to the bottom of this. The other two stood at the door looking out at the rain.

The sun was shining again, and the woodland gleamed, green and blue and fine after its bath, as Olav and Tore rode on in the afternoon. Olav was deep in thought. But at the bottom of his soul, deeper than doubt and disquietude, lay joy. He had seen that death had not yet parted him from her, and that his own youth was living somewhere in time and space, in spite of all he had done to kill it.

They did not reach Hestviken till night. Olav helped Tore with the horses—they put them in the stable, in case there might be another thunderstorm during the night. Then a strange thing happened as Olav reached over to pat the colt that stood in the stall next his saddle-horse: the animal plunged, making a great clatter, shied and backed. When Olav in surprise was going up to it, the colt went quite wild.

"It seems the horse is afraid of you!" said Tore.

Olav had to leave its stall; he said nothing.

He fell asleep as soon as he lay down. In the morning his memory of the vision was half faded, or as though it had happened long ago. But as he was about to dress, he went to the door of the closet to look over his shirt—he was afraid he had got ticks from the sæter. Then he saw with the corner of his eye that he was bleeding behind the shoulder—there was the mark of a bite. As he looked at it fresh blood oozed out of the little tooth-marks.

Once more the choking, bursting pain returned in his head and heart, and Olav had to clutch the doorpost until he had mastered the thought that this inconceivable thing was true—however it might have come about.

He had had a little scar there. Ingunn had bitten him once in wantonness—one night when he had been with her in her bower at Frettastein. It was an age since he had thought of it, for the mark had almost faded out with the years, and it was so far back on his shoulder that he could not see it without turning his head. But now the blood trickled red and fresh from the little pits left by her teeth.

I O

OLAV went about like a sleepwalker in his own house, while the daughters of Arne and his kinsfolk and friends made ready for the great bridal journey. His whole mind was turned inward, upon the memory of his vision. He had to think out what it might betoken, that she had come back thus.

The scar on his shoulder continued to bleed in the mornings. He felt nothing of it at other times, but if his thoughts ever strayed for a while from his meeting with his dead wife, it recalled itself to his mind by a little pricking or smarting.

His past now seemed so far behind him that he no longer knew what was true memory and what was dream. But he thought he remembered that she had said that night, laughing, that she would mark her own with a bite. And had she now come to remind him of that?

Now he would soon be left alone again. All that he thought he could never part with would soon have slipped out of his hands. Soon he would be as alone in the world and as free as when he bound himself to his child bride.

It was a long and weary road he had travelled since their young days. And when he thought of it, the time they had lived their life together as man and wife here in Hestviken was but the smallest part of it: for twelve years they had dwelt together, but the years of his outlawry in his youth had been near ten, and now it was over thirteen years since she died. Never before had he chanced to think about it—the time they had been suffered to live

together as married folk had really been short. It had appeared
to him that they had belonged to each other as long as he could
remember, and this did not cease with her death. It was only
when his own life began to dry up and wither, as a tree grows
old, hollow, and decayed, with fewer and fewer branches that
burst into leaf in spring, that he had ceased to feel they were
bound together, in a far deeper sense than he had ever been able
to see; but the brief years in which they had been suffered to enjoy each other's love, at Frettastein that autumn and the first years
here at Hestviken, had been but the visible sign of the mysterious
relation between them.

And had it now been vouchsafed her to fulfil her promise and
come to him—the living to the dying—and had she been permitted
to renew the mark she had put on him in wild girlish wantonness,
then it must have been in order to remind him that the bond between them was not yet broken, that their pact still held, and that
she could still claim him for her own.

If that were so, they could not be parted, unless God's judgment parted them as far asunder as heaven and hell—when finally
they had become as unlike each other as the free and blest spirits
in God's presence are unlike the Devil's fettered thralls.

Another thing he saw, though he knew not how it came about
that he could see it: that souls have no age. Sin and grace fashion
them and give them shape, but not as years and labour and sickness mark the bodily husk. Ingunn's ravaged body and his own
weatherbeaten, war-scarred frame were but as hard-worn garments; that was what the makers of images meant when they
painted souls as naked little children, the angels and devils taking
each their own as they issue from the mouths of the dying. Old
age does not survive death; but the blest and the lost shall receive
their everlasting destiny in the full force and wakefulness of
youth. And that too they had been taught by Brother Vegard—in
eternity all are ever young.

There were fifty in the company, with house-carls and serving-
women, when Cecilia Olavsdatter's bridal progress set out from
Hestviken. With pack-horses and cattle it was a brave train passing
through the countryside. Olav looked at it well pleased: as his
neighbours reckoned such things, he had prospered of late years.
Since the Swedish troubles he had enjoyed honour in the district;

all knew that he might have had power there, had he cared to use it; wealth he had, and his children had turned out so as to bring him joy and honour. To no man had he made complaint in the hard years, and none had seen him puffed up in the days of prosperity—*this* world had never been able to prevail against him.

So now he must follow the course that his heart had prompted all these years—fall at the feet of Christ crucified and confess that he had lived the whole time secretly at war with God and now knelt before Him, vanquished.

What might afterwards befall him he could not tell. 'Twas unlikely any man would care now to drag forth into the light his manslaughter of long ago. That was only a sting he had pressed into his own flesh—it had worked out again long since and was forgotten, but the wound had spread and consumed him.

The likeliest penance to be imposed on him would be to make a pilgrimage that might last until his death, old as he now was. And he thought upon it with an easy heart, at the very moment when he surveyed the marks of his prosperity—he would gladly leave it all, suffer hands and feet to be fettered, wander as a penitent pilgrim from sanctuary to sanctuary, begging his food—

But every time he thought of Eirik a thrill of anxiety went through him. His son was only present to his mind as he knelt before the choir of the convent church, erect and radiant in his bridegroom's attire. Eirik had given himself to God, without fear and without self-seeking. And as he came forward in the frock of a barefoot friar to bid the world farewell—in the eyes of his father, who dared now give free play at last to his love for his son, all the brightness of the scene was centred on Eirik's narrow, shining crown.

To him he would now say: "I am not your true father—your father's slayer I am."

If Eirik raised him up after *that*—then all would be well.

How Cecilia would take it was a question to which he gave little thought.

The wedding at Gunnarsby passed off bravely; it brought honour both to the Rypungs and to Olav. Cecilia Olavsdatter was so fair a bride that she shed a radiance about her when she appeared with the golden crown upon her loose and frizzly flaxen hair.

It struck Olav next morning, when he saw the young wife

attired with the linen coif—her hair had been the fairest thing
about Cecilia, and now that it was hidden away, she seemed much
smaller, so pale and light-eyed was she, and short of stature. But
the place was strange to her, she was unused to her condition—no
doubt she would be brighter when she was used to the married
state and to Gunnarsby. Jörund seemed mightily pleased with his
bride.

The sixth day of the wedding—Olav was to take his departure
the day after—the Kolbeinssons showed him and some of his nearest kin the jewels that their mother owned and that they would
one day share among them. She had a great treasure, Gunhild
Rypa, and many beautiful things.

The Kolbeinssons and the young wives of Aake and Steinar
grew very animated after a while. And again it came upon Olav
that he did not altogether *like* these folks. It struck him as im-
modest and unmannerly that they could not handle the valuables
in a calmer and more dignified way—their voices jerked up and
down, now loud and sharp, and the next moment smirking and
bland, as they watched each other with greedy and suspicious
glances. " 'Twill scarcely be an amicable division of the inheritance when the mother is gone," thought Olav. That at least they
had not failed in, the gentlefolk among whom he had been fos-
tered, nor himself either—not letting it be seen that either loss or
gain disturbed their serenity.

He chanced to look at his daughter. She stood silently by her
husband's side. Olav read in her eyes that her thoughts were the
same as his, and he felt a little sting as he recalled that tomorrow
he was to ride away and leave her behind with these folks.

In the evening he went out strolling with his daughter on a path
that led down to the lake. He himself had asked her to go with
him—he wished to find out how she was doing in her new home.
But Cecilia said nothing about that, and Olav could not bring
himself to ask any questions.

Only when they were going up toward the manor again did
the man say: "Now thus it is, Cecilia—you know that the day will
come, mayhap sooner than any of us looks for it, when you will
return to Hestviken, and then all will be yours. Bear that in mind
if it should chance now and again that you feel a longing for your
home at first."

"God grant you a long life, Father," the bride hastened to say.

"Have you never spoken of it with Jörund—that he should move to Hestviken in your lifetime?" she then asked.

Olav had never thought of this, so he remained silent. There was no great comfort in the thought: he did not believe he would care to live under the same roof as his son-in-law. So he merely answered:

"Likely enough when you have been some time here at Gunnarsby you will be unwilling to leave the place. Here you have young people in the house"—he meant to say something of young women of her own age, but shrank, when it came to the point, from reckoning Cecilia's sisters-in-law as an advantage—"wide lands and many neighbours. And you will be free to go abroad and will have much at your command."

To this Cecilia made no reply.

Next morning Olav left the table before the other guests; there were many who were to ride homeward in his company, so he thought he ought to see to the saddling and packing of the horses. When he came out on the steps of the barn—where their saddles and harness had been stored—he heard Cecilia's voice within; she was talking to old Tore. His daughter said:

"To think that you are to be parted from me—can you not come hither and dwell with us at Gunnarsby? Brynhild and Lucia have their own henchmen and waiting-women; they can scarce grudge me a man who can tend my horses and serve me."

"God forgive us, Cecilia"—the old man laughed—"could you not find a man who is even worse fitted to be a lady's henchman at Gunnarsby?"

Olav could not help smiling at the thought. Tore was a strange figure, he was so huge and broad in the chest and shoulders, but his legs were short and crooked, he had a round head with long grey hair hanging stiffly about it, his face was covered with little wrinkles, red and fleshy, and his eyes were dull as those of a boiled fish. He was strong as a giant and chose the hardest work, a man of few words and one to be trusted; one could not call his manner discourteous, but he was sufficient to himself and could never have learned such meekness as the servants at Gunnarsby had to practise—and now his age was three score years and more.

"I should be so *kind* to you!" Cecilia begged.

"You are as good as gold, I know that. But now I have served your father twenty years and more, and if the truth be told, 'twould be harder for Olav to get on without me at Hestviken than the man himself can guess, or anyone else."

" 'Twill be hard for me to do without you. No friend have I had so faithful as you, since I was so small that you let me ride on your back."

"When I am too old for aught else," said old Tore with a laugh, "I will come and be nurse to your children, Cecilia."

"Ay, will you promise that?"

Olav went in. Cecilia was sitting on the old house-carl's knees and had put her arm round his neck; she looked into his ugly face like a child begging for something.

Olav nodded to the two. "You are unhappy at parting from Tore, I can see."

Cecilia had risen hastily, and now her face was as calm and stubborn as usual.

"I have asked Tore, Father, if he would come and live with us here at Gunnarsby."

" 'Tis not sure, Cecilia, that it would go well with him here— old folk are ill matched with new customs."

Tore agreed with his master.

In going eastward the bridal progress had been compelled to follow the best roads there were, but on the homeward journey Olav, together with some of the guests who wished to travel rapidly, took the same short cut through the forest as he had ridden in returning from Gunnarsby the first time.

They rested at the same sæter as before. And while his companions lay and took their ease in the meadow above, Olav stole from them and walked down by the bank of the stream.

The sun was shining, and nothing was changed—only the willow-herb was pale and flowerless; it had begun to shed its seed, which drifted like silvery down in the breeze. Olav stood for a while gazing over at the scree, but today he could see nothing strange.

For the first time it occurred to him that his vision might have been a phantom—or something else: "*a negotio perambulante in tenebris, ab incursu et dæmonio meridiano*." Thus in the evening prayer one asks for help against the thing that walketh in darkness, and against the assaults of evil spirits at noonday. And in truth he had often felt that just in the stillness of the noonday heat there are many things abroad that one cannot see.

Or what if it had been she, but with some other purpose—to beg him take good heed, ere he gave away their only child—

Then Olav shook it from him. He would hold to what he had believed at first.

Coming through the church town Olav was told that there had been a fire at Hestviken. The great old barn to the east of the manor and the haystacks had been burned down.

It had begun in the forest away on the north side of the inlet—fishermen had made a fire over on the Bull—and then it had caught the heather, and the fir forest was burned up, but the flames were checked at the cleft that runs inland and is overgrown with lime and hazel. But for a while the wind had blown from the north, and sparks had fallen on the roofed haystacks outside the barn; then hay and barn had gone up in a blaze—for a time the houses beyond had been in danger.

It was strange how unhomely it had made the place look, thought Olav, as he stood next morning looking over toward the Bull—with the stumps of trees that stood out, jagged, blackened, and scorched red, or lay fallen on the burned moss. A thick band of charcoal and soot floated along the beach all the way.

The barn was the only building at Hestviken that belonged to the great days of the manor, so Olav was sorry to lose it. And now they would be in sore straits for fodder in the coming winter.

He had now to think of rebuilding and of getting in what might serve for fodder. Then came the seal-hunting and the fishing season. Olav had his hands full with one thing and another throughout the autumn and winter. His house-folk remarked that he gave unusual care to all that he did that winter. To Tore he had dropped hints that led the men to suppose he was minded to make another journey in foreign lands next summer, and perhaps he intended that Jörund Kolbeinsson should come to Hestviken with his wife.

Olav was happier at home than he had been in all the years he had been there. He liked the loneliness and he liked the busy activity, for he felt it to be a preparation for departure. He even got to like the view of the Bull's neck with the burned wood when he was used to it, especially after the autumn storms had cleared it and snow had fallen. It had a more open look.

That winter Einar and Valgard, the sons of Björn, Torhild's brothers, were away north in Haugsvik. Olav had often wished he could hear something of his son, the young Björn, and of the boy's mother. Now he sent off Tore, for he knew Einar and his brother well from of old.

Tore came back and was able to tell him that Björn had left home last spring: he wished to go out into the world and try his fortune. His uncles said he had gone away to learn the trade of a blacksmith—from childhood he had been more cunning with his hands than most lads—he had talked of going to a man in the Dovre Fell of whom folk said that his mother was a giant's daughter—but maybe that was not true; he was accounted a most excellent smith. With him Björn Olavsson would take service.

Torhild and Ketil prospered; there were three children born to them: a daughter and then a son and daughter who were twins. Nay, Björn had parted from his parents in all kindness, and his mother had bestowed on him saddle and horse and all he needed for the journey, in such noble sort for their condition that folk had called her overweening.

Olav had little to say to Tore's report, for over this son he had never had any rights.

I I

NEXT year, in the early summer, Olav put up a new barn and had it roofed by the time of bearing in the hay. He and his house-folk were busy haymaking in the meadows down by the mouth of the river—it was an afternoon a few days before Margaretmass [9]—when a strange man came up to him among the hay-cocks, gave him greeting, and said:

"I have a message for you, Olav, which is such that I may not tarry in the telling. Will you go with me a little apart, so that we may speak—alone?"

[9] June 10.

Olav did so, and when they came a little way from the others, the man said:

"I come from Gunnarsby. Your daughter is in travail of childbirth and in great jeopardy; it were well if you could come to her and that as swiftly as your swiftest horse can bring you."

"Is it so," asked Olav, "that they deem her life to be at stake?"

"There is peril of it," replied the other.

Olav ran back to the field, found Ragna and Tore, and told them how matters stood. He bade Tore bring Brunsvein from the paddock and Ragna fetch food; then he went down to the stranger and asked him to go with him to the house. As they went, Olav asked, of a sudden:

"But where have you your horse, man?"

"Nay, I have walked from Gunnarsby."

"Have you walked?" Olav looked at his guest suspiciously. He was a man in the thirties, looked like any other serving-man—Olav could not call to mind having seen him before, but that was nothing to go by, since they had so many folk about them at Gunnarsby; he had a trustworthy look. "Did Jörund send you hither with such a message and gave you no horse?"

"To tell the truth, Olav, 'twas not the Rypungs that sent me. But Cecilia helped me once when I was in bad straits, and then I vowed to God and Saint Halvard I would repay her if it were ever in my power. I thought I had a chance to do so now—if it be given her to see you and speak with you, before she may die—"

Olav was somewhat easier in his mind as he thought that perhaps his daughter was not in such a bad way after all, since it was neither her husband nor his brothers' wives who had dispatched the messenger. There seemed to be something strange about the whole affair, but however it might be, he was glad to have been told of his daughter's sickness, and he would ride to Gunnarsby at once. He asked no more questions of the stranger—Finn was his name—but on arriving at the manor gave orders that he should be well housed and cared for, and when he had taken his rest, they were to lend him a horse for his homeward journey.

An hour later Olav was in the saddle and stretched Brunsvein to the utmost—this was the swiftest colt in his stable, but he did not usually ride him himself, as he was not so handsome to look at as Bay Roland, his own saddle-horse. On reaching Skeidis parish he stayed for a few hours with his kinsfolk at Hestbæk and gave

Brunsvein a rest, but Olav mounted again long before sunrise, and late in the day he came to Gunnarsby.

But there he was told at once that Cecilia was doing well; she had given birth to a fine and healthy son; this was already a day and a half ago. No, Mistress Lucia replied to his questions, Cecilia had not had so hard a travail, she had been in no more peril of her life than any other young wife. Olav saw plainly that they were greatly surprised at his coming, and he was no more than moderately welcome at Gunnarsby this time. There was something behind this—he could not guess what—but so as not to betray this Finn he replied, when Lucia asked him where he had heard of Cecilia's illness, that he had met some folk at church who had kindred in these parts; they had told him that his daughter who was married at Gunnarsby last summer might expect a child about the time of Margaretmass.

"Ay, but 'twas not expected before Marymass [1]—" Mistress Lucia broke off in confusion, as though she had said too much, and there was an odd look on the faces of the others. Brynhild said the young wife had been sore afraid all the time she had been with child; maybe she had talked of it, saying she was afraid of this too, that it might come before its time—

It was strangely unlike Cecilia to be afraid, thought her father. But with women one can never know, and after all a man was no judge of these things. He could only be glad that Cecilia was doing well, and since he was here, he was glad too that he would see his daughter again.

It was fairly dark in the upper chamber where Cecilia lay, when Lucia took Olav up to see her in the evening. It rejoiced Olav to see that his daughter was glad he had come; she said that all was well with her now, and she was doing well in every way. The room in which they had laid her was spacious and richly bedight, and there was no lack of neighbours' wives and serving-maids to attend to her and her child.

Jörund spoke very lovingly to his wife and seemed exceedingly proud that he too had a son. And the women loudly praised the child. Olav took it in his arms when they handed it to him, looked at it—this was the little lad who would one day take his place at Hestviken, if God should suffer him to grow into a man—but he

[1] Assumption, B.V.M.—August 15.

had always thought that new-born babes were ugly little monsters to look at, all except Cecilia; she had been fair from the first day of her life.

Next morning Olav sat with his daughter again; they talked for the most part of those they knew at home. It was very little Cecilia had to say of how she liked her new home—only that there was far more bustle here than at Hestviken, and the folk of Gunnarsby were much abroad to feastings and the like—this had been a burden to her of late; but now, to be sure, she would stay more at home, as she had a child at the breast.

"Ay," said her father, "but a little lad like this will grow quickly, and soon you will be free again."

" 'Twas not of that I thought," replied the young wife hastily. "I must take after you, Father—I like best to live where there is no such crowd."

Her last word struck her father as strangely scornful; he was about to correct the child, bid her enjoy her youth while she had it.

At that moment one of the neighbours' wives came with the babe, to lay it to its mother's breast. Cecilia wore only a little vest covering her bosom and arms; as the woman raised her on the pillows, her father had a glimpse of her naked body about the waist, and he saw that her side was all black and blue. At the same time the sun shone in on the bed—there were snatches of brightness between the clouds—and he noticed that her face also bore marks, as of blows.

"Have you hurt yourself?" her father asked after the strange woman had gone.

"Yes, I fell and bruised myself," said Cecilia. "That is what made him come before his time."

Olav thought it so far well that a mishap of this sort had caused it—he had been afraid she might have inherited her mother's infirmity; and no doubt it was this fall that had made her uneasy.

"So then it was you thought of sending this Finn for me?"

Cecilia was silent for moment, as though reflecting:

"I did not ask him to go either—but perhaps he thought he owed me gratitude. And then maybe he took it into his head to repay me thus—when he heard I had fallen and hurt myself—"

"I wonder, though," said Olav, "whether he be yet returned—

have you heard? He was to borrow a horse of ours, so I could take it back with me."

"Finn will take good care that you have the horse back. But to tell the truth, Father, I do not think we shall see him at Gunnarsby. They are stricter with their servants here than we are wont to be, and as Finn ran off from here without asking leave—"

"Did he so?"

Cecilia nodded. "I wish I knew," she said, "what he will do with himself now. He has been a trusty man to me."

"Perhaps you wish me to take him into my service at Hestviken?" Olav asked.

Cecilia was silent for a moment, looking down at the child at her breast.

"Nay, *that* I wish not at all," she then said in her curt little voice.

Next day the boy was baptized, and Olav intended to return home on the day after. But in the evening, as he was about to bid his daughter good-night, he chanced to be alone with her for a moment. Then he made up his mind to ask her.

"Tell me now, Cecilia, while we are alone—have you aught on your mind that you would fain tell me?"

"No, I have not," said the young wife firmly. Seeing that her father looked disappointed, she gave him her hand. "But, for all that, I am glad you came, Father!"

On the morrow Olav set out for home. He had left the parish itself behind him and was now riding uphill by the bank of a little stream, on both sides of which were small farmsteads in the midst of green meadows. He was deep in thought when his horse gave a sudden start—a man had risen abruptly from beneath some bushes at the edge of the bridle-path. It was that Finn.

They exchanged greetings. But as the man said nothing, Olav thought he must.

"It turned out not so ill as you foretold, my friend," he said kindly. "My daughter is now in good case, and yesterday we christened Kolbein Jörundsson."

"Ay, so I have heard."

"Are you on your way down to Gunnarsby?" asked Olav.

"Nay, I am bound southward," said the man. He had slept at one of the little farms yonder, where he was known.

Olav reflected that it was this Finn who had brought him the news of his grandson's birth, so to speak. He said so and thanked him for it. He had brought with him ten English florins [2] that he had had by him since his voyage to England—to make a suitable altar-offering if there should be need of such. He now took out the two he had left and gave them to Finn.

The man accepted them, hesitating a little. Then he stood looking at Olav, and Olav sat looking down at him. Neither of them spoke. At last Olav said he must be getting on. "Maybe we are going the same way?"

They were, said the man. So Olav made Brunsvein go at a foot's pace, and Finn walked at his side, and not a sound was heard but the gurgling of the brook in its turf banks and the horse's hoofs when they struck a stone, and the faint summery murmur in the tree-tops; and the sun beat down, gleaming upon the foliage —and both men kept silence.

Once Olav asked if the other had had the loan of a horse from Hestviken, and Finn answered no, he had preferred to walk. After a while Olav asked whether Finn was from these parts, and Finn answered no, he came from Ness in Raumarike. With that their talk came to an end.

When they had journeyed together for an hour or more Finn said he must turn aside here—he pointed along a little path that led up a hill. So Olav thanked him for his company, and Finn thanked in return and was gone into the wood.

Afterwards Olav regretted that he had not tried to find out something. But he had shrunk from cross-questioning his daughter's serving-man.—So he rode on at a brisker pace.

Olav had had to promise that he would look in again at Hest-bæk on his way home. And this time they did not let him go so soon—it was six years since he had last been to see his kinsfolk here, said Arne, "and 'twill surely be six years ere you come again —and then I shall be under the sod."

Arne Torgilsson was now over eighty winters old, but his age sat none too heavily on him. He was like his father, Torgils Foul-beard, as he might have been had he not lost his wits; Arne was rather a small man, but handsome and well built; his hair and beard were white as bog-cotton, and his florid cheeks and sea-blue eyes showed brightly in the midst of all this whiteness. Torgunn, his

[2] A gold coin worth six shillings and eightpence.

youngest daughter, carried on the farm together with her sons;
she had been widowed many years already.

Arne gave a grunt when Olav told him that Cecilia had borne
a son.

"Then 'twill be the same as here—none but a daughter's son to
succeed you at Hestviken! To me God would not grant a son,
in spite of my prayers and vows—you had one, and he has turned
barefoot friar. You, Olav, who are so rich and have always stood
so well with the priests, could you not have sent to Rome and been
given dispensation? Then you might have married Torgunn and
carried on the Fivil race [3] in our old home."

"Could you not have thought of that before, kinsman," said
Olav with a laugh, "ere Torgunn and I were old folk?"

Olav had to stay at Hestbæk till the third day. It was near sunset when he came riding out to Hestviken. The sky was full of
clouds, which shone and blazed and cast red and yellow reflections
in the waters of the fiord. The rays of the sinking sun shot out
aslant, and the long shadows fell fitfully across the meadows, so
that Olav could not distinguish plainly who it was that came toward him through the fields; but there was something both familiar and strange in the tall, broad-shouldered figure, and the
cut of his dress had a courtly air ill suited to the place. By the
man's side walked a gigantic he-goat, black as coal, with a huge
pair of horns.

Then Olav saw that it was Eirik—Eirik who came to meet him
in a particoloured jerkin, half red and half yellow, so short and
tight that Olav thought it unseemly; he had a leather belt about
his waist, with a long dagger, a knife, and a pouch hanging from
it. The dark, curly hair had not yet grown so long as to hide the
tonsure. Olav could not quite rid himself of his first impression,
something devilish in the vision that presented itself, even when
he had recognized the goat as their own old he-goat.

Olav reined in his horse. Eirik ran forward the last few steps,
laid his hand on his father's saddle-bow, and asked, looking up
at him:

"Father—is she dead?"

"Cecilia? Nay, she is well." In silence they continued to look

[3] *Fivil* means bog-cotton, alluding to the fair hair and complexion of the
Hestviken family. See *The Snake Pit*, p. 338.

at each other, Eirik growing ever redder and more distressed. But there was no help for it, he had to speak out himself:

"I have come home, Father," he said in a tone of supplication. "As you see."

"I do see," Olav jerked at the reins, so that Eirik had to stand aside, but he walked beside his father's horse up to the houses.

Olav dismounted in the yard, replying to Tore's and Ragna's questions concerning Cecilia. Then he turned to the house door, where Eirik stood outside, waiting. The son followed his father in. Olav flung off his cloak, laid aside his arms; not till then did he turn to Eirik.

"Where have you come from?"

"You know that well," said Eirik in a low voice. "I left home—the convent, I mean—yestermorn—had the loan of a boat from Galfrid—"

"Have you lost heart for the cloistered life?" Or—have the friars sent you away? Have you done amiss, so that they will not have you?" asked Olav harshly.

Eirik was crimson in the face; a quiver as of pain passed over his features. But he answered very meekly: "The brethren thought I was not intended for the life. For you know, Father—'tis for that one has the year of probation—and my year was up two months ago. I was loath to part from my brethren; they let me stay awhile longer. But then they told me they believed I was not meant for a monk—I could better serve God if I lived in the world."

"You were to live in the world and serve God?" There was icy scorn in his father's voice. "Little must those brethren know you!"

He saw that his son shrank a little. But then Eirik answered as meekly as before: "Nay, Father—my brethren know me best of all —my father, Brother Einar, and the guardian. I shall not forget what they have taught me. Think not I am come home to take up that—iniquitous—life I led before. I—I—they have adopted me as their brother—as a brother *ab extra*. And you yourself know best that a man may live in the world and yet be mindful of his Redeemer and serve Him."

Olav stood looking at the young man in silence.

"What is this for—what garb is this?"

Eirik blushed again, all cramped and pinched in the ridiculous finery that was too tight and skimpy in every way.

"They gave it me in the convent," he said humbly. "They had

received it as a gift, and they all agreed to give it to me—that I might avoid falling into debt in the town for clothes to go home in."

"Ah."

Then Ragna came in with the food, and the household followed her to take their meal. Olav talked with his folk, but said no more to Eirik—scarce looked at him.

When the meal was ended Olav had ale and mead brought in —bade his house-folk drink to the welfare of Kolbein Jörundsson. Eirik accepted the horn, drank to his nephew's honour, and let it go further. But next time it came round to him, he let it pass, and soon after he stole quietly out of doors.

He must be gone to say his hours, said Ragna with feeling—he kept his hours and wore a great rosary round his neck underneath his jerkin.

It only stirred Olav to deeper scorn and anger when he heard it.

I 2

OLAV's exasperation had settled on him, as it were, at first sight of his newly returned son. He had accustomed himself to think of Eirik as though he were already half a saint, and utterly un-looked-for his son came strolling toward him across the fields at home, ridiculously tricked out, with a stinking black he-goat as companion.

And then came the thought of all the difficulties that Eirik's fickleness would bring in its train. A settlement with these bare-foot friars he must have too. According to their rule he thought they could not accept any endowment from the men who sought admission to their fraternity, so all that they had received when Eirik went to the convent had been given as alms; Olav could not demand its return. But if they tried to claim anything of what he had promised them when Eirik became a monk, then—! Olav was now angry with the whole crew of them; first they had strength-ened Eirik in his purpose as much as they could, and then—if in-deed he could place any reliance on what Eirik himself said—they had supported him again when he began to have scruples and to doubt his calling to the monastic life.

But there was something worse than this. It was Eirik's determination to forsake the world that had induced Jörund Rypa to
come forward with his suit—it was impossible to doubt that. And
in spite of all, Olav was not so sure—not even after his last journey
to Gunnarsby—that Cecilia's happiness was fully assured among
the Rypungs. If, then, they were justified in thinking that her kinsmen had not dealt quite honestly by them—

Olav said something of this to Eirik one day. He saw that it
made his son unhappy.

"But 'tis not unheard of," replied Eirik meekly, "for a novice
to be found unfitted to live according to the Rule."

Olav made no reply to this. What Eirik said was true, but then
most of those who entered the cloister became monks and nuns
in due time, and Eirik had been so zealous when he took the habit
last year, and he had formed his determination to become a monk
without persuasion or pressure from anyone.

"'Tis not sure either that I shall ever marry," he then said.

"Is it not? Do you think then to take up your old evil courses
again?"

Eirik turned red as fire. But he answered calmly and mildly:
"But you, Father, you have lived as becomes a Christian man in
all these years since our mother died—although you have neither
married again nor taken to yourself a leman."

"I?" exclaimed Olav, revolted. "I was a man well on in years.
And not even in my youth was I known in the stews or in the
haunts of dicers—"

Still Eirik spoke composedly: "I promised Father Einar, when
I parted from him, that I would keep myself from dicing and
overmuch drinking. Will you not believe, Father, that I have
learned *something* good and profitable in this year I have dwelt
under Saint Franciscus's roof and prayed every day in the presence of God Himself in the mystery of His holiest sanctuary?"

"Ah, well," muttered Olav, somewhat ashamed. "Time will
show, Eirik—how long you hold to *these* resolutions."

"You should not say such things!" Eirik sprang up and went
out.

But it seemed only to increase Olav's irritation that Eirik to all
appearance had now turned pious and meek. He never allowed
himself to be goaded into an angry answer, he neither boasted nor

told fabulous stories. His father kept him so strictly now that Eirik owned nothing he could call his own. Olav himself had always been a generous giver of alms, but none of his gifts to the poor and sick were allowed to pass through Eirik's hands. Eirik devised a means, however: he rendered many charitable services to his house-mates and to folk who passed through, showing thereby his humility and goodwill. That too was a vexation to his father, and it vexed him every time he noticed that Eirik withdrew himself apart, went down among the rocks by the waterside or into one of the outhouses to say his prayers alone. He told his beads daily and said the little hours of our Lady, most of which he now knew. By degrees Olav discovered that Eirik had set up little crosses here and there on the outskirts of the manor, in the places he frequented for saying his prayers.

In the course of the autumn a rumour came to Olav's ears that Eirik Olavsson had forsaken his convent because he felt a call to a yet stricter life of penitence. It was said to be his intention to build himself a cell in the churchyard and become an anchorite. The like had never been known in the parish before, so there was great talk among the folk—some made a mock of it, but others thought it must be a great blessing to the countryside. At last Olav guessed that in one way or another Eirik himself must have originated these rumours, and so he took his son to task. Eirik was thrown into dire confusion—and it was the first time since his return from the convent that his father had seen him falter and blink his eyes. But his answer was that he had never said he himself would turn anchorite; he had only spoken of something that had been read aloud in the refectory last winter, a book that was called *Vitæ Patrum*.

One day Eirik came to Olav and asked if he might bring the eldest of the Rundmyr children to Hestviken. The boy had become a cripple after an illness at the age of seven; when they laid him on the ground outside in summer he could just push himself about a little with his arms; he scarcely had the power of speech either. Before his sickness he had been a lively, handsome child— he bore no resemblance either to Liv or to Anki, but to a young and merry, red-haired and brown-eyed house-carl who had been at Hestviken the winter before those two were married. But that did not detract from Anki's paternal pride, and even now, when the boy was in this state, both Anki and Liv said they would rather lose all their other children than this one. But though they loved him so, and though they always received such abundant doles from Hestviken that they ought not to have suffered want, the sick child was covered with sores and lice and likely to rot away in his own uncleanliness. His parents did not neglect him, they stuffed him with the best morsels, but they could not cope with the filth.

Olav did not see how he could say no to Eirik's request, for the child was his godson and was called Olav after him. So he merely said that Eirik was not to bring him into the house until he could rid him of his lice and keep his sores so clean that they did not stink too foully. Eirik then kept Olav Livsson in the barn until the cold set in, but then they had to let him lie in the living-room. By this time Eirik had got him tolerably clean, and the boy had learned to swing himself along a few steps with a pair of crutches. In the course of the winter he acquired sense enough to be able to perform a little light work, such as soaking withies and deer sinews, or planing rough wooden implements. He also learned to speak better, but he was still a stammerer and tongue-tied. However, there were many drawbacks to having him in the house. Not that the house-folk were ever unfriendly with him; and if once in a while Olav Audunsson took notice of his godson, it was always in the way of kindness—as far as that went, Olav was not displeased that the poor creature was now looked after like a Christian child—but when he was vexed at the trouble the sick boy caused them, Eirik was made to feel his father's ill humour.

As yet Olav knew nothing of how the folk at Gunnarsby had taken the news that the son of Hestviken had returned. But he was a prey to misgivings whenever he thought of it, and it was never long absent from his mind.

In late autumn Olav found time to make a journey to Oslo, and while there he visited the Minorite convent. But he soon saw that he would be told nothing there of the reason for Eirik's defection. It was clear that the friars reckoned this as one of the convent's domestic affairs, and the silence of the cloister was as a wall. They had nothing but good to say of Eirik: they had grown devotedly attached to their young brother, but since it had been made clear both to himself and to them that God desired to lead this soul by other paths than that of the monastic life, then—

"Was it after the beating he gave that peasant at Tveit that you were clear about this?" asked Olav.

He had heard of this through Claus Wiephart. A pious widow at one of the farms of Tveit had sent word to the convent that she would give them some homespun cloth and victuals. Brother Stevne was to fetch the gifts and took Brother Eirik with him; he was to help carry them home. But when they were ready to leave, each with his load on his back, the widow's only son came home, and he had less love for the beggar monks than his mother, so he covered the two friars with abuse—till Brother Eirik could command himself no longer, flung down his sack, sprang upon the peasant, and dealt him a blow on the jaw that felled him to the ground. True, Brother Stevne had remonstrated with him on the spot, and Eirik had humbled himself before the peasant; at home in the convent, too, he had doubtless had to do penance— the barefoot friars would be ill served by a revival of the memories of their former combativeness. But the incident was talked of far and wide.

So Olav had thought to hit the mark with this. But the guardian never winced. Nay, said he, they could not send away a novice on account of a false step of that kind, if he showed true repentance of his sin. Eirik had made no attempt to excuse his hot temper, but had submitted to his penance in such a way that he might be called a pattern of obedience.

Eirik's father smiled incredulously.

Then at last the guardian told him—Eirik had come hither because he believed himself called to be a priest. But since there was a hindrance to this—

"Hindrance?" Olav turned suddenly red in the face. "Who has said, father, that there was any hindrance?"

"Such is the commandment of Holy Church, Olav. No man who has a blemish on body or limbs may serve before the altar. So with his maimed hand Eirik cannot—"

Olav said nothing. He had forgotten that Eirik lacked two joints of the little finger of his left hand. His first thought had been of Eirik's birth.

The guardian resumed, and now he spoke rapidly and with full assurance: Eirik had sought admittance to their order because he believed that God had called him to be a priest. But since God never gives a man a call that he cannot follow, it was clear that

Eirik Olavsson had been mistaken in this. But that placed the matter at once on a different footing. During the remainder of his year of probation Eirik had striven to ascertain whether he were chosen to serve God in the cloister as a lay brother; but in the end they had all been certain that it was not so.

With that Olav had to be satisfied. The brethren said nothing of the gifts they had received when Eirik came to them, but on the other hand they were silent as to what had been promised them later. So these questions were never broached.

But Olav Audunsson parted from the Minorites in but indifferent kindness. And after that time he always spoke of these friars with ill will. And since in all else he was known to be a pious man and one so well disposed to cloister folk and priests that not even Sira Hallbjörn Erlingsson had been able to quarrel with him, folk deemed that he must have just cause to complain of the barefoot friars' conduct in this matter.

It was true that the first thing to shake Eirik's determination was the knowledge that he could not be ordained priest.

He had thrown himself into the new life with such burning zeal that the master of the novices, Brother Einar, had rather to restrain him. Many of the monks were wont to stay behind in church after matins in order to pray until prime. Eirik forthwith asked leave to do this every morning, and Brother Einar had to order him to go back to the dormitory and lie down again.

Eirik himself thought he needed no more sleep than a bird on the bough. Were he never so tired when called to matins, the first breath of the cool air of the summer night which met him as he came into the cloister garth was enough to make him wide awake. To enter the cold, dark church was almost as it had felt when, as a child, he plunged into the sea for a swim. During matins the lofty vaulted building grew lighter and lighter. At midsummer the first rays of the morning sun swept clear over the hills behind Aker as the brethren left the choir and crossed the green courtyard to return to their dormitory.

But two mornings in the week he was given leave to stay behind in church after matins. As he knelt in prayer the images in the choir windows became clearer, the colours began to shine— then the sun fired the glass, and the reds and yellows glowed and sparkled, till the whole choir was filled with unearthly light and

warmth from the many-coloured sunbeams that splashed the paint-
ings on the walls and the altar cross and the candlesticks with
flecks of blue and violet and gold. When the brethren returned to
say prime, every corner of the church was filled with sunshine
and reflected sunshine—and then came the sound of footsteps in
the nave, echoing in the vault, as folk came in to hear mass.

Every time he was to join in the singing he felt the same surge
of joy: he looked forward every day to singing during mass, he
looked forward to Sundays and feast-days, for then they sang the
hours as well; he looked forward to all masses for the dead, for
then he joined in singing the vigil the evening before. He had always rejoiced in his own beautiful voice. Now he thought of
how he was turning this precious gift to account, and in holy awe
he set himself to learn to use it in singing God's praises. He was
then reminded of a verse, one of the first he had learned in this
house: *"Eructavit cor meum verbum bonum: dico ego opera mea
Regi."* [4] Eirik often chose the whole of the psalm that opens with
these words as a theme for reflection when he was allowed to stay
behind in the church; he did not yet know it word for word, but
there were riches enough in what he had learned.

The first image that had presented itself to him when he gave
himself over to prayer—when his Christianity appeared to him as
an upper chamber full of locked chests that he had never thought
of unlocking—remained with him. Every day new keys were
placed in his hands, and he saw that a man's life in this world is
never long enough to permit him to lay his hands on more than a
tiny fragment of the treasures that lie hidden in the secret stores
of the faith.

One day a book on paradise had been read out in the refectory.
Eirik recalled this chapter next morning as he knelt in the choir
and thought upon Gethsemane. He saw paradise before his eyes:
a garden like their own, where the hard fruit now clustered
thickly on the trees, while pot-herbs teemed on the rich mould of
the beds, and the flowers were beginning to bloom along the walls.
Thus had God planted and sown it for a possession for the first
human pair. One tree alone He had forbidden them to touch, but
that made them ready to believe the serpent, when he tempted
them and said this tree was the most excellent of all—and immediately they fell to plundering it. It was this garden that God gave

4 Psalm xlv, 1.

to the race of man as an earnest. But in Gethsemane the lean and dried-up branches of the olives straggled in the moonlight—in the convent they had some branches of olive trees that had been brought from the castle where their father, Saint Franciscus, was born; they were coarse and ugly, with hard and shrivelled leaves. Thus had men planted their garden, to receive God in it when He came down to visit them and redeem them from sin. Among these bitter, withered bushes He had lain upon His face, sweating blood, as He saw at the bottom of the chalice all the evil that the race of Adam and Eve had committed and shall commit from the dawn of the ages until the Day of Judgment. All the blood that had been spilt, all the robbery and murder and false swearing and deceit and lewdness and betrayal were in the chalice, and all this He was now to take upon Himself and atone for—and over by the gate lay His disciples asleep, but on the path from the castle Judas is already at hand, leading the servants of the high priest and the soldiers of Pilate with torches and with swords and staves to bind and smite and slay God.

There was no one else in the church that morning. Eirik crept forward on his knees to the tabernacle, loosed his clothes, and let them fall to his waist. Then he took the knotted rope he wore as a girdle and scourged himself with it till it was red with blood.

During the day he was sent out into the garden to weed. The sun was broiling hot. At first his back did not feel very sore, but by degrees, as he lay crawling among the beds and the coarse frock grew fast to the raw flesh, was torn away again and rubbed the wounds, and the sun beat straight down on him, it was like a burning fire across his shoulder-blades. But the pain filled him with a deep and humble bliss, for he thought it must feel almost like this to have a cross resting on one's back—and then he felt his own unworthiness, and it made him so humble that he could have cast himself down with his face in the mould. For the first time he began rightly to understand the meaning of all penitential exercises and all self-discipline—that such things were not an end, but the means: the body required to be chastened and taught obedience as one trains a horse; and he had a glimpse of the paths that are opened to the soul as it makes itself master of the flesh.

But when he spoke to Father Einar of this in his next confession, his master said seriously that these were matters in which a newcomer might easily go astray, and he ordered the novice not to

impose discipline on himself another time except after consultation with him.

The whole forenoon until dinner-time they were at work in
the cloisters, all those of the brethren who were at home. Only the
church and the east wing—the chapter-house and the scriptorium
—were yet built of stone, with a paved colonnade outside. To the
west and south of the garth stood timber houses, with a cloister
walk of timber. In the stone cloisters sat those brethren who read
or wrote, but outside the south wing old Brother Arnstein An-
tonius had his loom, and there stood Brother Sigvard and Brother
Johannes at their lathe and bench. In these forenoon hours
Brother Eirik had his place beside Brother Hubert, an old Ger-
man monk who had been an inmate of this house since its founda-
tion. He was to teach the novice booklore and Latin, and for the
sake of quiet they sat in the inmost corner of the cloister, close
beside the church door.

There was only one other young brother in the convent that
summer, Brother Arne, but he had been there since his seventh
year, when his father, Brother Sveinke, had taken the habit; the
mother with two daughters had entered the nunnery of Gimsöy,
and the elder of these sisters had already died, at the age of eight-
een, in odour of sanctity. Brother Arne was but seventeen years
old, but already an accomplished clerk, so Eirik had to take his
lessons alone, and he showed such aptitude that both his teacher
and the master of the novices were astonished. And then there
came a day when Eirik again had filled the tablet, and his writing
was so fair and firm on the green wax that Brother Hubert had to
show it to some of the others, before it was all smoothed out again:
"Great pity is it that Brother Eirik should bear such blemish that
he cannot be made a priest."

This was the first cloud of weeping that passed across Eirik's
bright summer sky. He had been so small when he lost that finger
that he had never felt the want of it, and it had never crossed his
mind that it might debar him from the service of the altar. The
novice-master remarked that the young man took it deeply to
heart, so he spoke to him about it, bidding him bear in mind that
it was a far greater aid toward perfection to suffer patiently the
trials that were laid upon him than if he himself sought out never
so many afflictions of his own devising. And there was just as

great need of his being a good clerk if he was to be a lay brother; their father, Saint Franciscus, had never wished to be other than a layman, and in the beginning he had intended to found his order as a company wholly of lay brothers.

Eirik listened meekly to the novice-master's speech and never spoke of the matter again, but for long after he was in deep dejection. And then autumn came on.

There was no more to be done in the garden. The pease-straw lay tangled on the grey, frost-gripped beds, and the fallen leaves under the fruit trees were whitened with rime. The monks had long ago taken to their little lanterns when they went to matins in the church. Quitting the scrap of warmth that was to be found under the thin coverlets of his couch, he had to pass through the cold dormitory and down into the cloister, where the raw frost-fog stung his nose and crept icily up his naked calves. Thick as wool the wintry mist lay on the convent; as soon as one entered it, it seemed to force its way in and dim the little lantern. But inside the church it was colder than cold.

Eirik was so cold that he thought his brain froze to a lump inside his skull. He did not grasp a word of the prayers he said during the office, for he was too cold to be able to think of their meaning. The fog forced its way even into the church; the candles by the choir stalls shone in a mist, and the friars' breath poured from their mouths like white smoke. But the nave was lost in outer darkness.

He now shuddered at the thought of the mornings when he had leave to stay behind after matins for private prayer. Stiff with cold he knelt with his eyes firmly fixed on the little lamp that shone before the tabernacle. Behind him he felt the body of the church, dark and empty, with the tombstones in the floor. Just outside the choir arch lay Sira Hallbjörn—and Eirik could not rid himself of the thought: what if the dead priest should appear to him one morning? If he were to turn round now and see Sira Hallbjörn standing behind him with the blood pouring down from his shattered skull over his pale, bony face, the chasuble in which he had been laid all besprinkled with blood—

Now and then he heard a low murmur from one or other of the brethren who had stayed behind as he had. But for the most part they knelt in perfect silence. They had led this life year after year, winter and summer, and now neither the marvellous glory of the summer mornings nor the dismal horror of the winter nights seemed to move them any longer.

He tried to keep a hold on himself with all his thoughts centred on the tabernacle. But even that mystery now inspired him with terror rather than consolation—that God had suffered Himself to be imprisoned in that little painted tower of wood and *was* there. Wide awake, in bodily substance, spirit and soul, he filled the church, looked into his own sinful heart and saw his drooping courage, saw all that stirred in the hearts of all—and in the omnipotence of his Godhead watched over the whole of this wintry land, filling every space: the icy convent—and the town and the fiord and the homesteads along the frozen shores—and Hestviken, Rundmyr, Konungahella—all the places he could think of. In summer, when he knelt here and felt the full sweetness of being able to speak with God so near, it had been joy upon joy to know that from the bodily presence of God in the sacrament he went out in His invisible presence wherever he might be—in the sunshine that filled the cloisters outside, baked the soil of the garden so that the young shoots expanded from morn till eve, poured down through the foliage—while the town fiord and the islands outside and the woodlands round about lay wrapped in heat haze. But now that winter had the world in its clutch, there was nothing but desolation—as though he divined the mighty, soundless struggle between Christ and Satan, life and death at grips. All things of sight and sense became lifeless trifles rocking to and fro amid the furious encounter.

He would not ask to be released from these hours of watching to keep which he himself had begged leave. But as time went on, Brother Einar remarked that Eirik no longer had any profit of them, and so he bade the young man go back to bed after matins each morning for a while.

But Eirik found it hard to fall asleep again. He could not get any warmth on his narrow couch with only one sack of straw under him and two thin blankets. Another effect of the cold was that he was late in falling asleep at night, so that he was always tired and short of sleep; and often what kept him awake in the morning was simply his dread of having to get up again for prime. And if by chance he got a little warmth in bed, the chilblains on his fingers and toes began to burn and itch intolerably.

He himself was in despair over his lack of spirit and tried to summon up courage: had he not been through much that was far harder, and without caring a scrap! He tried to think of rides in storm and driving snow, when at times he had scarce been able to see his horse's head. Or in a boat in wintertime—that night last year, just after he had come home, when they sailed to Tunsberg and a storm sprang up. Right ahead of them in the darkness was a loud booming amid the howl and roar of the stormy night—the white wall that seemed alive there must be the Hangman's Reef, and they were drifting straight onto it; with every wave that lifted their boat high into the air he thought the breakers came nearer. Everything on them had been sheeted with ice when at last, late in the morning, they were able to slip into shelter somewhere a long way south—he had thought that Knut, one of Ragna's sons, would not come through with his life. And had he now grown so soft that he whimpered at the itching of his chilblains, he who more than once had ripped the boots from his frozen feet, who had been used to feel the sea-salt bite into the raw flesh of his hands—

But such hardships were part of the day's work, and one took them as they came. And afterwards—if life were not in danger—there was the sweet delight of coming under a roof, thawing out one's frozen carcass, eating and drinking one's fill, creeping in under the skin coverlets somewhere or other, two or three men in a bed to keep each other warm, and sleeping like a log. And there was always a raciness in it: one never knew how things would turn out or what the next day might bring.

But here it was a choice made for one's whole life—after each summer's warmth and joy of heart one was faced by the winter, and one had to shiver one's way through it, watching, praying, fasting, from Holy Cross Day to Easter, so stiff with cold that neither the hours of rest on the hard bed nor the brief warmth of the refectory gave more than a breath of relief. One had just not to think of it, take the days as they came, for there would be no change until God sent warmth into the air again.

And Eirik discerned where the true sacrifice and severity of the monastic life lay: that a man had to will it himself and will it once for all, renounce playing with fortune and choose a life from which the unexpected was barred and where all was willed in advance. The submission of one's will was itself an act of will.

But then he thought he must give up—*that* was more than he could do!

At last he had to tell Father Einar how it was with him. The monk answered that a man's destiny must be thought to follow him even into the convent, or, to speak more justly, God might send him much that was unlooked-for, sickness or journeys abroad, for example. Eirik must pay for strength to overcome this temptation.

And Eirik prayed. But he knew himself that from deep within him, below the place in which he found the words of his prayer, a voice was pleading: "Show me not this grace for which I pray! Send me home!"

At times he thought, perhaps it was just in this that the Devil showed his profoundest cunning—in never tempting him with anything that pertained to the profligate life of his young days. He hated the thought of it and hated his old self. Even if he had to return to the world, at any rate he could never be like that again.

It was the memory of Hestviken that broke through and overwhelmed him, as he lay at night remembering, remembering with all his body and all his senses. No place in the world had just the same smell as their own beach; their corn when it stood in shooks and when there had been a frost at night was different from the corn of other fields—as he lay he thought he could catch the scent of their own haycocks and of the limes on the cliffs around the bay. Behind his closed eyelids floated visions of the land from which he had cut himself off: the sedgy paths up in Kverndal, the little dry mound where he found Lapp arrowheads, every crack in the rocks at home, the black wall of the Horse behind the houses, and the reddish, rounded side of the Bull rising from the sea, the surf at its foot, fresh and white on blue, sunny days, but on autumn evenings it sent out a lowing in the darkness, and through the night one could glimpse the dancing breakers and flying white foam.

Most of the calves that were born at Hestviken were brindled and usually had white markings—a heart on the forehead or patches of white on the sides or white feet. He remembered the look of them as they grazed on the salt pasture of the great level meadow by the shore at Saltviken and on the slopes where the wood had been cut down for burning charcoal. But the great junipers were left, dark and bushy. The salt-pans he remembered, and the homestead a little way inland, with its houses falling into ruin; only one was kept in repair so that the salt-boilers and mowers might sleep in it. His father left the farm to hay and pasture, but Eirik himself had always thought that when his time came he would take it up again—it might be much better for corn than the head manor at Hestviken.

And this that called and allured his very body and blood, this was no sin—this too was an honourable and Christian life. Generation after generation of men had lived at Hestviken who showed God reverence and obeyed His commandments; their hand had been open to the poor and to strangers, they had had both the power and the will to defend widows and the rights of lesser men —had been the first to fly to arms when the peace of the country-side was threatened by enemies from within or without the realm. If it fell to Jörund Rypa to possess the manor after his father, then much would be changed from the old ways—he knew his brother-in-law well enough for that. And what of himself, who all his life had had but one thought, of when one day he should be master of Hestviken?

Nor did he seem to be able to make any progress with his reading and writing now. Besides, he was now not the only novice under Brother Hubert; early in the autumn the son of a poor cottar from Eiker had taken the habit. Much then had to be repeated which Eirik had already learned, and the new lessons dragged, for this Brother Torbjörn was very dull of apprehension.

Little by little the novice-master, Brother Einar, began to lose faith in Eirik Olavsson's calling for the cloister. He had grown fond of the young man, doubting not that it was God Himself who had roused him and brought him from thoughtlessness to reflection. Eirik's early fervour, his zeal to submit himself to the rule of the order—this had been far more than a whim.

But now in the first place there was the fact that he had been driven to the convent gate by grief over a woman—even though there were much else besides. But it was the experience of the novice-master that those who surrendered their love to God because they had been disappointed of their desires in this world seldom made the best monks. And what had been the actual relation between Eirik and this foster-sister of his he could not tell; *now* the man said that nothing sinful had taken place, and he was afraid it was the Devil who had tempted him to think it worse than it was in order to frighten him into the convent without a true calling for it—in which case he would be a bad monk and a sure prey of the Evil One. Brother Einar had indeed corrected him severely for speaking thus: the Devil has no more power over a man than God permits and the man himself gives him, and he cannot rob God's household of its servants unless they themselves open the door to him. But there was something in what Eirik said; the novice-master perceived that Eirik was never wittingly untruthful, but it was clear that the man himself did not remember the real circumstances of the case. And he had seen the same many times before. Eirik had difficulty in remembering anything in such a way that he could tell the story of it twice alike. But if this was a fault in men of any condition, it was a grave fault in a monk.

And Eirik was of a variable disposition and no doubt would always be so. Brother Einar had seen enough and more than enough of such natures, and it was ever a misfortune for a convent to admit a brother who always longed for change—always de-sired for himself another office or other work than that to which he had been assigned, or yearned to be removed to another house, until he had tried all the convents of his order in three or four realms. Had not Brother Edvin Richardson been a sore trial to the fraternity, pious and pure-hearted man as he was, with the spirit of unrest that dwelt within him? In his case, indeed, there was a sort of remedy for his roving disposition—he had such fame as a painter of images that he was sent for from all parts, where folk would have him come and work for them. But a restless spirit such as his was likely to infect a whole convent. Brother Einar himself had been a Black Friar among the Benedictines of Björg-vin for ten years ere he received a call to join a stricter order, and he had now been a Minorite friar for more than thirty winters; but still he held that without weighty reason a monk ought not to abandon the convent where he first took the vow.

With the spring Eirik's affection for his convent was revived —but at the same time his longing for Hestviken grew stronger, and now he was utterly unhappy, for no path seemed open to him, and however much he prayed and disciplined himself, he was still torn in two directions by his longing. When therefore his trial year was at an end, it was so ordered that he was to delay his profession until the autumn, when the other two novices, Brother Arne and Brother Torbjörn, would take the vow. Then it was that he forgot himself and struck that peasant of Tveit to the ground. Had it been himself that this loon affronted, he believed he could have borne it now. But it was the house that he loved even more fervently, now that he had half decided to leave it, and the brethren of whom he was fond, and the habit of the order, which he had striven to wear honourably and well. He humbled himself before the man at the first word from Brother Stevne, he humbled himself at home in the chapter-house—but nevertheless it was this that finally turned the scale.

But on the day when all the brethren went to Brother Bjarnvard, the barber, to have their crowns shaved, and he was not to go with them—that gave him a pang. And the morning when he was once more dressed in hose and shoes, with the red and yellow jerkin, far too tight for him, and the belt and knife about his waist, he broke down altogether—he wept as he knelt in church, wept from shame and remorse, wished he had chosen to remain. But he knew in himself that now he would have regretted it, whichever choice he had made.

The brethren took an affectionate leave of him, promising him their prayers—for he would still belong to their fellowship as a brother *ab extra*. Then he walked down toward the quay, feeling naked and ashamed in his unwonted dress, and shrinking from the eyes of everyone in the armourers' yard. And his heart was ready to break with grief as he set sail and steered out among the islands, alone in the little boat that Galfrid had lent him.

But when he had passed through the Haaöy sound and come far enough to see the familiar places along the shore—no, then he had no more regrets. And when he saw the white surf at the foot of the Bull as he rounded the promontory and stood inshore—no, he had no more regrets.

And as he walked up from the waterside, bare and empty-handed—the sea breeze sporting before him, making the corn of the "good acre" sway like flames, with the sun gleaming on its silky beards—Eirik felt inclined to leap the fence and stroke the barley that the wind was lashing.

· · ·

His father's coldness did him more good than harm. It cost him
an effort to go about his daily life here at home in such different
guise from his former self. But that he was not suffered without
a struggle to live as he deemed to be right and worthy of a Christian man, that reassured him: he had chosen aright. He had not
fled from the convent to return to his old thoughtless and idle life
—there was yet a third way, and he had found it; it put fresh heart
into him every day to feel that it was not always easy to follow it.

So the winter went by without Eirik's showing the least sign
of lukewarmness.

About a week before Easter, Olav and Eirik went together up
to Galaby. Late in the afternoon, when the matters he had come
about were settled and Olav sat at table drinking with the Sheriff
and some others of the elder franklins, there was a noise in the
courtyard; the door burst open and a boy called to the men within
that Eirik Olavsson lay outside and had surely got his death-hurt.

Olav sprang up and ran out. Over by the stable a group of men
stood surrounding one who lay on his side in the snow, which
was red with his blood; his right hand still grasped his dagger.
Eirik lay in a swoon. Olav and another man carried him in, laid
him on a bed, and attended to his wounds. He had been stabbed
with a knife in the back and again in front near the collar-bone;
his face bore marks of blows. They were ugly wounds, but need
not be fatal unless the mischief was in it. While his father was
tending him, Eirik opened his eyes.

"Could you curb your manhood no longer?" asked Olav, but
not unkindly—he was smiling a little.

Eirik's eyelids dropped again.

Olav then heard how this had come about. It was two house-
carls who had fallen out as they were saddling the horses—they
seemed to have been old enemies—and it had come to blows; their
arms had been left indoors since the sitting of the court, so they
took to their knives. When Eirik had tried to come between them,
they had both turned on him, and then he drew his dagger, but
only to defend himself; neither of the house-carls had received
more than a few scratches. Now they lay bound in a cellar.

Eirik came to his senses for a while early in the night; he whispered that if this proved his bane, he did not wish a charge to be

made against the poor men, but he forgave them as he hoped God would forgive him.

To this Olav made no answer. Neither he nor Reidulf meant to spare the men if Eirik's wounds should take a bad turn. But all went well; Reidulf had sent for an old man who could stanch blood and was a good leech. A week later Olav was able to move his son to Hestviken, and there he himself and Ragna tended the wounded man so well that Eirik was on his feet again before Whit Sunday.

After this, peace was re-established between father and son. But while he lay sick Eirik had dropped out of the way of saying his hours and all his other practices; on getting up he did indeed resume them, but either kept them less strictly than before or concealed them better from his house-mates. And if Olav came upon him while he said his paternosters, or noticed that Eirik imposed on himself any kind of self-discipline, his son was sure to hear of it later in the day.

" 'Tis a good thing, Eirik," his father said with a quiet laugh, "that we have seen your hand still knows its way to your dagger. Else it would not be well for the rest of us to dwell under the same roof with so pious a man as you have grown."

Eirik turned red. It hurt him that his father should talk in this way, but Olav said it so good-humouredly, and he had never been able to resist his father when he showed him the smallest speck of kindness.

13

EIRIK lay awake in bed one morning at Gunnarsby. Jörund was putting on his clothes in another corner of the room. Cecilia came in from outside with something and exchanged a few words with her husband. Then he said:

"Will you not speak to your brother of that matter we talked of?"

"No. I have told you I will not."

Jörund muttered something in anger. Then he followed his wife out.

Eirik got up and dressed himself. When he came out Cecilia

was sitting on the earthen bench outside the house with her son in her lap. The child crawled over his mother and wanted to be caressed; Cecilia pressed the boy to her, but looked as if she were thinking of other things. Eirik greeted his sister and stood looking down at her.

"What did Jörund wish you to say to me?"

"Since you heard that"—Cecilia glanced up with her clear, cool look—"you must also have heard my answer."

"Was it about my leaving the convent?" asked Eirik. "Has that made it worse for you here at Gunnarsby?"

"Oh—'tis not that alone." Her eyes still rested on her brother's tall and handsome figure as he stood before her with the morning sun shining on the brown locks of his bent head. He was dressed in a dark-red gown that reached to the knees and fitted his broad shoulders well, a leather belt with silver buckle about his slim waist. *She* liked him better thus—it had revolted her to see her lively, handsome brother in the frock of a barefoot friar; never could she believe that was a life for Eirik. "There is much else—"

Eirik said: "Even with a sister's portion in Hestviken, Jörund will get more with you than his brothers got with their wives. Brynhild has four brothers, and Lucia's father had to make dear amends to the King for the foolish game he played when the Duke lay before Akershus."

Cecilia nodded. "Jörund knows that—they all know it. But that makes it no easier for Jörund now—we live here, the youngest of this crowded household, and we must bow to the others in everything."

"Is it Mistress Brynhild?" asked Eirik.

"Brynhild I like best. She says what she means. But true it is that she and Jörund have never been friends. And Aake and Lucia do not like me."

Eirik looked down at the young mother. He had guessed this during his stay here—neither Jörund nor Cecilia had an easy lot.

"Tell me withal what Jörund wished you to say to me," he asked her. "Tell me," he repeated, as his sister blushed but would not answer.

Suddenly, with a movement of impatience, Cecilia set the babbling child down on the ground. The infant rolled over and made ready to scream—Eirik took him up on his arm.

"Ay, 'twill be no longer than to Clement's mass [5]—and then I shall have another one like this." Cecilia drew two or three deep breaths. "I cannot deny—I would give much if I could be spared giving birth to the child here in the hands of these brothers' wives. Even if Hestviken is to be yours—could we not live there together? He and Aake, they could never *bear* each other. Jörund has wished this ever since we were married. He begged me—'twas one of the first nights we slept together—he begged me ask Father if we might take up our abode with him. But if he could wish that —if he would rather dwell with Father, who is so glum and hard to get on with, than with his brothers—then 'twould be all the easier one day when Father is gone and you are the master—you and he have been fast friends so long."

"Is it your wish," asked Eirik, as Cecilia had to stop and take breath, "that I speak with Father—ask him if you may come out to us by autumn?"

"Yes," said Cecilia, and blushed again.

Eirik handed her the child, which was struggling to get back to its mother. Then he turned and went to find Jörund.

All that forenoon the two friends were together on the outskirts of the manor; they walked hither and thither, sat or lay on the ground, and Jörund talked without ceasing. He swore that he had not taken it amiss when he heard Eirik was not to be a monk after all; *he* at least had never forgotten that probation was probation—but Aake and Steinar and their wives had uttered words that provoked Cecilia to retort—and Eirik knew well enough how stubborn and unbending she was when she thought differently from others. She often did so here, and it generally happened that there was some truth in what she said. But it *was* unbearable for them to stay here—the dissension between him and his brothers had become ten times worse since he had married Cecilia. But if they came to Hestviken, he was sure he could live happily with her. Then he began to talk of the table silver in Cecilia's dowry— Aake's wife had found out from Magnus, the goldsmith of Oslo, that this was the old silver that Olav had brought out at the betrothal feast; Olav had had it refashioned, but that, they declared, was cheating his son-in-law of the heritage—and Cecilia had given them an answer.

[5] November 23.

121

Eirik's head reeled with listening to Jörund's complaints when at last they returned to the manor.

As Eirik rode homeward he was determined that his father must yield, though it might be difficult to obtain the old man's consent. What happened was the only thing he had not looked for: Olav said yes without hesitating. So Jörund and Cecilia moved to Hestviken that autumn. They were given the women's house to live in.

Soon after, Cecilia gave birth to her second son. He was called Torgils—by mistake: the boy came into the world half-suffocated, and the women fetched in Eirik to baptize him in emergency. In his hurry he gave the child the first family name he could think of. Olav was angry—the boy ought to have been called Audun after his father and his little dead son, and he had no wish to have Foulbeard's name perpetuated in the family—though the man's own offspring had used it and two of Arne Torgilsson's daughters had named children after their grandfather.

One day Eirik said to his father: "Could you not be less curt of speech with Jörund? He thinks you like him not."

"No, I cannot," said Olav gruffly. Then he added, already a little more graciously: "Jörund can hardly expect me to treat him as if he were still our guest, now that he has taken up his abode here."

Olav had reached a point where he was no longer able to keep up his ill will toward Eirik. The young man had compelled a certain respect from his father: he was now in his second year at home, and the change that had come over him since his stay in the convent still lasted. Olav noticed that Eirik always tried to do what was right and had achieved a mastery over himself that Olav would have sworn Eirik could never attain. His father felt something like shame when he recalled that at first he seemed to have expected and almost wished that Eirik would relapse into his old bad ways.

Without any design on their part, without their even being clearly aware of it, they drew more closely together, all these people who for so long had formed *one* household. Since Jörund Rypa's coming they felt that they had grown into unity, and he was a stranger.

He idled among the houses, as though out of place—doing nothing. Nor had he a hand for any of the work that was to be done at this manor. He went out in the morning, stood at the stable door and watched his man grooming the horses that were his; if the weather was not too bitter he sauntered down to the pier, stood there awhile looking out and spitting into the sea. He had been out with the boats a few times, but then he would go no more. Then he lay dozing on the bench in his own house—there was so little sleep to be had at night with the two children, he complained. When Olav and Eirik came in with the boatmen— this was in the fishing season—he turned into the old house and sat there; but the men were tired and hungry and had no thought of beguiling the time for Jörund Rypa. When the season for catching auks came on he revived somewhat and went out with the others—but then they had a week of tearing northerly gales, and that put an end to it.

The others saw little of Cecilia; she spent her time in the women's house or with the maids in the cook-house and outhouses.

There was great shortage of fodder in Hestviken that year, as they had Jörund's beasts as well as their own, and they had had to make use of an old byre that had been in a tumbledown state as long as any could remember. It was mended in some sort, but the starving animals suffered horribly in it. Cecilia would come out in tears when she had been feeding the cattle there. Not often had anyone seen her weep for what might befall folk, but one evening as she came from the byre and met Eirik in the outer room, she threw her arms about his neck in the darkness.

"Eirik—you who pray so much to God, can you not pray that spring may come early this year?"

"I do so, you know it well."

After Olav had gone to bed that evening, Eirik went to him in the closet and told his father what he had been thinking—that they should take up the farm in Saltviken again. Olav thought they had more profit of the land, using it as they did now, for pasture and hay, than if they let it out at rent. Eirik replied that he did not mean they should take a tenant there, but should carry on the farm with men from here: "if Jörund is to keep ten cows and four horses here at Hestviken, then we ourselves must raise far less stock than before, or move some of it out."

At last he got a kind of consent out of his father. Eirik took with him Knut and Svein, Ragna's young sons, and rowed south only a couple of days later with two boatloads of fencing. They spent a whole week there, making ready what they could. No sooner was the frost out of the ground than he set off again, this time with some of the cattle; and before Halvard's mass [6] Eirik had fenced in most of what had been the home fields, with bush fencing if with nothing else. In time even his father would have to grant he was right—this could be made a good farm.

Olav Audunsson himself had been in to Oslo for the winter fair. And as usual he had made some bargains, which were to be completed by Halvard's mass. He would now send Eirik in to the town, and Eirik asked Jörund to go with him.

The brothers-in-law stayed in the town a couple of days over the feast; they had met acquaintances, and in the evenings they drank in one house or another. Eirik had a care of himself—he would not enter any of the places where formerly he had been too well known; this was one of the reasons he had asked Jörund to accompany him: if he was with a married man it seemed more natural that he should refuse to go to the common inns and confine himself to the halls of the guilds and the townsmen's houses. Another reason was that he guessed Jörund was weary to death of Hestviken.

The evening before St. Eirik's Day [7] they both came home late to the armourers' yard and they were in drink, so that Eirik overslept next morning. On that day at any rate he had meant full surely to hear mass among his own brethren—he had not succeeded in reaching the convent since the first day he was in town —but once more it was too late. The masses were now over in all the churches except St. Halvard's; he would have to go there, and to the Minorites' for vespers.

But as he prayed during the mass, the thought came to him that he would ask at the convent for some cuttings of the great cherry tree below the hill. Near the houses in Saltviken was a hollow beside a sunny ledge of rock, just the place where fruit trees might thrive. There were many places at Hestviken too, but his father had laughed at him when he proposed it: this was no knightly manor, that they should plant rose gardens or pleasances. But Eirik already thought of Saltviken as his own manor.

When he came back to their lodging he heard from Galfrid that Jörund had gone out with some men who lived in Brand's Yard. He went after him and found his brother-in-law in a house

[6] May 15.   [7] May 18.

at the far end of this yard, in company with some men who kept
cocks there. First they watched the cockfight, and then they
went into an upper chamber and drank. After a while some
women came in—one of them, called Gyda Honeycake, Eirik had
known in old days. She seated herself on his knees, and he drank
with her, fondled the wench too a little, thinking all the time that
the wisest thing he could do was to go his way, but feeling
ashamed because of the other men. Then the dice-box was brought
out. Eirik had no desire for gaming, since he had promised to keep
himself from such things—but it was not always possible. At the
same time he was shy of refusing before the others. There happened to be a man there, one whom Eirik did not know, who said
he cared not to throw dice, but was there anyone who would
play chess? Here he was freed from two temptations at one stroke,
since he could not play chess with Mistress Honeycake in his lap;
so Eirik declared himself willing and set the girl down, not without a secret regret at being rid of her. But the stranger, Helge,
was so good a chess-player that Eirik soon forgot all else in the
game. He would have liked to stay away from vespers too, but
when the bells began to ring he remembered the cherry trees, and
now he had set his heart on them. So he took his leave. Jörund
stayed on. Eirik saw that he was already far gone in drink; he
himself had been sobered by his zeal for the game as soon as he
had found how skilful an opponent he had. Jörund was playing
wildly, but Eirik gave little thought to that: the man was always
lucky at dice; besides, he was married now, he could surely take
care of himself.

And it had already passed out of his mind when he stood once
more in his own church and joined in the singing of *Ave Maris
Stella* and the Magnificat. After the service several of the brethren
came down to him and he went with them into the convent; now
he had to talk with them all, and soon the hour of the evening
meal arrived. The end was that Eirik was to sleep in the guest-
chamber that night; next morning after mass they could take up
those shoots for him. The fruit trees were far advanced, but Father
Einar thought that if the shoots were well wrapped in moss and
birchbark and he sailed straight back to Saltviken and planted
them that evening, they would take root.

Eirik was in church for complin and slept in the guest-chamber,
and in the light spring night he was roused by the monk who came

with his hood drawn over his head and whispered: "*Benedicamus Domino*." And he went to matins, and back to bed again, and to mass. Then for the first time he remembered the purse with the money he had received for his father—it lay at the bottom of his bed in the Richardsons' house—but surely it was safe enough there.

When once the brethren had procured the cherry-tree cuttings for him, they found many another thing to give him from their garden. Eirik carried the whole load down to the boat, got hold of an old sail, and wrapped his cuttings to keep them from the sun. It was high noon ere he returned to the armourers'. There he was told that Jörund had come in for a moment the evening before, but he had not been home that night.

Eirik walked into the town to seek out his brother-in-law. In Brand's Yard he met Helge, and from him he heard that late in the evening he had gone with Jörund Rypa to a house where no man would have liked to find his sister's husband. He was still sitting there when Helge left. Eirik asked Helge to go thither with him, but when they came to the house they were told that Jörund had gone home a little while before. So Eirik went back to their lodging.

There he found Jörund, engaged in packing their belongings. He looked somewhat the worse for wear. Eirik could not bring himself to say a word. He put together the last of their baggage. When he felt in his bed for the purse, it was gone.

"I have taken charge of that," said Jörund. "I could not tell how long you would be taken up with those brethren of yours—"

Eirik turned sharply on his brother-in-law. But then he swallowed the answer that was on the tip of his tongue. 'Twas bad enough as it was—would be made no better by talking.

So they went down to the boat. During the sail they did not exchange an unnecessary word. Eirik was glad enough they had none of the house-folk with them, so Cecilia would not hear of her husband's doings.

After supper that evening Eirik gave his father an account of how he had discharged his business. "Jörund has the purse with the money on him."

Jörund Rypa stood up. "Dear father-in-law of mine—sooth to say—I have not the money here. It fell out that I met a man who made a claim on me—I was in his debt for a mark and a half of silver—a dalesman it was, the man who sold me Greylag, but he had gone home when I had the money for him—so now I borrowed this money of yours, to be rid of the old debt."

Olav stared at his son-in-law till Jörund was out of countenance.

"Ay, we were throwing dice too—I am so used to having luck with me in my play; I had looked to win enough to pay this Simon what I owed him. But here is this stoup, which is worth much more than the silver I borrowed of you—" Jörund took a handsome little cup from the folds of his kirtle and placed it on the table before his father-in-law. "You must take this—"

Olav seized the cup, crushed it in his hand, then flung it right in the face of Jörund Rypa.

"I have not asked for your stoup. My silver I will have—neither more nor less!"

Eirik had leaped up. For a second he saw something in Jörund's face—and he was chilled through with fear—this should not have happened!

Jörund looked down at the twisted cup that lay before him. Then he put his foot on it and trod it flat.

"Take your stoup," said Olav, so that his son-in-law obeyed.

Then Jörund went out.

Eirik and Olav stood in silence without looking at each other. Then the father asked in a low, angry voice:

"And you—were you gaming too?"

Eirik shook his head. "He must have done this the last evening we were in Oslo. We went each our own way. He went to one of his kinsmen, and I was with the brethren, stayed there the night."

"Did you know no better," asked Olav cuttingly, "than to lie out there playing with your rosary—when you had *him* with you? *You* ought to know your friend. 'Tis an ill thing to set a sheep to herd a fox."

Eirik stood in silence. ("For all that, you should not have done it, Father"—but he dared not say it.)

Eirik could not fall asleep that night. He ought not to have left Jörund—his father was right there, more than he knew himself; for he did not know what sort of company it was he had left Jörund in. He might have tried to get Jörund to church with him, but he had shrunk from that; he had wished to be left in peace with those friends of his for whom he had a different kind of affection from that he felt for Jörund.

For all that, his father should not have done it—flung the stoup

127

in his face and treated him as a thief. Eirik gave a low groan—
Jörund would never forget this against his father. And if they
were now to live together here— He had a feeling that foreboded,
he knew not what disasters.

Then he bethought him of what he had lying in the shed at the
waterside, wrapped in a ragged sail. He must have it in the ground
as soon as might be, both Father Einar and Brother Hubert had
told him that. Eirik would just as soon avoid meeting either his
father or Jörund or Cecilia on the morrow. He got up and stole
quietly out.

The fiord lay pale and calm in the spring night, which was already turning to dawn. The gently heaving swell licked at the
yellow band of seaweed under the rocks, the gulls sat on the surface like white spots—now and then one rose and flew out. But in
the pine forest that filled every hollow of the mossy grey hills
along the shore, the song of birds awoke little by little. The pale-
grey clouds in the south were tinged with red and the north-
eastern sky turned to orange as he rowed along the broad, curv-
ing, white sandy beach of Saltviken. Inland was a great plain, poor
pasture, with a few alders that the salt-boilers had spared, and
huge old junipers, in shape like gigantic spearheads. Eirik rowed
past; he had a mind to look at the nets that he usually had lying
out off some rocks in the south of the bay—whether the boys had
seen to them while he was from home. As he rowed back again,
a score of fish lay floundering in the bottom of the boat.

The houses stood a little way from the beach, half-hidden from
the sea behind a low ridge of rust-coloured rock that looked like
the back of a gigantic whale. Inland the soil was broken by more
such whale-backs as it sloped up to the edge of the forest.

As he passed the door of his house, Eirik heard his dogs—they
knew of his coming. He let them out, received their joyful welcome. But the boys, his house-carls as he called them, slept heavily
—Knut and Svein in one of the beds and Olav Livsson on the
bench. Eirik had moved him hither, for he could see that his beads-
man was irksome to them at Hestviken; he would serve in any
case to mend their clothes while they lay out here with no
woman's help.

But he had to shut up the dogs again while he was planting—
they would scratch up the seedlings as fast as he put them in. He
had almost finished his work when he heard the boys going to the

byre. The sun had already been up some time; the fiord and the land on the other side lay bathed in the fresh, pale morning light. When the lads had brought out the cows and let them into the fenced field that he meant to sow with corn next year, his task was done.

He went down, greeted them, and gave orders about the fish. Then he threw his muddy garments to Olav Livsson, took a deep draught of the warm morning milk, and flung himself into his bed, feeling that now he would sleep on till evening.

14

EIRIK spent most of his time at Saltviken that summer. It seemed as if he had transferred all his affection for his ancestral home to this place; he no longer felt happy at Hestviken, and when he was compelled to stay there for some days, he simply longed to get back to the deserted manor and thought of what he would next turn his hand to there.

His father gave him angry words for it: "Soon you will be of no more use to me than my son-in-law."

"Ay, he can be no great help to you."

Olav laughed wrathfully.

Eirik worked hard to have the outhouses put in such state that some men could stay here next winter with half a score of cattle. He had only the two young lads and the cripple with him, but he made shift with them. Olav had two salters in the bay that summer, and they lay up at the manor.

At last, when Eirik had made an end of haymaking, Olav came over one day to see how it went with the salt-pans. He found fault with the appearance of the yard—a litter of building-materials and chips. The house itself was what one might expect where five men and a helpless cripple had their abode without a woman to look after them. He muttered disapproval of the ugly withered bush fences right up among the houses—and he wanted Eirik at home now, to help in the haymaking. He had little to say as Eirik went round with him, showing him what he had done and telling him what more he meant to do. But as they walked down to the boat, Olav halted a moment.

"You were right, Eirik. This farm here can be made much better than I thought. I see now that what you have done is well done."

Eirik turned red with joy. He said with a little smile: "Do you know, Father, this is the first time so long as we have known each other that you have acknowledged me right?"

Olav answered thoughtfully: "I am not sure of that. Did I not approve you when you would enter the convent? When you ran from home, desiring to go out into the world and try your fortune—I call naught else to mind but that I owned you right in that too, abeit I liked not your leaving me in that manner. And had you spoken to me of Bothild—maybe I had not refused you there either."

Eirik held his peace, in confusion. He saw that what his father said was true—but he knew that it was not the *whole* truth.

"Have you put the convent quite out of your thoughts?"

It was not easy to answer this. In a way he always looked back on that life with regret—and sometimes he had thought that when the farm at Saltviken was fully restored— If he could have taken his vows forthwith, he believed he would have done so. But he knew that he would have to go through the novitiate once more, and he could not support another whole year in which to make his choice.

"You are inconstant, my son," said Olav in a low voice as they walked on; "and I wonder whether there may not come a day when you will no longer have a mind to stay at Saltviken."

Eirik spat out the juniper berries he had been chewing. But then he checked himself and did not answer his father. Inconstant—Father Einar had said the same. It was strange—

"Since you have no more thought of the convent," said Olav, " 'twill soon be time for you to marry."

As Eirik made no reply, Olav pursued: "You are eight and twenty winters old, Eirik; 'tis well time. And I am over the half-hundred—at my age no man can tell if he will be above ground next year. I would fain know what will become of Hestviken when I am gone."

"Cecilia has two fine sons," said Eirik.

"Two and a half, I fear," said Olav curtly. "Ay, they are goodly babes, I hear the women say. But mouse-eared—like their father."

Eirik said: "Have you thought of any—? With whom you would have me married, I mean."

"Berse of Eiken has a daughter—"

"Gunhild? But there is enmity between you and Berse?"

"No worse but that we might be friends again." Olav smiled faintly. "If he could win the heir of Hestviken for a son-in-law, why—"

They had no more talk as Eirik rowed homeward in the summer evening. Only when they were at the quayside his father said:

"Then old Tore will have to be at Saltviken this winter with the cattle you will have there."

"Tore? But can you spare him here?"

"Better him than you." Olav paused a moment. "I should be loath to live here alone with Jörund." Eirik saw that it cost his father a good deal to say it.

Next day during the after-dinner rest Eirik went in to his sister. As she rose, Eirik saw that she was indeed as his father had said. It did not show much in her, except that she seemed to have difficulty in stooping—and at once it struck her brother that nothing seemed to change Cecilia: she only became unbending and stiff in the back.

She fetched flagon and cup and set them before him; then she sat down again to her sewing. The ale had stood; it was so flat that Eirik only drank so as not to offend his sister.

He scarce knew what to talk to her about. She sat perfectly straight, holding her sewing up close to her face; her fine pale mouth seemed hardened into a firm, straight line, and her cheeks had fallen in so that the powerful cheek-bones and the square chin appeared prominent. He saw that her bright eyes had lost their lustre; they were like little pale-grey pebbles on the beach.

Kolbein, her elder boy, came stumping in with something he had found—a strip of bark—laid it on his mother's knee. She said thanks, seriously, but shook her head when he wanted to climb into her lap; she was busy sewing.

Then he picked up his piece of bark and carried it over to Eirik. Eirik lifted up the boy and played with him; he had always got on well with children. Kolbein was fat and lusty—Eirik passed his fingers through the child's fair, moist hair. It was true, he had

mouse's ears; but still, it shocked him that the boy's own grandfather should say so. It had never occurred to him that Jörund's
ears were like that—he wore his hair so that they were hidden. It
was a sign that thralls' blood had found its way into a family,
folk said.

Eirik had a mind to ask Cecilia about Gunhild Bersesdatter—
they were of the same age—but did not bring himself to do so. He
had seen Gunhild at church many times, but could not remember
clearly how she looked—neither fair nor foul, he thought, and with
red hair.

He wished his sister would take her children on her lap, laugh
and play with them, boast of them as he had heard other young
wives do. But Cecilia did no such thing. She cared for them well,
but without a smile or a jest. She spoke to Jörund and of Jörund
—the little he had heard her say—as a good wife should. But always with the same cool gravity. He would rather she had made
complaint—for he knew that if she had anything to complain of,
it was not Cecilia's way to do so. He was uneasy on Jörund's
account and—not by such methods would she be able to keep
Jörund kind and in good humour, and if Jörund was now at
enmity with their father too—

His brother-in-law came in at that moment, greeted Eirik, and
poured himself out a drink of ale.

"Where is Magnhild?—bid her fetch us fresh ale!"

"I know not where Magnhild is." Cecilia put down her sewing,
took the flagon, and went out.

"Has he sent for you to help with the hay?" Jörund stretched
himself. "Ah, I have not stirred a hand—I'll not do it till Olav
offers amends for the insult he put upon me in the spring."

In the evening Eirik asked his father: "Has Jörund restored to
you the silver he borrowed in the spring?"

Olav snorted scornfully, did not even answer.

On Sunday, as the Hestviken folk were leaving church after
mass, Torgrim of Rynjul came up to them.

"Una says you might give your young folk leave today, Olav
—'tis so long since she spoke with Eirik, she says."

"With all my heart—" Olav swung himself into the saddle. He
and the servants rode off.

As Eirik gave his hand to Una Arnesdatter he saw that Gunhild was standing close by with the Rynjul children. She was just unhooking her cloak, which she handed with her veil to Torgrim's son. " 'Tis so warm today," she said to the boy. Her voice was bright and good—Eirik liked it.

He stole a glance at her while Una was greeting Jörund and Cecilia. She was not red-haired, as he had thought—her plaits were ash-coloured, but she had the fine red-and-white freckled complexion that often goes with red hair, and her skin shone like silk. She was tall, straight, and slender—and her reddish-brown habit fitted closely to the body, down to the silver belt about her hips; below that it fell in rich folds, which lay on the grass about her feet. The sleeves of her kirtle almost touched the ground and were split to the elbow, showing the ruffled sleeves of her pale-blue shift.

She looked no different from so many other healthy women of good birth who have been brought up free from care—her face was oval and full, her nose straight and rather thick at the tip, her eyes grey. But Eirik looked at this maid who was intended for him and began already to distinguish her from among all other women. Torgrim and Una must be privy to the matter, he guessed.

So when they were to ride away, Eirik lifted Gunhild Bersesdatter into the saddle. She thanked him frankly and kindly, looked down into his narrow, swarthy face, saw that the man's great yellow eyes were of rare beauty, and then she smiled very faintly and thanked him once more as she took the reins.

He had no chance of talking to her while they were together at Rynjul, but the fact that she *was* there seemed to fill the whole day for him. In the course of the evening the young people of the house, Astrid and Torgils and Elin, wished to start a game.

At first Eirik would not join them, he was so much older than Una's children and their friends; and he had usually held aloof from games and dancing since he came home. But he was fond of dancing—and his young kinswomen were bent upon having him sing for them. When he came into the chain, Astrid dropped Gunhild's hand and reached out for his. So it came about that he was placed between the two young maids.

The sun was about to set, and in the warm yellow glow the shadows of the dancers fell far across the grass. The song rang out finely in the peaceful summer evening, and Eirik felt the joy-ful intoxication of hearing his own good voice. All the time he felt Gunhild's hand lying in his—it was warm and slightly moist, and it sent a current of sweetness and goodness through his whole body. He looked forward to each turn, when the chain swung the other way; then he was brushed by her waving sleeves and the folds of her kirtle.

Once, when the dancers stopped to take breath, he chanced to look where Cecilia was sitting with Una watching the young folks' game. His sister had wrapped herself closely in her blue mantle; her face showed yellow as bone against the white folds of her linen coif. Games and dancing were over for her, and she was a little younger than Gunhild. Eirik dropped Astrid's hand and went over to the two married women.

He stretched himself on the grass at their feet, turned his face up toward Una as he talked. Soon after, the young people fol-lowed him; the rest went back at once, but Gunhild sat down by Cecilia, and the two talked together in low tones. Eirik heard her fresh voice behind him as the younger ones danced and sang on the green and he himself chatted to Una.

The brother and sister broke up as darkness was falling. Tor-grim said that Jörund had ridden away some time ago, saying he had business somewhere. When they entered the forest, Eirik dismounted and walked, leading his sister's horse. He ought not to have stayed so long at Rynjul, he was thinking—it was not prudent for her to be out after dark.

At Rundmyr he took the little path that ran by the upper edge of the bog; he had a message for Arnketil and dared not leave Cecilia, but thought perhaps he might see someone outside. Just as they were below the slope on which the houses stood, the door opened—the light of the fire shone out—and some folks came out, men and women; he could hear by their voices that they were vagabonds.

But among the crowd he caught sight of a particoloured kirtle that he thought he recognized. He had sold Jörund the clothes the Minorites had given him at parting; they fitted his brother-in-law.

Eirik was perturbed—did Jörund go to Rundmyr now! Hot about the ears, he recalled all he had himself told Jörund in old days of his adventures there—making them more wonderful than

they were. But he had a vague feeling that if Jörund sought diver-
sion there, worse things might be looked for. Though he had
never accounted to himself for it, he knew the coldness of the
other's nature well enough to be sure that if Jörund wallowed in
the mire, there was nothing in him that could be mirrored in the
puddles and lend them lustre.

Cecilia had seen nothing, thank God—she sat facing the other
way.

Arrived at home, Eirik put up the horses in the stable, where the
stalls were now all empty in the summer night. Then he seated
himself on a chest that stood by the door—he would be there
when Jörund came, try to get the man in without waking Cecilia.

Gunhild, Gunhild—she glided in and out of his thoughts the
whole time. His hands had scarcely approached a woman since he
left the convent. For more than three years he had kept a guard
on himself, in deeds, in words, in thoughts. When he had
been tempted of the devil, the world, and his own flesh, he had
fought.

Now he was set free to look at one, to think of one. He was
free to recall what it had been like to take her and lift her into the
saddle, to recall her hand, which he had held in his—a sweetness
and a promise of more, more—

Beneath the memory of these last serious years, when he
had trained his will and learned to use it against himself, floated
the shadowy memories of his youth, the embraces of venal
wenches and dreams of high-born maids—dreams that he dared not
jeopardize by frequenting any such. And Bothild—to think of her
directly he never dared, but the shame and the horror and the
pain of what she had betokened in his life lay dissolved and pre-
cipitated within him and had coloured all the currents that had
passed through his mind in these last years.

Now the bright image of Gunhild Bersesdatter began to take
shape against this dark-purple background. He had already abandoned himself to loving her.

It was past midnight and yet Jörund had not come. Eirik sat
and waited, grew anxious on his brother-in-law's account, thought
of Gunhild, and was happy.

Then he awoke and saw that he had slept a long time; it was
light outside. He looked out—up by the fence was Jörund's hand-

some dun saddle-horse; and in the shed outside, his saddle and bridle hung in their places. So in any case he could not have been very drunk.

His father did not allude to the matter until about a week later. "Have you thought over that of which we spoke lately? About a marriage for you?"

"It shall be as you desire, Father."

A day or two later Eirik again found occasion to visit Rynjul. Gunhild was still there. Not many words did he exchange with her, but she sat with Una while he was talking to his kinswoman.

Berse of Eiken was a cousin of Arne of Hestbæk, the father-in-law of Baard and Torgrim. But he and Torgrim of Rynjul had been estranged for many years—Torgrim was hot-headed and loose of tongue; in general folk paid little heed to his outbursts, for he was generous and the last man to bear a grudge, but Berse would not put up with an uncivil word, for he was mighty jealous of what he called his dignity. Olav Audunsson had also fallen out with him at one time: the two had been chosen as umpires in a dispute, but were unable to agree; and Olav had expressed his opinion in terms that were sharper than Berse considered becoming to his dignity.

Eirik had never before given a thought to this ill feeling among the three old men. But now, when the women had left the room, he asked Torgrim: "Are you kinsmen now reconciled—since the daughter from Eiken is here as a guest?"

Torgrim laughed and drank to Eirik. "Ay, I have shown the old man I dared be his enemy seven years. But, God's death, I'll now show him I am bolder yet—I dare be friends with him other seven years, if need be. But so long he cannot look to live—he is seventy winters old, all of that. And Gunhild takes after her mother—which is well for her." He nodded to Eirik.

So Eirik saw that Torgrim was the one who was to take the first steps toward the contract.

Some days after Bartholomew's mass [8] Una came out to Hestviken to visit Cecilia; with her she had her two young daughters and Gunhild Bersesdatter.

[8] August 24.

All the young people were sitting in the ladies' house with the women, when Una said to Cecilia that her first business was to offer to foster Torgils this winter: "since you are to have another child ere he is a year old, 'twill be too much for you, and now I have a foster-mother for him; Ingrid bore her child yestereven, and it was dead, poor young wife. She would gladly take your Torgils and give him the breast."

"Nay, nay—I will not send my son from me."

Then Jörund said: "Rather should you thank Mistress Una. You need your night's rest now, Cecilia, and maybe Torgils would be less sickly if he had a change of mothers."

Una said Jörund was right. Then she began to speak of Ingrid's misfortune. She had been Una's maid for many years and almost like a foster-daughter at Rynjul; from there she was married a year ago to a good and brave man who served with Gunhild's uncle, Guttorm of Draumtorp in Skeidis parish. Guttorm and his wife had been to a wedding in Raumarike, and they had with them a sack of valuables that had been lent for the wedding feast. In the forest by Gerdarud they had been surrounded by robbers—the master and his three house-carls had defended themselves well, but Jon, Ingrid's husband, died of his wounds a little later. The widow was almost out of her mind from grief, and one night she ran away from Draumtorp; alone with a little lad whom she had got to go with her, she came on foot to Rynjul.

They sat talking for a while of the robberies and ambushes that were reported in many parts of the country round Oslo. But then Una sent the young people out; she would speak a little with Cecilia privately.

Again Eirik felt that twinge of pity that his sister must be left, faded and cheerless, with the elder woman, while all the rest went out into the open air, where the sunlight flickered on the rocks, and the fiord gleamed brightly under the fair-weather breeze.

Astrid and Elin, they were as fair as their mother had been in her youth, sixteen and fourteen years, no more. Elin had carried Torgils out, defending herself laughingly against her sister, who also wanted to carry him—he was a fine, fair-haired little child, but pale and weak of limb. "You will have four foster-mothers when you come to Rynjul," laughed little Elin, pressing the babe closely to her.

"You have never been out here before?" Eirik asked Gunhild as they stood side by side watching the two young girls struggling for the child.

"No. I think I would fain go down and look at the sea."

"Perhaps you would like me to row you?" Eirik ventured to ask.

"That I would indeed."

They had lost sight of Jörund, so Eirik was alone in the boat with the three girls. Gunhild sat forward in the bow, raised against the blue sky, and her bright, slender figure was a little indistinct with the light behind her, but her movements were graceful when she turned and looked about her. On the thwart facing him sat the two young sisters: Astrid, who talked and laughed, and Elin, with the little child who had fallen asleep on her bosom; now and again she wrapped her cloak more closely about him and then drew it aside and peeped at the boy. Eirik would have liked to row far enough to give them a sight of Saltviken, but there was not time for that.

"Hestviken looks best from the water," said Gunhild as they walked up from the pier.

"But to live by the fiord—maybe you would not care for that?"

"Oh, yes, I think I should like it very well," said Gunhild, and again Eirik thought her voice frank and kind.

"Then you would not say no to a suitor—merely because he would bring you out to these parts?" He thought to himself it was awkwardly put.

"Oh, no—" Gunhild gave a little smile. "Not if there were no worse things to be said of him."

"What, then? That he—that you would have to live in the house with his married brother or sister, for instance?"

Gunhild shook her head.

"A maid who has had a stepmother since she was twelve," she said seriously, "has had time to learn to adapt herself. So I trow that would not scare me, if I liked the man in other ways."

"I would I knew," whispered Eirik—"if you think you could come to like me?"

Gunhild answered in a clear voice, smiling as she spoke: "I have never heard aught else of you, Eirik, but that you were a kindly man."

"So it would not grieve you if my father could be agreed with Berse?"

At this she laughed. "No! How should I take it into my head to grieve if Father were agreed with an enemy?"

Then Eirik laughed too.

That evening he ventured to lean his breast slightly against her knee when he lifted her into the saddle.

"I wonder when I shall see you again?"

"I cannot tell. I am to go home tomorrow."

Cecilia and Eirik accompanied their guests a little way across the fields. Little Torgils was asleep, well wrapped up, in Una's spacious lap. Before they parted his mother held up her arms. "Let me have him a moment, Una!" She kissed the boy, cautiously so as not to wake him. "I know well that you will have as good a care of him as I myself—"

Slowly the brother and sister walked back to the manor.

"But 'tis surely best that Una have charge of him this winter," he said soothingly.

"Ay, 'tis so; I know it. But—"

Eirik was wishing he could have taken her in his arms—or could have done something that would make her happy. It cut him to the soul that she should not be happy, now that he was. After the agitations of his talk with Gunhild he was quite unusually happy.

When he came into the room, his father sat there eating—he had not yet taken off either hat or cloak. Eirik paused for a moment.

"Father—cannot you be reconciled with Jörund? 'Twill be unbearable for Cecilia if you two go about here and never say a word to each other."

"Has *she* begged you to ask this of me?"

"Cecilia? Can you think of such a thing! But you must see—"

"Hm. She does not speak to me either, more than she can help. She takes Jörund's part, I believe. And maybe 'tis better so— We must wait awhile, Eirik, see how it goes. I have no great mind to be the first to hold out my hand. 'Tis not that I cannot forgive an enemy—but Jörund. If I do it *once*—yield to him when he is in the wrong—then I fear 'twill not be long ere he venture the same again."

So it was of no use. Nor was what his father said untrue. He would have to wait.

Not long after, Eirik saw Berse at a Thing in Haugsvik.

He was a giant in stature and bulky of body, with a mass of silvery hair and beard, his features large and handsome, but he was marked and blind of one eye from smallpox. He sat by himself on the raised seat; in his rich kirtle he seemed to have the bosom of an old woman, and his belly rolled out upon his knees. Olav and Torgrim sat on the side bench, and for the first time it struck Eirik that after all there was a great difference between seventy years and fifty. His father looked small beside Berse, but in spite of his white hair and scarred face he seemed young and elastic, straight and well-knit. But Torgrim with his lean and loose-hung frame and shock of brown and grey-streaked hair around his lively, angular face appeared to Eirik almost like a man of his own age. Then Olav called Eirik forward.

Eirik stood before Berse, answered with respectful courtesy to the words the old man addressed to him with the utmost gravity and dignity. Then Berse made a sign that he might go.

And well it was, thought Eirik. Out in the courtyard he came upon Ragnvald Jonsson.

"What makes you grin like that?" asked Ragnvald in surprise.

Eirik gave his friend a slap between the shoulders that made him gasp; then he could contain himself no longer; he burst out laughing so that he had to hold on to Ragnvald.

As they rowed homeward Olav asked: "What think you of Berse of Eiken, my son?"

Eirik bit his lip and struggled to look serious.

Olav said: "You know, 'tis a good old stock, many gallant men —great wealth there is, too. And the maid takes after her mother; Helga was a brave woman. In every bargain there is something one would wish to alter. And here there is Berse—"

On seeing his father smile, he dared to laugh too.

"But he is as old as the hills, is Berse, and 'tis a far cry from Eiken to Hestviken."

"Ay, Gunhild said the same."

"Have you spoken with Gunhild?" asked his father rather sharply.

"But little. We said a few words when she came out to us with Una. She let me know that she thought it pleasant by the fiord, and that Eiken lay far up the country."

"Ah, well. But beware of acting unwisely, Eirik—better have no more speech with her till all be in order. Berse will come—of that we may be sure—but we must let him come at his own pace, give him time to get his breath. 'Tis more seemly thus, you understand."

They looked at each other and laughed.

About Michaelmas it was cold for some days; the ground was covered with rime and all the pools were frozen over, now and again a snow-squall swept across. Then there was mild weather again; the hills were blue-black, splashed with yellow foliage, the blue fiord sparkled in the sunlight. The meadows along the shore were green with after-grass among white stubble-fields; there was light in all the groves, where yellow leaves shivered down and the alders alone still showed a faded green in their tops.

Eirik had come sailing in from Saltviken one morning. The weather was so fine that he stayed a moment outside the house door. The brindled cattle grazing in the green meadow were still fat from summer pasture, many fine beasts among them. They could well take five or six out to Saltviken.

He caught sight of Cecilia on the steps of the storehouse that had been assigned to Jörund for his use. She carried in her arms a heavy load of fur cloaks and other garments. Eirik called to her, ran up, and took it all from her.

"I thought I ought to mend our winter clothing ere I am brought to bed—the cold may soon set in in earnest." She turned toward the door of the loft.

"If there is more to come, take it out—I will come up and carry it for you."

Eirik came back, ran up the stairway whistling, and entered the loft. The sun shone in at the open door on his sister as she knelt by a chest. In one leap Eirik was beside her.

"Cecilia! Are you sick?"

"Nay—" She uttered a loud shriek of pain; she had flung down the lid of the chest so suddenly that it caught her fingers.

Eirik raised the lid slightly—saw a glimpse of what lay within. Then he put his arm about his sister's waist and supported her to a seat. He took her crushed hand and fingered it charily, to see if it were damaged. She panted and panted, wearily and painfully.

"Is there more you would have me carry down for you?" He flung the chest wide open.

Cecilia sent him one anxious glance. He saw she was trying to rise, but had not the strength.

"Jörund chooses a strange place to keep his silver."

He found his own hands shaking as he took one piece after another out of the homespun cloth: a great silver tankard in which lay a lump of silver that had been melted down, two smaller cups.

"I have not seen these things before?"

"Nor I either," whispered Cecilia. Then she collected herself. "This must be something he has brought lately."

Eirik nodded in spite of himself.

Cecilia went on in desperate eagerness: "He has always thought his brothers had dealt unfairly by him—twice when they divided an inheritance. That is why Jörund thinks he can never get silver enough. They set more store by such treasures at Gunnarsby than — So Jörund will always buy all he can."

Eirik nodded again. Jörund had been like a hawk after silver —though often enough he lost it again in play. But never had he thought it could lead to such a thing as—as what he was afraid of; though to be sure he knew nothing as yet.

He took up the clothes that Cecilia had dropped beside the chest and gave his sister his hand. She was trembling all over.

"Erik—in God's name—what will you do?"

"Speak to Jörund. Have no fear, Cecilia," he begged her.

Her brother helped her down the stairway, took her into the house, and laid her on her bed.

"Shall I find Magnhild for you?"

Cecilia shook her head.

"Is it not imprudent that you be left alone now?"

"No, I can well be alone."

Out in the yard Kolbein ran straight into his legs. Eirik picked up his nephew; with the child in his arms he went back to the women's house and put his head in at the door.

"Kolli wants to go to his mother, he says—may he come in?"

"I would rather be alone."

He played with the boy, sang to him, and sought to allay the dread in his own heart. Till he saw Jörund's boat outside; then he carried Kolbein in to the women in the cook-house. Eirik was waiting by the fence of the "good acre" as Jörund came up from the sea.

"You have come home?"

"Yes, I came this morning. I shall have to stay here awhile. There is a thing I must speak with you about." They walked together across the yard. "We can go up into your loft."

Jörund backed away from him. Eirik looked the other in the face till he succeeded in holding the shifting eyes a moment.

"Remember, Jörund, I have been your friend since our young days—many a time ere this have I rescued you from a tight corner. And now we are in the same boat; your welfare is ours. And if you have behaved foolishly, your misfortune will be my sister's and ours.—Nay, you can go first," he said when they came to the stairway.

Jörund took his hand from the hilt of his dagger and obeyed.

On entering the loft Eirik went straight to the chest and opened it.

"What have you been doing in my chest?"

"Nothing. Cecilia came to look for some clothes and I helped her to carry them down."

"Cecilia—!"

"Ay. But she was not the cause of this—I believe God Himself so ordered it that we might be rescued from this danger. And if you mean to make Cecilia suffer for this, you may go straightway and be shriven."

"Do you threaten me?"

"I do."

"Do you think I am afraid of you? A holy hound like you—turn the other cheek if a man smite you under the ear—"

"True, I have curbed myself at times these last years when I was provoked. But you know very well, in old days I was never slow to take up a quarrel—unlike you. You never had cause to fear me—but I know well you are none of the bravest."

"Where have you left your piety today?" Jörund tried to sneer.

"Have no care for that. We have to speak of what is to be done with this silver."

"The silver I have bought—"

"Ay, so I thought. You have bought it of the folk you met at Rundmyr on the evening of Suscipimus Deus Sunday?"

"I should have remembered they are your thralls"—Jörund flared up; "and of course you would keep the nest for your own with all that are in it of thieves and whores—"

"Be quiet now," said Eirik calmly. " 'Tis true you ought to have remembered that these folk are faithful to us, and if you are such a gull as to believe all the tales I once told you for entertainment's sake—how could I tell you were so credulous; 'tis not like you. But it so happened that I was riding past and saw you come out with someone— They have said nothing; I advise you to remember that! Was it the thieves themselves, or was it their fences?" he brought himself to ask.

"It was a woman," said Jörund curtly.

Did you think that bride had inherited the silver she carried along the road?—but he kept the question to himself.

"I have thought of a way, Jörund. We will bury these things in the ground by Rundmyr. And then we must find them again when they have lain there awhile, and bring them to Guttorm at Draumtorp."

"I have bought them," said Jörund angrily.

"I will give you Agnar in exchange"—he instantly regretted that he had not thought of something else; Jörund was not always good to his horses. "I wager he is worth more than you gave that woman," he said rather scornfully. "Cannot you see, man, 'tis your own honour and welfare that you have to save by this?" he went on earnestly. "What use have you of silver that you must keep hidden?"

He wrapped the treasure in the cloth again, put it under his cloak, carried it down, and hid it in his bed.

In the course of the afternoon, when he had seen Jörund go out, he slipped into the women's house to hear how it was with Cecilia.

She sat sewing at some of the things he had brought down for her in the morning. Eirik was afraid to ask the question, but at last he said nevertheless:

"Has Jörund spoken to you of what we talked of this morning?"

"Yes. I must thank you, Eirik, for giving him your help. He says he cannot guess how he could be so thoughtless as to let them trick him into taking these things. But in sooth it was because he wished to restore to Father what he owed him."

"That must be a lie," thought her brother. He leaned over her and stroked her wimpled head once or twice as she bent over her sewing.

In the evening, as he and his father were going to bed, Eirik said:

"Now I have a boon to ask of you, Father, and 'tis the same I asked before—be reconciled with Jörund!"

"I have already given you my answer."

"Yes. But now I say to you—this is worse for Cecilia than you think. For the love of God who died for us all—grant what I ask of you this time!"

Olav looked at his son, but made no answer.

"Ay, there is yet more I would ask of you. When Cecilia is over her churching—let her rule here as mistress of the whole manor!"

"What say you! When you yourself are to bring a wife into the house at John's mass! 'Twill leave but a short space for Cecilia to wear the keys."

"Oh, I know not.—I had thought that Gunhild and I might be at Saltviken most of the time."

"No, Eirik! Saltviken is far too small for the daughter of Eiken."

"I am not sure of that. One day Hestviken will be ours in any case—and then we shall be thought no less of for having kept to its desert and dependent manor for some years."

"I told you," said Olav slowly, "last time we spoke of these things—I believe Jörund is a dangerous man to give in to, when he is in the wrong."

"Father!" Eirik rose, stood facing Olav, and spoke with vehement insistence. "I beg this of you, with all my power! Think of our mother! Have you ever felt pity for her, in the years when she lay here broken and powerless—and you must have—did you ever rue it that you made her lot more grievous—Father, Christ knows I do not speak thus to accuse you, I know your own lot was hard enough—I know you would not have taken her, but they forced the marriage upon you, ere you were grown up. But even if you did not love her, you must have pitied her; do not then so order it that Cecilia's lot must be as hard as Mother's!"

Olav had listened to his son—with an expression that bewildered Eirik.

"What has put this into your head? That I did not love your mother?" The strange smile that spread over the man's whole face reminded his son, as it died away, of rings that spread over a sheet of water. "I did so. And for her sake I will do as you ask."

When Eirik had gone to bed—he lay on the silver and thought he would rather have had a nest of vipers in his bed-straw—his father came to the door of the closet.

"Will you stay at home now?"

"I thought I would sail across tomorrow with Tore—give him directions there. Then I could come back on the second or third day."

"That were well."

In the midst of all the misery on which he lay brooding it suddenly occurred to Eirik: things had so shaped themselves that he now counted for not a little at Hestviken. And he was not sorry at the thought. And by John's mass, his father had said. He lay sleepless that night, in a fever of dread and disgust over the affairs of others, in a fever of joy over his own.

About midnight he stole out and made his way up toward Rundmyr. He found the hiding-place he had in mind, buried the Draumtorp silver there. On coming home he waked Tore, and when Olav came out in the grey dawn, they had loaded the boats and were ready to sail.

At Saltviken they were met by Olav Livsson. With his two crutches and his thin, dangling limbs the cripple made one think of a huge creeping spider. But his face was handsome, narrow and refined, with great brown eyes. Eirik remembered with disgust Jörund's asking whether he were father to the lad. When Eirik laughingly replied that he must have been but twelve or thirteen at the time, Jörund smiled slyly—"Well?" Eirik could not make out how he had ever liked Jörund Rypa. But he had been fond of him, for all that.

He had a busy day. Out here he had to lend a hand with everything. The dead leaves were still stacked outside, but now they were dry; the good, bitter-sweet scent of them carried a long way. In the spring, when they had dung enough and could take up more cornfields, the ugly bush fences should be replaced by rails. He went to look at his cherry trees too—there was no fruit on them, nor could that be expected, but only four of the ten trees were dead, and two of the rosebushes were alive. He plucked a sprig of mint, crushed it between his fingers, and smelled it. Some fine, blue-green leaves had also come up—they must be the herb that Brother Hubert called aquilegia; no doubt there had been some of its seed in the mould about the roots. There would be great bright-blue flowers on it—had Gunhild ever seen the like before? She would be surprised when she saw that he even had a garden to his manor.

Before he fell asleep that night, the thought came to him that from here it was not nearly so far up to Eiken as from Hestviken. And next morning he saddled the bay and rode inland.

He had never before seen Eiken except at a distance—no high-road passed near it. Now he turned his horse into a side-track that led in the direction of the manor.

It stood secluded on a hill that came down in a tongue between two converging watercourses, close under a dark wooded height.

Eirik rode up and past it. There was no one about among the houses; the manor lay as though deserted below its wood, with many houses, and beyond them stood great oaks with browned leaves against the sky.

Above the manor the road led upward into the forest. The weather was fine and it amused Eirik to ride thus into the unknown; he had a mind to see whither this track might lead—whether perhaps he might come out on a height, from whence he could have a view of this part of the country—it was unfamiliar to him.

He came upon some great slabs of rock where the forest was thin, the firs broken at the top by wind or weight of snow. Heather and moss grew thick over the ground, and among the rocks were patches of bog with dying, hoary trees and gnarled and yellow birches around tarns that mirrored the blue sky.

Up here, in the shadows, all was white with rime, and a few little snowflakes in the bog showed that a shower had passed over the forest. But now the sky was clear and blue, scored by white fine-weather clouds, and the sun shone on the autumnal woods. Eirik let his horse get its breath, sitting at his ease and thinking of nothing—when there came a call from beyond the bog, a loud, clear woman's voice. She was calling a goat, cried something, a name it must have been, in a sad and plaintive tone; then came the call again.

Eirik listened intently. Then he crossed himself—if this was other than human, it would have no power over him against his will. But indeed it might be someone from Eiken.

The calling came nearer. Now he could hear: "Blaalin, Blaalin," she was calling. Now he caught sight of a woman clad in green; she came out upon the stony ground on this side of the tarn, stopped by some yellow stunted birches.

Now she had seen that a strange horseman had appeared on the mountain—she stopped, hesitating. Then he turned his horse and, taking up her luring tone, he called her name in a voice that rang: "Gunhild, Gunhild—" and rode toward her.

"Have I frightened you?" he cried when he was near enough for her to know him.

She came forward to meet him, still hesitating a little. "Are you *here*? On this side?"

"Ay, I had business—" He checked himself. Of all his good resolutions, the most difficult to keep was that he must always speak the truth instead of saying the first thing that occurred to him. "I had a mind to look around here for once. I have never been east of the Kambshorn road."

Her kirtle was green edged with red, but simple in cut as a serving-woman's working-shift: the sleeves did not reach the wrist, and it was so short that her ankles showed; she wore coarse shoes that were black with wet and besmeared with bog mire. Dry twigs and leaves were caught in her dress and in her plaits, which were half-undone. Eirik thought she looked younger and as it were nearer in this simple dress.

"But—is it not rash of you, Gunhild, to roam the woods thus alone?" He knew there were many bears on the hills hereabout—and mountain-folk too, 'twas said.

Gunhild looked up into his face; he saw that she had been afraid. "My goat did not come home last night—one that I have had from a kid."

"Then shall I join you in the search?" The goat had been taken by a wild beast, he thought, but it might be they would find a trace—

"Thanks, will you? Then perhaps it were best you turned your horse into the paddock by our summer byre—'tis just here."

"But you will come too? I like not your being alone here in the forest."

He carried the bridle on his arm, and she walked at his side. They still kept a few young cattle and goats up here, she said, and when her father and stepmother set out from home two days ago, she had come up hither to see how it went. Yesterday morning Blaalin had given but little milk; she had thought nothing of it, but since then the herdsman said she had walked so strangely, almost as if she were drunken—and then she did not come home with the rest at evening. And Gunhild had scarcely been able to sleep for uneasiness—Blaalin, poor creature, lying out in the open. Eirik swallowed her every word—she spoke to him as if they had been friends a great while.

The path ended in a meadow, where some old black houses were falling to pieces. Since he had repaired the old houses at Saltviken, Eirik could never see a ruinous building without thinking of what he would have done with it—so also here. Building was now become his favourite occupation.

"But we ought rather to go over to the other side, Gunhild—the wind was from the south-west last night."

Gunhild did not know that—the goat always goes against the wind.

So they set off in the other direction. They kept within sight and sound of each other and answered each other's calls the whole time.

The fine, loud notes resounded in the clear autumn weather. Eirik ran over crunching dry moss, down the face of screes, where the bracken was shrivelled and the wild raspberry still bore blood-red fruit, but its leaves lay fallen among the stones, showing their silvery undersides. He leaped into swamps, so that the mud splashed and his spear-shaft sank deep when he wanted to support himself on it; he came upon frozen ground where the thin ice broke under his feet at every step, into thick spruce forest, where he lost sight of her. Then he called:

"Are you, are you, are you there, Gunhild, Gunhild, Gunhild, my Gunhild—"

And she called back to him: "Are you, are you, are you there, Eirik, Eirik, Eirik—"

He could tell by her voice that she had forgotten her sorrow in the sport, and he leaped with joy and let his pure and flexible voice ring out under the blue sky. Once they came to a place where the echo answered so plainly that they stayed shouting and singing at the rock and forgot all else.

They were walking on a slope where great trees lay over-thrown by the wind, with shreds of mossy soil clinging to their roots, and among them the cranberry shone red. They walked in sight of each other—when she gathered up her kirtle in both hands and ran slantingly toward him, leaping and climbing over stocks and stones. At the same moment he too heard the feeble, piteous cry—he too ran in the direction of the sound. They met by the little pit—within it the rime lay thick upon moss and with-ered leaves—and there they found the little black-saddled goat. She lay with her legs stretched out and her neck turned back; there was not much life in the poor creature. But Gunhild flung herself down and got the goat halfway up in her arms, fondling it and talking to it the while.

Eirik lifted Blaalin out of the pit and carried it, and Gunhild took his light spear and walked at his side. It would have been better to kill the poor beast, which was nearly dead already—and the goat was a heavy burden after a while. But he was too glad of the chance of walking thus with her to say anything of this; every moment Gunhild had to caress Blaalin in his arms.

At last they found their way back to the summer byre. Eirik fetched a truss of hay for her to strew under Blaalin, and she had found an old ragged coverlet to spread over the goat.

Then she said: "But you must come in, Eirik, and rest. I have naught else to offer you than goat's milk and a slice of cheese."

"Did you sleep here last night?" he asked in a low voice—they entered a little dark hut where the daylight crept in between the logs. The hearth was a hole in the floor, and the couch a pallet of cleft logs with hay and a few blankets spread on top. So she was not proud—gentle she was and full of care for all that was in her charge, faithful and diligent. Eirik looked at her, full of tenderness and wonder, as he sat on the edge of her poor couch and drank the smoky goat's-milk.

He made up the fire for her, and she put the kettle on. While she waited for the milk to be ready for curdling, they sat side by side on the pallet, chatting together like old friends. Till Gun-hild said all at once—and turned red as she spoke:

"I wonder, Eirik—the dairywoman may come back soon—she might think it strange that I have a guest in the hut."

Eirik rose rather reluctantly. "But go with me across the paddock, Gunhild, if you can leave the kettle."

He took his horse and led it through the gate into the forest. Then they must needs part.

"You have soot on your hand—" he held it between both his. They stood looking at each other, smiling slightly. She made no resistance when he drew her close to him, and so he threw his arm about the girl and kissed her on the mouth.

She let him do it; then he kissed her all over her face, pressing her tightly against him—till he felt her struggle.

"Eirik—now you must let me go."

"Oh, no—?"

"Yes—let go!"

He let her go. "Are you angry now, Gunhild?"

"Oh, I know not." So he drew her toward him again. She flung her arms about his neck an instant. "But now you must go—nay, nay, what are you doing?"

He had thrust a hand down under the neck of her kirtle and pressed it for a moment against her smooth breast. Half laughing and half embarrassed she pushed him from her, and fished up the hard, cold thing he had slipped under her dress.

"Nay, Eirik—you must take this back—so great a gift I may not take from you yet." She held out the gold brooch he had taken out of his shirt.

"Oh, yes." He swung himself into the saddle; when she came up, gave him his spear with one hand, and tried to force the brooch on him with the other, he bent down and once more brushed her smooth, cool forehead with his lips. "You are to have it—you must keep it till you can wear it!"

Then he let his horse go. Time after time he turned and nodded to her. When he saw her for the last time, as the path turned down into the thicket, Gunhild raised her hand and waved to him.

Eirik smiled to himself, laughed quietly now and then, as he rode back toward the fiord. At intervals he hummed the notes of the call, but very low, and he dared not sing her name aloud. This was the happiest day he had known.

15

ON the last Sunday but one before Advent, Cecilia Olavsdatter held her churching, and when they came home to Hestviken her father gave her the keys of his stores in the sight of the whole household, asking her to be pleased to take upon herself the duties of mistress of Hestviken.

Olav and Jörund now spoke to each other—not very much, but at any rate Olav was not unfriendly toward his son-in-law. And he had visited Cecilia several times to see this last child of hers; the folk of the place thought he must be glad there was once more an Audun at Hestviken. And indeed it was a fine big child. Cecilia was pale and thin, but seemed in good health—she took charge of the house as a capable wife, and the old serving-folk, who had known her from a child, were eager to comply with the behests of their young mistress and loved her little sons.

Eirik's joy was such that not one of these quiet people in this quiet household could fail to be cheered by it—though he himself was calm enough at this time. Since that day in the forest he had spoken only once with Gunhild—at church—and then he did no more than ask after Blaalin—Blaalin was dead.

But Olav had told him that now Torgrim had received Berse's answer; they had his leave to come and speak with him of the matter after the last day of Yule—he held it unbecoming to conclude a bargain of this nature during Advent or in the holy-days. The betrothal ale might then take place before Lent, and if Olav Audunsson desired the wedding to be held so soon as the early summer, Berse would not oppose it, seeing that Eirik was not so young and Gunhild had already completed her twentieth year.

And Una said both she and Signe would so order it that he could meet Gunhild Bersesdatter at Yuletide: "for you two ought to hold some converse ere you be bound together in betrothal—since it is now agreed you are to wed Gunhild."

He was troubled enough in his mind over what he had buried in the ground at Rundmyr. That hiding-place was known to others besides him. True, he had long ago forbidden Arnketil to harbour dishonest folk, but here was proof that at Rundmyr they held his commands but lightly. And Jörund had challenged him more than once, demanding to know what he had done with the treasure. Eirik put him off, reminding him that he had bought the silver of him for the price of a good horse, and saying that it lay in a spot that it was unsafe to visit even in broad daylight. Moreover, he tried every means of keeping Jörund in good humour—took him out hunting and in his boat and found pretexts for making visits to all the houses where he had friends or kinsfolk. It was no longer quite to his mind to roam about so much, but he saw that the quiet life at Hestviken was dangerous for Jörund: the man was as full of humours as a bull, and if he turned vicious, Eirik was afraid Cecilia would suffer for it.

But he himself was too happy to let any of this take a real hold of him. When he brought Gunhild out hither, he thought that in some way the others' troubles and difficulties would also grow less. She brought such gladness with her.

Then one morning, a fortnight before Yule, when Eirik came out into the yard he saw that a thin coat of snow lay on the ground. The morning moon shone like a bright speck behind the drifting mist, promising a heavier fall. Eirik made up his mind that today he would take up the silver again; otherwise the snow might force him to wait he knew not how long, and he yearned to be rid of it.

He asked Jörund to go out hunting with him during the day, and when the two came home at dark Eirik had killed a fox and carried with him a little bundle in an earthy homespun cloth.

He did not know whether to tell his father of it or not. But he had no desire to lie more than he could help in this wretched affair. And he was afraid it would trouble and distress Cecilia if there were once more talk of this silver—she had enough hard work in any case, making ready for Yule, and at night she had little rest, for the infant child.

So he merely said to his father that Jörund had business north in the next parish and he had promised to accompany his brother-in-law. Then they rode to Draumtorp.

They arrived there at evening, and Eirik was ill pleased when he heard that Berse of Eiken was there with two of his sons, Gunhild's own brothers. It had increased his indignation over the affair from the first that Guttorm of Draumtorp was her uncle. But that he should be compelled to utter his lying tale in the hearing of those who were soon to be his brothers-in-law, that was a thing he had not looked for.

But it went well. When Eirik had once made a beginning, he told a smooth and credible story of his fox-hunt and of his dog that had stuck fast in an earth and of the find they had made, which Jörund and he at once had thought might be a part of the Draumtorp treasure.

Guttorm was glad to get back some of his silver, so Eirik and Jörund were given the best of welcomes. The attack in the Gerdarud forest was then discussed at great length. The brothers-in-law from Hestviken listened to the old men and replied no more than there was need—this seemed to please Berse; he grew very friendly; he even jested with Eirik, saying mayhap they would be better acquainted in time—and in the end Eirik was vouchsafed the honour of escorting Berse to bed. Now that he was rid of his ugly secret, Eirik's mood soon became light and gay, and he had drunk all he needed, so it was with a right merry heart he helped his father-in-law that was to be. Even when he was overwhelmed by the frailty of his nature, this old Berse contrived somehow to preserve his dignity in the midst of his throes.

Guttorm of Draumtorp had a long talk with Eirik next morning. He seemed to be a wise and sober man. He spoke of Berse, calling to mind that the old man had been honoured for many years as the franklins' leader, and with every right; he had been a generous, brave, and shrewd man in his younger days. Now in truth he had grown somewhat odd with age—and his young wife, the third, whom he had married when he was already sixty winters old, had no little sway over him, though he would not allow it. And his children by the first wife had brought great sorrow upon him. The son, Benedikt, had blamed his father for his sister's misfortune, and he had ridden from Eiken in anger; Berse never saw him again, for he fell the year after in Denmark. But Eldrid did not die, 'twas not so well.

"But all the children he had by Helga, my sister, are good and virtuous folk, Eirik—and now I am glad Gunhild shall make so good a marriage."

Eirik guessed from this that all the maid's kinsfolk knew of the agreement; her younger brothers, Torleif and Kaare, also greeted him as one who was soon to be their brother-in-law.

Guttorm had once met Olav Audunsson at Hestbæk, and in

taking leave he bade Eirik bring greetings to his father. So when Eirik came home he had to say he had been at Draumtorp and to tell Olav of the finding of the silver. Olav was angry when he heard that such things had been found in his woods. Eirik replied that he had already reproved Anki and Liv and that he would not fail to keep a watch in future, but he begged his father to spare them this time.

At Yule Eirik met the folk from Eiken, and now they greeted him in such wise that all could see what was in the wind. When they rode to church from Skikkjustad on the eighth day of Yule, in driving rain on a road slippery with ice, Berse bade Eirik ride beside Gunhild and keep an eye on her horse; and at Rynjul they were allowed to sit by themselves over the chessboard a whole evening. It was a strange game, for Gunhild was as stupid as could be at this play, but this too became her well in Eirik's eyes—he had never before played chess with any woman but his sister, and she played better than most men.

That same evening Olav of Hestviken and Berse of Eiken spoke long together in another house on the manor—though it was a holy-day—and kinsmen and friends on both sides were present. Afterwards Olav told Eirik of the agreement they had come to regarding the bride's portion; Olav was to come to Eiken on the eve of St. Agnes [9] with his son and his witnesses, and next day Eirik Olavsson was to betroth Gunhild Bersesdatter with ring and gifts.

On the following morning Gunhild was sent home together with her stepmother and her eldest, married brother, but Berse stayed behind at Rynjul with his two younger sons. It was the finest, clearest winter weather, and so Eirik proposed that they should ride into the town, as many as were minded to see the great procession when the King visited the Church of St. Mary on the day of Epiphany—for it was reported that King Haakon was in Oslo.

All the young men wished to go—Berse's sons, young Torgils Torgrimsson and his cousin, Sigmund Baardsson from Skikkju-stad. Then said Torgrim himself, the master of the house, that he might have a mind to go. "What think you, Olav, shall we two join company with the young folk for once?"

Olav laughed and shook his head. He must be thinking rather

[9] January 20.

of returning home. "Long enough has Cecilia been left alone at Hestviken."

Then Berse himself spoke up. He had served in King Eirik's body-guard and afterwards in King Haakon's, and now he would do his King a last homage and would take his place in the procession.

Thus they made slow progress, and when they came to the town it was so late that Eirik could not go to his convent and seek lodging there, as had been his intention, but followed the rest of the company to a yard where Guttorm's son-in-law owned a house.

Late as it was, the upper room into which they came was full of men, and the tables were full of food and drink. The men flocked about Guttorm to tell him the great news that was over the whole town: three nights ago the men of Aker had descended on the den of those miscreants who so long had made the forests around Oslo unsafe. Last autumn the ruffians had fallen upon a little farm in a clearing by Elivaag, where two brothers dwelt with their wives and a young sister; they had plundered the place and slaughtered the cattle, ravished the women, who were alone at home—but one of the robbers seemed to have liked the young girl so well that he had visited her since. She received him with a show of kindness and at last coaxed him into telling her where was the robber stronghold, and so her brothers had gathered the peasants and led them thither; six of the robbers had been slain or burned in their house, but four men and one woman lay in the dungeon of the old royal castle waiting to receive the reward of their misdeeds on the rock of execution. The girl had claimed as her meed to be allowed to hold her ravisher's hair clear of the headsman's axe.

At long last, when the men had said their say and drunk their fill, all came to bed. Eirik lay on the outside in a bed with Jörund Rypa and Kaare Bersesson; they two fell asleep at once, but he lay awake, in a torment of dismay, trying to tell himself that he need not be afraid, ere he knew whether there were aught to be afraid of.

He took the rosary from his neck and held it in his hands. But in all these years he had never been wont to pray *for* anything— he had only prayed in order to feel that God was there and that he could speak to Him, but he had been content with all that fell to him from God's hand. Ah, yes, he had prayed for Cecilia. But now he knew not what he might do—if what he had done were wrong, then he could not well pray God to help him conceal the truth, if it were meant to come to light.

He stood down by the castle quay, caught in the press of people, so that he could scarce see anything of the procession—listening to folks' talk around him. It seemed impossible they could speak of aught but the robbers.

The church was full of folk, so there was no room to kneel down, and he could not follow the mass, for his heart was in too great a tumult. But he stayed behind when the church began to empty. Then he saw that he had been standing close to a side altar, and on the wall beside it was painted Mary with her attendant virgins: Margaret, Lucy, Cecilia, Barbara, Agatha; last of the band stood Agnes with her lamb. She was to have been the witness of his plighting his troth to Gunhild; he had been glad of that, for he had had a special affection for this young and childlike martyr ever since he had heard her legend. So he approached her with a prayer: "Pray for me for what is best." He grew calmer on the instant; it was as though he had taken counsel with a little sister.

Someone touched him on the shoulder, and he rose at once—it was Guttorm of Draumtorp. Eirik had expected this, it seemed to him. They went out of the church together, but as they stood outside the porch looking up the street, Guttorm said suddenly:

"We may just as well talk inside. Something has come up of which I thought I would fain speak with you in private, Eirik Olavsson. Maybe you guess what it is?"

Eirik looked at the other, but made no reply.

"I wish to hear," said Guttorm, "if aught else had come to light about my silver, the rest of it. So we went out to the castle this morning between matins and mass—Berse was bound thither in any case, and so I went with him. Sir Tore then had the prisoners brought up into the hall, so that we might question them."

Eirik pressed his hat between his hands, but answered nothing. Now they were standing by the same side altar—and on the wall above him he saw the painting of the holy virgins; lithe and slender in their bright kirtles they stood in a ring about their Queen, smiling upon the King's Son in her lap. Eirik was reminded of the verse: *Ego mater pulchræ dilectionis, et timoris, et agnitionis, et sanctæ spei,*[1] and of the response: *Deo gratias.*

Guttorm scratched his head.

"Sooth to say, Eirik—it mislikes me to have to speak of these things— And I am thinking—could you not say it yourself?"

"I—?"

"You can guess I questioned them closely of that hiding-place of theirs out in the Hestvik woods." He looked searchingly at the young man who stood with a calm, white face looking down at the floor. "For, to be brief, it would seem that as you found my silver, you knew where to look?"

Eirik nodded slightly.

"I have got you back your silver, Guttorm," he said quietly. "Can you not be content with that?"

"Is it true that you had bought it?"

"Yes. But you will hardly think I bought it of any unknown," he went on, in a more lively tone. "The place where—where I got wind of this affair—is the dwelling of poor and ignorant folk —the man was like a foster-father to me when I was a boy. They have little wit—and all kinds of beggars and the like frequent their cot, some of our own beadsmen among them, good folk, such as have served in our boats, all kinds of vagabonds besides. Guttorm—could you not forbear to look more closely into this matter, be content that I have borne the cost of getting back your goods—and leave me to sit in judgment at home over my own folk?"

"No, Eirik—'tis useless that you try to give out that it was one of your folk—"

Eirik broke in: "In God's name, if you know more, then you must know that I have special grounds for dealing with the matter as I have done—secretly."

"That may be so." Guttorm paused awhile, turning over something in his mind. "You know not if there be more of my silver to be found up there?"

"No.—I have given no thought to that. I cannot believe it either—but if you will, you could come out to us when the snow is gone, I will gladly help you to make search."

Guttorm looked at the young man sharply—he himself red-

[1] "I am the mother of fair love, and fear, and knowledge, and holy hope." Ecclesiasticus, xxiv, 18.

dened as he spoke. "Better we make an end of it," he then said. "Jörund Rypa says there were four cups—the great tankard and four small ones—"

Eirik looked at Guttorm, bewildered. The lump of silver, he thought; then it was Jörund himself who had melted down some of the booty—this grew worse and worse. He shook his head.

"I have seen it in no other shape than as it was when I gave it to you. So I know not who has melted down your silver cups."

"There should be four cups and the lump of silver, says he," Guttorm rejoined in a low voice.

Eirik stared—slowly a blush crept over his pale face.

"Then Jörund's memory is at fault."

"That horse you gave him in exchange," asked Guttorm warily —"that was worth more than the silver you brought me—'twas the one he rode yesterday?"

"Since you know *who* it was," said Eirik hotly, "can you suppose I was minded to haggle over the price?"

Guttorm was silent for a few moments. Then he asked slowly: "Then you know of no more than the silver that I received back from you? You give me your answer here, where we stand, and I take your word for it."

Involuntarily Eirik looked up at the wall—it flashed through his mind that he had heard of pictures that found a voice: Mary herself and her Son had witnessed from painted lips and mouths of stone that the truth might be made manifest. But no change came over the gentle faces under the golden crowns, and the holy virgins stood motionless, showing forth the wheels and the swords that had once torn their bodies asunder.

"No. I know naught of more," he said simply.

Guttorm held out his hand. As Eirik made no move to take it, he seized the young man's, pressed it hard.

"I believe you, I say. But that I had to get this affair straightened out—you cannot bear me ill will for that?"

"No. You had to do it—"

" 'Tis cold standing here," said Guttorm. "Come, let us go out."

Outside, the smoke whirled up from all the white roofs—it was mild, the sun shone, and the sky was blue. The thin coat of fresh snow that had fallen during the night had been trodden down, so that the street was slippery. "I shall have to take your arm," said Guttorm.

Eirik could utter nothing in reply. He saw what the elder man meant, but it was bitter to have to swallow such amends when he had been forced to put up with so immense and undeserved an insult. Arm in arm the two walked up West Street. In the square outside St. Halvard's Church Guttorm met some men he knew; he leaned heavily on Eirik's arm while he spoke to them. Eirik stood dumb as a post. But when they reached the house by Holy Cross Church, where they were lodged, he said to Guttorm:

"Ere we go in—*I* would fain ask you of one or two matters."

"That is fair enough."

They had passed behind the yards, where the river ran between clay banks. Eirik bade Guttorm tell him what had passed in the hall of the castle that morning, and who had been present.

Guttorm said Berse had been there with both his sons, Torgrim from Rynjul and Jörund Rypa, himself and his son-in-law Karl. Of the castle folk none had been present but Sir Tore and the men-at-arms who brought in the prisoners.

None of these had taken part in the attack on Guttorm and his company—the robbers either had been killed or had left the band before this winter. But the woman had been ready to make known what had become of the Draumtorp silver; she had sold it to that man who stood there, Jörund Rypa. The two had known each other of old. Then Jörund had straightway confirmed her words, but said that Aasa had declared to him it was her heritage, which she had just fetched from home, and he had believed her, for he knew that she came of good family. He bought the silver of her because she said she would then see about leaving her man— married they were not—and she would amend her life.

To this the woman had replied that nothing had been said of where the silver came from, nor had she seen any sign that night of Jörund's zeal for the improvement of her morals.

Then Jörund said that she was lying, and he had never a thought but that she had inherited the silver from Aasmund of Haugseter. So much was true, that she was this man's daughter, but she had fallen into evil courses and had run from home. It was only when Jörund had shown Eirik his purchase that his brother-in-law had hinted it might be stolen goods. Thereupon Jörund would keep it no longer, but Eirik offered to buy it of him for the black gelding he was now riding—and there was a great tankard, four smaller cups, and a lump of melted silver. But afterwards, when winter was come, Eirik had said he dared not keep it any longer—since he was now to marry Guttorm's niece, he thought it safest to restore it to the master of Draumtorp ere the betrothal took place.

Eirik stood inertly leaning his back against the fence. The snow-covered fields across the river sparkled so that it hurt his eyes with the glare of blue and white—and if he looked down, where the river ran dark between its snow-clad banks of clay, he turned giddy. A raging headache had come upon him all at once.

"What said Berse?" asked Eirik.

"Berse—oh, you may well guess. But tell me, Eirik, what manner of man is this brother-in-law of yours, Jörund Rypa?"

"You must have heard of the Rypungs of Gunnarsby. He and I were friends for many years—"

"Are you no longer so? It struck me, when he spoke of how you had no thought of giving me back the silver until there was talk of coming affinity between us—you know, he need not have said that; 'twould have been more natural if he had *not* said that of his wife's brother. Unless he purposed thereby to *prevent* your marriage with Gunhild—?"

Eirik looked at the other a moment.

"It is hard to believe such a thing—" he whispered feebly. Then he straightened his shoulders, shook himself slightly, and flung his cloak about him. "But now I will go and find Berse," he said briskly.

Guttorm put out a hand as though to detain him. "One thing you cannot fail to see, Eirik—that which we had in mind for you and Gunhild, there can be naught of that now?"

"But you will speak on my behalf, Guttorm," asked the young man eagerly—"tell Berse you believe I am an honourable man?"

"That I will do, be sure of that. But there is—the other, Eirik. So surely as we believe you to be true men, you and your father and all your kinsmen beside, even so must we fear all the more to be linked in affinity with that one—"

Eirik stared at Guttorm—he had turned white about the mouth like a sick man.

"I will find Berse, for all that," he said, and began to walk rapidly back toward the street.

• • •

But when they came back to their lodging they were told that Berse had ridden away with all his company. And Jörund had left immediately after. It was Torgrim of Rynjul who had taken Eirik's part, said Karl, Guttorm's son-in-law; but when Berse utterly refused to believe that Eirik was as innocent as the babe unborn, Torgrim had flown into a rage, saying 'twas an ill thing Berse had been given no wits, for now he had great need of some —and so the old man had swept out of the house in great wrath. Torgrim's parley with Jörund had ended in the franklin's seizing a cowhide whip that lay there and striking Jörund across the face with it—

"And would God and Saint Olav had guided my hand so that I had found a spear instead and run him through," Torgrim bewailed when they spoke of it.

Then he turned his wrath upon Eirik, who had made no answer to this outburst. "You sit there moping like a big-bellied bride— or like an archangel that has had his wings stripped of feathers by the devils! Better be off at once to the friars and beg them to give you back your frock! Then Jörund will have got what he sought!"

Karl whistled—Guttorm looked up sharply.

But Eirik replied calmly: "Whatever may befall—'twill not be in *that* way that I go back to the convent—if I go."

It was Torgrim who said they ought to ride away at once— acquaint Olav with the turn of events. "You are an upright man, Guttorm, so you will come with us." Guttorm promised.

"It had been better if you had asked counsel of your father," said Guttorm to Eirik as they rode across the ice of the Botnfiord, "or ever you came to this!"

"You who know him," replied Eirik hotly, "how think you Father would have taken it? 'Twould have been unbearable for us all to live together at Hestviken thereafter. God help my sister and her children now—"

A little way from Draumtorp one of Guttorm's house-carls met them; he announced that Berse had arrived and demanded speech with the master ere he rode farther on the way to Eiken.

"Let him wait," said Torgrim, and Guttorm answered that he would return home next day.

.   .   .

It was dark when they came out to Hestviken. As the company rode up to the door of the house, Eirik saw that someone stood up on the lookout rock, black against the last green light on the horizon. As his father came down toward them Eirik was reminded of One who was haled from one judge to another—"I have not strength to bear it, God, my God, help me to have strength!"

It was so dark that they could not see the expression on Olav's face when he came, but Torgrim had leaped from his horse and ran toward him.

"Has he come home, this Jörund, and what has he said?"

"Not a word that I believe," Olav answered scornfully. "But come in!"

It was dark in the great room; only a little red eye glowed on the hearth. But then a light appeared in the anteroom—Cecilia Olavsdatter entered, bearing a candlestick with a lighted candle in each hand. Eirik stood by the door, leaning on his sword, still in his travelling-cloak. "This is the worst," he thought as he saw his sister's stony face. She set the candles on the table, knelt by the hearth, and began to feed the embers with bark and chips of fir, while Olav greeted Guttorm.

"These men will surely sleep here tonight?" she asked when she had made up the fire; "and will you talk together first or wait till you have supped?"

"In God's name, let us say out what has to be said," cried Torgrim.

At a nod from her father she turned to the door. At the same moment Jörund appeared and came forward into the light. He looked around at the new-comers.

"Eirik has mustered a troop, I see—of his friends, young and old. Now we shall hear his tale—and we all know he was ever good at making up a fable to beguile the time, so I look for naught else but that you will believe him, you, Olav, and all his kinsmen. I have no such gift, so I know I shall be the loser—I cannot devise a more likely tale, when the truth sounds unlikely."

Behind them they heard a crash—Cecilia had barred the door. Now she stepped forward and placed herself by her husband's side.

"Then 'tis best I begin and tell what I know—since it was I who found the silver, and it was my fault that my brother was mixed up in our affairs."

Jörund turned upon her furiously. "You witness against your own husband—"

—and Eirik was at his sister's other side: "Nay, Cecilia—you are not to say anything—"

Cecilia pushed both men away.

"I witness what is true—thereby we are all best served," she said calmly, "you too, Jörund! But first I beg you all to be silent on this matter, as you hope the angels on the Day of Judgment may be silent on those of your sins which you would be most loath to hear cried aloud at the summoning of souls!"

"We shall do what we can, mistress," said Guttorm, "that this evil business may be kept close." The others agreed.

Then she told of the finding of the silver.

Torgrim asked: "Are you certain there was no more in the chest than these three cups?"

"Ay, for I had taken all out—the cloak I sought for lay at the bottom. But now I must go and attend to my duties—you must be both hungry and thirsty, since you have ridden so far today."

Jörund turned and would have gone out with his wife. Olav said: "Nay, Jörund, wait awhile—we have not yet had our say on this matter."

Cecilia turned in the doorway. "Remember, Father, what I have said to you—Jörund was taught full young that he could not depend on his own nearest kinsmen. Ill it is that it has turned out so that he now believes you and Eirik to be among his enemies, and he thought he had something to avenge."

"And a swingeing vengeance he took!" Torgrim cut in.

"You too, kinsman, may have helped to give my husband the belief that all here wished him ill. 'Tis not easy for a stranger to know how little you mean of all you say when the rage is upon you."

It was an uncomfortable meal—the men ate and drank all the good things that Cecilia and her maids set before them, in silence for the most part. Olav had scarcely spoken—not a word did he address to Eirik, and Eirik and Jörund sat there silent as stones. Cecilia stayed in the room, going round herself and filling the cups. But when the maids had carried out the meats, and more ale was brought in, the mistress of the house turned to Guttorm:

"I have a boon to ask of you, Guttorm, and a great one it is, but there is none other I can turn to—my kinsman Torgrim would stand me in no good stead. Will you ride with me to Eiken to-morrow? I will speak with Berse himself."

"Berse is at Draumtorp under my roof, mistress."

"Then let me ride home with you. Sigmund Baardsson here will do me the kindness to come with us and bring me back."

"I ride with Guttorm myself tomorrow," said Olav.

"So much the better—"

"Nay," said her father; "we cannot take you with us, my daughter. It was never our custom at Hestviken to let women speak for men."

Eirik stole out a little while after his sister had left the room. He found her in the cook-house—she had just put out the fire and was leaving. Eirik took her in his arms. "Cecilia!"

She stood still for a moment, with her hands on her brother's shoulders. Then she freed herself.

"I must lock up here, Eirik—'tis time I go in to bed."

"Can you not sleep—in the upper chamber?" he asked eagerly. "Cecilia—you cannot go in—lie by *him* tonight!"

"I must," she replied with a sort of laugh. "You have little sense, all of you. Could you not leave Jörund in peace?" she said hotly. "I know not if I can quiet him, but— Remember, I have three children by him."

Eirik silently pressed her to him.

"I am not afraid," said Cecilia in a little dry, frozen voice, and tore herself away.

Torgrim with the two young lads, Torgils and Sigmund, rode homeward next morning, as soon as they had broken their fast. Then Olav sent out word that they were to saddle the horses for Guttorm and him. Eirik brought the men their cloaks and arms. Guttorm went out first; as Olav was following, his son entreated him:

"Father—!"

Olav looked up into the young man's white, despairing face.

"You must remember, Father—it was not I who cast my eyes upon her—Gunhild. It was you two, you and Berse, you wished it. We knew, both of us, when we met, what was your will—that we should take kindly to each other. Remember that, when you speak to her father—"

Olav shook his head. "What you have in mind, Eirik—can never be."

"Oh, yes!" He clasped his hands vehemently. "Now all the countryside knows there is to be feasting at Agnes's mass. Will you gain anything by it, you and he, if you set all the folk talking, when it comes to naught—? Think of that, Father, if you will think of nothing else! Be not too harsh when you speak with Berse—"

"It is a great thing you ask of me, Eirik," said Olav quietly.

"And we have great things at stake—"

"If I can, I will think about it," said Olav as before.

" 'Tis not much you promise," muttered Eirik.

"To none other would I promise so much, my son." Olav went out, and Eirik followed.

Guttorm was already in the saddle. Eirik came forward to hold his father's horse while he mounted; at that moment Cecilia came out of the door of the women's house. She was dressed in her dark, fur-trimmed hooded cloak. She carried her infant in her arms, and Kolbein walked by her side, holding his mother's cloak.

"Will you saddle Brunsvein for me, Eirik?" she asked. "My grey is lame of one hind leg, I saw this morning. I shall but take the children up to Ragna—"

"Nay, Cecilia," said Olav. "I have told you, you cannot do this."

"I must, Father. It touches me more nearly than any other of you. If Berse will not listen to you—to me he *must*, as he is a Christian man—when I plead for my husband and my three young sons."

Olav stood and looked at his daughter.

Then said Guttorm, as he sat on his horse: "I believe the woman is right. Let your daughter ride with us; I think she knows best."

"You have not strength enough, Cecilia." Her father went up close to her. "In this cold. And 'tis not certain we can reach home this evening. It may be I must stay the night at Hestbæk. 'Twill be bad for you with milk in your breast—"

"Oh, yes, I have the strength—" with a fleeting smile she took her children over to Ragna's house, and Eirik turned into the stable.

As they rode into the forest by the mouth of the stream, Eirik moved toward the women's house. His heart beat fast at the thought of meeting his brother-in-law; even now it seemed he had no right to judge Jörund's actions—the man was Cecilia's husband, and so long as they were all alive, he was one of them.

At that moment he chanced to recall that it was here in this anteroom he had stood with Bothild that evening. He had half forgotten it—the man he had been in those days of madness, when his only wish was to hurt that poor child, had become a stranger to his new self.

Suddenly, like gleam after gleam of summer lightning, there flashed across Eirik's soul—all the forgiveness and all the gifts he had received in these last years. And even if it were now his lot to forfeit his happiness in this world, that did not diminish the value of what God had done for him: never more could he become as he had been when he persecuted her—he realized in wonder how his raw and immature nature had ripened to hard grain. And as he opened the inner door he felt a burning compassion for Jörund's perfidy.

The moment he crossed the threshold, Jörund struck at him—Eirik fell back a step, so that the blow fell on the door. In another instant he dashed in, seized his brother-in-law round the waist and arms; he wrenched the sword from him and flung it across the floor. Jörund had been hiding behind the door.

"Stop it now, Jörund—you have done yourself harm enough, man!" The other stood panting and scowling, and for the first time Eirik saw clearly what a change had come over Jörund of late years—he was bloated in both face and body, slack of feature, with eyes closed up, and it seemed he could not look folk in the face. Eirik shuddered—then he crossed the room, picked up the sword and handed it to his brother-in-law. "You have done enough folly—do not make it worse. You were ever too fond of your own life—you can scarce have reflected ere you risked it to be revenged on me. If you think you have cause to seek vengeance, you will hardly pay such a price for it."

"I forestalled you, for all that," scoffed Jörund Rypa; "do you think I could not guess what you had in mind? I heard you lurking here outside the door—"

"As you see, I am unarmed—but better sit down."

Jörund shot a queer, hesitating glance at his brother-in-law. Then he raised his sword threateningly. Eirik smiled faintly and shook his head.

"I could cut you down on the spot—and fly to the woods—"

"That may be. But 'twill be hard to support life in the woods at this season—for one who is a stranger hereabouts. 'Tis not so sure either that you would get so far. Maybe you would not escape from the manor—"

"Am I guarded like a prisoner?" shouted Jörund. Eirik saw that his eyes looked like a hunted rat's.

"Oh, no. But it might make some noise—the men are outside—"

Jörund threw away his sword, crossed the room, and flung himself on his bed. He lay leaning on his elbow, staring at Eirik. "What *have* you come for, then?"

"To tell you," replied Eirik, "that you will not be rid of me in this way—if that is what you intend. Whatever I do or do not, you must surely see—Father is an old man, Cecilia has no other near kinsman but me. So long as your conduct is such as to make me fear she has no happy life with you, there is small chance I shall go off and be a monk!"

"Cecilia is a whore!" said Jörund viciously.

"Beware of saying that again!" replied Eirik, still calm. "I believe the Evil One has taken away your wits—" No sooner had he said it than he was afraid—Jörund's look was such that one could believe it to be true.

"I am not Kolbein's father," roared Jörund; "I have it from her own lips! I begged her to tell me I was so—not a word did I get out of her in answer!"

"You could scarce expect an honourable woman to answer such a question." He felt sick with horror and disgust. Then Jörund began to howl like a dog, howled and howled—then broke into sobs and tears, while the words poured bubbling from his month: all had treated him faithlessly, his brothers, their wives, every friend and kinsman he had in the world, Cecilia and Olav and all here—Eirik scarcely understood one word in ten.

"Do you trust *none*, Jörund?" asked Eirik when the other paused for a moment in his rage.

In answer Jörund gave a yell as if he had been kicked.

"Jörund," said Eirik impressively, "your wife has gone to beg Berse of Eiken hold his peace about this affair, so that your good name may be saved. She will not find it easy to plead to him—I fear you know that better than any of us. Never a word of complaint has she uttered to us her kinsfolk. You will be well advised to believe what I tell you—in our family we have never been wont to deal in guile or treachery; we may have enough to answer for without that, but we have always had a name for keeping our word—"

Jörund Rypa buried his head in the bedclothes, weeping and gasping for breath. Then, quite suddenly, he began to snore. Eirik was afraid he might be taken sick—tried to turn him so that he lay more comfortably. The eyes in Jörund's red and swollen face half-opened for a moment, but closed again at once—it was sleep.

Eirik sat for a while by his bedside, but Jörund slept on. So he stole out, with a mind uneasy and oppressed.

An hour before nones Eirik came out, dressed for a journey. He looked into the women's house—Jörund filled the room with his snoring. Then he went to the stable, led out the bay, and saddled him.

The sun was so low that its rays tinged the fields and the snow-covered woods behind the manor with red and gold when Eirik came in view of Eiken. He asked leave to put up his horse at a little farm by the highroad. He must venture it, even if it came to Berse's ears.

He went on foot across the fields up to the manor, past the road that led to the houses. The sun had now set and the white ground had turned to a greyish blue, but the sky was orange, with a few golden clouds floating down in the south, and up in the vault some stars peeped out already.

The road he had taken when he was last here, up to the ridge, had been lately used—there were sledge-tracks and wisps of hay along it. For some distance it followed the fence that divided the farm from the forest. He waded up to the fence and stood there scanning the houses. It struck him as an evil omen: he had never been received here.

He waited, uncertain whether to go down and ask if he might speak with Gunhild. Then a door opened—a woman and a man and a dog came out.

In a low voice Eirik gave the call—the same they had used last autumn. *She* started, the dog set up a bark and darted up to him, the man after.

"Is it you, Kaare?" cried Eirik.

Kaare Bersesson came up to him. "Are *you* here?"

"Yes. Will you ask your sister if I may speak with her? I will wait in the road here."

It had already grown much darker—the sunset had faded to yellow and pale green and there were many more stars. She came up, wrapped in a long, hooded cloak; her brother and the dog were with her.

"You must let Gunhild and me be alone awhile, Kaare," said Eirik. His sister said something to the boy, who turned back again, followed by his dog.

Then he came forward and took her in his arms. She burst into tears. "What is this, Eirik? I know not what to make of it."

He held her close and felt miserable—he was so little used to women's tears. But after a while he released the girl and began, quite calmly, to tell the whole story, of which she had heard something from her brothers.

Gunhild had checked her tears. "Nay, *that* I knew—what they said could not be true, my brothers do not believe it either. But what does he aim at, Jörund Rypa?"

Eirik told her something of Jörund's strange fancies and how he thought they were plotting against him at Hestviken—"but this is what I wanted to say to you, Gunhild. I had thought —I make bold to think you will not oppose my wish—that the compact between us be carried out?"

"I think I have let you see that—perhaps more than I ought." She withdrew herself when he tried to take her in his arms again, but let him hold her hand.

"There will be nothing of it at Agnes's mass. We must wait, that is sure. But I cannot but think that when your father has well considered it, he must see that this marriage is so desirable in every other way that—"

Gunhild squeezed his hand. "I hope we may not have to wait too long," she said in a timid little voice, which sent a thrill of joy through the man. " 'Tis not good to live with a stepmother when one is a grown maid. And I have had this trust in you ever since we first met—*you* will be good to her who is to live with you!"

Then she could not prevent his clasping her in his arms once more.

"There is one thing besides that I would say to you," he went on after a moment. "You know there was a time when I desired to be a monk—I was over a year in the convent. So I know something of church law and such matters. Should it go so hard with us that Berse brings forward another suitor, then know that a marriage is no marriage after God's ordinance and the law of the Church unless you yourself have consented thereto. If you dare to hold fast and refuse to say yes, they cannot force you—and it is the bishop's duty to take you under his protection, if you make complaint to him."

"Nay, force me to take one I will not have!" said Gunhild impulsively. "Rather will I fly from home—rather will I seek refuge with Eldrid, my sister—"

It flashed upon Eirik: no, not that in any case. His Gunhild, pure and proud, in company with that old— In seven parishes there was not a woman who bore an uglier name than Eldrid Bersesdatter. That must never be.—But all he said was:

" 'Twill not be so ill as that—I only thought, *if* it should drag on so long that there should be talk of another marriage. God bless you, Gunhild—it cannot be that your steadfastness will be put to so hard a proof."

"I am cold," she said after a pause; she was shivering and treading the ground.

"Come—I will wrap my cloak about you." He drew her to a pile of logs that lay by the wayside, seated himself, and took her on his knees. "Are you still cold?" he whispered.

"My feet are like ice—"

He took hold of her under the knees, lifted her so that she lay huddled in his embrace, wrapped his cloak about her feet. He felt the whole weight of her young, healthy body against his, she filled his arms so well, and his face sought her soft, cold cheek inside the fur-bordered hood. And he felt his own youth and vitality, and that they two were warmed with the warmth of their blood in the chilly freshness of the winter night.

A little frightened by his firm grasp and the heat of his kisses, she struggled to reach the ground. "Eirik—I dare not stay out longer—"

So he had to let her down at last—trembling and panting a little from the violence of his last embrace. He went with her as far as the entrance to the manor.

"It may be long ere we meet again—?"

Gunhild gave him her hand. "Be not afraid, Eirik—they shall not bear me down!"

"May Christ and Mary Virgin bless you—if only I am sure of that, we shall find a way!"

It was already dark and a thousand stars were shining as he hurried down toward the highroad. Piercingly cold, so that the snow cried under his feet—the Milky Way spread so brightly across the black, starry vault. But the cold was good—it gave him a feeling of his own strength and warmth.

They were about to go to rest at the little homestead when he came and took out his horse. And the night was far spent when he reached Hestviken. He looked in upon Jörund—it was icy cold in the women's house, the fire had died on the hearth. Eirik listened to the sleeper's breathing—went to his own house, lighted a lantern, came back and looked at his brother-in-law. Jörund looked as if he had not moved, but his sleep seemed healthier now.

Eirik spread the coverlet over him, collected some skins and blankets, and made a bed for himself on the bench. He pulled the boots from his feet, stiffened with cold, took off his belt, wrapped himself in his frozen cloak, and soon fell asleep.

He did not wake till Jörund shook him. "Will you not come and eat?"

Eirik sat bolt-upright. Jörund was quite different today—quiet and shy, and his voice was very gentle. When they had broken their fast, Jörund asked, avoiding the other's eyes:

"Tell me—Eirik—is it true that—did I try to come at you—did we come to blows yesterday?"

"Can you not recall what we spoke of yesterday?" asked Eirik seriously.

"I know not rightly—whether I was dreaming or not. Sometimes my head aches so intolerably that I remember nothing afterwards—"

"Are you better today?"

"My head still pains me—but not in the same way."

And as soon as they had finished their meal he went back to bed and fell asleep again. Eirik went in several times to look at him.

About midday Olav and Cecilia returned. Eirik went out and met them. He searched his father's face—Olav seemed not to see him, gave him no greeting, but dismounted and went straight into his own house without looking to one side or the other.

Eirik accompanied Cecilia to Ragna's house. When she had laid

Audun to her swelling breast she gave a little sigh of relief. Eirik
picked up her cloak, which had fallen on the floor.

"You are waiting to hear how we have sped?" She looked
down at the infant's head. "We might have fared better—but we
might also have fared worse. Berse promised to hold his peace. But
I will not conceal from you he said things to us— Ay, Father—
Father curbed himself in a way. But I wish—I wish he had been
spared this—now that he is an old man too. You had better not go
near him."

"I must—" Eirik stroked his sister's cheek. "You seem to think I
have less courage than you have, Cecilia," he said mournfully.

"I know not." She moved the babe to her other breast. "There
may be some things that a man can do better than a woman. And
others that a man cannot do so well—"

But when he came into the great room, Olav still sat there in his
travelling-clothes, with his hands on the hilt of his sword and his
chin resting on them. He threw a fleeting glance at Eirik, but said
nothing; and so Eirik did not venture to speak.

16

So it went by, another winter—one day after another. Not a word
had Olav ever uttered about his meeting with Berse at Draumtorp,
and Erik took good heed not to ask him questions. Indeed, they
seldom spoke to each other; their footing was the same as it had
been when he was a boy: his father sat and stared, and Eirik did
not know whether the man was looking at him or through him at
something else; if he had to speak to Olav about anything, it
seemed as if his father only listened to him with half an ear, and
a breath of ill will and unfriendliness smote him in the presence
of the old man. Eirik remembered that in former days his father's
manner had nearly driven him frantic. Now he thought: God
knows, perhaps even then he had had a secret burden on his soul.
And he felt that his affection for his father had grown firmer of
late years, like all else within him—had, as it were, solidified into
pith.

It was bad for Cecilia and Jörund that he should be so unsociable, but there was no helping it.

As far as he could, Eirik associated with the young married couple in the women's house. He had given up pondering over his brother-in-law's behaviour—was inclined to think the man must have been unsettled in his mind during the autumn and winter, and now he seemed to be rid of his venom for this time. All through the latter part of the winter Jörund Rypa was in good humour, chatty and cheerful, like his old self. He played with his children, showed affection for his wife—sometimes in a way that made Eirik blush; nor could he help thinking that Cecilia disliked it too, but she did not betray herself. She discharged her share of the household duties with the greatest diligence, and Eirik saw that the house-folk would have been ready to go through fire for their young mistress. Cecilia could even force her father to rouse himself, when she wished to consult him.

Never did Eirik see a sign that Jörund gave a thought to what had happened at Yuletide, or troubled himself about what rumours it had given rise to. There was talk among the neighbours, Erik could tell that, but no one hinted anything to him. This too he knew: had it been two poor men who had been involved in a case of receiving stolen goods, they would not have escaped without being branded for life, at the very least. But they were the sons of Gunnarsby and Hestviken, and their kinsmen were Baard of Skikkjustad, who was one of the mightiest men of the countryside, especially since he had married off all his four daughters so wisely, and Torgrim of Rynjul, who could say and do as he pleased—most men liked him, for all that, and bore with his rough tongue; even he who was the victim of it could console himself that tomorrow another would be made to feel it.

Eirik acknowledged the truth of all that had been said by the holy fathers—the judgment of men, worldly prosperity, and all such things now seemed so small in his eyes that he could only wonder how anyone cared to strive so hard for them as they did —with pain and grief, with cunning, treachery, and violence. Had it not been for Gunhild and the love that was between them, had it not been that Cecilia and Jörund needed his support, he would gladly have let all else go, and today rather than tomorrow. But he was now beginning to see the meaning of being in the world and not of the world—he felt there was nothing more that could subdue his innermost freedom and peace of mind.

One day early in spring Eirik accompanied his sister up to

Rynjul; she wished to see her child that was being brought up there. He sat with Una in her weaving-room, watching Cecilia as she led her son across the floor—Torgils Jörundsson had learned to walk since his mother saw him last. Then Torgrim came in.

After a while the master of the house said: "You may have heard, Eirik, that Gunhild has a new suitor?" He mentioned a man whom Eirik did not know even by name, one from Agder. "Berse will not learn wisdom by experience. He had his way with Eldrid's marriage, and it turned out as it did. In spite of that he means to sell Gunhild into the hands of another old troll."

Brother and sister rode homeward in the twilight; beyond the thick tangle of the alders' foliage the first great stars were shining in the clear sky. It was a mild evening—the raw scent of earth rose from the bare brown surface, and the birds sang in every grove. They had ridden a long while in silence when the sister said:

"Eirik—that news that Torgrim brought you of Gunhild. It is our fault that you are to lose her."

"Gunhild will not submit to be forced," said Eirik.

"Forced—there are so many ways," answered Cecilia.

After a pause Eirik said: "Since we have begun to speak of such things—and do not answer if you are unwilling—has Jörund ever troubled you with his suspicions that everyone is against him?"

"How have you found that out?" she asked with warmth.

"That time last winter—when he seemed beside himself, accused everyone—you did not escape either—"

"Oh, I am partly to blame for it myself," said Cecilia. "I was so young then. I knew no better than to provoke him by my silence and provoke him by what I said."

Young, thought Eirik—"she is not so old as Gunhild."

Cecilia said after a while: "I acted wrongly, too, I doubt not. The others were going to a feast; I refused to go with them. Chiefly because I was so far gone with Kolbein at that time— but I knew too that they had a guest in that house, one whom I was not minded to meet. But in the evening he came to Gunnarsby, and I went out nevertheless and spoke to him by the gate. Nay, we said not a word that Jörund himself might not have heard—that is not *his* way. But Jörund came to hear of it, and he knew the man had known me at Hestviken—You know him not.— Then I was stubborn—and Jörund lost his temper. He has never done such a thing since—it gave him a fright when Father came. Indeed Jörund is a reasonable man between these fits of his."

"But it can never be a sin," thought Eirik, "if I urge Gunhild to resist—"

Some days later Eirik went down to Saltviken. All through the winter he had looked forward to doing the spring work on his farm. Now he set about it, but at the same time his thoughts wandered to other things. He could not get over what he had guessed from his sister's words—even that insult had been offered Cecilia, who had certainly never let any man touch her even when she was a child. And then there was the thought of Gunhild.

It was the finest of weather every day. Now the manure was spread and dug in on his new dark-soiled cornfields, blending its good warm smell with the acrid scent of growing grass in the meadows. Where the soil was thin over the rocks, the pansies already showed blue. The first shoots on the trees shone bright as pale-green flames against the sunlight—little green leaves had appeared already. The boughs of his cherry trees were pearly with buds; here and there a branch beside the sun-warmed rock had burst into white blossom. In the midday rest Eirik went down to the bay, undressed, and swam out. The water was still cold, but otherwise it was like summer down here on the beach.

The day he had finished sowing he stopped work at nones and changed his clothes—he kept a blue kirtle here, so that he might go to church without passing round by Hestviken. Then he rode inland toward Eiken.

There had been a flock of children at the homestead where he had put up his horse when he was last in these parts. He now made his way thither, found a half-grown girl who was washing clothes in the brook. He took out some small silver coins and asked if she would go an errand for him.

"Then run away to Eiken, see if you can speak with Gunhild alone. You are to ask her if she has any message for the owner of this token."

He took out of his bosom an embroidered shirt-sleeve; Gunhild had given it him at Yule when they were togther at Rynjul, and promised him its fellow for Easter.

He lay on the grass above the little farm. The woman came up and began to talk to him; from her he learned that Berse and his wife were not at home; they had gone southward down the fiord a week before, but the place was being made ready to receive guests on the return of the master and mistress. So it was a good thing after all that he had made his way hither, he thought.

At sunset the little girl came running down the road. Eirik went to meet her; she handed him back the token:

"Gunhild bade me bring greetings and say you are to ask the owner of this token to ride to the Ness with all speed and wait there; he shall there be given all he is to receive according to the covenant."

Eirik stared at the child—this took his breath away. Never could he have imagined it.

Eirik rode southward as the shades of evening gradually deepened to a pale-grey spring night and the birds sang jubilantly all through the forest. It was cool and good to ride at this late hour, and he had never been afraid to travel by night.

And, to be sure, he was glad. But at the same time he was not a little dismayed. That Gunhild should make good so wild a threat—could any man have thought it!

He saw quite clearly that now they would both be placed in a difficult position. If it became known whither Gunhild had betaken herself and that they had been there together, the worst would certainly be said. He must take her away from her sister's house as quickly as he could. But where could they seek refuge?

The law was even as he had said—it was a bishop's duty to defend women against forced marriages—but very few bishops were ever called upon to fulfil this duty, even when their rule was a long one. He knew pretty well how welcome Gunhild Bersesdatter would be made in the Bishop's castle or with the strict Lady Groa at Nonneseter if she were sent thither. Ask any of his father's friends in the town or in his home parish to receive a woman whom he had carried off by force, that was impossible. Torgrim and Una would do it no doubt—but he could not drag them into such difficulties. And Rynjul was too near both to Eiken and to Hestviken. For his own father would scarcely be better pleased with this than hers.

The best plan he could think of was to take her to his kinsfolk in the Upplands. He had not parted in friendship from Steinfinn Haakonsson of Berg, but he knew enough of his cousin to be sure that if he sought his support in such a case as this, he would find a loyal kinsman in Steinfinn.

This plan involved difficulties enough and—the way was long; they might be pursued, and then in God's name the encounter could scarcely pass off without an exchange of blows. But if they had a start, and travelled by unfrequented paths— There was more than that—he knew it well enough as he rode here in the spring night and breathed the acrid scent of growing leaves and grass and felt the warmth of his own sound youthful body. Already he had visions of the chances he would have of kissing his fair bride and clasping her in his arms as they rode together unattended for five or six days and nights, through forests and remote country districts. But it was well he was old enough to know that he must be on his guard. What would be said of them he knew; but she must know it too, and yet she had chosen to accept this hazard. But to be forced to weep over a secret sorrow of his causing—he would not bring that on Gunhild.

His heart failed him at the memory of thoughts he had once had—no, in Jesus' name, Bothild was enough.

It was clear he would have been wiser to have sent her back a message that she must not think of keeping so ill-considered a promise. But that would surely have offended her. And what kind of man would he have to be who should be capable of such prudence?

If at least he knew where this Ness was to be found! Somewhere on the border between Saana and Garda parishes. He had ridden past it once with old Tore, when he was a lad—one saw the homestead on the farther side of a lake. Now he did not even know if he were on the right road—he was in the depth of the forest, where patches of snow gleamed here and there and the birches had not yet burst into leaf and the cold ground breathed the raw scent of early spring from the musty slime that covers the ground as soon as the snow recedes. It was already past midnight, and the song of birds, which had been silent awhile, began to be heard again, but the notes of the night-birds were not yet hushed, the night-raven croaked—and in some bogs that he had passed the capercailye was calling. Eirik was sleepy—and the bay was tired and a little lame.

He leaped from the saddle and led his horse down a steep descent, where the water streamed over the path, past some small farms—and soon he came out on a broader road. A little farther on, this road led past a little lake.

The black forest surrounded the whole piece of water except on the north side, where a solitary homestead stood on a point of land that jutted out into the lake. A mist was rising from the surface of the water and from the marshy meadows around the homestead, so that only its green roof showed above the haze. From the head of the lake a track branched from the road across the marsh. Eirik rode along it—the worst bog-holes were bridged with logs; the birches were dripping wet, with a strong and bitter scent of bursting leaves. He passed many places that had once been meadow, where young green fir trees had sprung up. The dawn was now so far advanced that the sky was white and the surface of the water like steel between the driving mists. In the field before the homestead the grass was already high and lush, grey with moisture in the thick air, and here too birch and alder were almost in leaf.

He could not wake folk in a strange place at this time of the morning, but he saw a little barn standing at the edge of the wood. He turned his horse loose outside, went in and lay down in the empty barn.

When he awoke, the sun was shining in through every crack of the logs. Outside the open door all was gleaming green and gold in the sunlight, and in the doorway stood a woman holding the bay by the forelock. Eirik sprang up, shook out his wrinkled cloak, went forward and greeted her:

"Can you tell me, mistress, if this house be the Ness, where Eldred Bersesdatter lives?"

As he spoke he was sure that this must be Eldrid: she was dressed like a working-woman and looked like—he knew not what, but not like a woman of the people.

She was not very tall—not so tall as Gunhild, and thin, broader across the shoulders than across the narrow, scanty, mannish hips, and she held herself straight as a wand. Her brown, weatherbeaten face looked as if the flesh had been scraped from under the skin —the forehead was smooth, as were the strongly arched cheek-bones and the fine, straight nose. But the longer Eirik looked at this ravaged and aging woman, the more clearly he saw that she must once have been beautiful—so beautiful that not one of all the fair women he had seen could compare with Eldrid.

"I am Eldrid of the Ness—have you an errand to me?"

"I have—one that will seem strange to you, I fear." Then he told her who he was.

"Are you a son of Olav Audunsson of Hestviken?" Her voice too was beautiful, rich and ringing. "You are not like your father. I remember him—he came home to these parts the year before I disappeared from—"

She asked him to go up with her to the houses, and Eirik saw that the place looked well, now the sun was shining; trees and meadow were nearly as far advanced as at home. But it was strangely deserted and lonely—and shut off, with the dark forest behind it, which was beginning to invade the old meadow-land, and the narrow lake in front, where the reflection of the high wooded slope on the south side darkened half the surface even on a bright May morning like this.

The ness on which the houses stood was almost cut off from the shore, by a neck of land so low that the water came over the grass on both sides. In flood-time it came right across, Eldrid told him.

"Then you must use a boat?"

"Boat?" Eldrid laughed mockingly. "We have naught to take us abroad, we who live here."

The houses lay irregularly on the little mound, according as there had been room to build them. They were small and might have been kept in better repair. A bent old woman with her coif drawn low over her surly eyes glanced at the two as they went past.

The walls of the dwelling-house were only three logs high; there was a penthouse of upright timbers which formed a sort of anteroom, and only a single room within. Instead of the central hearth there was a fireplace by the door, and the wall in that corner was covered with slabs of stone and daubed with clay; at each end of the other long wall was an untidy bed. Other furniture there was none, but on the bench that ran round the walls all kinds of cups and platters, garments and pots and a butter-churn were piled in confusion.

Eldrid cleared a seat for him at the end of the room. "You must be hungry."

He was—now he remembered that since he rode from home the day before at noon he had tasted nothing but a drink of milk at the cottage by Eiken. So he relished what Eldrid set before him on the bench: curds, oaten bread, and old cheese. Then he had to come out with his message:

"I come from your sister, Eldrid—from Gunhild of Eiken—"

"My sister!" Eldrid gave him a strange look. Then she took a spindle from the jumple on the bench, thrust it into her belt, and began to spin. "That sister of mine whom you name I have neither seen nor heard from until now. And I wonder who can have spoken to her of me. Not her parents, I trow. What would she, then—Gunhild, my sister?"

"She begs you to save her. They will give her to an old man, a widower, whom she has never seen. And now she thinks—perhaps you will take pity on her. There is none other in the world from whom she may look for kindness."

Eldrid looked at him with a shadow of a smile on her brown and broken lips. "Hm. And you—maybe you are he whom she would have?"

"It was agreed that I should be betrothed to Gunhild last winter. But then her father broke with us."

"And maybe it was too late?" said Eldrid as before.

Eirik guessed her meaning; he was annoyed with himself for turning red, but replied in an even tone: "Ay—so long as we thought we had only to wait a year or so, and the old people would have made up their differences—we should have been content. But if Berse will once more give his young hind to an old buck, he will find it is too late, he shall not so dispose of Gunhild. She will not submit, and I will not suffer that man to get her."

"But what help do you look to me for?" asked Eldrid. "Shall I go to Berse and invoke a curse on him?"

Eirik had sat and watched her. Although she looked as if she had been dried over many fires, there was still something fine about her; her hair was not wholly hidden by the stiff coif: it was dark, streaked with grey, and a lock of it fell with a strange charm over the broad, smooth forehead, across which ran two sharp furrows. Hollow as her cheeks were, he had never seen anything more beautiful than the rounding of her jawbone and the curve of her chin. The eyes were deeply sunk in their great sockets, and there were many wrinkles about them, but they were large, dark, and grey. Her mouth, however, was brown and scaly, with a deep red crack through the underlip. And the hands that span were red and cracked and knotted with gout.

Yet he could not believe that everything he had heard about her was true. And even if she had erred—gravely—they must first have wronged her cruelly. And however that might be, it was a pitiable sight to see this fair and high-born woman, banished and aging, dwelling in so miserable a cabin.

Then he began and told her the whole story of his courtship from beginning to end.

"So it was she who sent you hither?"

"Yes."

"And you expect her to keep her word and come hither?"

"Yes. But if you will tell us of a place where we can find lodging till she be rested, we will gladly betake ourselves thither, if you would rather have it so."

"If I am afraid to have to do with this affair, you mean?" Eldrid laughed. "Rather will Gunhild be afraid, when she comes from Eiken and sees how her sister lives."

"She will think as I do," said Eirik quietly. "It should not be so. And it must be mended."

"Do you seek to tempt me with a reward?" asked Eldrid mockingly.

"I know not if you will call it a reward if I do what I can to see my sister-in-law righted. I have heard that your brother tried, but he fell—"

Eldrid let her hands sink into her lap. But then she said: "You seem to have no fear of defiling yourself, Eirik, if you touch pitch. But if you purpose ever to be reconciled with Berse, you must throw over both that brother-in-law of yours who deals in stolen goods and the sister-in-law who is a whore. Ay, Berse was the first of all men who called me by that name, and he told no lie of his best friend's wife. Better that no man hear of it, if it should come about that you lie with your young bride at the Ness any night."

"I thought to ask one other boon of you," said Erik. "I will ask you to show Gunhild such kindness as to ride north in our company. None will think it of you that you sold your young sister to dishonour."

Slowly Eldrid's face flushed red. But then she laughed. "I should have to ride my grey bull then—I have no horse!"

"The bay will carry both Gunhild and me," said Eirik imperturbably, "till we get one for you on the way."

Eldrid only laughed again.

"Must you do your spring husbandry here without a horse?" asked Eirik after a while. "Or do you borrow one of your neighbours?"

"I have mattock and spade," replied Eldrid shortly. "And basket and pannier."

Now he was told that she lived here alone with the old hag he had seen, a palsied old man who was her kinsman—she had taken him in because he was Berse's enemy—and a half-grown lad who herded for her and helped with whatever there might be.

"But then we must seize the opportunity while I am here with my horse," said Eirik. And when she would not hear of it, he laughed and said she must take it as if she had a brother come to the house. Then he jumped up and ran out.

When she came out awhile after, she found him down in the cornfield, where only a little work had been done in one corner. He had dragged out an old plough and was engaged in putting it in order so that he could harness the bay to it. His long cloak and his blue holy-day kirtle lay on the ground, and Eirik stood in nothing but a red homespun shirt, short breeches, long hose, and riding-boots.

"Are you going to plough in those boots?" asked Eldrid.

"No, if you could lend me something else to wear on my feet, it would be better."

"How old are you, Eirik Olavsson?" asked Eldrid.

"Oh—I am not young—nine and twenty."

"One would not think you were nineteen."

"When I was nineteen," replied Eirik with a laugh, "I was far wiser—as folks reckon."

Late in the afternoon Eirik said he would ride northward—to see if anyone were in sight.

"How did you think she would come hither?" asked Eldrid.

Eirik said he did not know—perhaps she had someone at the manor who was faithful to her.

"I believe you think she will come!" Then she said: "It will be late ere you come back?"

No, said Eirik, the bay was tired—"but I can go into the barn and lie there, as I lay last night."

"No," said Eldrid curtly; " 'tis not often we have guests here, but since you are come, I will not suffer that you be treated otherwise than is fitting. I shall make ready the outer bed for you and leave the door unbolted."

It was nevertheless later than he had thought when he returned. A white mist was rising from the water and the bog as he rode across from the end of the lake; all was still at the homestead. Eirik stole in quietly. The room was dark and warm; he guessed that Eldrid was in bed.

He had not said his hours since prime, so he knelt at the foot of the bed and prayed—seven paternosters for each of the lesser hours, fifteen for vespers, and seven for complin. The last he said for her who gave him hospitality: he had seen something of her loneliness, and he swore that if it were in his power he would better her condition.

He had taken off his outer garments and was climbing into bed when Eldrid's voice came from the far corner:

"I have left milk and food for you on the hearth—you played truant from your supper."

"Thanks, I am not hungry. 'Twas ill of me to wake you."

"Is it your practice every evening—to pray so long?" she asked again.

"Yes. But I have told you, I had as lief sleep in the barn. Then I shall not disturb you with my practices."

She gave a little laugh. "Nay, you may freely keep your practices for me."

The days went by. When Eirik thought of Hestviken and Saltviken and of his people there, it all seemed strangely far away and long ago. He wondered at times what they could think had become of him. And he wondered a little how Gunhild would contrive to come hither. Now it would soon be a week—

But he felt it was as it should be, that he was living here at this strange and lonely homestead in the depth of the dark forest. Every morning when he came out, the ness lay like an island in a sea of white mist, and above it rose the hills, dark with firs. Then came the sun and drove away the mist, and all day long it shone on these awakening fields, the corn that she had sown before he came was already green, and the leaves grew denser in the thickets, and the grass in the meadow was long and glossy. He determined to do all the work for her that he could find—and there was enough to put one's hand to here. Her poverty astonished him—she had scarcely any meal in the house, and of her cows three gave no milk and the other two but little, though they were in better condition than most cows in springtime—she had pasture for many more cattle than she owned. Most of her sheep had been taken by wild beasts the year before, and her corn had frozen; houses and implements were as might be expected in a place where there was no man and no horse to bring in materials of any sort. To make up for the shortage of food she had nets in the lake and snares in the woods, and Eirik undertook to look after both for her.

It dawned on Eirik that this place had a strangely familiar air— as though he had once lived here, long ago. It was the first home he could remember that now came back to him—it was long since he had thought of it, but now it stood forth; that too had been a place far out of the way and deep in the forest, but he did not recall any water. And Eldrid became merged in a strange way with a dream he had had when a child—of a woman in a blue mantle, half human and half bird; he had been afraid of her, but she was beautiful too, and he had called her Leman, for he was so small he knew not the meaning of that word, but he thought it was something that flew. Ay, he had confused this dream vision with his mother—he knew not how it was, but now it came over him that the Ness was like that first place he remembered in the world, and Eldrid reminded him of Leman in his dream.

But every evening he rode out along the road by which he had come, to meet Gunhild, and back he came across the marshes, when evening had deepened to grey spring night and the white mist from lake and meadows was rising about Eldrid's farm.

On the seventh day it clouded over—there had been some showers, but toward evening the sun gleamed fitfully over the Ness. Eirik was sawing up some logs that lay on the woodpile—from where he stood he could see Eldrid at the door of the byre; she was calling in her cows. Last of all came the little shaggy grey bull, splashing through the mire. Eldrid waited for its coming, laid her hands on its cheeks, and leaned her forehead caressingly against the bull's head.

Eirik went in to put on his kirtle and cloak. There was food left for him on the step of his bed—she took care now that he had something before he rode out. He did not hear anyone coming until the horses were just outside the house; then he started up and ran to the outer door.

Outside, where drops of rain now glittered in the sunlight, two men had dismounted from their horses. The second one, a young lad, swung himself back into the saddle, took his master's horse by the bridle, and rode off into the fields; but the first was a tall, elderly man of fine presence; it was Guttorm from Draumtorp, and he hurried in out of the rain.

"'Tis wellnigh more than I had looked for," he said as he stepped into Eldrid's house, "that you should be here!"

Eirik had turned white in the face. "Have you come!"

"Ay, it is I who have come. Gunhild has yet so much kindness for you—though God knows how you deserved it!—that she turned to me and neither to her father nor her brothers. You may well suppose they would not have met you without drawn swords in their hands."

"I should have liked that better." Involuntarily Eirik's hand went to his sword-hilt.

"Silence with such talk! Can you expect we should think much of your manhood—do you call it manly to try to entice the child out of her kinsmen's keeping—to such a den as this?"

"This is her sister's house—"

"Did you think Gunhild would submit to be ruled by you, because she is sister to Eldrid? But they are not daughters of the same mother—"

"Can you not say what you have to say, Guttorm, without abusing a woman?"

"You may be right, there. Not many words are needed either. Gunhild bade me give you back this—that says enough, I think."

Eirik took what Guttorm handed him, scarcely looking at it. Then he let the gold brooch drop and it fell at his feet.

Guttorm spoke again, sadly: "Ay, it made me angry to hear this, Eirik Olavsson—never would I have thought such a thing of the son of so upright a franklin as Olav is. I took you for an honourable man—I believed you on your bare word, though appearances were against you."

"You do not so now?"

"We will not speak of that," replied Guttorm hotly. "I have delivered my message and now I will go. How would you have me judge your conduct toward my niece?" he flared up; "you have lain in wait by the fence like a barn-door thief, decoyed the child out to you late at night, visited her at the sæter and sat with her alone in the hut as if she were a hireling—you hear, she had to make a clean breast of how she came by your brooch. And because she is innocent and childlike, you thought you could decoy her to you—hither!"

"Will you not greet the mistress of the house, man!" cried Eirik furiously.

Eldrid had gone in, clad as she came from the byre. Calmly and proudly she returned Guttorm's greeting.

"You have received a message from my sister, Eirik?" she asked gently.

"Yes, I have brought him a message."

"But so far as I understood you, Master Guttorm, this sister of mine has told you it was Eirik's device that they should seek refuge with me? Eirik told me it was Gunhild who prayed him to come hither, saying she would follow—"

"Said he *that!*"

Eirik himself replied; he was pale even to the lips: "Yes."

"Shame on you, then!" Guttorm spat.

Eldrid spoke. "So said Eirik—and that he purposed, as soon as she was rested, to take her away to his rich kinsfolk in the Upplands, give the maid into their charge, until he might be reconciled with Berse. I believe he too thought that Gunhild had chosen unwisely when she appointed this as their trysting-place."

"Gunhild has heard nothing of his rich kinsfolk in the Upplands, so far as I know. But 'tis not amiss if he has since thought better of his design."

Eirik said, calmly and earnestly: "Does it seem so strange to you, Guttorm—'tis known to every soul in the parishes hereabout that Berse sold his eldest daughter to—to—Jephthah's daughter in Jewry had a better bargain than the mistress here. I had conceived a love for Gunhild—and I know she liked me well. When therefore I came to hear that Berse had allotted the same fate to her—would give her to a hideous ancient who had already worn out one wife at least—"

"What stuff is this?" Guttorm interrupted angrily; "old—he is a year or two older than yourself, a courteous and goodly man. Ay, he was married ere he was of age, but Mistress Hillebjörg lived but a year or two—"

"Was it when she heard this of her new bridegroom," asked Eldrid, "that my sister gave up her sinful project and took counsel of you?"

"No," replied Guttorm reluctantly, dropping his voice. "I got wind that the child meditated a mischief. But since she has seen Sir Magnus she must needs admit that her father has sought to provide well for her in every way.—But enough said of this. Good night."

"Nay, tarry awhile, master—" Eldrid followed Guttorm out.

In a few moments she came back; Eirik had not moved.

"Nay, he would neither rest nor take food," she said. She looked up at the tall, dark man, who loomed huge in the dim light of the room. "Now I trow 'twill be long ere you believe a woman's word again?" she asked, with something like mockery.

Eirik turned from her and went out.

It was now raining quietly and steadily, and the growing scent of spring seemed even heavier in the wet evening. Eirik thought that now he could only leave this place—but he felt so strangely weak and empty, almost as when he had been stabbed with knives up at Haugsvik and came near bleeding to death. He wandered along a path through the meadow, down toward the lake. He thought of taking the boat and rowing somewhere.

Then Eldrid came running after him in great haste and seized him by the arm. "Eirik—where are you going? Man, you do not think to drown yourself for such foolishness as this!"

"No, no." He shook her hand off. "I had not thought of that."

"Come up now," Eldrid begged him. "Do not go moping here in the rain."

Eirik looked at her; then, rather unwillingly, he went back with the woman.

She had heaped fuel on the fire—the light of the flames played over the walls and roof in the low room with the heavy beams

under which a grown man could not stand upright, except under
the roof-tree. Eirik drank a little of the milk she offered him, absently thinking it was not so ill to have the fireplace in the corner,
as here—the rain did not fall into the fire when the smoke-vent
was open as now.

"Let us go to rest," Eldrid then said. "You need no more ride
out at night."

Eirik undressed, so far as was his habit. But then he remained
sitting on the bench at the foot of his bed, with his arm around
the carved horse's head, staring at the embers that shrank together
in the fireplace. Eldrid already lay under the skins in her bed.
"Lie down now," she bade him more than once, and Eirik answered: "Yes," but stayed where he was.

Then she sprang out again and came over to him, barefooted,
in her coarse, dark under-kirtle. She seized him by the shoulders,
forced him to sit upright, so sharply that his neck struck against
the log of the wall.

"Do not sit staring like this!" she said impatiently. "You have
not a little to learn yet, Eirik!"

"Learn—" He took hold of her wrist. "Shall I learn of you
maybe?"

She looked down into his distorted face. Her nostrils expanded
and her eyes grew wide. "Oh, ay—I could teach you much—"

Then he pulled her down to him, crushed her broken lips with
kisses.

17

EVER since he was at the convent Eirik had been used to wake at
the time when the brethren rose to go to matins. And he did the
same now, when he slept in Eldrid's arms.

Now the caller passed through the dormitory whispering
"*Benedicamus Domino*," and the friars answered softly: "*Deo
gratias*," as they slipped from their pallets. He himself had been
one of those who filed quietly down into the bright choir to sing
the hymn of praise at daybreak; he himself had knelt and prayed
from the first faint streak of dawn until the sun ruled in all its

power and all men had gone to their labour. And now he had strayed hither, and what this woman had taught him was such that he had felt a blast of the heat of hell.—And yet, he thought, with a strange rigour of pain, what had befallen him was a destiny that had been laid on him from his birth, and now it was accomplished. More and more clearly he felt the familiarity of this forest wilderness: it had all been in his dream—even the little cornfield with the withered bush fence about it; in his dream he had ridden the bay, when Leman came flying on her broad blue wings, plucked him from his horse, and flung herself upon him with the wild, hot caresses that terrified him. Ay, now she had him under her wings, had beak and claws in him, struck at his heart and drank his life-blood.

He knew of no return. This time he could not tear himself away from Leman and fly as in his dream—he had no strength for that now. Of the women he had possessed, she was the first he loved—and the first who had desired *him* and not a penny in reward. And then—to ride away from her one day and leave her alone, deserted and in want, that he could never bring himself to do.

And in the midst of his misfortune it dawned upon him—this was not the end. He had been drawn down into evil before, but he had been saved, his feet had been set on the firm rock and he had been made a freer man than before. And He who had saved him then would save him again. From his destiny no man can fly, but above his destiny is God. And so in what had befallen him it could not have been designed that Leman should strike her beak into his heart and drink him dry and empty, but he began to think he might be called to set free Leman from her semblance.

It had lasted for more than a week. He continued to work for Eldrid in the daytime, and he had become acquainted with his three house-mates, the hag, the herdboy, and Holgeir, Eldrid's old kinsman. They seemed not to be surprised—folk were not likely to be surprised at anything with Eldrid. Nor was he himself surprised, somehow—all that lay between his childhood in the forest and the present, when the forest had recaptured him, seemed like a dream.

Once or twice he had taken bow and arrows—the house was well furnished with arms; when he asked Eldrid who was their owner, she merely answered: "I." Then he went hunting.

He came home toward noon on the tenth day after Guttorm's visit to the Ness, bringing Eldrid two wood-grouse. Then he asked her abruptly, with no beating about the bush:

"Will you marry me, Eldrid?"

Eldrid gave a little laugh. "No, I will not."

"Why not?"

"Do you know how many men I have had?" she asked mockingly.

"Scarce so many, I warrant, as that Mary of Magdala."

"Ho, ho! Is that your aim? You may spare yourself the trouble, Eirik. A monk too I have had—when I made him go the way I would, he was the worst of all."

"Ay, that is likely enough," said Eirik. "Since he had broken a holy vow. But none can say that of me—it must be held that Gunhild has released me from all oaths and promises."

Eldrid had dropped her work and stood staring at her young lover.

"Well, how had you thought this would end?" asked Eirik.

"Oh—some I drove away when I grew tired of them—others were tired of me first and went of themselves. Which it will be with you I have not yet thought."

"Eldrid," said Eirik, "I have seen it in your eyes, every time I took the bow and went into the woods, you were afraid I would not come back."

She stared at him, red and speechless. But then she broke out:

"Afraid! Ay, 'tis true—and think you I am afraid to be afraid? Did you know—I learned what it is to be afraid while you were yet sucking your mother's breasts—afraid!" Eldrid's great eyes flashed. "Take yourself off, little lad, when you will, and go back to saying your hours and creeping to the cross and doing penance—not for me! I prayed, the day I rode as a bride to Harald's house—the storm came upon us on the way, I prayed God to send his lightning and save me. I prayed Mary Virgin—to take me in her keeping—I too was a virgin of fourteen years as she was when the angel visited her. I prayed her send the angel with the flaming sword and save me. It had struck the great ash in Castle Cleft, we saw the marks of the lightning in the grass as we rode up; but there was no mercy for me. And you talk to me of being afraid—" She stalked hither and thither in the little room.

"*You* say 'afraid' to me—I think 'twould scare you from your wits were I to tell you all the vengeance I took upon Harald, with his own house-carls, before his eyes, while he lay palsied and speechless. That might have been enough—the rest I have regretted; maybe 'twas stupid, not worth the pains—after Harald was dead and his children had driven me out and I dwelt at Sigurdstad wasting myself and my estate—but I rejoice whenever I recall Harald, as he lay there babbling and glaring—"

Eldrid stood facing Eirik, with a sneer on her dry, brown lips. "Go! You are afraid of *me* now—milksop, puny creature that you are—your face is grey and white as a flock of wool!"

Eirik shook his head. "I am not afraid." He smiled faintly. "And I mean to stay here and be married to you."

Some evenings later, when old Holgeir was with them in the room, Eirik said to him:

"I have asked Eldrid if she will marry me. She is a widow and can dispose of herself, but 'twere better she acted in accord with one of her kinsmen. Therefore I now ask you."

Holgeir answered that if Eirik would make him a promise in the presence of witnesses that he should remain here in the same condition, even if Eldrid took a husband, he would give his consent. To this Eirik agreed.

When Holgeir had gone out he turned to Eldrid. "Say yes, you too—'twill be tiresome for both you and me to be talking for ever of the same thing."

Eldrid replied hotly: "You are like the witless beasts, Eirik, like a horse or a steer; 'tis vain to try to save them from the fire—they run straight back into the flames."

"May I take that for consent?" asked Eirik with a little laugh.

"Take it for what you will!"

Then he sold to Holgeir the little silver chain with a cross on it which he had worn round his neck under his clothes since he was a boy, and bought meal and malt. Eldrid brewed and baked and they killed a calf; she made preparations for the betrothal feast with a gloomy air and strange words, but every time he held her in his arms he knew why she was thus—it was because he now had power over her: she still thought this marriage was madness, but she could not lose him.

One night she asked him: "What will you do with me when you go back home to Hestviken?"

"'Tis not sure it will ever be ours to dwell there, so long as Father lives," said Eirik. "But you have had a greater manor than that under you ere now."

She was so thin when he pressed her to him that it made him think of grouse he had sometimes shot—they had once been winged, but had lived on and supported themselves in a fashion long after.

Just before marrying, then, Eirik invited the neighbours to a feast, and then he went off to the parish priest at Saana church. Eirik had lent Holgeir the bay, and himself walked behind with the two peasants from the little farms up in the woods.

Holgeir was spokesman. Eirik gave his name and his father's name and his home parish. Sira Jon promised to publish the banns of marriage in lawful manner and he also promised to come to the betrothal feast.

It was held three days before Knut's mass [2] and all went well. Eirik betrothed Eldrid with his ring; for surety's sake he turned his words so as to say: "I take you to wife," so that he might be sure the marriage was now made, since he had already lived with the woman. Eldrid used the same form of words in her response.

Sira Jon then said some prayers, blessed them with holy water, blessed the company and the food. The feast passed off right well. The poor peasants who were witnesses seemed to have known but little of their neighbour ere now, but they made good cheer at her table. The priest was allotted the high seat; now that he and his two assistants had removed their white vestments he grew very talkative and very cheerful. He was himself the son of a poor peasant of the neighbouring parish, and he had often been at the Ness in his childhood, for it was of his aunt's husband that Benedikt Bersesson had bought the farm for his sister. He boasted greatly of what the Ness had been in those days and gave Eirik good advice as to what he ought to do now that he was to be master here, at the same time enjoining him to show gratitude to God for having been raised to such prosperity.

It dawned on Eirik that the priest took him to be a man of naught who had taken service here and was now to get a farm

[2] July 10.

and a wife who came of great folk, though she was somewhat the worse for wear. All the guests thought the same—they had seen him working here in a rough frock that Eldrid had made for him and shoes of rawhide that he had made for himself. None but Eldrid and Holgeir knew more of him than that. This roused all his old love of giving play to his fancy—he grew very free and said not a word that might lead any of them to suspect the truth, but talked and behaved as though he were a poor serving-man who was now being received into the ranks of landowners.

The priest said among other things that nowhere in the land was better fish to be found than in this lake, especially the perch. Eirik promised to render his fishing-tithes well and duly, and said that if one day he caught some fine perch in his nets he would bring the priest a little present.

The banns had been called twice for Eirik and Eldrid. But one morning during the week before the third time of asking, Eirik had a great catch of fine fish in his nets, and so he thought he would now fulfil his promise to the priest and bring him some fresh fish for the fast-day. He strung the biggest of the perch together, took his horse, and rode off.

But no sooner had he entered the door of the priest's house than Sira Jon came at him, looking as if the eyes would start from his head; he took the string of fish and flung it away, as though it were a string of vipers:

"Man of ill omen—you have befooled me abominably and made sport of me—so you are none other than the only son of Olav Audunsson of Hestviken!" He waved his hands in dismay.

"Nay, Sira, have I befooled you? I told you my name and my father's name and where I came from—"

"Ay, Eirik and Olav—there are many of those names. Then I send word to your parish priest, to know if you were unmarried and in no affinity to the woman—and this is what I hear!"

"Ay, but you cannot possibly have heard of any lawful hindrance?"

"His only son besides, and heir to an estate—and you will be married to Eldrid Bersesdatter!"

"Ay," smiled Eirik, "since I hold myself to be an equal mate for her."

At this Sira Jon exclaimed that never in this world would he say their bridal mass, nor would he publish the banns the third time.

"That you have no right to refuse us, Sira!"

"Right—ay, I know you have had your nose inside a convent and have smelled at the books they had there—you may complain to Dean Peter or to the Bishop, if you dare!"

All that Eirik could say was of no avail—that he had long been of full age and that Eldrid was a widow and had betrothed herself to him by the counsel of a kinsman, and that their cohabitation was already binding marriage by the law of the Church and could not be dissolved without mortal sin; and since neither Olav nor Berse were sheep of his flock, he could not see why the priest was so afraid of them. It was all of no use, even when he tried to tempt Sira Jon, promising to remember him when once he was master of Hestviken.

So nothing came of the wedding. Eirik cared little—since Eldrid seemed not to take it to heart. What had been done was enough to satisfy the law of God, according to which they were husband and wife; and what view the law of the land might take of their cohabitation mattered little, as yet anyway.

But his talk with the priest had nevertheless forced him to remember that there was a world outside the Ness on Longwater. And one day in the course of the autumn he told his wife that he would have to ride home and see his father.

The morning he set out, Eldrid accompanied him a little way across the marshes.

"Do not look at me like that," he said with an embarrassed smile as they parted. "I shall be home again by the evening of the third day at the latest, but it may well be I shall come sooner."

It was past midday when he came out by the river-mouth and saw once more the bay and the fiord outside and the rust-coloured rocks by the shore. He had ridden through the fields. They had finished cutting the corn here, and the cattle were loose in the paddocks. He knew every beast, and he knew every foot of ground; there was not a bush or a heap of stones or a tussock in the meadow that he had not gone round with scythe and bill-hook. And yet he did not feel at home here any longer, in the way he was at home at the Ness, at the farm where he was always coming upon corners that were unknown to him, on the lake, to the farther end of which he had never yet rowed, in the woods around, where he was always striking tracks that led he knew not whither—and yet wherever he went he had the feeling that here he had been born and brought up, that he had seen it all before, either when he was a child, or in his dreams.

As his horse's hoofs struck the rocks of the yard, Ragna came to the door of the cook-house. She cried aloud and ran toward him. Then others of the house-folk came out and swarmed about him, and last came Cecilia with a little child on her arm. It gave Eirik a shock to realize that it was Audun and that he had not grown much since he last saw him. It was not yet a year since that day in the storehouse loft.

Then he saw his father come to the door of the house. Olav stood there a moment, looked at his son, then turned in again.

Eirik kissed his silent sister on the lips. "I will come in to you, when I have spoken with Father."

He followed Olav into the living-room. His father sat in his seat. Eirik remained standing by the door with his hat in his hands.

"I have come home, Father—"

"Ay, I am growing used to that now."

"Nay, Father, I know you have good reason to chide me for leaving home without warning and staying away so long—"

Olav interrupted him: "A vagabond you are, and never will there be aught of you but a vagabond and a bird of passage. I make no complaint—'tis your nature. A fool I was to believe time after time that each new whimsy would last. I believed you when you said you would be a monk, I believed you when you said you would live at Saltviken and restore the farm there, I believed you when you thought you had set your heart on Gunhild Berses-datter—But one thing I did not believe of you—that you would take so paltry a revenge on Berse. As when you went off and de-bauched his daughter, who was so situated that you knew no man would defend her—"

"I am married to Eldrid, Father."

As his father made no reply, Eirik said again: "I thought you had heard that—since our priest had to make inquiry about me here in my own parish—"

"I heard of it. But I thought you would act according to your wont, as like as not—as when you were to take your vows in the convent. But it falls worst on yourself. God knows how you will carry it on the day when you begin to feel galled by a bond that cannot be broken."

Eirik stood still, looking at his father. Again he seemed to be wondering—all that his father said was true enough, and yet he knew that the truth was otherwise.

"I do not blame her," said Olav bitterly. "I would not have done what Berse did—given away a fair young child to an oldster who had buried two wives already—and an ugly sight he was with the big white bumps on his skull grinning out of his tousled hair, and never have I heard that he did a kindness to man or woman. Maybe other wives would have transgressed as much as Eldrid, had they not lacked the courage.

"And naturally she was ready to marry you, if she could bring it about. For all that, I will not have such a woman established in your mother's seat here or taking precedence of your sister here at Hestviken—not while I am master. When I am dead or unfit to have control, then you may come back, and then it may be more honourable that you bring with you the wife you have chosen rather than thrust her into a corner—if you have not done so already before that time comes. But till then you two must keep away from my domains."

"As you will, Father."

"Nay, I do not mean it so," said Olav curtly, "that I would drive you from home. You may stay here as long as you wish—I suppose you will fetch such things as are yours, visit kinsfolk and friends. I will not deny you that. Nor that you come hither to visit your sister—but you must come alone. But *dwell* here you shall not again in my time. I am tired of this; no sooner do we think you are settled somewhere than we have you back—and when we think you mean to stay at home, of a sudden you are gone.—But put off your cloak now," said his father, as he would speak to any other guest, "and take your rest."

Cecilia had ordered food and ale to be brought to her house for her brother. Jörund had gone to Gunnarsby to see his brothers, she said. They talked together, first of her children—all three were thriving—and then of the manor and the summer and of folk they knew, but not of his affairs.

Eirik asked whether Jörund and their father were on better terms now.

"They are not at enmity," replied the wife. She turned red. "He has begun to do more on the farm—Jörund has not had his baleful headache so much this summer. Father talks of moving out to Saltviken," she added, "letting Jörund have charge here."

Eirik lifted Kolbein onto his knees. "You know," he said quietly, "my wife has never had a child—and now she is not so young either. I had it in my mind to tell you this—so you may know, you and Jörund, if you are now to take over all the work here—'tis most likely that this little lad will one day have Hestviken after me."

"Eirik—that you could undo yourself thus!" said Cecilia in a horrified whisper.

"It is not as you think," replied Eirik; and what shocked his sister most was that she could not read the expression in his eyes, but it was not one of sorrow or remorse.

Eirik took his departure late in the afternoon of the third day. He had packed a saddle-bag with such of his things as he needed most; more he would have sent after him, for he was to ride home alone and he could lead no pack-horse with him—there was no fodder for more than one horse at the Ness. But Gisti, one of his old dogs, he would have with him; it had followed its master's heels wherever he went these three days, jumping up at him whenever he snapped his fingers. He was glad, for he felt the want of a dog at the Ness.

Cecilia wished to ride with him part of the way; she could then see to her child at Rynjul at the same time.

His father said farewell to Eirik in the yard. They parted kindly, but Eirik knew that from now he was a stranger here.

Brother and sister rode inland together; Knut Ragnason, who was now Cecilia's henchman, followed at a little distance. As they passed Rundmyr, Eirik asked Cecilia to take care of Olav Livsson, the sick lad: "He is fit to do a little woman's work." Cecilia promised.

They came to where the road branched off to Rynjul. Eirik did not wish to go and meet his kinsfolk there; so they took leave of each other. He had dismounted. His sister laid her hand on his head, forced it sharply into her lap.

"Eirik, Eirik," she whispered despairingly, " 'tis as though they would draw you back to elf-land!"

Eirik gently freed himself. "What fancies! I am content with the lot that has fallen to me."

It was dark when he reached the end of the lake. The Ness stood out black against the pale surface of the water. He made out a figure walking toward him on the road. Eirik leaped from his horse.

"Here am I, Eldrid."

She did not take his hand; he heard her breathing heavily, and then she burst into tears. She sat down at the edge of the road, bent double in the dark, and wept convulsively. Eirik stood still, leaning against his horse, and waited. At last he went over, took her by the hand and raised her.

"Now you must weep no more, Eldrid!"

Then they walked together across the marshes, home to the farm. The bay walked in front and Eirik's dog followed at his heels.

"I have made ready no food," she said when they had entered her house. "I had done so yestereve—you remember you said maybe you would be home so soon. But it made me so sick to see it standing there useless. Now I will go and fetch—"

Eirik watched his wife go with pensive eyes.

As he supped and afterwards unpacked his saddle-bag, they spoke some words of his journey. Eirik said that his father had not received him too badly. But it had been agreed that he was not to move home to Hestviken at present.

No sooner had Eldrid come to bed than she began to weep again. And she wept on and on—she wept under her husband's caresses, she fell asleep with her face against his shoulder and sobbed in her sleep, and woke and wept again. Eirik lay still and let her weep her fill.

"Would I had died," she lamented once, "ere you met me!"

"You must not say such a thing," he begged her earnestly. "You must not wish you had died while you hated God and all men."

"Yes! Rather that than that you should lie here, cast out from your heritage and kin."

"You are she who was set apart for me from the first. From here I am come, and hither I was to return."

Then he told her his dream of the bird-woman, Leman.

But next morning, when Eirik came in to his meal, Eldrid asked dryly: "Did you hear aught of that sister of mine, Gunhild—what has become of her?"

Eirik looked up.

"Nay," he said, taken by surprise; "that I clean forgot to ask!"

18

OLAV moved out to Saltviken.

The work afloat had to be done from Hestviken; here was no other quay than the little boat-pier of piled stones, no boathouse or warehouse, but only the little sheds by the salt-pans. And it would be a great piece of work to make a harbour in the open and shallow bay. Saltviken could be made a good corn-growing farm. Eirik had been right there.

Olav sailed up to Hestviken, went on board his own boats, spoke with Cecilia on dark winter mornings on the quay, but did not go up to the manor. Yet he knew that his son-in-law let fly abuse of the old kelpie that haunted the beach.

He knew that his daughter's husband could not cope with any of the things that had been placed in his charge. He had to depend on his old tried folk and on Cecilia. But it had come to this, that he thought himself obliged to pretend a trust in Jörund Rypa even though he had none.

What folk said of it all—it was clear that he himself was the last who would hear that. But it could not possibly be any secret that he had chosen ill in choosing a husband for his daughter. And as to Eirik's conduct, Jörund had let him hear what all thought of it: he had meant to take revenge on Berse—and a dastard's revenge—so he only got his deserts when he found out that the old adulteress was too sly and that he was the one who was caught.

Olav was wearied to death of everything. This turmoil in which he had been caught up, when he had had to swallow Berse's insults—and he had controlled himself, for Eirik's sake he had controlled himself more than he believed possible—and then Eirik behaved like a hothead, without a thought of honour or of aught but his own caprices—when at last this turmoil had calmed down, Olav felt that now he cared for nothing more. Now it was all one to him.

But he would not give up, for all that; he would have to continue the fight against disgrace and misfortune. He would stake all the respect he had won in the country round against his neighbours' judgment of Cecilia's husband, affect to think that Jörund was worth his salt and that his shield was untarnished. And at the same time, while living at the deserted manor, he tried secretly to keep an eye on everything, to direct and advise—whether Jörund liked it or not. It might well be that thus he might bring about better times for Cecilia and her children. Now that he could play the master at Hestviken, Jörund had found friends; they were not the best men of the neighbourhood, and he himself was quarrelsome and unamiable—with luck he might come by a few inches of cold steel.

And Eirik, who had acted in such a way that there was no excuse for his conduct—he must be banned from home. And it was better so—would he might never have to look on this creature again while he lived. He should have foreseen it, that time when he came home and found Ingunn with calamity incarnate in her womb—that he would be haunted by this spectre throughout his life and never find peace: he had hated him, despised him, hardened his heart against him, wished him dead—and longed for him, believed in him when the other deceived him, wished him well as soon as he had allowed himself to be deceived—this stranger had been more his own than the children whose father he was. Time after time he had believed that the curse was turned to—well, to something else—the bastard to a son of whom he was fond—and then the changeling had always swung to the right-about—and he himself was left deluded, the victim of scorn—and of what was worse and smarted more keenly.

But now it was finished. And well it was.

Yet ever and anon he caught himself thinking of Eirik. He longed to tell Eirik what was in his mind, without restraint. He longed to see him.

Time seemed long to him out at Saltviken a whole winter. He

lived there alone with Knut Ragnason and the young wife the
lad had lately married.

One day in spring Galfrid Richardson came unexpectedly to
Saltviken to see him. In the evening he told Olav his business.

There was a man who sought the hand of Galfrid's youngest
daughter, Alis, and Galfrid himself was willing enough to have
the man for a son-in-law, but he wished to speak to Olav first:
"For it is that Björn, the son of Torhild of Torhildsrud—so 'tis
you who are his father."

Olav answered he had gotten this son while his wife was yet
alive, so he had no right over the man, but if Björn needed help
to establish himself, he would not refuse—

'Twas not so meant, said Galfrid; he only sought to know
whether Olav had anything to say against the marriage. Björn
was doing well, and his mother and stepfather were now prosperous. He had become acquainted with the young man last
autumn, when Björn hired the smithy in their yard. He was to
make the ironwork for the new doors of St. Laurence's Church;
it was some of the knights of the King's body-guard who made
this gift to the church. Björn had acquitted himself of the task
in such fashion that one of the knights would have him forge two
branched candlesticks and an iron-bound coffer for the chapel
of ease that stood on his manor. But when Björn brought these
things to Sir Arne and claimed his reward, the knight deemed it
too high and would chaffer. Björn made answer that if Sir Arne
could not afford to give what the smith claimed, he could afford
to present the knight with both coffer and candlesticks; but he
held that none other than himself could judge what his work was
worth. Then Sir Arne gave him the sum he claimed. Now Björn
Olavsson had bought himself the houses he needed in the old Gullbringen Yard—Olav knew it, next below Fluga Yard, between
Sigrid's Yard and the river.[3]

After this, Olav had a strong desire to see Björn once more. At
Margaret's mass [4] he found that he had business in the town. And
on Sunday, when he came from mass in St. Halvard's, he went

[3] That is, the little river Alna, on the bank of which stood the ancient
town of Oslo.
[4] June 10.

down toward the yards that lay at the bottom of the slope, by the river bank. Gullbringen was the largest, and it had three court-yards, one beyond the other.

The houses around the innermost yard stood on the very bank of the Alna. There was a smithy, a stable with lofts, and a fine stone house. A great rosebush grew against the wall of the dwell-ing; beside it stood a young man and two women, who bent down and smelled the roses. Olav recognized the young slender one with the long auburn plaits; she was Alis Galfridsdatter, he had seen her at her father's house. The other was one of her married sisters.

Alis had seen him; she whispered something to the young man. Then she turned and went, giving Olav Audunsson a shy greet-ing as she slipped past. She had a fine, healthy, freckled face, wore a rose in her bosom, and carried roses in her hand.

The man came up slowly and greeted Olav: "Have we such great honour?"

His smile was boyishly self-confident—he must be twenty now, thought his father.

"I had a mind to see you again—"

"And indeed 'tis long since the last time. And the years seem to have dealt hardly with you—you are grown old, Olav Auduns-son! But go in—"

So he sat on the bench in the smith's house, and in the corner opposite sat the man who was his only son.

The lad was handsome—as he himself had been in his youth—a good deal bigger in stature, but not so shapely and well-knit. But he had the same fair complexion, the bright silvery sheen of hair and eyebrows, the white skin, and the clear grey eyes rather far apart.

Olav soon found that it was no easy matter to converse with Björn—he had nothing to say to him. His mother, his stepfather, his brothers and sisters, they were all well and prosperous; and so was Björn himself. His house declared plainly enough that the young man held his own.

"You are young to be a householder and practise your craft as your own master?"

"Oh, I have stood on my own feet since I was fifteen."

Olav said he would fain see proofs of Björn's skill—he had heard it greatly praised. Björn replied that he had nothing here which was worth showing: "but you can go up to Laurence's Spital and look at the ironwork on the south door of the church and the three candelabra that hang in the nave. They are the best I have wrought till now. I have no leisure today or I would have gone with you—"

"Is it true," asked Olav with a little laugh, "that the master of whom you learned your craft is of giant race?"

"He told me naught of that. And I never ask folk uninvited questions." This was meant for a reproof, his father saw, and he was inclined to smile. Never had he seen a man so heartily self-sufficient as this lad.

"But a good smith he was—none better in Norway," said Björn. He went across to a chest, came back, and handed Olav a lock and key for a coffer. "This I wrought while I was with him. The locks I make now are more cunning. If you like it, you may have it, Olav."

Olav thanked him and praised the work.

"'Tis not from your father's family you have this skill," he said tentatively. "We were never good handicraftsmen in our race."

"My father's family I know not at all," replied Björn in a clear voice.

"And that you resent?" said Olav in the same tone.

Björn looked him straight in the eyes, with his pert young smile. "Nay, Olav, that I do not. You begat me—and I say you did well in that. And have you done no more for me since—then I hold you have done me no ill there."

Olav looked at his son—wondered whether the boy knew what he was saying, or were these words put into his mouth?

Björn got up and went to the shelf over the door. "But you must think I am inhospitable." He filled the cup and drank to his father: "Hail to you, Olav Audunsson! It cheers my heart none the less to know you have sat on my bench for once."

Olav accepted the drink, with a little smile. "I cannot say your looks betray it, Björn!" It was wine, and good wine.

"Ay, but I mean it—and I wish you to have a token to remind you of it." Again he went to the chest. This time it was a brooch, fairly large and gilt all over; in the centre was an image of Mary with the Child, and around it a wreath of bosses, each of which bore an angel's face.

"Nay, Björn—that is far too great a gift, I will not have it!"

"Yes, take it now. Do you not remember I had a gold ring of you once?"

"Is it that you wish to quit scores with me, then?"

"No, no, not that either. I may tell you, Olav, 'tis with that ring I shall plight my troth to Álís Galfridsdatter at Clement's Church door on the eve of Laurence's mass."

" 'Twill be honoured, then."

As Björn went with him to the door, Olav asked: "Your mother —she is well content with your choice of a wife?"

"Mother—" For the first time Björn's smile was purely gay, with no challenge in it. "Mother is content with me, whatever I do."

"That is well," replied Olav. "Then I know that you have always done what is right and manly."

They pressed each other's hand at parting and Olav went.

Olav walked over toward his inn, half smiling. He might rest content with this Björn. Young and overconfident—but they were faults that life mends in a man—and God grant the lad might lose little of himself in the mending. So that the man might fulfil the promise of the boy, when once he was full-fledged.

What Björn had said was true—he might have done more for this son of his. Other men treated such matters differently—had their bastards brought up in their own homes or in those of their friends. He had indeed given the mother her farm, but Björn seemed to count that for nothing—and true it was, she owed her prosperity to herself and that husband. And if Torhild had not married, perhaps he and Björn would have seen more of each other. Although the true reason was that he felt he could not bear to look a son constantly in the face whom he had no power to bring into the family and set in his place—and so all else he could do was nothing worth.

And whatever the lad had meant in saying it, there was truth in his words: that, if he had done nothing for Björn but beget him, he had thereby done him no ill. The son who stood outside the family and would not call him father—he was also outside the family misfortune.

19

For the third time Eirik brought in the corn frozen and half-ripe. It froze down here by the lake earlier than anywhere else in the country round. It was not so great a disaster either—they could always make gruel from it, and grain for malt and bread they could buy. Meat and fish were the foods they had in plenty, and in Lent it was all to the good if they had to go a little hungry.

He smiled when he thought of the first year's Lent. He kept the fast as had been his custom since he was in the convent, drank nothing but water once a day, and put a piece of ice in his mouth if he was too thirsty at other times. At night he slept on a sack of straw in the porch. He did not ask what Eldrid did. But one morning when he came in he saw her lying on the floor—she was still asleep. Then she said that she lay there every night, after he had gone out to rest, and as she saw that he went barefoot in his shoes, she did the same.

"You must not, for you are not used to it."

Eldrid said she had been shriven every year in Lent and had received *corpus Domini* on Easter Day—but she had only done so to avoid being cited.

"It is well that you have left such evil ways," said her husband.

"Nay, I made a vow that night I waited for you on the road—when you had been out to Hestviken."

"Then they did some good, the foolish thoughts you had. But I had told you I should be home again the third evening."

"Had you not kept your word," said Eldrid, "I know not what would have become of me."

"God help you, Eldrid—but you ought to know better than most, that no man is worth much as he is in himself."

"You are not like other folk."

"Oh, but I am. In most things I have not been-better than my fellows, and in some I have been worse."

But he had never spoken Bothild's name to his wife.

Now he knew the lake from end to end, and the woods around, the paths and the wastes. There was not much to be done on the little farm, so he had ample time to roam about to his heart's content. When he found, the first winter, that Eldrid had skis—they made it easier for her to move about among the outhouses, so long as she had no horse—he too had to make himself a pair. When he had accustomed himself to the use of them he liked this mode of travelling so well that he ran on skis oftener than he rode. There were times when he was out from morning to evening; often he did not come home till late at night—until it chanced that there was some piece of work or other that he could postpone no longer. Then he would find a host of other things that it might be well to get done, and for a while he would not leave the houses, had scarce time to swallow his food and none at all to rest; in the evenings he sat by the fire with knife and chisel, awl and sinews, and worked, while Eldrid sewed and span, as silent as her husband.

They never talked much together, beyond what the work required. They knew not much more of each other's earlier life than they had known when they met. But he felt that her life had gone up in his, she drifted with him as a boat drifts with the stream, and both were content it should be so.

He had been two years at the Ness when Brother Stefan came to preach at Saana church for a few days in Ascension week. On the last day Eirik persuaded him to come home to the Ness and stay the night there, and the next morning he accompanied Brother Stefan by a short road through the forest into the next parish.

They sat talking for a long time on a ridge, whence they had a view of tarns and forest, but never a homestead under the broad sky, and Eirik's dogs lay in the moss at his feet. Eirik cleared his mind to Brother Stefan of all that he had not been able to bring out in confession, because it had not to do with sin or grace, but with the All in which all things move and have their being.

While they were talking thus, Brother Stefan said he counted it a gain that Eldrid was no longer bound in thraldom by her own hate. "But it will not be your lot to live all your days here at the Ness—have you thought of how it will be when one day you two move out to Hestviken?"

"No," replied Eirik. "It must be as God pleases—*if* we ever come there. Father may live to see eighty years. Moreover, Eldrid is a discerning woman, and open to reason. The finest and most promising foal may be spoilt by cruelty and foolish treatment."

"You must not liken a Christian soul to an unreasoning beast," said Brother Stefan.

"That old Ragnhild you saw at our house—she told me—Harald Jonsson once bound Eldrid to the post of the loft ere he rode from home; he would have her stand there till her feet swelled so that she could bear no more—if he could make his wife so meek that she would show him kindness. Ragnhild set her free the second night and tended her—she was sixteen at that time, Eldrid. She had been Harald's leman, and he sent her away when he wedded Eldrid, but afterwards he took her back to Borg; she was to help him break in Eldrid—this Ragnhild."

They sat in silence for a while, both of them.

Brother Stefan said they had grieved, all the brethren, when they heard the course Eirik had taken: Brother Arne had vowed to scourge himself every Thursday evening so that the blood flowed about his feet, till he heard his brother had repented.

Brother Arne, who had been the companion of his novitiate, was the one for whom Eirik cared most of all in the convent—he was but a young lad and had been with the Minorites from a child. Eirik now bade Brother Stefan take Arne his greeting and his thanks.

When they came down into the neighbouring parish, at the first fence about a green field Eirik said farewell to his friend. Brother Stefan gave him his blessing; then the monk went on toward the village, and the solitary hunter, with his bow over his shoulder and his hounds at his side, turned back to climb the hill again.

That summer went by at the Ness, and most of another winter. In Candlemas week there was severe cold. Eirik was up on the hill in the daytime, felling timber; but one night he woke to find Eldrid trembling by his side. She said she had fallen into the spring that day, as she was fetching water for the byre, and thought she must now be too old to go about in ice-covered clothes. Eirik then found out that the old serving-woman, Ragnhild, had a way of being out of temper with her mistress at times, and then she shut herself up in Holgeir's cabin till the mood passed off. While it lasted Eldrid herself did all the work of the farmyard; they had no herdsman in winter.

Soon after she grew hot as coals all over, had some bad fits of coughing, and then began to be light-headed, wailing and muttering and throwing herself hither and thither. For some days she lay grievously sick. The first evening she began to be better, on seeing her husband come in with the milk, she asked after Ragnhild. Eirik laughed and said the old hag's wrath had fallen on them both—none knew why—so she still sat in her corner, and he had seen to her duties.

"Nay, Eirik, this is too bad—milking and cleaning byres is no work for a man."

"Who milks in the monasteries, think you?" asked Eirik with a laugh.

Next day came Gaute Virvir, Eirik's old friend from home. He had had business in the neighbourhood and so bethought him that he would visit the Ness. He found Eirik occupied in feeding the cows. Eirik gave his guest such welcome as he could, his wife being sick. Gaute had just had judgment given against him in the matter of an estate, so he was in a gloomy mood and the news he gave of his neighbours at home was told with a sad mien, like a tale of disaster. Olav still dwelt at Saltviken, and Cecilia's last child had died just after baptism, and Gunhild Bersesdatter was now Sir Magnus's wife and dwelt in the Lady Ingebjörg's bower —the knight was one of the Duchess's liegemen.

Eirik thought that, all in all, the tidings he had from home were not bad. It was hard on Cecilia that she had lost a child. But it seemed they managed just as well without him; his father and Cecilia together had the whole charge of the manor, he could guess, and Jörund was allowed to play the master—so doubtless he had become more tractable.

Three summers he had lived here, and soon the third winter would have gone by—Eirik was thinking of this one evening as he stood at the outer door looking out into the blue-grey dusk. The whole ness, which faced the sun, was brown and bare of snow; the eaves dripped a little; this evening was so mild that no icicles hung from them. In the forest the snow still lay deep, but the surface of the lake was black with melting ice, and along the shore the evening sky was mirrored in clear water—which had grown broader since the day before.

Then he became aware of something black moving over the ice down by the end of the lake—it looked like two figures, and they had dismounted and were leading their horses. Eirik ran toward them—he must stop them, bring them in to land at the only place where the ice could be called anything like safe. As he ran down, calling to them to stay where they were, he wondered a little who they might be—there was no other house but the Ness on the whole lake, so they must be bound thither.

As he hurried across the flat among the glassy pools of water, he saw that one of them must be a woman. But not till he had come close to them did he recognize Cecilia.

"In God's name, let me help you ashore. Take the horses, Svein, and I will lead Cecilia."

He thought he could see in the dim light that there was something wrong with her, wondered whether it was only fear when she saw how unsafe the ice was, or whether it was something else as well.

When they reached land, Eirik said: "You can find the way now, Svein. My wife will be asleep already, but you must go in and wake her, tell her who is coming." He took Cecilia's horse. "You must mount, Cecilia—the snow is knee-deep here across the marshes."

Then she threw her arms about her brother's neck and clung to him, and he could feel how she was trembling.

"I am come to beg you go back with me," she said in despair. "It has come to such a pass that I can bear no more." She gave a violent shudder. "I cannot bear to look upon Jörund again."

Eirik pressed her to him. " 'Tis best you come indoors first," he said; "take off your wet garments. For it must be a long tale you have to tell, I am afraid."

"The end of it is," said Cecilia, as she released her brother, "that yesterday he struck Olav, Anki's son, so that the lad died this morning. Then I bade Svein saddle my horse—"

Eirik stood aghast:

"The cripple! Can such things be!—What have you done with your children?" he asked abruptly.

"Tore has them. But he has never done aught to the children—

I charged them at home," she went on, as he led her horse along the shore, "to send no word of this to Father. I dare not—till you are there. You are the only one who can help us—perchance."

Eldrid met them at the door of the house. Eirik could see afar off that she had swathed her head in her long, snow-white church-coif. She gave Cecilia her hand and bade her welcome.

Indoors Eldrid had stirred up the fire on the hearth; she led Cecilia to the warmest seat on the bench, took her wet cloak, and thrust a pillow behind her guest's back.

"You must be tired, Eirik's sister—you have ridden all the way from Hestviken in this heavy going, your man says."

Eirik saw that his sister looked about her with wondering eyes —the room was tidy and snug, even if it were small and low, and the beds were well provided with bedclothes and skin coverlets —and then she looked up at her brother's wife. Eldrid had not aged in these three years, and in her kirtle of dark colours, with the white linen headdress falling low over her back, she looked like a fine elderly woman.

"I think, Cecilia, you had better go to bed at once, wet and cold as you are—and I will bring your supper." She took the young wife to their own bed, knelt down, and drew off her footgear. "Your feet are like ice—you must take the coverlet from the other bed, Eirik, and warm it; then I can wrap it about your sister."

Cecilia sat clutching the edge of the bed with both hands; the tears now ran down her cheeks as she wept almost without a sound; and when Eldrid had wound the warm skin coverlet about her legs and laid her down, she turned to the wall and buried her face in the pillows. She lay thus till her sister-in-law came with the food.

"Now you must come out with me, you—Svein was your name, was it not? I shall go to Holgeir's house and sleep with Ragnhild tonight, Eirik—I think your sister would fain speak with you alone, you have not seen each other for so long."

With that Eldrid bade them good-night and went out.

Cecilia ate and drank.

"Shame on Gaute—he has put it about all over the countryside that you go in rags, half-naked, and live like the meanest cottar, and your wife is so infirm she must ever take to her bed—"

"Then Gaute is a worse tattler than I am myself," said Eirik.

"Had I known the truth of your condition," replied Cecilia, "I am not sure I should have come hither to complain of my trouble. I thought you could not be worse off than you were."

"Then it was well that Gaute spread his tale."

But when he had taken away the empty cups and seated himself on the bed by his sister, while the embers fell together in the fireplace, he felt a dread of what he was about to hear.

Between whiles Jörund had been tractable and kind, said Cecilia. But he scented covert injuries and distrust of himself in all that their father and the old serving-folk said and did, and it was often hard for her to intervene. Then there were Anki and Liv— he had conceived a hatred for them since that unfortunate affair, and he would have them out of Rundmyr. Olav said he would not hear of it—then Jörund was beside himself, made the most incredible accusations against their father, said it was known to the whole countryside why he kept such a den of thieves close beside his manor, but now they should go or he would set fire to the whole nest. This happened last autumn, while she still lay in after her little daughter who died—her father had come over to see her. Shortly after, it came out that Gudrun from Rundmyr, who had been helping at Hestviken during the summer, had not returned to her parents as she had left them, and Jörund had offered money to Svein Ragnason and several other men to take the blame on themselves. "I have never told Jörund of it," said Cecilia, "but I went up thither one day lately—Anki takes it much to heart, for Gudrun is not ill-looking; her at any rate he had thought to marry off, and she is but fourteen, so the poor child could scarce help herself."

But Jörund had gone quite wild when he got to know it. And for Olav, the cripple, he had always had a loathing. And yestermorn Olav had been in the fields with the children—he was cutting willow pipes for them—when Kolbein came running home; the boy cried and said his father had come upon them, so angry, had snatched Olav's crutches from him and struck him with them.

Cecilia had dashed out. There lay Olav, with the blood running from his nose and mouth. "I said to Jörund what first came into my head." But Jörund was like a raging bull and not like a reasonable being. Then Svein and Halstein came up, and he let her go. They carried Olav Livsson in to Ragna, and Cecilia had sat by him all night, but in the morning he died.

At last Cecilia fell asleep, and Eirik went and lay down in the farther bed.

He had no doubt that Jörund was distracted at times—he ought to be watched, perhaps put in bonds. And Cecilia could not live with him any longer. Either she must move out to Saltviken with her children, or he himself must go thither and take his brother-in-law with him, while his father returned home to Hestviken and stayed there with Cecilia—that he must decide when he had seen how things were on the spot.

Next morning at daybreak Eldrid stole in to change into her working-dress. Eirik said he would have to ride over to Hestviken that day—"and I fear it may be some while ere I come home to you."

"Ay, so I thought."

Cecilia insisted on riding back with Eirik, though both he and Eldrid begged her to stay at the Ness till her brother sent for her.

Not much was said between them on the journey; the roads were in a bad state, and Eirik could see too that Cecilia already repented of having said so much as she had.

When they came to Rundmyr, Eirik asked his sister and Svein to wait in the old houses that stood by the roadside; he would go on to Anki and Liv. He knew not what he should say to the poor folk. As he hurried on foot along the familiar path over the bog, he recalled how here he had played with fire, blinded by childish anger against his father, filled with a vain desire to make himself acquainted with all that was evil—and he himself had come off free, in a way, while those who had less sense and less guilt lay writhing, burned beyond help.

Two sheep were in the tussocky field, seeking what pasture there might be; they ran off as he came up. The door of the cottage was barred, and there was no answer to his knocking. And the little byre was open and deserted. Eirik's anger was kindled—had Jörund driven them out after all?

As they rode into the yard at the manor, the house-folk appeared from every door. They collected about Eirik as he sat on his horse, looked up at him, grave and anxious. But no one said anything, until Tore came forward and held the bay while Eirik dismounted.

"You have not come too soon either, Eirik!"

To that he could answer nothing. Then he asked: "Where is Jörund?"

At first there was none who answered; then someone murmured that he must be indoors; but at last a half-grown lad whispered fearfully—Jörund had gone down to the waterside awhile ago, he had seen—

As the men were about to follow him, Eirik forbade them, and to Svein, who handed him an axe, he said: "I have my sword, as you see—but I look not to have use for it."

He did not take the road, but went down the hill below the front of the dwelling-house. Between the spur on which the manor was built and the waterside there were only a few small scraps of arable land; the rest was rocky knolls and scrub, briers and juniper. Eirik crept along stealthily so that the madman should not see him coming. But as he went down he could not help seeing how much farther advanced the spring was out here by the sea; everywhere fresh green appeared among the withered grass in the crevices of rock, there were great red shoots on the brier bushes, and the goats that picked their way on the hillside had already recovered from the winter. And outside, the fiord gleamed in the afternoon sunshine.

He saw no one on the quay. But as soon as his steps were heard on the planks, a man dashed out from behind a shed, flew past him, bent almost double, and leaped straight into a boat that lay alongside. Eirik did not stop to think, but ran after him and jumped into the boat in his turn, just as Jörund had cast off. They both stood up in the boat. Jörund seized an oar and struck at his brother-in-law, and in an instant the boat capsized.

As soon as they were in the water the other flung his arms about Eirik; he guessed that Jörund was trying to hold him under —he had swallowed a mass of water, and his cloak and sword and heavy boots hindered him; he was dizzy and choking already. But in spite of that he was more used to falling into the sea than Jörund; he contrived to free himself from the other's hold and get his head above water. They were not far from the shore; he reached the slippery seaweed, clambered up, and sat down on the rock.

Eirik spat out the sea-water, took off his dripping cloak, and shook himself, so that the water splashed inside his boots.

"Can you get ashore by yourself?" he called out as he saw Jörund's head above water. "Or shall I come and help you?"

Then Jörund scrambled in; Eirik gave him a hand and pulled him onto the rock. There they stood, with the water pouring from them.

"I believe your madness is half feigning," said Eirik. "Do you think thus to escape from your misdeeds more lightly?"

Jörund sent him the ugly look, like a scared rat, that Eirik had seen before, and it made him wince inwardly.

"Anyhow, you failed again to take my life," said Jörund scornfully. As Eirik made no answer, his brother-in-law went on: "I knew very well you have hated me and planned revenge and sought my life all these years. Ever since that night at Baagahus, when you had drunk your wits away and struck at Brynjulf Tistill —and I saved you from the dungeon!"

It came back hazily to Eirik—an old memory of some half-forgotten brawl in the castle. They had both been mixed up in it, he and Jörund, but he it was who had to pay the penalty, and Jörund had got off free.

"Let us go up now," he said impatiently; "we are standing here like a pair of wet dogs."

"And since I found out what you meant by having such folk settled at Rundmyr—and I can guess 'twas irksome for you and your father that you were not suffered to pursue this noble trade in peace—"

Eirik had drawn his sword and was drying it as best he could with heather and tufts of grass. "If you do not go home, I will baste you with the flat of this!"

"More likely you will run it through me, now you have me unarmed." But he began to move.

Eirik did not know what to think: whether Jörund himself believed all this or was only feigning.

The house-folk in the yard stared at these two as they walked up, all wet. Eirik bade one of them tell Cecilia that they must have dry clothes. Then he followed Jörund, who went toward the great room; as he came in he saw that they must be living here now. He hung up his sword and seated himself, opposite Jörund; and there they sat in silence.

But when in a little while Cecilia came in with her arms full of clothes, Jörund looked up with an ugly smile at his young wife. "Have *you* time to give *me* a thought? I did not think you could tear yourself from the corpse of your bold paramour, the six-legs that I chastised yesterday."

"Nay, Jörund," said Eirik below his breath, but with a shake in his voice, "if you are never so mad—you can still go too far. That you could raise your hand against a poor cripple—"

" 'Tis her way to have a fancy for cripples, this wife of mine." Again he smiled, that horrid, imbecile smile. "The first one she played the whore with, he was a limping cripple too—"

A sudden change came over Cecilia's face; there was an icy green glint in her great bright eyes. Instinctively Eirik sprang to his sister's side.

"I saw it myself," the man went on, "the halting misshapen wretch—and she big with my own child—"

Cecilia's cold voice was sharp as a knife: "If you thought you saw aught unseemly—how was it you did not come forward till this halting cripple was so far away that he could not defend me when you trampled me underfoot?"

Eirik seized his sister by the arm. "Come out!" In a flash he had seen the depth of Cecilia's hatred of her husband, and he was afraid.

"Nay, I cannot bear the touch of Jörund's clothes," he said, when they had come into Ragna's house. "There are some old things of mine in the chest above in the loft.—Did you not once learn of Mærta," he asked as she turned to fetch his clothes, "how to brew draughts that send a man to sleep? Better mix something of the sort in his ale tonight. I will go over and find Father this very evening; and I am afraid to leave this house unless I can be sure that he is fast asleep."

When he had changed into some of his old clothes, he went up into the loft in which they had laid Olav Livsson on straw. There were two candles burning by the dead man's head, and he was wrapped in a good linen cloth. Eirik uncovered the face only: that too bore black marks of ill usage, but the narrow white features were peaceful, as though the lad had fallen asleep. Under the winding-sheet the body looked ungainly in its length, with its thin, withered limbs.

Eirik kissed the ice-cold forehead, knelt beside the bier, and recited the prayers and the litany for the dead; and those of the household who sat there murmured the responses: "*Ora pro nobis*" and "*Te rogamus, audi nos.*"

Afterwards he spoke in a low tone with the house-folk. They had not dared to send word to the priest, but they themselves had sat by the corpse the night before, and they promised to take turns at watching tonight as well. Eirik said that he would make provision for the funeral when he came back on the morrow, but now he must go out to Saltviken and speak with Olav. They had heard nothing of Arnketil and Liv; the houses at Rundmyr had stood empty since yestermorn, so they must have fled with all their flock from terror of Jörund, for he had threatened them with fire and murder.

He had asked Halstein to take supper in to Jörund and stay with him till he fell asleep—Halstein was a big, strong man. Now Eirik looked into the room before going down to the boat. Jörund was asleep. The door of the house could be locked from the outside; Eirik gave the key to Halstein and bade him bring Jörund his breakfast betimes in the morning.

When he landed in Saltviken it was already dusk. Nothing was left of the sunset but some copper-red edges below the grey clouds that lay over the west country. The sea was dark, crisped by the evening breeze, and broke against the faintly gleaming curve of the beach with the low rippling murmur he knew so well.

The gravel crunched under his feet and the wind whistled in the bent grass; on the scanty strip of pasture with its tall junipers lay some bullocks. Ah, he had not set foot here since the day he rode out to seek Gunhild. And now there was not a thing in his life that he had forgotten so completely as Gunhild.

He had expected the folk to be in bed at the farm, but as he came up between the fences he saw a dark figure standing by the gate—his father.

"It is I, Father"—instinctively he wished to forestall the old man, so he spoke hurriedly: "I come from Hestviken; it has come to such a pass there that Cecilia thought we must all take counsel what is to be done; she sent for me."

"It has long been so," said Olav. "But of you we heard never a word. It can hardly be worse now than it has been all this time, when you felt no call to see how things were at your own home."

But it was his father himself who had forbidden him to come. His youthful anger reverberated in Eirik: could his father never be fair and just toward him? But he controlled himself—to justify his actions would only make bad worse.

"I never heard other than good tidings—but you may be right; one can never trust hearsay."

Knut and Signe slept in the living-room, said Olav—they would have to go into the upper chamber, where his own bed was. It was dark as the grave in the room above, and Eirik stumbled and ran against things that lay scattered about. And in the darkness, with the door ajar to the spring night, they sat and talked together. Eirik told of what had happened at Hestviken and what was in his own mind: "Cecilia cannot live with Jörund after this."

"No, that must fall to you and your wife. And 'twill be a merry life at Hestviken when you three share it."

The bitter scorn in the voice that came out of the darkness put an end to Eirik's patience. "There has never been a merry life at Hestviken, Father. You wore down Mother—I know not whether of set purpose or not. Since then you have done all in your power to wear us down, till we were of the same mind, Cecilia and I— that anything was better than to dwell in the same house with you. Remember that, when she comes to live here—and be like a Christian man and not like a mountain troll to her children—even if they have mouse's ears."

"Would to God I had never seen you!" came in his father's voice, shaking with passion. "Would to Christ and our Lady I had let you stay where you were, at the back of beyond!"

"That was in other hands than yours—I came whither I was meant to come. But for that I say it would have been as well for me to have stayed there—and for you too: in one way or another it seems you were fated to deal unjustly with every child you have begotten."

"You I have not begotten! You are not my son!"

"Shame on you!" Eirik sprang up in his wrath. "What is this strain that is in such men as you and Jörund? When the world goes against you, you cry shame upon your own wives with infamous words—"

He heard Olav breathing hard in the darkness and restrained himself.

"But this is an ill season for us to take up our old quarrels, Father—and I beg you forgive me if I spoke too hotly. But you might spare Mother your insults"—he was on the point of firing up, but checked himself again. "Let us to bed now, Father—best that we set out for Hestviken as soon as it is day."

With that he rolled himself up on the bench. Sleep was impossible—his mind was in a whirl: the long day's ride, and Jörund, and his struggle with the madman in the water, and the dead lad in the loft, the deserted cottage at Rundmyr, and Cecilia—the sudden distortion of her pale features into the very face of naked hate, the icy glint in her deep clear eyes. Fear for his sister made him shudder—never could Cecilia stray on those false paths that Eldrid had followed, but it dawned upon him that hate knows many roads, and they all lead to the same goal at last.

Then he recalled his father's words—and he recalled his childhood's terror of one day being driven out as a bastard. Could it be that there had been some reason for his fear, that he had once heard words of which he had forgotten all but the fright they gave him—that his father had suspected his poor mother, persecuted her, as Jörund persecuted Cecilia, as he himself had persecuted a woman to death with shameful suspicions?

A longing for his home at the Ness came over him, an irresistible temptation to take flight. But thither he could never more return, he knew that. But at the same time he knew that if he and Eldrid were forced back into this foretaste of hell, he had a wife on whom he could rely. Never had he put so secure a trust in any human being as in her, whose soul had breasted torrents unbearable.

His father was not sleeping either, he felt sure. And now his anger gave way to pity for the old man.

Olav waked him—just as he had fallen asleep, he thought. The sun rose as they rounded the Horse. Then Olav broke the silence:

"When we come up," he said, "I must ride inland at once—Svein and I. They cannot be left out in the woods with all their children and Gudrun. I must get Anki and Liv back to Rundmyr first of all—you will herd Jörund meanwhile. He shall be made to pay the full penalty for the lad he slew and for their daughter whom he has debauched. Then, I think, next time his wit is about to fly from him, he will remember to catch it by the tail."

As Eirik held the boat against the pier for his father to step out, he heard Olav say: "What is afoot, Halstein?"

The house-carl looked strange and pale. He waited till Eirik had joined his father.

"Jörund is dead this night, Olav," he said in a low voice.

After a pause Olav asked: "Is it—?"

"The wound is from a dagger. Straight in the breast. More I know not."

"He was wild and out of his wits," said Eirik hastily. "God have mercy on his soul—he cannot have been in his right mind when he did it."

The house-carl gave him a look but made no answer.

Father and son went together into the living-room, Halstein followed them. He had not touched the body. Jörund lay in the south bed—his great naked body with the left leg and arm and shoulder hanging out, the head bent to one side: it looked as if he had tried to get up. There was a wound in the left breast below the nipple, and blood, but not very much, on the white skin, clinging to the tuft of curly hair. On the bench by the bedside still stood the food that Halstein had brought in when he found him.

Eirik was almost as pale as the dead man: in his father's face he read nothing but the same hate as he had seen in the eyes of Jörund's wife. This had been his friend—the thought of the other's derangement and ignominy and miserable death broke his heart as he lifted the ice-cold body and disposed it with the head on the pillow; he tried to close the dead eyes and press together the nostrils.

Olav raised the coverlet, felt about the body. "Where is the dagger?"

The wound was three-cornered, as though made by one of those foreign daggers with a triangular blade; it was clean, and of such size that the weapon must have been thrust in with force right up to the hilt.

Halstein crossed the room quietly and barred the door.

"I must say what has to be said—you are the next friends of the dead man—and it was I who was to answer for him. But when Eirik gave me the key yestereven, I knew not there was another way into this house—"

"Another way—" Father and son said it together.

"When I came in this morning," whispered the house-carl, pointing to the north bed, which had been Eirik's when he lived at home, "it was all tumbled in a mess of straw and bedclothes, half across the floor, and the hatch was not quite closed, for some straw was caught in it."

The two stood stiff and speechless. The north-western corner of the house did not rest upon the rock, but upon a wall of masonry, and when Olav Ribbung built it after the fire, in the time of the Birchlegs, he had made a postern here toward the sea, with a hatch leading to it from the bottom of the north bed. In Olav Audunsson's time this secret passage had never been used, but it was certainly known to the oldest members of the household, and Eirik himself had sometimes tried it when a boy.

He saw his father was leaning his hand on the table, stooping lower and lower—it looked as if the old man would fall forward in a heap. Eirik took hold of him—Olav half raised his head, and the grey, scarred old face looked as ancient as sin; the mouth was open, but the eyes were close shut. He raised one hand, gently pushed Eirik aside, and went toward the bed, swaying like a blind man.

He bared the breast of the corpse again, fingered the wound, and pushed aside some bloody hair that clung to one of its corners. Then he felt again all over the bed, searching for the dagger.

When he turned round, his son saw that the sweat ran down his forehead below the soft white hair. He looked hither and thither as though at a loss.

"Father?" said Eirik inquiringly, seized with anxiety—but he could not guess what this was.

Olav was moving away, with a strange padding gait, like an animal caught in a pitfall.

"Father," said Eirik again, "we must go and find Cecilia."

Olav supported himself against the doorpost of the closet, which was carved with the figure of Gunnar:

"Go you— I shall come—"

"We must make fast the door," replied Eirik in a low voice, "till we have collected men to view the corpse." He saw the terror in his father's eyes. "Remember, his brothers must be fetched."

Olav gave one loud groan. Then he went out, following his son.

. . .

When they entered the women's house, the widow sat crouching in the farthest corner of the room. Ragna, the old serving-woman, was with her. Cecilia shrank yet closer to the wall, staring at the men with eyes that were wild with terror.

Eirik went forward to embrace her. She resisted:

"Have you seen him?" she whispered.

Eirik nodded, and took her in his arms in spite of her efforts; she was trembling as though seized with spasms. Then he lifted her up like a child, carried her to the bed, and laid her on it. And the father stood watching the two with the same look on his face, which seemed to have been struck inhuman.

Cecilia lay trembling. Little by little her convulsions ceased and she lay still, but her eyes were just as wild and staring as before. Her father had seated himself on the bench; as though absently he still held his old barbed axe between his knees, with his hands resting on its head.

After a while Eirik went out. He called together the men and gave them orders: one was to ride first to Rynjul for Torgrim and Una, then to summon men hither, neighbours who could view the corpse; another he sent up to the churchtown to ask the priest to come at evening and keep vigil over the two bodies. The slain and the slayer—for he would have to persuade Sira Magne that Jörund might be given Christian burial—the deed was done in madness. The message to Gunnarsby he could send on the morrow.

It was some time before he had given his men all instructions. Then it struck him that he must try to make Cecilia take something, if it were but a drink of milk. He went in with the maid who carried the bowl. His sister still lay with staring eyes, and his father sat as before.

She put her lips to the bowl, but pushed it away at once. "I cannot—'twill make me sick—"

Eirik seated himself on the edge of the bed. The serving-women had gone out.

"Sister!" said Eirik all at once. "If you could but weep!"

"Ah—if I could," she replied tonelessly.

At that her father raised his head. "Would I could help you to *that*! Would I could help you to it ere it be too late! Better you were burned alive at the stake than that you should fare as I have fared! Never believe you will benefit your children by holding your peace and hardening your heart and soul. Eirik spoke more truly than he knew when he said it had been better for you to live with a mountain troll who devours Christian children than with me!"

The son and the daughter stared at him, uncomprehending.

"I too was young then," Olav went on; "not many years older than you are now, Cecilia. And 'twas not so grave a thing as this. My deed—I know not if it were a crime; myself I thought to have right on my side. But I concealed it. At first I thought, when the time came that I *could* do so, I would make confession, repent, and purge my sin. Now the time for that is long past. It has corrupted me, and all that I have touched and taken in my hands has been tainted with my corruption."

Still Cecilia did not understand, but Eirik:

"Jesus Christ—Father!" he whispered, pale about the mouth.

"Now I *cannot* repent," said Olav firmly. "The light that I once had has been taken from me—my repentance is now as the sight of a man whose eyes have been put out. But now I will make my confession nevertheless; Cecilia—you and I will go together, and one fate shall fall upon us both."

Then she understood. She sat up in the bed with a start.

"I!—Think you that I—!" Her voice was wild and sharp.

Eirik had leaped up and stood in front of his sister. "Father—stop!"

"Then the same fate can fall upon us both," Olav repeated. "If you must flee the country, we will go together."

"With you!" His daughter shuddered. "Rather will I do as Jörund has done!"

Olav asked: "That foreign dagger you had of me once, when you were a little maid—where have you that, Cecilia?"

"In my coffer." She stepped out of bed, went across the room to her chest; her brother saw that she was now trembling again, but her mouth was hard set and her eyes flashed. She took from the chest a little coffer and turned out on the bench all that was in it—brooches and chains, a little coral rosary, several knives.

"It is not here. Perhaps Jörund took it," she said; her teeth were chattering.

"We can go in and search once more," said Olav quietly.

"No!" she shrank back.

"Dare you go in to him with me?"

"No—" Cecilia bowed her head. "I must not look upon a corpse, as I am now," she whispered almost inaudibly.

"If you are innocent, it can hurt neither you nor it."

Her whole body seemed to give way. Her father went on:

"If you are innocent, then go in with me, lay your hand on his breast—"

"No." She shrieked: "I *will* not—"

"Monster!"

Eirik sprang to his sister's side.

As Olav took his daughter by the wrist, she started back, tried to tear herself free, but slipped and fell. She lay on her knees with bent head, struggling with the other hand to loosen her father's grip. To Eirik it looked as if he dragged her over the floor.

Then he seized Kinfetch, rushed at his father with the axe raised in both hands. Olav saw it, let go his daughter—and, straightening himself, he raised his forehead to the blow—

But she too had seen it, flung herself against her brother's hip; Eirik stumbled, and the steel rang upon the stone curb of the hearth.

"Eirik!" Cecilia's piercing cry reached him.

He looked into his father's bloodshot eyes and felt that they gave him his death: it was not hate, it was not anger, it was not the wild and tense excitement of a while ago. He knew not what it was—these were the eyes of a man who came from a land that has never been seen by the living.

The axe fell from his hand. He flung his hands before his face, staggered to the bench and dropped upon it, sat half turned to the wall, with his head hidden in his arms.

He heard that one went out at the door, and at the same moment Cecilia lightly touched his shoulder.

"Eirik—how could you!" She looked as if she could not bear much more. "He is our father—"

"Yes." He moaned faintly without looking up. "I know it. The Lord have mercy on us. I know it."

Then he raised his face to her for a moment. "I know it. I would have killed him. I would. My father."

She broke into violent sobbing and threw herself down beside him. With her face pressed against her brother's dark hair Cecilia wept and wept, till he drew her down into his embrace and, clinging to each other, they wept with terror at the life in which they were entrapped.

But at last Eirik pushed her from him. "I must go and find him."

As he went out, she followed, took him by the hand, and squeezed it—they went together like two children scared out of their wits. Outside the door of the great house he hesitated a moment; then they went slowly on, hand in hand, as though seeking their way in a wilderness. When they had reached the end of the houses, they looked down and saw Olav just rowing away from the pier.

"Eirik—what will he do?" she whispered.

He shook his head. "I know not."

"Eirik," she whispered again, "could you grasp what he meant —what has he done?"

Again he shook his head. "I know not—"

Their father was rowing northward round the Bull. Then the two turned and went slowly back to the houses. Outside the door of the great house Eirik paused.

"He shall not lie there alone like a heathen dog. I will go in to him—"

Cecilia caught her brother's arm in a close embrace.

"Then I will go with you. I am not afraid if you are with me—"

Cecilia felt that a shock ran through her brother's frame—a strange look came into his face—he too must have doubted. But she would not admit the thought. So brother and sister went in together to the dead man.

20

OLAV had never rowed up to Oslo before. Now and again he rested on his oars for a while; the water gurgled underneath the drifting boat. The fiord was calm today, and there was not a craft to be seen.

A light mist had floated up from the south, turning water and sky to grey; the wooded hills grew dark, and the new green of oak and ash made feathery patches against the blue-black firs. Olav plied his oars again.

The flaming terror that had caught his spirit had now burned itself out; he was tired and drab within. He was now on the way to do the thing from which his whole life had been a flight, and this time he knew he would do it; he knew this as surely as he had known all the other times that he would flee from it as soon as he saw a way out. But his soul was grey and cold as a corpse.

He had heard a thousand times that God's mercy is without bounds, and in secret he had relied on this: what he fled from was always there, waiting for him when he took courage to turn, since it was all that was outside time and change: God's arms spread out on the cross, ready to enfold him, grace streaming from the five wounds, the drooping head that looked down over all creation, watching and waiting, surrounded by Mary and all the saints with prayers that rose like incense from an unquenchable censer. His servants were ever ready with power to unlock his fetters; the Bread of Life was ever upon the altar. God was without bounds.

But he himself was not, he saw that now. It was too late, after all. The bounds that were in himself had set and hardened into stone—like the stones folk had shown him here and there about the country which had once been living beasts and men.

Now he *could* no longer repent. There was no longer any love of God within him, nor any longing to find his way back; now he would rather have gone on and on away from God, everlastingly. That was hell. That was the realm of eternal torment, he knew it, but the home of torment had become his home.

The game was played out, and now he might indeed confess and do the penance imposed by the Bishop—it would be of no avail. Absolution cannot absolve him who has no repentance within him. He had lost his faith of a Christian—though he knew that what he had once believed was all that is and was and shall be, and he himself was what was not; but so many times had he chosen himself, and that which was naught, that he had lost sight and sense for that which was Life.

But for Cecilia's sake he would do it nevertheless. He had learned to know his daughter in these last years; and now it seemed as if he had been long aware that she might end by doing a deed like this. He ought to have acted before.

Eirik had something of this in him; he saw that now. He had hated as a travesty of himself the changeling's mendacity, hated his lax nature, hated him for never being able to carry through any of the intentions he had formed. Ah, yes, he had married that adulteress. Eirik too had done that. And he had loved Eirik, who lied and boasted and followed every fancy and turned again from every path he had set out on—loved this incubus that he had got on his back, this goblin that had sucked blood of him till they were as father and son after the flesh. The murdered man's son had avenged his father as secretly as he himself had slain Teit.

He thought he had seen all this in a flash when Eirik rushed at him with the axe lifted to strike and he had held up his head to the blow—with something akin to joy he had seen the end coming. Then the axe had been turned aside in the hand of the son avenger.

And he knew that this had happened for Cecilia's sake. *How* it was to benefit his daughter he could not tell. But she was young— she had a long life before her in which to be hardened and die, if she did as he had done. He saw the horror of what he wished to bring about—and he thought of the three little sons who would grow up as children of a mother who had killed their father. But worse still that they should grow up under her hands while she carried such a secret within her. In one way or another he knew it would be the saving of them all if he now laid at Cecilia's feet the corpse he had dragged about so long: Behold—and take good heed, ere it be too late for you to do the like.

The afternoon was far spent when he rowed westward along the quays of the townsmen: Claus Wiephart's quay with his warehouse—where he was wont to land—the quay of Mickle Yard, of Clement's Church, Jon's quay—on to that of the Bishop's palace. And he gave a cold and snappish answer when a young fellow came down and called out to him discourteously that he must not put in there with his boat. Olav replied that he intended to tie up his boat here, and that he had business in the Bishop's castle —as he spoke he remembered that neither in clothes nor in person was he fit for a visit to town, and it vexed him as he crossed the green.

Half an hour later he stood in the narrow square between the Bishop's palace and the wall of Halvard's churchyard.

The Bishop was at the point of death. None had time to listen to him or answer his questions—folk hurried hither and thither in the palace: the Lord Helge's sickness had come upon him so suddenly, and with the Easter festival at hand. True, tomorrow was Palm Sunday, he had forgotten that.

He had never thought that *this* could happen—that when at last he was ready to throw down his arms, there would be no one to receive his surrender. And now he felt that his deathlike calm was nothing but extreme suspense, for now he was cold and trembling—and in despair at being forced to take the plunge once more; this postponement seemed to him unbearable.

Olav knew not what to do with himself. The mist had condensed into a fine drizzle. The great stone buildings around the square—the wall of the Bishop's palace and the churchyard fence and the mighty mass of the cathedral with its heavy towers and leaden roof glistening in the rain—loomed even greater in the dark weather. But the bursting poplars that reached over the churchyard wall seemed to curl up their new and fragrant leaves, and the grass grew luxuriantly among the cobblestones of the pavement.

He could not face going out to Claus, sitting and listening to the merchant's chat. Nor to the armourer's either. He had only been in Oslo once since Galfrid's daughter was married to Björn. They had one child—unless there were more since—but it was as though he scarcely dared to hear of this grandson of his; if he had been a leper he could not have been more afraid of thrusting himself into Björn's life.

A church bell began to ring close by with loud clangour—it was from St. Olav's Convent; the tower rose from the end of the churchyard wall. At that moment two preaching friars came round the corner; with their heads well shrouded in their hoods they hurried homeward to shelter from the rough weather, their black capes fluttering away from the white frocks. Olav watched them go; the short one must be old Brother Hjalm, but he would hardly know him now, it was so many years since he had set foot in their convent.

Olav followed the same way; he could at any rate go into St. Olav's Church and so pass the time. Afterwards he would have to think of a place to spend the night, where he would not be forced to speak of what had happened at home in Hestviken.

In the church door he was met by a great sandy dog that came rushing toward him, followed by the lay brother who had chased it out; they nearly ran into each other. "Nay, is it you, Olav Audunsson?" said the monk joyfully. "We have not seen you here since— But you are come to look for Father Finn, I can guess— ay, he will be glad to meet you—such a good friend of his father you were, I mind me. Ay, now he is preaching to the townsmen, the sermon that he gave us in Latin this morning—" the talkative lay brother nodded and slipped through the side door into the choir.

It dawned on Olav that the tall, middle-aged monk who stood on the steps of the choir preaching—he must be the second son of Arnvid Finnsson. The last time he saw Finn he was a pupil in the school at Hamar. Now the close-cropped hair that bordered the monk's shining scalp was silvery grey, the narrow, weather-beaten face marked with wrinkles.

He did not resemble his father—none of Arnvid's sons had done so; they were handsome, as he had heard their mother was. Father Finn was erect and thin; he stood very still as he preached, clad in white, with the heavy black cape over his shoulders; he had a fine, clear, and gentle voice:

"—but that part which lay buried in the earth is to remind us of God's invisible power and hidden counsel. That part may be likened to the root of the cross; unseen by the eyes of men, it bears the trunk of the cross, its branches, and its precious fruit. Such tokens are given us that we may be able to hold it fast in our minds that our salvation has sprung from the root, which is God's unseen counsel.

"But what availeth it us, good brethren, to interpret in words the token of the cross if we do not show in our works that we have interpreted aright the words of our Lord: 'He that taketh not his cross and followeth after Me is not worthy of Me'? He taketh up his cross and followeth in His footsteps who feareth not to suffer pains and hardships for love of God and his even Christian and his own soul. We may bear the cross in two ways, with our body or with our soul—"

It was a *sermo crucis*, such as was usually preached in the conventual churches during Lent. Olav looked about him—it was long since he had been in this church. The nave was long and narrow and somewhat gloomy now that no candles were lighted; the windows were darkened by the great ash trees of Halvard's churchyard and the mass of the cathedral beyond. There were not many folk either—under the misrule of the last Prior the convent of St. Olav had lost much of its ancient reputation.

Father Finn Arnvidsson's sermon was intended in the first place for the brethren of the order, Olav could understand; he had so much to say about penance and discipline:

"—in this way every man must beware of himself, for here lurketh the danger which is inward pride: causing us to look down on those of our brethren who are less able to bear fasting, watching, frost, and scourging. We cannot render like again to our Lord for the pain He suffered, scourging for scourging, wound for wound—in chastising our own body we must take good heed lest we deem ourselves to be vying with Him. But if others offer to scourge us, to wound or use us despitefully and deliver us into the hands of the tormentors, then must we bear such things with gladness, remembering that we are thereby vouchsafed an honour of which we are unworthy."

A scud of rain lashed the windows of the church; Olav heard that a wind had sprung up.—A thought had dawned within him—should he tell Finn Arnvidsson what it was that had brought him to Oslo? Although his case was such that he could make no valid confession to any other than the Bishop, unless he were at the point of death—he might say to Finn that he was here to confess an old blood-guiltiness, a secret slaying committed at the very time of their last parting, when Finn was yet a boy; he remembered now that he had bidden the lad farewell outside the schoolhouse on the day of his setting out for Miklebö. That would be the same as breaking down the bridge behind him.

"We bear our cross in the spirit when our heart is grieved for the sins and sorrows of other men, as Saint Paul maketh mention: 'Who is weak, and I am not weak?' saith he; 'who is offended, and I burn not?' Good brethren, it is not for us to wonder whether the Lord hath laid it upon us to bear the sins and sorrows of others or to atone for the transgressions of our brethren, though He hath made all atonement for us all. But when we are tempted to ask why then must we atone, we ought to remember that He bears heaven and earth as an orb in His hand, but He deigned to lay aside the royal robe of His omnipotence and array Himself in the poor kirtle of Adam. He fainted by the way as He bore the cross out of Jorsalborg, that a great boon might be bestowed upon Simon of Cyrene, in that he was held worthy to help his God and bear the cross with Him. Blessed above all other men who have lived upon earth was this countryman. But it is given to all of us to taste of Simon's blessedness, when God calleth us unworthy sinners out of the multitude standing by the wayside to watch the passage of the cross, and biddeth us share its burden with Him—"

No sooner was the sermon over than the old lay brother who had recognized Olav came back. Bustling and loquacious, he led the way to the parlour; now he would go and tell Father Finn.

It was a little square room with a groined vault; a narrow pointed door stood open to the cloister. Olav went and stood in the doorway, watching the rain, which was now pouring down upon the bare green carpet of the cloister garth; the rain came in under the arcade, sending up splashes from the stone-paved floor. A strong south-westerly gale had set in, and well it was; this early spring had made him uneasy—it was not to be relied on so long as no rain came to carry away the snow in the woods.

The heavy black clouds that came drifting over the sky made the evening dark for the time of year, and there was a pale and shifting glimmer in the air from all the wet leaden roofs. A soughing came from the great ash trees, whose tops, tufted with blossom, towered above the ridge of the church roof; the wind whistled and shrieked in the windlass of the well in the middle of the grass plot. Then the bells of Halvard's Church began, with a hollow booming, the shrill little bell of the convent church joined in, and soon all the church bells in town were ringing.

Behind the pillars on the other side of the garth came a white monk—Father Finn Arnvidsson walked briskly toward him with outstretched hand. "Hail to you, Olav Audunsson—'twas a kindly thought to come and seek me out!"

They sat in the parlour—they had not seen each other since the one was a boy and the other a young man. That was more than thirty years ago.

Olav asked after Finn's brothers and after his kinsfolk, the Steinfinnssons and Haakon Gautsson's children from Berg. Finn replied that he could give no tidings that were new: he had lately come to Norway from a journey in foreign lands which had lasted two years, and before that he had been subprior in Nidaros, but now he was to go home to his convent at Hamar.

"But now it is almost the hour of complin. Shall you be in town for a time?"

Olav said he did not know. "My son-in-law is lately dead—"

"Where do you lodge—nay, surely you have a house of your own here in Oslo?"

When he heard that Olav had not yet secured a lodging for the night, Father Finn thought that he might sleep there. The guest-house was full, but there were some guests' cells in the upper story —he would go and ask the Prior:

"I have many things to set in order in these days, ere I set out for home, but I would gladly have more speech with you—you were my father's best friend. And it will be easier to find occasion for converse if you dwell under this roof."

Olav sat in the guest-chamber eating his evening porridge. There was no other in the room but a sick man who lay in one of the beds, groaning in his sleep; the other guests had gone over to the church to hear the singing. Olav pushed the bowl from him, leaned the back of his head against the wall, and stared into the light of the candle; from the church came the notes of the choir, and outside the rain splashed and the wind howled.

Then came the sound of footsteps on the flags of the cloister— the monks returning from church. And a young lay brother with a lantern in his hand stood in the doorway and signed to him: now silence would reign here till after early mass next morning.

The lay brother went before him up a creaking stair and along a passage, opened a door, and set the lantern on the floor of the cell.

It was a tiny room with grey stone walls. There was a narrow sleeping-bench against one wall, and a desk with a kneeling-rail and a crucifix under a little bow-window, which was closed by a shutter with a parchment pane. The shutter shook and rattled in the wind. Olav opened it and looked out into the stormy spring night—over the shining wet roof that covered the cloister, down upon the green garth with the well and the windlass, which creaked with every gust. It was so long since he had been in a room as high up as this that he felt as though imprisoned in a tower.

He took off his outer garments and lay down on the bench.

Sleep he could not; he lay listening to every sound from the blustering and rainy night outside.

The night before, he had lain at Saltviken—knowing nothing of Cecilia's mad deed. 'Twas no longer ago than that. As he tried to gather up in his memory all that had happened since he met Eirik by the fence late in the evening, the hurry of events seemed like a headlong plunge. He had come to the end of the road and over the edge.

His thoughts went to the words Finn had spoken of Simon of Cyrene—had he been thinking of his father? Arnvid had been a man who suffered himself to be called out of the crowd to succour anyone who was driven past to his doom. And it must have been for this reason that he had always held Arnvid to be more than other men. Arnvid was so stout-hearted that he was not afraid to bend his back if any man would lay his cross upon him. He had not been afraid to follow so closely in his Lord's footsteps that he had his share of folk's spitting and abuse.

Had he himself been as fearless as Arnvid, then he would have proclaimed the slaying of Teit at the first house he came to. And he had condemned Ingunn to hide her child far away in the wilderness, deprived of rights, of name, of kindred—till he saw that the wrong she had done was breaking her down, and he tried to mend one injustice with another. He should have defended the boy's right from the first—the right to be called Ingunn Steinfinnsdatter's son, though a bastard, to be his mother's heir and to look to his mother's husband for support and protection. Had he been as Arnvid, he would only have asked what was right; would have been man enough to live with a seduced wife, to honour her to whom he had plighted his troth before God, and to love her to whom he had given his affection since he had the wit to prefer one person to another.

Nay, he might have had the courage to hearken to his own conscience when it pleaded for Teit: "the fool knows not what he has done, he is naught but a witless whelp as you yourself were when you went to your bridal bed ere you were out of your nonage.

"But, the sin once committed, he would in any case have had the courage to stand by it: while I cleared myself by lying of the injury I did my foster-father, when I was young and wild and thoughtless; but the man who was so thoughtless as to injure me,

him I struck down. For I thought I could not live if another had
stained my honour and I let it go unavenged. I thought it easier
to live besmirched if I myself had stained my honour—so long as
none knew of the stain. For such a cause as this I turned Judas
against my Lord, armed me with the hardest sins, if but they
might be hard enough to weigh upon my weakness like an
armour."

Such fear had he had of the judgment of men—he who had believed himself indifferent to what folk might think of him. For he
did not desire to wield a chieftain's power over them, nor to be
a rich man among them, if he should use craft and suppleness to
gain riches, nor friendship with any man whom he could not like
outright, nor such good fortune as makes a man fat and lazy—he
had only desired to stand among them as the oak stands above the
brushwood.

And he saw that such was the lot intended for him. God had
given him as a heritage from loyal, brave, and pious forefathers
that which He has promised to the offspring of the righteous: a
mind and a heart that hated cruelty, that feared not luckless days,
that faced any foe undaunted—only those he loved could scare
him into anything.

"God, my God, who lovest us all, who loved me—whom I once
loved; had I chosen Thee, I should have chosen my deepest love."

He saw that in a way he had had a right to judge of himself
as he did—he had only forgotten that he held all that was good in
him as a vassal holds his fief under the sovereignty of the King.
And he had rebelled, had broken his faith and laid waste his land.

He *should* have grown as the oak, patient and spreading, with
light and shelter for all who sought its wide embrace. Such was
his destiny, nor had he been able to grow otherwise—his inward
hurt had only cankered the pith in him, so that he had become
hollow and withered and barren. Not one had he been able to
protect to any purpose: from Ingunn herself down to such as
Anki and Liv and their children, he had tried to act as a provi-
dence for them, and it had been in vain. He had wasted his wealth
in the struggle with his rightful Lord—but as a man who is born
open-handed, generous even with stolen goods, he had taken in
all who came to his door—though all he offered was a beggar's
feast and a mumper's wedding.

Simon of Cyrene—now he recalled that the image of this man

had been shown to him once before, many years ago in England; then he had seen in a dream his own soul wounded to death, and he had been compelled to stand outside the band of poor men who went forward to receive the body of the Lord.

How, he wondered, would he have felt on Easter morn, that countryman from Cyrene, if he had refused when they would have him bear the cross, if he had slipped away and hidden himself in the crowd of those who mocked?

He too had had children—Alexander and Rufus were their names. He had once heard what became of these sons of Simon, saints and crowned martyrs.

Olav still lay awake when he heard the distant singing from the church. As he listened to the strains of matins, drowned now and then by gusts of wind, he fell asleep.

Morning was far advanced when he awoke. There was singing again—they were blessing the palms, he knew, and then would come the procession round the church. Olav still lay abed—once more he was assailed by bitter regret, that he had left home in the clothes he stood in. When at last he came down in his coarse old everyday clothes and heavy boots, the service was already far advanced; the words rang out from the choir:

"*Passio Domini nostri Jesu Christi secundum Matthœum.*" [5]

From where he stood he could not see the priests who were singing. And today was the long lesson, so he could not follow it from memory, but only knew some fragments. Wrapped in his old brown cloak he stood far back by the door, and as the clear and powerful male voice intoned the gospel, rising and falling and rising again, he was carried along past words and names he recognized—*Pascha—tradetur ut crucifigatur—Caiaphas*—beacons that told him where they were now. Jesus and the disciples were in Bethany, in *domo Simonis leprosi*, and sat at meat; now Mary of Magdala came in at the door, bearing a box of ointment, that she might pour out the most precious thing she could find before God. And the voice of Judas snarled at the woman with miserly scorn.

Then another voice, fuller and richer, answered with the

[5] On Palm Sunday the 26th and 27th chapters of St. Matthew's gospel are sung (on Tuesday in Holy Week the story of the Passion according to St. Mark, on Wednesday according to St. Luke, and on Good Friday according to St. John).

Master's own words as He took Mary under His protection and praised her loving-kindness.

Olav waited for the words he knew, the words that were branded upon his heart with red-hot irons—would they not come soon? They were not so far away. Ah, now they were coming—now He was sending the disciples into the city to make ready the supper. Now—

His heart beat against his chest as though it would burst as the great, rich voice pealed from the choir:

"*Amen dico vobis, quia unus vestrum me traditurus est—*"

The voice of the Evangelist followed with a short strophe, and then the whole chorus of disciples broke in, harsh and agitated:

"*Numquid ego sum, Domine?*"

Olav felt the sweat break out over his whole body as the voice of Christ rang out. And then they came, the words that were burned into his heart:

"*Væ autem homini illi, per quem Filius hominis tradetur: Bonum erat ei si natus non fuisset homo ille.*"

The evangelist sang: "*Respondens autem Judas qui tradidit eum, dixit*"—and the loud voice of Judas followed:

"*Numquid ego sum, Rabbi?*"

The voice of Christ replied: "*Tu dixisti.*"

Olav had bowed his head upon his breast and thrown the flap of his cloak over his shoulder, hiding half his face. The coarse homespun smelt of stable and boat and fish. Among the crowd in festival attire he alone was unprepared.

Words that he knew flowed on in the chant. Now they were going to the Mount of Olives—but Olav seemed to be watching from afar: as Judas stood somewhere in the city spying after them. Now he was thrust out, now all his companions knew what had only been known to God and himself when he came in and sat at supper with the others.

The visions floated farther and farther into the darkness. Among the trees God Himself falls upon His face: *Tristis est anima mea usque ad mortem*— But the disciples are asleep and take no heed. From a gate in the city wall come the watchmen with torches and flashing spears, while Judas goes before and shows the way. Saint Peter leaps up out of his sleep; in the boldness of youth he snatches his sword from the sheath to fling himself between his Master and His enemies—lays about him like a fool, strikes off a servant's ear—and when he sees that they are overpowered and hears the calm answer of the Lord, to him incomprehensible, he throws down his sword and runs away; they all run, all the disciples who but a while ago promised so stoutly. Christ is left standing alone, holds out His hands unresisting, lets them bind Him—passing comprehension. But who has seen that part of the cross which was in the ground, who knows the root of the cross—?

Round about Olav men and women stole a chance of sitting or kneeling awhile—there was no end to it, this hateful arraignment by men of their Maker, the voice of the people in shrill chorus: "*Crucifigatur!*" And again: "*Crucifigatur!*" The long road out of the city up to the hill of Calvary, the horror of the crucifixion—and the reviling, which did not cease even there.

After the last loud cry from the cross, when He gave up the ghost, the singing stopped abruptly and the congregation sank on its knees, as though struck down by this dead silence.

Strangely quiet it sounded when the Evangelist's voice began again, assuming now the customary Sunday tone, and sang the narrative of the grave and of the Pharisees' timid consultation with Pilate.

The mass followed upon the gospel as though out of a gate—manifesting again the vast and awful mysteries of man's deceit and God's mercy. It was Holy Week advancing upon mankind, Maundy Thursday and Good Friday; Saint Mark and Saint Luke and Saint John would each in turn bear witness. And Easter Day on the far side of this week of evil seemed infinitely distant.

When Olav came to the guest-house, he found it so crowded with folk that he hesitated to go in. Two lay brothers hurried forward with steaming dishes, followed by two more with cans of ale: it was past midday and the good folk of the inn were pale and pinched about the nose and hungry as wolves.

One of the lay brothers was the same young man who had conducted him to the guest's cell the evening before. As soon as he saw Olav he took him in hand, made room, and pushed him into the place of honour—the franklin was a friend of the Prior of Hamar. He tried to force food and drink on Olav, but Olav could get nothing down.

As soon as decency allowed, he rose from the table, went up

to his cell, and lay on his bed. He fell asleep at once and slept till the young lay brother woke him: "Now Father Finn has time—"

When Olav came down into the parlour, where Finn Arnvidsson sat waiting, there were several others in the room: two young monks, so much alike that Olav guessed them to be twins, sat there with a woman, their mother, and some young maids. The whole band of kinsfolk had the same fiery-red hair and freckled complexion, upturned noses, and pale-blue eyes; their talk was of news from home—Olav heard it with half an ear while he listened to what Father Finn told him of his father's last years.

Olav sat with eyes cast down; his hands clutched and clutched at his dagger, he pulled it half out of its sheath and thrust it back again. Then he cut short the other in the middle of his calm and quiet narration:

"Ay, Finn—your father knew something of that which I am now to tell you. He counselled me, before he died, to do that for which I am now come." Without thinking, Olav rose to his feet and stood erect, and as he raised his voice the company on the opposite bench ceased their talk and listened to him:

"I once slew a man in my youth and I have never confessed it. Arnvid, your father, knew of it, but at that time, I would not do what he begged of me—confess my blood-guiltiness and purge my sin by penance. But this that lately happened in my home—my son-in-law has been killed in his sleep and we know not who did it—this drove me hither to seek the Bishop. I knew not that *you* were in Oslo."

Finn Arnvidsson had also risen. They stood looking each other in the face. Then Father Finn slipped away to the other company, who stood staring, and whispered a few words to the two young monks. A moment later all the red-haired folk were out of the room, and Olav stood alone with Arnvid's son.

The monk laid his hands on his shoulders.

"God be praised," he said warmly.

"Did your father speak to you of this?" asked Olav, looking up into the other's face. Finn was a much taller man.

"No. But now I understand much better one thing and another with which he charged me—that I should say a Miserere daily for all men who are burdened with an unshriven sin, for instance- -and other things besides. God be praised that you have now resolved to do this.—But you should not have spoken of it in the hearing of those strange women."

"I am not sure that I had said it to you if we two had been alone. But now I have broken down all bridges behind me." Olav smiled faintly.

The monk stared at him a moment. Then he nodded in silence.

"Now that the lord Helge is at the point of death," said Olav, "and none can tell me who acts in his stead—whether official or penitentiary or what he may be called—"

"I myself will find that out tomorrow, Olav."

"But now I will go. I would rather be alone now—"

"Yes indeed. I understand."

They took each other firmly by the hand. Olav went up, lay down on his bed, and fell asleep at once. He slept till the young lay brother came up with his supper. Olav ate and lay down again. God, my God, how good it is to have thrown down all bridges behind one!

When he came down into the cloisters next morning, on his way to church, Finn Arnvidsson came toward him.

"Olav—know you not that so long as you have not confessed this sin in lawful manner, you must not enter the church? I remind you of this, for, you know, you will only have more to answer for if you set at naught the interdict—"

Olav stopped, overwhelmed. Assuredly he knew it—he was banned just as wholly as if excommunication had been pronounced on him in church. But so long had he defied the ban, stealing in where he had no right to be and committing sacrilege, that at last he had forgotten.—He answered nothing, turned back and walked down the cloister.

Father Finn followed him, took him by the arm. "You must remember, Olav—ay, you know Latin, I think?"

"A little I know—"

"You must remember these words of Saint Ambrose: '*Novit omnia Deus, sed exspectat vocem tuam, non ut puniat sed ut ignoscat*. God knows all things, but He waits to hear your voice, not to chastise, but to forgive.'"

Olav nodded.

On coming to his cell he threw himself on his knees at the little desk with the crucifix.

Assuredly he had known it—but he had forgotten. This was the first thing he would have to bear—that he must stay outside the church door. He saw that it was there he had sought nourishment during all these years—as the outlawed Danish lords had lived by making descents on their own land.

He took the crucifix from the desk and kissed the image of the King.

"Lord—I am not worthy that Thou shouldst take pity on my repentance and show me grace!"

He had made his confession mentally so many times, the whole chain of his life's sins—from the time when his pride was young and childishly thin-skinned; he had faced the men on whom his boy's heart was set with white lies and petty deceit that they might think him a man. In the beginning it had meant no more than that he was afraid they might smile if they found that he was only a young, hot-headed, obstinate and weak-spirited lad, while he wished to be taken for one who was resourceful, prudent, and strong. But he had carried this playing with truth to such length that he became a secret slayer, perjured and sacrilegious; link by link he had wrought his fetters, stone by stone he had built his own dungeon. Till it had come to this: that every time his thoughtless daring sprang up, the fetters held it back, and every time his heart would fly out to meet all who called it forth, it beat its wings against the stone walls and fell back.

Repent—now he saw that life would not be granted him long enough to see fully all of which he had to repent. If he had chosen loyalty to his Chieftain and been able to bear such burdens as he need never have repented taking on his shoulders— He could not repent having opened his door to everyone who craved shelter by his hearth, and never could he sufficiently repent that he had so acted toward himself that it was to a man full of leprosy that he let them in.

Nothing could be undone. Cecilia sat out at Hestviken with the body of the husband she had slain; the three fair-haired, mouse-eared boys stood about her, the fourth child lay under her heart, and she, their mother, had killed their father.

How could he have been deaf to his own heart, which told him: trust not a man who was false to his friend as a boy? So long had he strayed in shadows that he could not believe his own eyes —Jörund was not a fit husband for his only child. And afterwards he had done nothing—although he felt now that he must have known something might happen. This husband whom his daughter defended in word and deed, true as the sword is true to its master—he would be sure to try her patience once too often, and then Cecilia would turn against him. He remembered what she was like as a child: a dogged little spitfire, with her sharp bright eyes under a shock of flaxen hair. How could *he* believe Cecilia would change her nature, even if she were tamed and tutored by life? One can tame both bear and hawk; it does not make domestic animals of them.

Now it was too late, and he could only pray God to help him. Pride and presumption it would be if he now prayed God to use him as His instrument. For him it only remained to sever himself from the company of men—a lonely pilgrimage of penance. And to be thankful it was granted him to do it.

To take Cecilia with him was not in *his* power. Rather follow Jörund than go with him, she had said. So be it; perhaps she would think otherwise when she heard what he had done.

This was the first bitter cup he had to drain—to see that his conversion came too late in the evening for him to hope that God would send him back into the fray as His man. His work in the world was ended, and he could not undo it. He had rejected the glorious task of Simon of Cyrene; now he could only humble himself sorrowfully before the cross.

Olav took the crucifix in his hand again, stood looking at it. Somewhere, beyond the long week of pain and conflict, bided the Easter morn, and beyond death and purgatory it would be given even to him to see the glorious victory of the Cross. But here on earth it would never be his to see the radiance of a standard under which he might fight with the powers that were given him at his birth.

Olav looked up from the desk and turned half round as the door opened. It was Finn Arnvidsson who entered. His speech was dry and strangely cool—Olav guessed he was trying to conceal his emotion.

The monk said he came straight from St. Halvard's Church, where he had spoken with Master Sigurd Eindridson, who was delegate during Bishop Helge's illness to confess homicides. And he would hear Olav's confession in the sacristy after mass.

"So you have a day in which to prepare yourself. I too shall watch tonight, and pray that you may make a good confession. But remember that you are an old man, Olav—lie down and take your rest when you can watch no longer. It is of no use to constrain your body more than it can bear."

Olav compressed his lips. But it was true—he was old; even on his bodily strength he could rely no longer. Arnvid's son knelt by his side and remained on his knees a long while with his face in his hands. Then he rose silently and went out.

The hours went by. Now and again Olav caught sounds from outside—footsteps in the paved cloister as they fetched water from the well. The rain continued to splash on the roof and pour off it, gusts of wind beat upon the house, with a roar in the tree-tops, a creaking and crashing everywhere—then the blast died down for a while. The bells told him how the day was passing; the distant singing from the church showed how the life of the convent followed its wonted way.

A day and a night—the time of waiting seemed unbearably long. He held the crucifix in his hand and looked at it from time to time—but it seemed to him that his prayers fell from his lips as withered leaves flutter down from the trees in autumn. Was it so hard to wait?—but He had been kept waiting thirty years. From the beginning of time until the last day, God waited for mankind.

At dusk the young lay brother came, bringing him food— Olav saw that the man guessed something of what was afoot. He drank up the water and ate a little bread. Then he knelt down again and waited.

Night fell outside, the house grew silent, only the rain continued to pour down, the wind rose and fell. Once he went to the window and looked out. In an upper window of the opposite wing a faint light glowed through a little pane. There was one man who watched with him tonight.

As morning advanced on the next day it looked as if the southerly weather would soon have spent itself for this time. There were short fine intervals and once the sun peeped out strongly enough to be reflected from the wet roofs.

Olav sprang up as Finn Arnvidsson appeared at the door. He

took his hat, threw his cloak about him, and followed the monk down the narrow stairway that led to the cloister.

From the parlour someone came flying toward them in great haste—a tall man in a dark-red cloak with the hood drawn over his head. He was as wet as he could be. It was Eirik.

"Father! Cecilia is innocent—" He greeted as though absently the preaching friar who stood by his father's side. "Ay, Father, there is so much I have to tell you—but this comes first—she is innocent!"

Olav stared at his son—slowly he turned crimson in the face.

"God be praised—thanks be to God—" His voice became unsteady. "Are you *sure*?—You are not to tell me this now if later I am to hear—for I cannot bear it a second time—"

"They have found the man who killed him, Father. It was Anki. The poor wretches were so frightened that they ran away with their children and all they possessed, hid themselves in the woods by Kaldbæk. But late in the evening of Sunday, Anki came down to Rynjul and asked Una to go with him to Gudrun. Poor child, she was already dead when Una came. Then she sent a message home, and Torgrim came over himself with the men who were to carry the bodies to the village. Then they found both the dagger and Jörund's brooch in the bog-hole under Gudrun. Arnketil denied nothing—seemed rather to be glad it had come out, says Torgrim—they were to know that his children were not left unavenged."

Olav swayed so strangely as he stood; a stifled rattling sound came from his lips, and they had turned blue—the whole face was blue. Then he fell, like a tree that is blown down.

Eirik threw himself down beside the strange monk, who was already loosening the clothes at the neck, raising the shoulders in his arms. His father's face was dark, the whites of the eyes showed yellow and bloodshot under the lids, the breathing was stertorous. Eirik could not read the look in the monk's face—despair or horror that he fought to repress—but it added to the son's fear.

"Is he dying—?"

"No," said the other hastily. "Help me to take hold, so we can carry him in."

PART TWO

The Son Avenger

I

𝔐 IDSUMMER was gone before Eirik was able to visit his home at the Ness.

Across the bogs the sunshine blazed on the shining leaves of the osiers, and the new blades of grass were agleam in the little tussocky meadows. The lake reflected the woods on the other side and the warm blue sky and the clouds, which were already turning to gold—it was the end of the day.

As he approached the gate of the paddock a scent of new-mown hay was wafted toward him. Eirik dismounted, but paused for a moment before opening the gate: the days of the evening sun were yellow as gold, and the cluster of little houses on the ness threw long shadows over the meadow, where Eldrid and old Ragnhild were spreading hay.

His wife had seen him; she put down her rake and came to meet him. She walked lightly and erect, barelegged in her working-clothes. Erik thought once more that he knew nothing finer than Eldrid's forehead above the great eye-sockets and the rounding of the cheek, though the face was brown as wood, the skin drawn tight over the bones, and she had deep furrows right across her brow, many wrinkles about the great eyes, and cracks in her rough lips.

Never had he felt so intensely that here was the home he would have chosen; he liked best to dwell in the forests. This was the last time he would come *home* to this place. But it was not that he thought with any regret of the destiny that was now bearing him away from here. At one time he had loved Hestviken so that it sent a tremor through mind and sense if he did but come near anything that belonged to his home. Now he loved Hestviken because the manor needed him, the old folk looked to him and expected him to take control as master; he was the brother who was to care for Cecilia and her children, and he was the son, bound to stay by the old man who lived on, stricken and swathed in his dumbness and mysterious calamity as in a cloak of darkness.

Man and wife gave each other their hands in greeting, but their manner was the same as if Eirik had ridden from home the day before. Eldrid asked how his sister fared now, and Eirik answered: well. And Olav? There was no change, said Eirik.

As soon as he saw that it would be long ere he himself could come home, Eirik had sent Svein Ragnason over to the Ness. The young man had told Eldrid all he knew of what had taken place at Hestviken in the spring, and it did not occur to Eirik to tell his wife any more or even to inquire how much she had heard.

He lay awake that night and felt how securely Eldrid slept in his arm. He was glad he should be at home for a while in their own house, before they had to move out to Hestviken and live in the same house as his father. He remembered full well that their life together had begun in a flame of passion, when they had rushed into each other's arms as though each would devour and suck the other dry. A change had come over them by degrees, and now they lived together as if the hunger and thirst of both were appeased. Eldrid was the first human being he had known with whom he felt so safe that he could hold his peace. It had been so from the very first days, before they were married—nay, from the days when he was a new-comer here and never had a thought that she was to be his. Not even then had he been tempted to talk wildly and at random or to assert himself noisily when he was in Eldrid's company.

These were not new thoughts—he simply felt that with her he had enjoyed silence, calm like that of the forest, and freedom. The bond that bound him to her was the first to which he had submitted without feeling the strain.

He had seen Gunhild again at church, one day in spring. Ay, surely, she was fair—like a bell-cow with her jingling jewels, honest and capable she looked. But they had not been suited to each other after all. He was thankful to have got a wife of whom he would not tire.

He did not reflect upon what Eldrid might have found in him. He saw her calm demeanour, watched her sleeping securely by his side, and that was enough for him.

He and Svein mowed the grass on the marshes during the next few days; at evening he rowed out with Eldrid and set the nets. During the midday rest he lay on the green by the wall of the house, and most of the household did the same. Eirik listened to the two old folk and chatted with them. Holgeir seemed well pleased that he and Eldrid were leaving the place. When Svein married and came hither, Holgeir would be more of a man at the Ness, being the mistress's kinsman. Eldrid wished to take Ragnhild with her; the woman was in two minds about it: now she would go with her mistress, now she would not. Young Svein slept with his cap over his eyes. Eldrid sat a little apart, mending a garment or spinning.

Eirik said to her one day when they were alone: " 'Tis no easy lot I have in store for you at Hestviken, Eldrid. There you will find much that is not well."

But he said nothing of what the difficulties were. It was long since Eirik had thought of speaking to anyone of the difficulties that might await him. Perhaps he had never done so, but formerly he had tried to deaden his own feelings with talk and with fussing about other things. Now he had taught himself the calmness with which one must go to work if one would unravel a knot.

It was terrible to see his father in such a state, but he dared not show that he felt it—dared not even show him special care or affection: in the man's present plight this would only add to his torment.

Olav had been almost entirely paralysed in one side when he came to himself. Little by little he recovered sufficiently to be able to walk, but he was bent quite over on the left side; he could just move his arm, but could not control it, and the scarred and ravaged face was now quite distorted and awry. When he tried to speak, it was almost impossible to catch a word; his lips only gave out a babbling. But now he no longer tried.

One day, about a month after Eirik had brought him home to Hestviken, he made signs that he wished to be shaved of the ragged white beard that had grown over his face. Apart from that, Eirik saw how it hurt Olav to be obliged to accept help; he was always making impotent attempts to do without it. But he made an ugly mess of his beard when eating—that was the reason.

As far as Eirik could tell, his father's understanding was not darkened. Perhaps it would have been easier if it had been.

When Olav lay sick at Oslo, Father Finn Arnvidsson had said he would give him extreme unction and the viaticum if his life were in danger—he had proved his will to confess his hidden sin.

But if he was destined to recover and live on for a time with the seal of this secret doom upon his lips, then let no man venture to think there are limits to God's mercy or that he can fathom God's mysterious counsel. As a king receives his faithless liegeman back into his friendship, but bids him dwell awhile without the court until he be sent for—so must Olav await with manly patience a sign from our Lord.

Eirik had lodged with his own brethren during the last days at Oslo. There he made his confession to Brother Stefan and took counsel with him. And next morning, when he went forward and received *corpus Domini*, he prayed:

"O God, Thou who art King of kings and eternal Love. No king of this world, be he never so hard, refuses a son who would ransom his father; rather will he take the son as his father's hostage. Lord, look not upon my sins, but look upon Thy Son's sacred wounds and have compassion upon my poverty, that my offer may find favour in Thy sight, so that I may do such penance in his stead as my father should have done."

Brother Stefan said that he too must wait for a sign.

One of the greatest difficulties was that Cecilia could scarcely bear to look at her father—and Eirik guessed that affection had little part in the horror she felt for him.

None could fail to see that Cecilia had rallied and grown younger again since her husband was no more. She had grown so fair in these three months of widowhood—it was as though she had been stifled in a dungeon and were now set free. What she had said when her father would force her to lay her hand on the corpse was not true. And well it was not, thought Eirik; it would have been dreadful had it been so with her, after the ugly death that came upon Jörund.

She was a faithful mother to her two little sons. The second boy, Torgils, was still at Rynjul, where the old people would not let him go. Kolbein was now six and Audun three winters old. They were handsome and healthy children, obeyed their mother like lambs and held her in high honour; but among the folk of the manor they were full of sport and high spirits, and when they came to know their uncle, they followed at his heels wherever he went. They were not at all afraid of their grandfather, Eirik saw—they scarcely noticed him.

Early in the autumn Eirik came again to the Ness, and this time it was to bring his wife home to Hestviken.

There was a diversity of opinions among folk when Eldrid Bersesdatter came back to the country where she had lived in her youth and took her place as mistress of one of the greatest manors. But for the most part they thought it was well. True, she had done much that was ill, but that was very long ago; it was right that she should be taken out of the humble cot in which she had lived for fifteen years and restored to such condition as became her birth. Her kinswomen, the daughters of Arne and their families, received her, Una and Torgrim cordially, Baard and Signe more coolly, but in very seemly fashion.

She was still a handsome woman and carried herself so well when she mixed among folk that those who were old enough to recall Eldrid's beauty at the time she was given to old Harald Jonsson revived the memory of that marriage. And many there were who could tell tales of her evil courses when she was mistress of Borg and later at Sigurdstad in a different way. Now she was an elderly woman, nearing the half-hundred. But she and Eirik were not so ill matched a pair to look at, for all that.

He was so big and bony that he began early to look more than his age. Tall and broad-shouldered, he stooped a little with his bulky chest and long, powerful limbs, and his back was rounded by hard work. His thin and narrow face, with its indented nose and prominent jaw, was brown, tanned, and furrowed; though no one would have called him ugly, it was not easy to see that he had once passed for a comely youth. Only the great light-brown eyes were unusually handsome; but his dark and curly hair was strongly marked with grey.

With the passing of years Eirik Olavsson had grown very like his father, folk said—not so much in outward appearance; the tall, dark, rather loose-limbed man had indeed remarkably little in common with the father, who had been so fair-complexioned, shapely, and well-knit. But folk could clearly recognize the father's nature in the son.

Like him, Eirik was taciturn; they were all so in that family. As Olav in his time could stand quite motionless by the hour together on the lookout rock or leaning over the fence of a cornfield, so the son now stood gazing in the same places. But he was a much more capable master of Hestviken than Olav had been. Not that the father's management had been other than careful and wise; the family estate had not shrunk in his time. But with the son everything went with more life and spirit, and success attended him. The manor of Saltviken, which had been left untenanted in Olav Half-priest's time, had been reclaimed, and he had helped the young folk whom he had established at Rundmyr to clear the land around.

He had brought Liv and her remaining children south to a house in Saltviken. It was indeed a better abode than the woman was used to; nevertheless she was loath to leave her cot. But Eirik said it was better that Anki's children should live farther from Hestviken when Jörund's sons grew up.

Anki had seized a chance of escaping from the men who were to carry him bound to the Warden. In the first two years rumours were heard from time to time that the murderer had appeared, now here, now there, on the outskirts of the parish and in the neighboring country; he must have a haunt somewhere in the forests. And when Liv had a child a year and a half after the disappearance of her husband, she gave out that he was the father— he had looked in at home a few times.

In the third spring after Jörund's death three men of the parish were taking a short cut through the woods on the way to Gardar. Close to the Black Tarn they found in a scree the remains of a corpse, badly mangled by beasts. But one leg in a boot had been caught fast among some stones. The men then searched the forest around, seeking for traces of the dead man's hiding-place, for they guessed him to be a robber. And, sure enough, they found a little way up the hill a kind of hut built on a ledge of rock. It looked as if the man had not been so badly off there; the couch was well covered with clothes and a great food-box stood there, still half full of food.

Now, there was one of the men who thought he had seen that box before—the low, flat carving of interlacing vines looked like the work of Eirik Olavsson of Hestviken, and there were runes cut on the pin that held the lid in place. One of the men was scholar enough to make out what was written: it was "*Eirekr*." Then it occurred to them that they had seen Eirik of Hestviken wearing boots that were patched in just the same way as the one the corpse had on.

They got Arnketil's remains up to the village, and the murderer was laid in earth just outside the churchyard wall. Then they carried what they had found to Hestviken and told Eirik the news: "The thrall was true to his nature, a thief to the last."

"Anki did not steal these things," said Eirik. He fixed his great, clear eyes on the peasant who had spoken. "Thrall or thief, he avenged son and daughter in such way as he was able. And it is for God to judge how great was his sin."

No one sought to find out more. If Eirik Olavsson had secretly helped the slayer of his brother-in-law, that must be his affair. The Hestvik men had always shielded their dependants—even when they were in the wrong. It came out afterwards that he had caused masses to be said for Anki—ay, the dead man might well need that.

They had always been good Christians there and open-handed with alms. Olav had been generous while he was master, and Eirik was the same. But Olav always seemed to listen to the woes of poor folk with but half an ear and in helping them looked as if he were thinking hard of something else. Eirik said loans must be given with a laugh, and gifts with a joyful countenance. Though he was not much more of a talker than his father, one could see that he listened to what folk said; there was nothing oppressive in his silence. In every way he was more friendly than the old man had been.

The day after these men had been with him Eirik rowed south to Saltviken; he wished to give Liv the news himself.

Before setting out for home he went up to the manor to find Cecilia. He knew that she had not yet held her churching, and she still kept to the same upper chamber where she had sat with her father on the night when she had fetched him home from the Ness.

The spring sun shone in through the three small bayed loop-holes and fell straight upon the woman's coifed head; she sat on a low chest, bent over the sucking child. When her brother came in at the door, she looked up and smiled in greeting. But her eyes went back at once to the new-born boy at her breast—she looked young and thoughtful and happy. Her face had grown rounder, but her eyes were clear and her lips had recovered their bright-red hue.

She listened calmly to her brother's account of Arnketil's death.

"Ay, that was bound to be the end," she said sorrowfully, "since he never *would* follow your advice and take himself away from here."

Then she asked after Kolbein and Audun and Eldrid, also after her father. But all the time she was looking down at the child who now lay full-fed and asleep in her lap. Eirik was strangely moved to see this mild and blissful animal-look in the young mother's eyes; she had never been like this when she sat with her other children.

She was fond of them. She had made clothes for them and sent them across during the winter, with a message that when she was over her childbed they might come and visit their mother. But he guessed it was something new with this little Gunnar. Him she had borne under a cheerful heart.

Una came in with ale and food for the guest. She had grown older and more portly, but was as cheerful and active as ever. She went over to Cecilia, had to look at the child—it half opened its eyes, and at once the two women were delightedly busy over the little thing.

Una took the boy in her arms and brought him over; Eirik must take a good look at him. She unswathed the back of the little head: was it not finely shaped?

"Ay, 'tis a goodly child," said Eirik. "But he has red hair," he laughed teasingly.

Cecilia looked up, her cheeks flushed deeply, and her brother saw she was on the point of flying into a rage. But then she laughed too. "Certainly he has red hair. 'Tis as I say—my Gunnar has every fine thing you can think of." She came over and took back the child.

Eirik said he could not wait till Aslak came home: "but give him my greeting!"

Cecilia Olavsdatter had not been a widow more than a year when a suitor announced himself; it was Ragnvald Jonsson, the friend of Olav's youth. He had been out and tried his fortune at Hestviken before, when the two young maids were there; first it was Bothild Asgersdatter he would have, and then Cecilia. Nothing came of it; then he took a wife who brought him an estate at the head of the fiord, and there he dwelt now, a widower with two little daughters.

Cecilia was not unwilling—she had known Ragnvald from childhood, and he was upright, kind, and a fine man to look at—even if there were many wiser than he. And Eirik could see no cause to refuse him if Cecilia herself desired this marriage.

He guessed it was a little hard for his sister to have to share her authority with Eldrid. The two women liked each other; they associated without friction. But the fact was that Cecilia had held sway as mistress of her father's manor for the greater part of her grown-up life, and now Eldrid had to take precedence of her; she was so much older, and she was his wife. But he doubted not that Cecilia longed above all to escape from the proximity of her father.

When Eirik laid Ragnvald's suit before Olav and gave his own opinion, his father nodded assent. So he and Ragnvald came to terms. The betrothal ale was to take place during the summer.

At Botolph's mass [1] Cecilia herself went into Oslo to make purchases for the feast. But on the evening of her return Eirik saw, as soon as his sister stood up in the boat, that something had happened. "What is it?" he asked as he helped her onto the quay.

"That I will tell you later."

Change after change came over Cecilia's face, usually so unruffled—she seemed to be listening, with a youthful, faraway look in her eyes; then her features contracted in mournful brooding.

Eirik was about to see his father to his bed; Eldrid was already bending down to loose her shoestring when Cecilia came in upon them.

"Stay awhile, Father—there is a matter I would fain have disposed of this evening, so I beg you will listen to me now. Nay, do not go, Eldrid—I wish you to hear it too. It is that I cannot marry Ragnvald."

"You cannot!" Eirik turned round to his sister. "He has our word already, Cecilia!"

"I know it, but he must release us." She looked at her father, and he looked at her with his one ice-blue, bloodshot eye; the other was half closed by the palsied lid.

[1] June 17.

"You remember Aslak Gunnarsson, Father; Jon Toresson he called himself the winter he was with us. I met him in the town; he had heard that I was now a widow, and he was on his way hither. He has not married. And now I have promised myself to him."

Eirik saw that his father was attacked by the spasms which sometimes occurred in the dead side of his face and the palsied arm.

"You have promised yourself to two men—" He checked himself and said quietly: "It is far too late to speak of this tonight. Wait till tomorrow."

"There is no need of much speaking. 'Tis true that I have promised myself to two men. But only one can have me. And that will be Aslak."

"But Father and I have given our word to *one* man. We did so with your consent. And we will not break our word."

"*Once* I have been married on the advice of you two." The green flash that came into her eyes seemed no more than a reflection, but it reminded Eirik of the time when he had believed his sister capable of killing her husband. "I shall never give Ragnvald my troth. And if you will not betroth me to Aslak, I shall go northward with him in spite of you."

"You must not say such things, Cecilia—you have three sons."

"Ay, I have thought of that. But they must stay with you— they are your heirs. What say you, Eldrid?" She turned to her brother's wife.

"I say that no good can come of breaking one's word. But 'tis not good either to marry against one's will. You ought to wait awhile—"

"Aslak and I have waited long enough. What say you, Father? Think you not we have waited long enough now?"

Olav nodded.

"Father!" exclaimed Eirik. "Do I understand you rightly—do you wish us to withdraw from the bargain with Ragnvald?"

Olav laid his sound hand heavily on his son's arm and nodded again.

"Ah, if that is the way of it, then— You are the master, Father."

Not much more was said of the matter. Eirik had to ride to Ragnvald and tell him of the turn it had taken. At first Ragnvald was very wroth, but before long he said it was all one about the marriage. "If Cecilia has made up her mind to a thing, I am loath to be the one who should try to force her away from her purpose."

So it was not Ragnvald who came out to Hestviken at St. Olav's vigil,[2] but Aslak Gunnarsson. As the guest dismounted and came toward him, Eirik saw that Aslak halted a little. The brother felt a slight shock, of aversion, or he knew not what.

They were betrothed in the course of the autumn, and the wedding was held at Hestviken in the following spring; by that time Jörund had been dead two years. Aslak had no home of his own, but lodged with his brothers at Yttre Dal. He bought up horses from the districts where the farmers carried on the breeding of foals, sold them in Oslo and along the border; he was now a man of substance and owned shares in many farms in the Upplands, but liked none of them so well that he would live there. So it was arranged that he and Cecilia should live at Hestviken.

Eirik and Aslak lived together in amity and concord. The new brother-in-law was prudent and upright, an active and companionable man—Eirik saw that. But it could never grow into any warm friendship between the two men, they both knew that. And when Aslak and Cecilia had been married over half a year, Aslak came and said he thought they might as well move to Saltviken —for in any case he or Eirik must constantly be there to see to the work of the farm, and here at Hestviken they were already so many, and now that Cecilia was with child—

Eirik guessed that the two would be glad to enjoy their happiness in a place where they would not be reminded of all the past mischances, and where Cecilia could be mistress in her own house and need not have her father before her eyes. So he and Aslak were soon agreed.

Eirik thought of all this as he came down from the upper chamber and remembered his sister's face as she sat bending over the child she had had by Aslak. And he remembered the day in late autumn when they moved out hither; he had sailed them round himself. It was raining heavily, and the road between the fences was under water in places; Aslak lifted up his wife and carried her right up to the manor, though her feet were already as wet as they could be and the man was lame—though not so badly. And he remem-

[2] July 28.

bered the blaze of anger in Cecilia's eyes when he once happened
to mention Aslak's defect: "He got it fighting one against five; at
last a man threw him from behind so that he broke his leg."

He did not believe there had been a shadow of truth in Jörund's
talk. It was not like her—nor like Aslak either. With this man his
sister was in good hands, and the manor was in good hands. He
would have liked to go up to the stream and look at the mill Aslak
was building—he was tired of carrying his corn round to Hestviken by boat, he said. But he felt he never had any desire to seek
out his brother-in-law, though they were always good friends
when they met. He liked Aslak and thought well of him, but
there was no help for it.

He had said to Eldrid one day: "I know not what it is, but when
I am in company with Aslak it always comes over me that the
man finds life irksome."

"That is likely enough," said his wife with a kind of smile. "But
I do not believe he finds it so irksome as you do."

Eirik looked at her in surprise: "No! You are right there," he
replied with a laugh.

He went over to the cherry orchard and looked at it. The first
cuttings he had planted were now trees with trunks as thick as a
child's arm, and glossy bark; ground shoots had come up all about
them. The little plantation was full of yellow buds ready to burst.
In time there would be a whole grove here as in the convent
garden.

He rowed homeward in the course of the afternoon. On the
shore, before one rounds the point of the lookout crag, there is
a little strip of sandy beach below the rust-red rocks. Eirik saw
that his father stood there with his little bow; he was struggling
with it once more, trying if he could train himself to use his half-
palsied arm and hand. It hurt Eirik anew whenever he saw that
Olav *could* not give up—again and again he attempted to conquer
his disability.

He lived in continual anxiety for his father when the stricken
old man was wandering out alone. Far away over the high ground
to the south he dragged himself; the housefolk had seen him sitting there looking down into Saltviken. But when Eirik asked if
he should sail him out thither one day so that he could have a
sight of the manor, Olav shook his head. Round the whole bay he

walked, up Kverndal or along the ridge of the Bull. He might easily fall over the edge or have another stroke, lie there and perish. But Eirik dared not send anyone after him to keep an eye on the old man—he had seen that nothing would distress his father more. And he must be left to go his way—he could not possibly endure to sit ever indoors or drag his crippled body about among the houses of the manor.

Not a day passed but Eirik renewed his prayer to be allowed to bear the penance in his father's stead. And each time he felt it with a deeper thrill—disablement, helplessness, inactivity—it made him afraid. For he knew a man cannot feel it otherwise than as a humiliation—a more bitter shame than being a bastard. Never before had he seen so clearly that of all vainglory the sweetest is that which springs from pride in one's bodily strength and perfect health.

But none other than Eldrid guessed that he laid upon himself penitential exercises; he had to use such measure that none might observe any change in him in his daily work. Then his wife said to him one day:

"Now all is otherwise than when we first met, Eirik. Then we were driven on by such desires as are kindled by hate and anger and scorn. I will speak no more of it now, but you must know that I am willing, whenever you wish that our life together shall come to an end."

"You must consider well, Eldrid," said her husband quietly. "What you have in mind would be a good issue, but not unless we are both agreed on it."

2

ANOTHER winter went by, and then came the spring—early that year. As soon as the ground began to be clear of snow, Olav's unrest came upon him again; he wandered abroad early and late, though he no longer went so far as before. From the manor they constantly saw the dark, bent, and crooked figure moving slowly against the sky on the sun-baked rocks by the shore or under the brow of the wood beyond the fields. He often went to the river-mouth, where the Kverndal stream falls into the bay. A little way from the beach there was a stretch of dry sward below an over-hanging crag—Eirik had haunted the place, digging for Lapps' arrows, when he was a boy. There they often found Olav sitting.

It had become the custom for Eldrid to go out and fetch him home to meals. From her first coming to Hestviken Olav had met his son's wife with a lingering shadow of the quiet and charming courtesy that had become him so well in his younger years—whenever he was willing or remembered to show it. Eldrid had slipped into the life of the manor much more easily than, for instance, Aslak, and Eirik guessed that Olav liked his wife. By degrees it had come about that Olav seemed less worried at accepting help from the mistress of the house than from anyone else.

Olav was taking his usual walk across the fields one fine morning. Along the high balks the pale grass of the year before lay crushed, but the bright new blades had come up so well in the last few days that soon they would cover the old. Every time Olav had to stand still for a moment, he stared at it, unseeing—the dark spines of withered meadowsweet and angelica were surrounded at the roots with thick wreaths of new crisped leaves. He leaned heavily on the spear that he used as a staff. He had grown used to the pains in his legs, till he felt them without a thought; his sound leg ached in the joints and was always tender and tired, but the half-dead one was full of a dull pricking and shooting.

The trees at the edge of the wood were breaking into leaf, but some of them were already quite green. Every year it was the same trees that came out first—earliest of all hereabout was the young wild cherry that grew at the foot of Hvitserk's mound up in the great field. Today he noticed all at once that it had grown into an old and ample tree, spreading wide its summer foliage.

Birds winged their way among the thickets; their piping and chirping came from the wood. Some osiers down by the river were yellow as gold with blossom, and their scent hung in the air, mild and over-sweet.

Olav crossed the bridge, struggled up the hill to his seat under the rock. Then he heard that at the bottom of the slope a band of children were bathing in the sea. He dragged himself farther, stood behind a clump of bursting alders, and looked down at the youngsters.

The same stretch of dry sward ran here between small rocks up to the wood on the flank of the Bull. Here the bay was shallow, with a bottom of fine light clay, so that the water had a milky look about the naked bodies of the children who splashed and played in it. Kolbein was one of them—he knew his grandson's straw-coloured mop of hair. The boy was now ten, so thin that the bones of his chest showed plainly, and his joints were knotted like growing glades of grass. The others were the children of the new foreman who had succeeded old Tore, and some no doubt belonged to the new folk Eirik had taken in at Rundmyr.

Kolbein was swimming a race with another boy—blowing and kicking far too much, thought the old man. Right up on the edge of dry seaweed toddled a little one—it was the foreman's youngest, a boy, he saw, the little tot that grubbed about in the courtyard at home every day. Now and then he gave an angry yell, for the rocks pricked his feet, but no one turned round to look at him, and so he managed to get along by himself. His sister, who must have been in charge of the little ones, sat on a big rock far out in the water, and before her a tall, handsome boy stood in the water up to his middle. Those two were older than the rest, perhaps twelve or thirteen. The girl took the mussels that the boy opened and handed to her—she was white and fair, her bosom slightly rounded already; her dark hair dangled down her back.

All at once it seemed it could not be half a hundred years since they had been the two biggest of the band of children who played about the tarn in the forest to the north of Frettastein. It was more like a dream he had dreamed, and not so long ago.

The fat little boy had come right up to the grassy slope. Solemnly straddling, with stomach thrust out, he came along—and at that instant Olav descried, just in front of where he stood and right in the child's path, a great adder sunning itself on some stones. He went forword—instinctively he walked more steadily as he hurried to where the snake lay. But as he was about to thrust at it with his spear, it raised its head, hissed, and struck at the flashing steel—then glided in under the stones.

The little child had set up a howl. When Olav looked back, the children stood at the edge of the water staring, while the big sister dashed toward them, splashing the water all about her.

Awhile after, as he lay beneath the crag, the children came walking past along the path hidden by the bushes; they were on the way home. The big sister was leading the little boy by the hand, hauling him after her, as she chatted to her friend:

"Nay, afraid of him we are not. Mother says we have but to make the sign of the cross when we see him, then he cannot harm us. But an ugly sight he is, Olav the bad. He has been like that since he stood before the church door in Oslo to take his oath upon the book—a false oath it was, and then he was *struck* so. His left hand is *black!*"

Instinctively Olav looked at his palsied hand—black it was not, nor does one make an oath with the left hand. It was surely nothing but child's talk. Although—could children have made up that about the oath, and the name—Olav the bad?

The sign, the sign that he waited for—he watched for it everywhere, in odd or even. In the games of a band of children and the words of a little girl—

In the evening he saw the child again; she was walking with her mother and one of the serving-women toward the break of the woods, and they carried pails and pans, were going to the summer byre. No, there was nothing in her now that recalled Ingunn. He had never noticed before what they called her—Reidun, said her mother.

When Reidun found that he was looking at her, she seemed confused and furtively crossed herself.

Olav had slept but a short space, he thought, when he was awakened by the sharp pain under his ribs—but tonight it was worse than ever before, and he was cold too; an icy chill had lodged between his shoulder-blades, and when he breathed, it seemed to run over, making the cold sweat trickle down his body —his hands and feet were as cold as clammy stones.

He must have lain too long on the grass today, he decided, old wreck that he was.

Then came a sudden wave of heat—hotter and hotter till his head and body were aglow, but his limbs were still as cold as lead. The heat seemed to stream from the great lump of pain that lay embedded in his body at the edge of the chest; it was as though he had a red-hot stone there, and the stinging pains that shot out from it, up into his lungs and through his entrails, filled his whole frame with torment. A ceaseless flight of sparks went on within him; now the rain of sparks reached his head and flew around within his skull; the skin outside was all acreep; now he *saw* the sparks, they swarmed in the darkness, which turned round and round, and the couch beneath him turned, but the ball of pain under his chest was in a ferment, so that he trembled with the effort not to groan aloud, and the sweat ran off him in streams. Till the qualms forced their way upward, dilated chest and throat, filled his mouth with blood and loathsomeness, and then the surge of rusty blood burst the dam of his clenched teeth.

It gave relief as soon as the vomiting was over. He lay relaxed, feeling the pains ebbing back to their source, and now it hurt him in a clean and honest way, like a wound. He was now shivering with cold too, between the sweat-drenched bedclothes, but that did him good. If only he had been able to wipe away the blood that he lay in—it smelt so foully.

Then all at once he was on a path that led through a gap with screes on both sides and spruce firs growing in the crevices. Beyond the gap he saw water far below; it was grey weather, the land on the other side was shrouded in mist—and he knew the place again; he was at home on the shore of Lake Mjösen, and as he walked he seemed to see himself, at sixteen, clear and distinct as a raw lad in the coolness of his youthful health.

Now he saw that Ingunn was walking a little in front of him —in her old red kirtle; her heavy light-brown plaits fell half-loosened down her slender back. He began to walk faster; she sauntered ahead without hurrying, but press on as he might, he did not gain on her—it was still just as far between them.

He carried a spear on his shoulder—it was one he had hafted for her, with a red shaft and a short point, but after he had given it her, he had always to carry it for her. It had grown so heavy—heavier and heavier it grew, till his shoulder ached and he was bent double—and Ingunn walked there before him, and he could not come up with her.

Then they came down to the shore, walked along a bay. There was a beach of fine white sand with a dark edge licked by the waves, and the waters of the lake were grey. He still saw Ingunn far away, and the spear he carried on his shoulder weighed him down, and in his chest he had a smarting wound from which the blood gushed out—he saw it run down upon the sand, which sucked it up with a thousand greedy little mouths.

Olav awoke in pitch-darkness, knew that he had cried out. He heard someone tumble out of bed in the room beyond and strike a light. Soon after, Eirik appeared in the doorway with a burning torch in his hand, naked in his cloak, with the flaps of it tied about his waist.

"Are you sick, Father?"

Eldrid appeared behind her husband. They threw the light on him.

"He has thrown up again." Eldrid found a rag, wiped him and the bed, while Eirik raised his body. He was heavy with sleep and went clumsily about it, so that Olav could not repress a low groan: the sparks of pain began to whirl within him again.

" 'Tis all blood and clotted gore."

"He has been in a sweat. Better lay more over him." Eldrid fetched a skin coverlet.

"Shall I carry you in, Father—to the other bed?"

Olav rolled his head in refusal—he lay powerless among the pillows.

"Then I must lie in here—it were unwise to leave him alone to-night," said Eirik to his wife.

Olav rolled his head again, raised his sound hand deprecatingly.

The two went back and lay down. Again Olav's pains receded to their centre fairly quickly; after he had lain motionless awhile, it was no longer so bad. If only they had thought to give him a drink of something— And it was hot with this coverlet—Olav pushed it onto the floor.

Otherwise he did not suffer so much now; only for the pain that was lodged under his ribs and seemed to swell over his chest with every breath he took. Presently he thought his body was like an old craft that lay half sunken on the beach, and every wave that lifted it loosened the planks more and more from the timbers, and his spirit was like a bird sitting on a floor-board awash within the rotten boat, and when the board came clear and floated off, the bird would fly away. But after a while the tide lapped him to sleep.

His thirst awoke him—he was not so much in pain now as feeling ill, and he himself was afflicted by the close, cold smell of age and death about him. He could not remember if he had dreamed or what, but he had come out of his sleep with a feeling that within the worn and tortured old body that now wrestled with Death, he himself was a young prisoner.

At the foot of the bed was a loop-hole in the wall, closed with a wooden shutter. Olav lay tormented by thirst and shortness of breath and thought he would get up and open it. Two or three times he raised himself slightly, but as soon as he moved he felt that the pains were making ready to rush upon him.

Then he did it in spite of them—one wrench and he was on his knees at the foot of the bed. Flung forward over the bedstead he lay waiting till the excruciating throes aroused by the sudden movement had raged their fill.

A fresh whirl of pain sparkled over him as he took hold of the pin of the shutter and pulled it toward him. It was stiff—Olav clenched his teeth, swallowed his cries, as the red-hot devils raged within him, but then he sank back against the horse's head of the bedpost with the pin in his hand; it seemed the hardest pull he had given in his life, and the tears poured down over his ravaged face as he breathed the morning air that blew in upon him. Outside it was light, a white morning, and the birds were awakening.

He swung himself out of bed and staggered to his clothes. In a way he was himself aware that he was only a mortally sick old man struggling with a hand and a half to hitch on some wraps in a dark room, and it hurt him so much when he moved that tears and sweat ran off him, and he ground his teeth lest he might howl aloud and wake them in the outer room. But at the same time he felt that within him was himself, engaged in breaking through a ring of foes, trying to ride them down—memories of all the fights in which he had borne arms loomed before him as presaging dreams—but now it was earnest, and he struggled furiously to force his quaking limbs into obedience.

Groping along the wall, he came out into the great room, found his way to the door of the anteroom, and opened it. From there he reached the outer door and accomplished that. Then he stood on the icy doorstone, barefoot in cloak and kirtle. The morning air blew into him and filled his aching chest; it hurt, but more than that, it did him good.

He looked up at the cliff that rose behind the roofs of the outhouses, with green grass and bushes clinging to its crevices, and every leaf was still and waiting; the fir forest above waited motionless against the white morning sky.

The fiord he could not see, but he heard it moving gently at the foot of the rocks, and the murmur of the wavelets over the shingle. He must see the water once more.

Supporting himself with his hand on the logs of the wall, he made his way along the line of houses and stood leaning against the corner of the last in the row. The path leading to the water-side wound lonely and deserted by the side of the "good acre's" brown carpet, which crept into the shelter of the lookout rock; the corn was sprouting thickly with green needles. Down below, where the path came to an end, the sheds leaned listening over the sea, which swirled with a faint splash about their piles.

Olav let go his hold of the corner of the men's house. Swaying, he walked on without support. A little way up the lookout rock he climbed, but then sank down and lay in a little hollow, where the dry, sun-scorched turf made him a bed.

The immense bright vault above him and the fiord far below and the woods of the shore began to warm as the day breathed forth its colours. Birds were awake in woods and groves. From where he lay he saw a bird sitting on a young spruce on the ridge, a black dot against the yellow dawn; he could see it swelling and contracting like the beats of a little heart; the clear flute-like notes welled out of it like a living source above all the little sleepy twitterings round about, but it was answered from the darkness of the wood. The troops of clouds up in the sky were flushing, and he began to grow impatient of his waiting.

He saw that all about him waited with him. The sea that splashed against the rocks, rowan and birch that had found foot-hold in the crevices and stood there with leaves still half curled up—now and again they quivered impatiently, but then they grew calm. The stone to which his face was turned waited, gazing at the light from sky and sea.

From the depths of his memory words floated up—the morning song that he had once known. All the trees of the forest shall re-joice before the face of the Lord, for He comes to judge the world with righteousness, the waves shall clap their hands.—He saw that now they were waiting, the trees that grew upon the rocks of his manor, all that sprouted and grew on the land of his fathers, the waves that followed one another into the bay—all were waiting to see judgment passed upon their faithless and un-profitable master. It was as though the earth were waiting every hour of the day, but it was in the quiver of dawn that the fair and defrauded earth breathed out so that one heard it—sorrowful and merciless as a deflowered maid it waited to be given justice against men, who went in, one by one, to be judged. Every hour and every moment judgment was given; it was the watchword that one day cried to another and one night whispered to the next. All else that God had created sang the hymn of praise—*Benedicite omnia opera domini Domino*—he too had known it when he was young. But those whom He had set to be captains and lords of the earth forsook God and fought with one another, betraying God and betraying their fellows.

The bird in the tree-top on the ridge still poured out its stream of notes—and he too had been given his life in fief, and authority had been his, the rich Christ had placed the standard in his hand and hung the sword over his shoulder and set the ring upon his hand.—And he had not defended the standard and had stained the sword with dishonour and forgotten what the ring should have called to mind—he must stand forth and could not declare one deed that he had performed from full and unbroken loyalty, nor could he point to one work that he could call well done.—Lord, rebuke me not in thine anger, neither condemn me in thy justice.

Above him he saw the whole vault of heaven full of white clouds, they stood thick as an immense flock of lambs, but they *were* folk. They were white and shone with a light that was within them and filled them as sunshine fills the clouds. Slowly gliding, they moved high above him, looking down on him—he recognized his mother and certain of the others too, Ingunn was there—

It was the sunrise, he knew that—but it was like a writing. Thus he had stared at the fine pattern of letters on smooth white vellum, until all at once he knew a word—that time when Arnvid tried to teach him to read writing.

Then the very rays from the source of light broke out and poured down over him. For an instant he stared with open eyes straight into the eye of the sun, tried even, wild with love and longing, to gaze yet deeper into God. He sank back in red fire, all about him was a living blaze, and he knew that now the prison tower that he had built around him was burning. But salved by the glance that surrounded him, he would walk out unharmed

over the glowing embers of his burned house, into the Vision
that is eternal bliss, and the fire that burned him was not so ardent
as his longing.

Eirik found his father lying in a swoon far up the hill when he
went out in the morning, alarmed at the old man's absence. He
carried him in and put him to bed.

Death could not be far away, he saw. Olav's hair was parted
in strands, his cheeks had fallen in, and he was white about the
nose, but he seemed free from pain. Eirik sent messages—for the
priest, for the old people at Rynjul, and to Saltviken. The messenger was to tell his sister that this time she *must* come—Cecilia
had not set foot in Hestviken since she moved out with Aslak a
year and a half ago, and whenever Eirik had asked her to come
and see her father she had excused herself.

They were gathered about him within the closet, his kinsfolk
and household, when Sira Magne entered in alb and stole and
recited:

"*Pax huic domui,*"
and the acolyte who bore the crucifix gave the response:
"*Et omnibus habitantibus in ea.*"

Kolbein and Torgils were allowed to hold the candles. They
stood looking intently at their grandfather, who was about to die.
The children had always known that there was something sombre
and mysterious about the old man who dragged himself around
on the outskirts of their life, crooked and shrunken and speechless, but at ordinary times they had not thought much about him.
Now they took no notice of the molten wax that ran down on
their fingers as they stared at him; in the soft light of the candles
the waves of smooth white hair showed brightly against the
brown pillows, Eldrid had combed him so finely. The grey face
with its scarred cheek, one eyelid half closed and the mouth
drawn awry, but clear and unmarred on the other side, was like
the head of one of the statues in the doorway of St. Mary's
Church, for that too was shattered on the left side.

Quivering with excitement, the boys watched to see if anything would happen, if any change would come over the old
man's ruined face when the priest absolved him of his sins in God's
name. Beside the standing figure of the priest knelt Uncle Eirik,
motionless as a statue; he kept his grizzled head bent, and in his

hands, which were hidden by a cloth of fine linen, he held the manor's best silver cup with six little tufts of snow-white wool. In a clear voice he said the responses together with the acolyte; the boys understood nothing of the prayers, but remembered to bow their heads whenever they heard the name of Jesus or *Gloria Patri*.

Then came the questions in Norse to the dying man, who had not been able to make any confession; at each act of repentance, faith, hope, and love the dying man smote his breast and made a bowing motion with his head. In his one living eye, which reflected the flame of the candle, the boys looked into a world of which they could form no idea, but the shattered half of the face was not made whole, as they had almost expected. Afterwards the priest and their uncle said the *Kyrie*, and Sira Magne read out of his book a long, long prayer and called their grandfather by name, Olavus, while Eirik lowered his head yet deeper, and behind them they were weeping, Una loudest of all.

Eirik's forehead nearly touched the floor as the acolyte said the *Confiteor*—they knew that, and then came the absolution, *misereatur* and *indulgentiam*.

They had never before seen a dying person anointed, and their eyes followed the priest's fingers as he took the tufts of wool one by one out of the cup in Eirik's hands, moistened with oil and smeared the sign of the cross over their grandfather's eyes and ears, nose and mouth, and the backs of his hands. Last of all Eirik, otherwise remaining motionless, raised with one hand the blanket from the dying man's feet; thus with the chrism of mercy were blotted out all the sins he had committed with sight and senses, with word and hand, and every step he had taken from the right way.

And now the children waited with a sore longing for it to be over, for they were tired of standing still and holding the candles, and Eirik's back and shoulders kept moving as though he wept, and his voice was husky as he said the responses.

In the afternoon they were out in the courtyard; they knew they must not play any game, for Sira Magne was to come back at evening and bring *corpus Domini* for their grandfather. But after a while they forgot themselves and made a good deal of noise—it was not so often that Kolbein and Audun saw their brother Torgils, and then they had to discuss with the foreman's children the wonderful thing they had seen that morning. Reidun had been in the closet with the rest, and she had seen that the black hand of Olav turned white when the priest anointed it, and Kolbein and Torgils agreed—they saw it turn lighter, at any rate.

Then they were sent for to the women's house; the old people from Rynjul were resting there, and their little red-haired brother, Gunnar, had learned to walk since the big children had last been at Saltviken. Audun remembered that this was the first time Gunnar had been here, so they took him out into the yard. Till Aslak came and told them to be quiet.

Eirik and Cecilia sat alone in the old house. The smoke-vent was open, and the evening sun shone down and gave colour to the thin column of smoke that rose from the last dying embers. Higher up, the trailing smoke began to curl and wave, then it spread out under the roof in a light cloud. The two sat watching the play of the smoke, and from outside came the sound of boys' shrill voices and little feet running on the rock.

Presently the son got up, went into the closet, and looked at the sick man.

"He is asleep now," he said as he came back. And after a moment: "When he wakes, you would speak with him alone awhile, I doubt not?"

"Speak with him is more than any can do now, Eirik."

"Say to him what you have on your mind—"

"We have already bidden him farewell, all of us. What more is there to say?"

"Cecilia," said Eirik, dropping his voice, "can you think that Father has not noticed it?—in all these four years you tried not to see him. If he came into the room where you were, you left it if you could.—Nay, I have not forgotten that he did you grave injury that time—"

"That I forgave him long ago," said Cecilia quickly. "'Tis not that. But can you not understand, brother—if it was gruesome for you and Eldrid to have him before you here neither alive nor dead, then it must have been worse yet for me, when you remember all that happened before his life came to such a close."

"Do you remember *I* raised the axe against him?—and God knows 'twas not my fault I did not kill my father. Judge, then, if it has been a light matter for me to see him in this state for four years—I who remember how he was of old—the noblest man I have set eyes on, the goodliest and the most generous."

"So you say now, Eirik. I remember naught else but enmity between you—in all the years since you were a little lad, until the day you turned your back on home and took a wife without asking his counsel. Never could you endure to live here with us; as often as you came home you went away again almost at once —and for that you blamed Father; you said he was the most un-reasonable of men. And in that I thought you were not so far wrong—unreasonable he often was with you, and hard to live with for all of us. But I tell you—I have forgiven him with all my heart, as a Christian woman should."

"It is well that you have forgiven him as a Christian woman should"—Eirik could not help smiling faintly—"but do you not think that is little enough between daughter and father?"

All at once Cecilia's eyes filled with tears. "I *have* been a good, obedient daughter, Eirik. None of you knew Jörund rightly. God rest his soul—but I have wondered many a time that I did not do what Father believed I had done. I think it was no sin in me that I was not minded to stay here and have him before my eyes as he haunted this place like a ghost of all the torment that was worse than being broken on the wheel—when at last it had been given me to share my lot with Aslak and I could say, I too, I am glad to be alive! Above all, since I do not believe Father has longed to see me more than I have longed for him!"

"That you cannot tell! 'Tis true that Father was harsh and silent at times—but judge him by his deeds, Cecilia. I warrant you never saw a man who acted more nobly and as becomes a Christian in all he did. The first to hold out two full hands to the poor, the first to open his door to widows and whosoever craved his protection—methinks your Aslak could bear witness to that: 'twas not so safe then, in the days of old King Haakon's power, to har-bour an outlawed manslayer. You have no right, you and he, to bear a grudge because Father did not give him you as well, as soon as the boy cried for you! Have you heard that Father ever won a penny of goods or a foot of land by dishonest dealing or oppression of an even Christian? Not the veriest scoundrel in the countryside has ever dared to utter a word that could stain Father's fame or honour. But if any, man or woman, were in such case that his name and fame were cast as carrion to the birds of prey—then, if Father could say nothing to silence evil tongues, he held his peace. An ill word fell ever to the ground if it came to Father's door—unless one of us others took it up and flew with it. Have you forgotten that Father was the first man to take up arms and rouse the yeomen to resistance when the Duke's army scoured the country, and the last to come home to a plundered manor, wounded and unrewarded by his King?

"God help me, Cecilia—I have no right to chide you; you have been a better daughter than I a son—I rendered him naught but disobedience and a fool's defiance. I had no more wisdom than to be vexed when I thought we were aggrieved by his silence and severity. Though not many times did he chastise me as I deserved —on you he can never have laid a correcting hand. I ought to have known better—"

Eirik raised his left hand a little, looked down at the stump of the little finger.

"I remember when Father had to cut it off. I was so small, I did not see that my life was in danger if it were not taken off at once. When I saw the red-hot iron I was so beside myself with fear that I ran hither and thither about the room, bellowing and kicking in my struggles, so Father had to seize me forcibly. Do you think he tried to soothe me with sweet words? He spoke harshly to me, did Father, but when that was of no use he took the red-hot iron and pressed it into his own flesh to put heart into me."

The son hid his face in his hands, uttering stifled sobs. But presently he looked up again:

"God forgive us both, sister mine—never did we recognize what a man our father was. But you will find it true, as you grow older: the best inheritance he leaves your sons is the memory of his good name—that is God's reward to the descendants of an upright man."

Cecilia sat with bent head; her cheeks had reddened and her expression was unusually mild.

"You are right, brother—Father was more of a man than we guessed. And yet," she whispered after a moment, "for half his lifetime he bore the guilt of an unshriven slaying—and when he would make amends for it at last, God took judgment into his own hand."

"We may not inquire into such things," replied Eirik in an

earnest whisper—"God's hidden counsels. But never will I believe it fell upon him because Father's sin was worse than most men's. Mayhap it was done to show forth an example—the rest of us take so little heed of our misdeeds. And God made choice of father to do full penance, since He knew his heart—stronger and more faithful than we poor wretches who would not be able to swallow one drop of His justice."

Cecilia said in a low tone: "Aslak has heard something—at home in the Hamar country. There was some talk about Mother, that time she was young, about a clerk or a pupil in the school. He disappeared, and some thought that Father might have had a finger in it—"

"Are you not ashamed?" whispered Eirik indignantly. "Do you and Aslak pay heed to folks' gossip about your parents—?"

"You yourself have said he was hard on her."

"I was only a child when she died—what I thought of the things I saw counts for nothing. Perhaps that was what weighed most heavily on him—to endure his marriage with patience. They were so unlike, and she was ailing from her youth. God must judge between the two. Without sin no man goes through life."

Eirik rose, took a few paces toward the door of the closet, and came back to his sister. "It may be as well that I tell you now— I had meant to announce it to you and Aslak at the funeral ale. When Father is committed to the earth, I shall go back to the convent. So that all he leaves behind him will be yours—except that which Eldrid and I will give for the repose of his soul."

Cecilia was silent a long while.

"Is Eldrid at one with you in this?" she asked at last, a little incredulously.

"Yes. She goes to Gimsöy. Whether she will take the veil I know not—she knows not yet herself. But she will take the vow of chastity and dwell there."

"Is it for Father's soul you do this?" asked his sister again.

"Ay, and for my own." And for Jörund. And for you and your children. For all of us who are rebellious and defiant, when God lays a heavy burden upon us, and who forget Him wholly or in part when He showers His bounties upon us.—This he left unsaid.

"Have you told him this?"

"No. Father was never a man to care much for words and promises. Time enough for him to see it after he is dead."

A moment later Cecilia started up—they heard Gunnar scream-
ing outside in the courtyard. His mother hurried out. Eirik went
into the closet to the sick man. In the dim light he saw that Olav
lay with one eye open—he was hot and his breath was laboured,
but Eirik guessed that he was conscious—and wondered whether
the old man had heard anything; he looked at him so strangely—

Olav had lain awake and had heard sentence passed on his own
life by the mouth of his son. Meanwhile an image hovered before
his vision—it was the frenzy of fever, but not so violent that he
did not know it for what it was. He saw a cornfield, overgrown
with tares and thistles, willow-herb and brambles—the weeds
flaunted their red and yellow flowers in the sun, and the corn was
so choked by them that none could tell that the ground had been
sown. But out in the field there walked *one*—sometimes he thought
it was his guardian angel, but sometimes it was Eirik—a friend
who did not ask whether the dying man had done him wrong, but
thought only of gathering up the poor ears of corn that he could
save among the thistles. It should not have been so, his life should
have been like a cornfield swaying clean and bright and ready for
the sickle. But one there was who had been able to find a handful
of good corn and would lay it in the balance—

Kolbein came to the door and eagerly announced that now they
could see Sira Magne's roan horse down by the bridge. Eirik
lighted the candles, gave one to the boy, and they went out.

The crag that rose behind the line of outhouses seemed to stand
out vaster and more immovable now that it was bathed in the
late yellow sunlight. The firs shone with their hard red trunks
and branches washed light after the winter's snow, and above was
the burning blue vault of heaven. Eirik thought that never before
had he seen so plainly how infinitely deep was the ocean of sky,
and against this depth the firm rock was more rock and the firs
were more intensely firs than he had ever guessed before. The
wakeful Eye that watched over all rested upon every single one
of the midges that danced before him in the air and knew every
pulse-beat in his body. And in the likeness of the bread He came,
borne by the priest on the great horse that was now mounting the
hill by the barn, to give Himself as food for His own.

The groom who led the horse rang the little silver bell; the
house-folk had come out and were kneeling in the yard. Cecilia
had her little son in her arms, Aslak and the boys by her side.

Kolbein and Eirik knelt before the door of the house with their candles, whose flames were almost invisible in the sunshine. Eirik knew that the fire that now consumed him was destined to die down, to hide beneath the ashes, to blaze up again in bright flames, but never would it be quenched within him.

At the funeral feast for Olav Audunsson, Eirik announced his and his wife's determination, and at midsummer he and Eldrid had made division of their estate. He accompanied her to Gimsöy, and thence he went straight to Oslo and resumed the habit of the order in the Minorite convent. The ceremony was a quiet one this time, on a weekday morning during one of the first masses. No others of his family were in church than Aslak Gunnarsson and Cecilia. This time his sister seemed less opposed to her brother's turning monk.

Aslak and his wife husbanded the Hestvik estate so well that all Olav's grandchildren were abundantly provided for—Cecilia had three sons and three daughters by her second husband. Of Jörund's sons, Kolbein and Audun turned out well; Torgils was a wild lad, but he was drowned at an early age.

Eirik always impressed it upon the youths, when they visited him at the convent, that their worldly prosperity was a reward for their grandfather's pious and manly life, and he could quote many sayings from Scripture to this effect. The boys were fond of him and had great respect for him; they had never known him except as a barefoot friar. And he was a pious friar, diligent in tending the sick, whether in body or soul; book-learning he also acquired with years, and he was the convent's gardener most of his time. But his nephews knew from what they heard among the neighbours that in his youth Eirik had a name for being somewhat wild. Cecilia never spoke to her children of her brother's former life.

Olav's fame among men was not so lustrous as Eirik would fain have made it—all the young folk knew that well. A bold warrior he had been and a good, honest franklin, but odd and unsociable, a joyless companion in a joyful gathering.

The great pestilence came and made riddance in the family, but it was still numerous after the sickness had passed. Its ravages were not so severe in the south as in the north country. In the Minorite convent of Oslo not much more than the half of the brethren died, but in the house of the order at Nidaros only two monks were left. It was therefore decided that Brother Eirik Olavsson and three young friars from Oslo should be transferred thither. Eirik was then threescore years old, strong and hale, though he had always treated himself with great rigour. But the friars were exposed to violent storms in crossing the mountains, and a few days after he had arrived at his new convent Eirik expired in the arms of his brethren.

KRISTIN LAVRANSDATTER
Sigrid Undset's masterful trilogy

"No other novelist has bodied forth the medieval world with such richness and fullness."   —*New York Herald Tribune*

The acknowledged masterpiece of the Nobel Prize–winning Norwegian novelist Sigrid Undset, *Kristin Lavransdatter* has never been out of print in this country since its first publication in 1927. Its narrative of a woman's life in fourteenth-century Norway has kept its hold on generations of readers, and the heroine, Kristin—beautiful, strong-willed, and passionate—stands with the world's great literary figures of our time.

THE BRIDAL WREATH

The first volume of this masterwork describes young Kristin's stormy romance with Erlend Nikulaussön, a young man perhaps overly fond of women, of whom her father strongly disapproves.

FICTION/0-394-75299-6

THE MISTRESS OF HUSABY

Volume II tells of Kristin's troubled and eventful married life on the great estate of Husaby, to which her husband has taken her.

FICTION/0-394-75293-7

THE CROSS

The final volume shows Kristin still indomitable, reconstructing her world after the devastation of the Black Death and the loss of almost everything that she has loved.

FICTION/0-394-75291-0

Available at your local bookstore, or call toll-free to order:
1-800-793-2665 (credit cards only).

THE MASTER OF HESTVIKEN

Sigrid Undset's
ACCLAIMED EPIC

"Powerful, intense, and memorable . . . a triumph! . . . [Undset] combines a supreme identification with the manners, the morals, the feelings of a particular age and [with] an understanding of fundamental human character."
— *The New York Times*

THE AXE

Set in medieval Norway, a land torn by pagan codes of vengeance and the rigors of Christian piety, the first volume in this epic tetralogy introduces us to Olav Audunnson and Ingunn Steinfinnsdatter, whose youthful passion triggers a chain of murder, exile, and disgrace.

Fiction/Literature/0-679-75273-0

THE SNAKE PIT

After years of bitter separation, Olav Audunnson and Ingunn Steinfinnsdatter begin what each hopes will be a new life—but in Ingunn's past lies the shame of an illegitimate child and in Olav's past lies murder.

Fiction/Literature/0-679-75554-3

IN THE WILDERNESS

Bereft by the death of his wife, Ingunn, and haunted by the memory of his sins against her, Olav Audunsson leaves his estate at Hestviken on a journey of adventure, temptation, and repentance.

Fiction/Literature/0-679-75553-5

THE SON AVENGER

In the concluding volume, Olav, now in the last years of his life, must watch his grown children reenact the sins of his youth, with consequences even more fearful.

Fiction/Literature/0-679-75552-7

Available at your local bookstore, or call toll-free to order:
1-800-793-2665 (credit cards only).

Printed in the United States
by Baker & Taylor Publisher Services